When Will This Cruel War Be Over?

The Civil War Diary of Emma Simpson

BY BARRY DENENBERG

Scholastic Inc. New York

Gordonsville, Virginia

1864

Times gone by

Wednesday, December 23, 1863

Brother Cole returned home today.

I cannot fully convey the pain that pierced my heart as Nelson and Amos carried his coffin from the cart.

Mother is inconsolable — her hopes so recently raised by the intelligence that he was recovering from his wounds in Richmond.

We received word that he was on lookout duty late one evening when a ball from a Yankee sharpshooter's rifle wounded him in the chest. His condition, although serious, was not thought to be life threatening. We were told that when he was well enough to travel he would be given a furlough and returned home.

Only two weeks later we learned that, while recuperating in the hospital, he died from pneumonia.

As I write this I wonder how I can remain so calm. Perhaps the full knowledge of what has happened to our family has not been wholly realized.

What words can I use to express our profound grief? How can I adequately describe the apprehension, fear, hope and, finally, despair that has filled our days?

As if it were not enough to learn of his suffering,

what solace are we to find in knowing that he met his demise not in glorious battle defending our beloved land, but was touched by the hands of fate in such a tragic manner?

Mother urges me to trust in the Lord, for He is our protector.

Brother Cole is safe in heaven, now. Surely the Lord is with him. He was a good son and a gentle brother. I fear we shall not see his kind again.

Friday, December 25, 1863

There will be no Christmas celebration this year.

My thoughts dwell on times gone by. My memories beckon to me, pulling me back, reminding me at every turn of how our lives used to be, reminding me of Christmases past.

Even Father, who usually tolerated no variation of his arduous daily duties, considered Christmas a special time. He and Brother Cole would go with Nelson to choose a proper tree, which Father insisted be put up as early as possible so that we could decorate it appropriately and enjoy it for the longest possible time.

The house would be a beehive of activity for weeks before.

Mother was even more occupied than usual: seeing

to it that everything was just so, supervising the negroes, talking to Dolphy about readying all the beautiful silk and satin dresses we would be wearing — we all dressed with such care then — to Denise about preparing the food, and Iris about the endless list of housekeeping chores.

The guest rooms on the second and third floors had to be put in perfect "apple-pie order," as Iris called it. Everything was washed, swept, dusted, cleaned, and polished until each room sparkled.

The house was filled with the merry sounds of loved ones and warmed by a feeling of hospitality that lightened the heart. The children gleefully anticipating their gifts — candy and toys, a wagon with horse attached, a monkey in a box, a hobbyhorse, dolls, and diaries.

The hams, turkeys, mutton, and bacon were brought from the smokehouse by the negroes, and the tables piled high with pies, cakes, cookies, and candies.

It seems only yesterday that we anxiously awaited the arrival of Uncle Benjamin, Aunt Caroline, and Cousin Rachel from Richmond. Father enjoyed Uncle Benjamin's company immensely, taking out the chessboard immediately upon his arrival. Aunt Caroline is so much like Mother, both in appearance and manner — one would think they were twins. And Cousin Rachel, whom I have known nearly all my life, grew dearer to me with each visit. O how glorious was their arrival, made all the more glorious by the knowledge that they would remain with us to greet the New Year. There was so much to talk about; those days seemed to just fly by.

Could it be only three years ago that Father, Mother, Brother Cole, and I stood on the front porch greeting the constant stream of friends, neighbors, and relatives arriving to celebrate the Christmas season? I can see the scene so clearly in my mind's eye, as house servants darted in and out, attending to the gift-laden carriages, making sure that all the guests were nicely settled in their rooms.

Those visits were the most joyous memories of my life. Alas, now they are only that, memories.

I can remember that Christmas Eve, after our sleigh ride — how gloriously Mother sang hymns for us that night, while Aunt Caroline accompanied her on the piano. Mother has such a melodious voice, and she and Aunt Caroline are the picture of harmony.

Cousin Rachel had to be coaxed for quite a time but she finally agreed to grace us with her delightful flute playing. She, like Mother and Aunt Caroline, is so talented.

I wish I were as gifted as they, but I am afraid that I am not musically inclined.

They each have such beautiful, wavy brown hair — I am envious. I wish mine looked more like theirs, rather than this common, straight, dark hair that I, like Brother Cole, seem to have inherited from Father.

All of us drinking eggnog as Father offered a toast to everyone's lifelong health and happiness.

And O how hard it was to wait for Christmas morning. Brother Cole and I would wake everyone at dawn, eager to see what was in our stockings.

I can still remember the surprised look on Cousin Rachel's face when she unwrapped her gift, revealing the two lively, little white rabbits that she immediately Christened Agnes and Annie. That night we stayed up until the early hours of the morning, talking and feeding them apples and cabbage leaves.

And Cousin Rachel was such a delight to converse with. I know I tend to be on the quiet side. Mother accuses me of being much too serious and thinks that Cousin Rachel is a proper antidote for me, since she is such a chatterbox. Mother is, of course, correct in her supposition, for I am truly comforted when Cousin Rachel is around to entertain me with her endless conversation — she has an opinion on everything.

Everyone seemed so happy then. How could I know that would be the last time I would see Uncle Benjamin? How could I know it would be the last Christmas we would all celebrate together?

1863 was the most dismal year of my life.

The house seems so empty now, for indeed it is. Father has been gone for over two years. And my dear, sweet Brother Cole is in the kingdom of the Lord.

Once it wasn't that way.

Now our land is in a distressing state. Our struggle with the Yankees, is, they say, going poorly, even after two years of this infernal fighting.

Friday, January 1, 1864

I have decided upon my resolutions for the New Year. I have always had the habit of writing down my resolutions and referring to them from time to time throughout the year.

Those I made in years past seem so childish: wash my hair more, take better care of my appearance, watch sweets, tend to the horses, rise earlier in the morning.

This year I have decided to concentrate on fewer areas in the hope that I can be more successful.

I have resolved to faithfully keep my diary, which was begun at Mother's suggestion. She hoped it might help develop my writing skills and improve my penmanship.

I strive to take my time — although there is so much I want to say that sometimes my pen flies in my hand and I have to remind myself to take care.

My only other resolution, which is truthfully the

most important one, is to try and help Mother more. I must confess, I have felt overwhelmed many times over the past two years. I fear I have been more of a burden to Mother than a help. So much has fallen on her shoulders. This coming year I vow that she can depend on me more.

My most fervent prayer is that 1864 will be a happier year, although I do not see anything on the horizon that would support that hope. I trust that the Lord will provide.

One does not know what to expect these days

Sunday, January 3, 1864

The thermometer reached only seven degrees today. There were icicles hanging from the house and the trees — and the milk freezes if left exposed. It was so cold we did not attend church.

It has been difficult without Father.

Father and Mother always had their responsibilities strictly defined, unless Mother required his assistance with the more troublesome negroes. Father saw to the farm and the fieldwork while Mother saw to the house and the house servants — everything ran like clockwork. My world seemed so safe and secure then. I thought it would always remain that way.

Now all responsibilities have fallen to Mother. She has done her best, but Father's lengthy absence has shown us how various were his tasks. I fear that Mother cannot replace him in all areas, try as she might.

Nelson has been a great help to Mother. He, along with Amos and Iris, is proving to be one of our most reliable negroes. He has helped Mother see to it that the tobacco, corn, and other crops are properly cared for and that the horses and livestock are tended to. These tasks had become a time-consuming part of Mother's day. As always, Amos assists Mother with her garden.

Our negroes, bless them, mind Mother as they always have and I cannot think of one instance in which they have not helped in every way.

Still, I think they miss Father's understanding but firm guiding hand. When Father was home contentment and order reigned supreme. Father always treated our negroes with compassion — using force only when called for.

There is constant talk now, especially by Mr. Garlington and Doctor Harris, of a growing spirit of rebelliousness among the negroes in the area. I have not seen any evidence of this. However, one does not know what to expect these days.

Monday, January 4, 1864

We are so isolated here — seldom seeing the number of visitors we used to, and I miss that very much.

Mrs. Broyles and her daughters, Lily and Lucy, came by today. Although they are a year and two younger than me — Lily is the elder — they are quite pleasant company. Both Broyles boys have gone off to fight the war.

Last fall Mother told me that Mrs. Broyles thought I was a proper influence on her two girls, and Mother hoped I would do my best to be courteous to them. I do find them both sweet and kind, although it is no use talking to them about anything serious. I hope I am not being too harsh — Mother says I am too hard on people.

I told Mother it would be fine if she invited them to see the beautiful new colt that Falla had just given birth to. Falla was named such because when she was born Amos said she would "falla" him everywhere.

They helped me feed Falla some corn and care for the new colt. They seemed to take to the horses right away, and I think they enjoyed themselves.

Later I suggested that we all go riding. I rode Little, who will not let anyone but me ride her, and Lily rode Plum. Lucy began by riding Boy, who, however, proved too much for her because he enjoys galloping and can be skittish. Lily manages the horses better so I had her ride Boy and put Lucy on Plum.

We all had a delightful time, and that night ate apples, which we baked on the hearth, and roasted eggs, which we cut in half so we could remove the yolks and fill the cavity with salt. We also helped Denise make ice cream and molasses candy in the kitchen.

During this more recent visit, Mrs. Broyles and Mother talked at length in the parlor. Mother told me later that Mrs. Broyles feels quite alone. They have not

12

seen a white face for nearly a month. She is quite concerned about her two boys, whose decision to join the war has left her in a dreadful state. She lost her husband at Gettysburg last July. She learned of his tragic death when she saw his name in the newspaper's casualty report. Mother counsels her that the Lord will not forsake those who put their trust in Him.

The story takes me far away from my own troubles

Tuesday, January 5, 1864

I have decided to commence reading again. I read only one book last year, which is quite odd for me, and was due to my melancholy state. The one book was *Emma*, by Jane Austen, which Mother gave me for my birthday. It was inscribed: "To my own lovely Emma." I told Mother I hoped she didn't think I was anything like that Emma. She is forever poking her nose into everybody's affairs and paying too little attention to her own. Mother laughed when I told her this and assured me that she did not think that about me. She thought only that it would make an appropriate birthday gift because her name was the same as mine, and that I might like the story, which I most assuredly did.

Mother has been insistent that things remain, whenever possible, as they were.

As before the war, Mother and I breakfast alone, after she has spoken with Iris, Denise, Dolphy, and Nelson. As I mentioned, the time she spends with Nelson is necessitated by Father's absence. So we begin our day by eight o'clock — an hour later than usual.

After Iris serves us biscuits and apple butter for breakfast, we read from the Bible — which mother is quite adamant about — and then we begin my studies. I do not care much for arithmetic, geometry, rhetoric, or French lessons, preferring the time we spend on reading.

Although I think Mother is, at times, concerned with my lack of attention to some of my studies, we both take great delight in my reading list, which Mother attends to with great care. Books are becoming quite difficult to obtain, but our library, which Mother takes as much pride in as her garden, affords a wealth of possibilities. Mother has composed quite a respectable list for me.

I do love reading so and intend to devour everything on Mother's list this year. I know she was disappointed by my inattentiveness last year, and the great amount of time I spent idly in my room.

Each morning, after Mother reads a chapter aloud, we discuss the book we are reading. We began this year with *Wuthering Heights*, which, I must confess, I am having some difficulty with.

For one thing, I am, at times, confused by the characters. Perhaps I am foolish, but I do not understand how anyone can be as dark and troubled as Heathcliff. Nor

15

do I understand why he would care so much for Catherine, who seems quite frivolous to me and unworthy of all that attention.

I am, however, enjoying *Wuthering Heights*, for the story takes me far away from my own troubles.

Wednesday, January 6, 1864

Try as I might, I cannot seem to stop thinking about times past. The long walks, the buggy rides into town, the dances and fancy balls after which we would feast on cake, strawberries, and ice cream, the sparkling conversation, the laughter and the merriment — there is none of that now.

Although I have vowed to keep my mind on the tasks at hand and not dwell on the past, as I did last year, so many little things remind me of the way things once were.

Just this morning I was fixing my hair — which seems to vex me no matter what I do — and I realized I was using Cousin Rachel's comb, the one she lost last summer.

That, now that I think of it, was the last time we went into town to shop for new dresses at Mr. Breckinridge's store. Even then there was little to choose from. Mother says we have the Yankee blockade to thank for that. Despite Mr. Breckinridge's diminished selection, Cousin Rachel and I spent sufficient time making our choices and then rushed home to try them on in preparation for dinner.

That night Cousin Rachel and I drank, I think, too much strong tea and were up till three o'clock in the morning talking about personal matters, the war, and marriage — which has become one of Cousin Rachel's favorite topics. I can only attribute this to the fact that she is three years older than me.

The next day we went riding at dawn in order to avoid the heat of the day. Cousin Rachel insisted on riding Sultan, although I cautioned her against it. Sultan can be as stubborn as a mule when he sets his mind to it. And the more he is whipped the more stubborn he becomes, turning every which way and moving off at whatever pace suits him. Of course, he is a superior animal. In the open field I have never ridden a horse that can best him. He flies like the wind.

It was a beautiful morning. The ground was covered with dew and there wasn't a sound to be heard above the horses' hooves.

Just when we were about to return home, Cousin Rachel's comb fell out of her hair. When she jumped to the ground to retrieve it, Sultan jerked the bridle out of her hand and made for the house, happily riderless, his mane flying in the wind. Cousin Rachel immediately

17

took off after him, her now loosened hair also flying behind her.

I followed slowly behind, laughing at the scene unfolding before me. When we finally reached the house, the negroes working in the field stopped to watch the spectacle. Sultan had been put back in his stall, from which he stared balefully at us, although I thought I could detect a twinkle in his eye.

That night we regaled everyone with the story of Sultan and the lost hair comb which, I realized this morning, I had retrieved, but never given back to Cousin Rachel.

It gives me some welcome relief to allow my mind to dwell on those pleasing memories of the past. Alas, there are, all too often, frequent reminders of sadder memories. The saddest are those of Brother Cole.

Each morning I am reminded of the competition between Father and Brother Cole to see who would be the first to wake in the morning. Brother Cole played the game, I must say, with little success.

Iris, too, took great delight in watching the two of them, as she would gleefully report to Mother and me on those rare occasions when Father would descend the stairs to find his son sitting in his customary seat at the breakfast table.

Iris brought us near to tears trying to imitate Father's

18

shock, followed by his heartfelt laugh and Brother Cole's beaming smile.

Aunt Caroline and Cousin Rachel's company has been the only thing that truly takes my mind from the trials of the past two years.

I was gravely disappointed that they were unable to join us this Christmas, due to the situation in Richmond and the general fear of traveling that has caused so much consternation in the area.

My diary has become my true friend

Saturday, January 9, 1864

My diary has become my true friend.

Expressing my thoughts in writing, especially during these dark days that have descended on our sunny land, is a great comfort to me.

Sunday, January 10, 1864

Attended church today. Amos placed a warm brick and extra blankets in the carriage to keep Mother and me as comfortable as possible. It is snowing lightly.

I washed my hair today.

Monday, January 11, 1864

I wonder if anyone will ever think me presentable — although I know this is a silly question to ask, especially at this time. I certainly hope I am not becoming vain, but it is useless to try and put these thoughts aside once they arise. I wonder if ugly people are able to find other ugly people and are actually attracted to them — although I am not so foolish as to think I am ugly. At times I feel quite pleased with myself, especially if I am wearing a pretty dress and my hair is done in a fashion I think is flattering.

I wonder if pretty girls feel pretty all the time?

I know that all of this sounds quite foolish but I feel it is better to write in my diary — where no one will ever see it — than speak to anyone about such foolishness.

Wednesday, January 13, 1864

I never realized how happy I was until this war besieged our land.

The moon had never shone as brightly

Monday, January 18, 1864

I wonder if I will ever fall in love. He will have to be someone whom I feel is worthy. I must confess I do have an image in my heart. I do have a weakness for beauty. I care nothing of what others might think, but I do desire to gaze on a face I find pleasing. Should I be different? I am not sure I can be.

Of course he must have other characteristics. He must be intelligent and possess a sense of honor. I could never marry anyone I did not respect. The most important thing is to be sure you love the one you marry with your whole heart.

It is hard for me to believe that a year ago, at this time, Tally and I had not even met.

I miss him more and more as the days go by.

Last year, in July, when Aunt Caroline gave birth to Baby Elizabeth and we learned of Uncle Benjamin's tragic death, Mother decided we should make the journey to Richmond, despite the dangers. The journey, although arduous, was without incident and we arrived exhausted, but happy to see our beloved relatives.

Early the next morning Cousin Rachel had the carriages brought around and we spent most of the day in town. Richmond is so much larger than Gordonsville; I felt quite overwhelmed.

That evening we chose our dresses — I wore the one with the wreath of roses and a white lily in my hair — for the reception that Aunt Caroline was giving in honor of Baby Elizabeth's birth.

One boy, whose name I cannot quite remember, which is no wonder, boldly introduced himself to me.

Like most boys, he seemed to take great pride in misunderstanding everything I said, twisting it this way and that and politely pointing out precisely where my thinking was in error, although I honestly do not recall talking about anything that warranted such attention.

There is nothing that troubles me more than people who go out of their way to criticize everything you say, holding each sentence under a magnifying glass and repeating it back to you in a completely unrecognizable fashion.

Like most boys, he was more interested in debate than discussion, more concerned with the sound of his own words than what others were saying. He employed what I can only call a kind of false voice when he was about to orate on a particular subject.

I do not know what it is about boys that causes them to think this behavior impresses girls but, frankly, it vexes me quite a bit.

I endured it for as long as I could — it seemed as if

23

we had been chatting for an eternity — finally excusing myself by telling him that I had to attend to a private matter, which, I could see, put him in quite a state.

I slowly ferried my way through the gathering, which had, by now, grown quite sizable. I badly needed some air, and I hoped the portico would provide some. Before I arrived at my destination Aunt Caroline beckoned to me. She introduced me to a handsome young man named Taliaferro Mills.

He was, as I said, quite handsome, but even more compelling was the sense I felt that Tally — as he requested I call him — was different from other boys.

We immediately and effortlessly engaged in a discussion about a variety of subjects: books, education, religion, politics, slavery, and the war. One thing I liked about Tally right off is that he was not ashamed, as are most boys, to admit how much he enjoyed reading.

Tally appeared eager to hear my opinions, which I considered quite flattering. It is not that I consider myself brilliant, but I know that my views are just as profound as the ones boys put forth as if they are in private possession of the wisdom of the ages.

More than anyone else I ever met, Tally seemed to challenge me with his seriousness. At first I found this quite disarming, causing me to blush, I fear. I also found it, however, quite refreshing.

24

He also has a way of looking sad, which made me care for him even more.

He asked if I would like some night air and perhaps a glass of punch, and I readily agreed to both. We made our way to the portico, which was lit by a full moon. It seemed to me that night that the moon had never shone as brightly.

Later that evening, when we finally bid everyone good night, Cousin Rachel and I retired to her room. She sleeps in a beautiful four-poster bed and still keeps the steps beside it that she used as a little girl to get in and out.

I learned from her that Tally's parents were tragically killed two years ago in a fire while he was away at school. They have joined the ranks of the blessed. Perhaps this accounts for his serious manner.

She chided me for flirting with him, pointing out that I hardly spent a minute with anyone else during the entire evening.

I replied that I simply preferred, having found someone to my liking, to spend time with him, rather than have one silly conversation after another.

Cousin Rachel said that she herself preferred having one silly conversation after another — which caused us both to laugh uproariously until we embraced, tears of mirth running down our cheeks, both of us, I fear, feeling the effects of the wonderful punch.

25

During the long journey home all I could talk about was Tally. Mother, as she often does, warned me not to judge people at first sight. I must confess that she is right; I do tend to do that, but I trust my instincts and I do not think that will ever change.

Looking back now on meeting Tally, I can see that he was disturbed by the war and concerned about doing what was honorable.

At the time I did not understand all that was happening to us and I am not certain that I do now. Perhaps I could have convinced him that he need not have gone off to fight. I am not sure, however, that that would have been the proper thing to do.

The next week he left Richmond to join General Lee's Army of Northern Virginia, which I learned about later when he wrote me this letter:

> *Dear Emma,*
>
> *I felt it my duty to personally acknowledge my debt of gratitude toward you for helping me make what, for me, was a grave and difficult decision.*
>
> *Your frank comments on the subject of this war, which is surely a plague on our land, helped me formulate my own often complicated views of my responsibilities as a citizen of the South.*
>
> *By the time you receive this letter I will have joined my Confederate comrades, who are fighting to remove the Yankee invaders from our land.*

May I humbly and earnestly request that I might be allowed to write you from time to time, if my letters can find their way, and that perhaps you might do me the honor of a reply, if time permits. My warmest regard to your father and mother.

Sincerely,
Taliaferro Mills

Lord knows when he will return — when all our gallant boys will return.

She has called upon me to take her place

Friday, January 22, 1864

Mother is not feeling well due to a fever, and she remains in bed. I pray the Lord will provide.

Iris helps me tend to her throughout the day — she is quite devoted. I sat up with Iris for the past two nights while Mother slept peacefully. Iris urged me to go to bed and get some rest, but I am more comfortable being with her and Mother and I think I do doze from time to time on the sofa.

Mother's night table is now cluttered with bottles of medicine and various liquids, including quinine, which Doctor Harris says will help reduce her fever.

Sunday, January 24, 1864

This morning Mother was well enough to sit up in the large chair in the corner of the room by the big bay window.

I brushed her hair, as I know she likes to look presentable.

She was quite grateful.

Mother has asked me to see to it that the weekly classes with the negro children continue as before her illness. Mother has always seen to the education of her little scholars. I know she feels badly that she is unable to leave her bed chamber and is quite distressed that she cannot carry on her duties as before, but Doctor Harris insists she rest.

I am proud that she has called upon me to take her place.

I tried my best with them but, I must say, it is a trial. They are more interested in playing than hearing stories from the Bible and it is quite tedious reading to them while they fidget about.

Iris helps as we begin class at ten each Wednesday morning, although few of the children arrive on time. Iris's darling daughter, Dinah, is a shining exception, arriving promptly and eager to begin.

I have resolved to do my utmost to ease Mother's mind while she recuperates.

I pray each night that Mother's fever will be gone.

Monday, February 1, 1864

I have been unable to write for the past week. Mother's illness has caused me to sink into a melancholy state. Doctor Harris says she needs time to regain her health and that nothing will help more than rest and quiet. He reassures us that merciful are the ways of the Lord.

Wednesday, February 3, 1864

Aunt Caroline, Cousin Rachel, and Baby Elizabeth have come from Richmond to stay with us. We had to put up the crib for the baby, who stays in Father's room.

Aunt Caroline says they have come because of the state of affairs in Richmond, but I think they have come because of Mother's condition. I keep these thoughts to myself, however, not even mentioning them to Cousin Rachel.

Baby Elizabeth seems to be the only one who is truly happy these days. I gave her a warm bath this morning, which she seemed to enjoy immensely. Afterward she played with the doll I made her for Christmas, but never sent. Tending to the baby helped take my mind briefly from my concern for Mother.

Saturday, February 6, 1864

I feel so very helpless. Thank the Lord for Aunt Caroline and Cousin Rachel. I do not know what I would have done without them. Their presence is such a comfort.

When will this cruel war be over?

Sunday, February 7, 1864

I am finding it difficult to obtain ink. We no longer have any coffee or salt, and Aunt Caroline says that everything is high priced these days.

Tuesday, February 9, 1864

We hear that more negroes have gone off to join the Yankees. God bless our negroes, who remain loyal.

When will this cruel war be over?

Sunday, February 14, 1864

Cousin Rachel is quite disturbed that she has not received any Valentine's Day cards. She said that previously she received over a dozen — which was more than anyone in her school.

Monday, February 15, 1864

Mother has improved somewhat — which is a great relief to me — although she has lost weight and still looks quite tired. She is so weak she cannot hold a book in her hands. It is quite distressing to see her in this state. I know how much Mother dislikes being ill and unable to perform her duties. It would be a great comfort to her if Father were here.

I am reading to her each morning and she naps in the early afternoon.

Tuesday, February 16, 1864

There are many reports of smallpox in the area.

Friday, February 19, 1864

Mother is feeling better today. How merciful are the ways of the Lord. She says she enjoys my reading aloud to her so much that it is the first thing she thinks of when she awakes each morning.

We are reading *Wuthering Heights*, which Mother listens to with rapt attention, sometimes requesting I reread a particular passage. This morning she asked to hear Catherine's speech to Isabella concerning her infatuation with Heathcliff.

As I have said, I find Heathcliff a loathsome creature and fail to understand what attraction he holds for these two women.

Saturday, February 20, 1864

Aunt Caroline has been a dear help to Mother in managing the servants.

The household continues as before, thanks to her efforts. Mother, thank the Lord, has been well enough to spend some time in the morning with Dolphy, going over the clothes that need mending so badly. It is impossible to get new ones and we are fortunate that Dolphy is such a wonderful seamstress.

Iris sees to it that all the rooms are in order, everything dusted and swept and the beds made, although we are, of course, expecting no one. Father would have wanted it that way, she says.

I asked Cousin Rachel if she wanted to pull the breast bone of the guinea hen we had for dinner so we could see who would marry first. She said she would prefer not, as she thought it a silly thing to do and that she considered marriage just as silly.

I must confess, I was startled by this. Cousin Rachel is rather high bred and seems to be putting on airs quite a bit of the time. Perhaps it is because she is older than me — although only by three years.

Sunday, February 21, 1864

The baby is cutting a tooth and Aunt Caroline is awake most of the night tending to her. I help when I can.

Monday, February 22, 1864

Colonel James has been killed, although there was no notice of it in the papers. Mrs. James's oldest son was killed the first year of the war and now she is a widow with three young children to care for.

Tuesday, February 23, 1864

Mother remained in bed all day.

Saturday, February 27, 1864

Aunt Caroline has had great difficulty all week due to problems with her teeth. Six had to be extracted and the long and painful operation, without the benefit of gas, has left her with a grave shock to her system. This coupled with her exhaustion due to the baby has caused Aunt Caroline to look wan and tired.

I simply want Tally to return safely

Thursday, March 3, 1864

O glorious day — a letter from Tally.

The letter was dated Christmas Day, and he seemed disconsolate.

He says the weather is quite cold and when the rain and sleet fall icicles hang from their hats and clothes. Many of the men are badly frostbitten, and some have froze to death along the roadside. He has seen enough of the glory of war, and he marvels at the ability of those around him to get used to the deprivations they are forced to endure.

I hope it is not childish to think of my own feelings when the war is being waged about such grave issues — but I cannot help that I simply want Tally to return safely.

He reports that they have been expecting an engagement for the past two weeks but that, thus far, it has not come — which is just as well with him. They are in winter quarters and the men are quite restive. One soldier on lookout duty was found asleep at his post. He was, Tally says, brought up before a court-martial but his life was spared.

Everyone believes the Yankees are just in front of them and the battle is looming. He says that the fighting has resulted in great slaughter on both sides and that he has lost many friends. He has seen quite enough of a soldier's life. The Yankee artillery is so fearsome — felling every upright thing — that one of his comrades was killed by a shattered tree limb.

There has been little to eat and what they do have — mostly cornmeal, crackers, and bacon — is not enough. They are forced to catch squirrels and rabbits and birds, which they roast at night on sticks since they have few utensils with which to cook. Many of the men are suffering from dysentery and malaria but Tally only has blistered feet.

Even more than good food, he craves sleep. They are constantly kept in a weary state — at night they sleep on the hard ground.

He says it is difficult to remain and fight knowing that those back home are suffering every day. But he feels this is his duty and cannot forsake it. Some men are so desperate to return to their homes that they have taken extraordinary measures. He observed one man who purposely shot off his finger in order to obtain a furlough. Sometimes it is as if he is in a dream and he wonders what it will be like when he wakes. Many of the men are growing sick of the war and are deserting. He says a battlefield is the saddest sight he has ever seen.

38

Writing paper is quite scarce, and he is writing in between the lines so he can say as much as possible. It is indeed difficult to read. My letters are a great comfort to him and he hopes I will not tire of writing.

He has sent me a ring which I must confess was quite a surprise, although a pleasant one. He says he will be home soon — although I am afraid to believe that that is true. I fear that my faith is not that strong. The ring is too small and I have placed it on a silver chain which I wear around my neck, but only when I am in my room alone, as I fear it would upset Mother — thinking Tally too forward and too old for me — as if eighteen were that much older than almost fifteen. I know we have only met once, and then briefly, but I know my heart.

The ring is too dear to me to just place it in a drawer.

Saturday, March 5, 1864

The Broyles brothers have both returned home due to wounds received fighting Yankees at Deep Creek.

39

We have grown accustomed to having no men around

Monday, March 7, 1864

The war has been going on far longer than anyone thought, so long that I fear we have become accustomed to it. We have grown accustomed to having no men around, accustomed to things we had taken for granted — coffee, ink, flour for baking — all becoming precious, and accustomed to all the gaiety having vanished from our lives. We seem to have lost all hope, as if this is the way it will be forever.

Thursday, March 10, 1864

Another letter from Father today. It was difficult for Aunt Caroline to read it. She said she did not think it wise to show the letter to Mother, who has not been well lately and has once again been confined to bed by Doctor Harris.

Father remains confident that our cause will triumph

in the end. He says the Abolitionists may rave as much as they like but the fact is that the negro race is inferior to the white race and must remain so. He says the negroes have thrived in the South due to our ever watchful eyes and are better off with us than with the Yankees.

He is proud to hear that our negroes have remained loyal and that their behavior proves his argument, for if slavery were as bad as Northerners would have us believe then surely all the negroes in the South would have abandoned the plantations and gone north by now.

Sadly, he informs us that Jack Fellers was severely wounded and, although the surgeon said there was no danger — which at least allowed him to have a peaceful night's sleep — he was beyond all human help by morning. Father requested that we tell the grievous news to the Fellers family. Father says that the suffering his brave and noble troops have had to endure will prove justified in the end, for their cause is a righteous one. To keep up their spirits, his men recently engaged in a fierce snowball battle. He urges us to pray to God so He will not forsake us during these dark and bloody days. Father has the utmost faith in General Lee, whose dignified presence is a solace to all around him and fills the men with pride, knowing that they are guided by his calm hand. Father has not been wounded and believes God has kept him in the hollow of His hand.

41

I do not know if Father is aware of Mother's condition. Each day she seems worse than the one past, and I fear it is becoming too much for me to bear.

Father wonders why we don't write him, which is curious because we have. I cannot help but think that our letters are not getting to their proper destination. The mail — like everything else — seems to be suffering lately.

Sunday, March 20, 1864

Cousin Martha's daughter Bettie has the measles. The whole family fears they may get it also.

There is little to say that is of any real help

Monday, March 21, 1864

We visited Mrs. Fellers today. Their home is understandably filled with sadness. They were married last year, just previous to Mr. Fellers' leaving. Mrs. Fellers does not even have any children to remember him by. This is what this terrible war has brought to our land.

Needless to say she was beside herself with grief. Aunt Caroline did her best to console her but, as we all know, there is little to say that is of any real help.

Wednesday, March 23, 1864

Mother is still feeling poorly.

Thursday, March 24, 1864

Cousin Rachel has been quite a trial since she arrived. For some time I thought she was cross with me — but now I know that that is not so. Like all of us she is shaken because her world has been pulled out from under her. I think her father's death affected her greatly, although she says nothing about it directly.

We talked in my room until late in the evening, drinking tea sweetened with brown sugar, which helps relieve some of our anxiety.

She is greatly disturbed that she has had to leave her school. Knowing that she may never return distresses her. The school was closed due to the war. Cousin Rachel, however, explained to me that she had to return home even before that, having become ill with what the doctors say is a weak stomach.

She went on about the school quite at length. It is apparent that she liked it a great deal.

Cousin Rachel lived with four other girls in a large room. She took drawing classes, French, piano, flute, and musical composition, in addition to other studies. Her French teacher was Mademoiselle Vaucher, who was from France.

In the evenings there was a two-hour study period, during which time Cousin Rachel said she and her roommates studied little, preferring to debate the merits of marriage and gossip about the cadets at the nearby military academy. Precisely at ten o'clock the lights were turned out — a practice that was strictly enforced by proctors patrolling the halls.

44

She misses the theater parties, the fancy balls, the Friday evening musical soirees, and eating with her friends in the school dining room — although she was quick to point out that the school's fare compared quite unfavorably to what she was accustomed to at home.

From time to time they had Sunday dinner at Susan Anne Taylor's home, where they feasted on oysters, turkey, fish, venison, pound cake, strawberries, and marmalade. Susan Anne was one of Cousin Rachel's roommates and her closest friend. I gather that she misses her company, and I am afraid I cannot provide Cousin Rachel with that kind of companionship, try as I might.

Although I have always appreciated the fact that Mother sees to my education, I have, nonetheless, been curious about what it is like going away to school, as Cousin Rachel did, and I quite enjoyed listening to her.

She admitted that she has been behaving sourly.

Cousin Rachel has a great many opinions that she holds quite strongly. She says she will never be governed by what others think, and she will do what her conscience dictates.

She thinks that boys hide their real feelings and true characters and are not to be trusted, and that many girls foolishly marry boys who are unworthy, something she says she has no intention of doing. She maintains that girls are in every way superior to boys, and she believes that married life is infinitely taxing and she will never embark on that course.

It would be foolish, she says, to agree to marry with the war raging over our land. You might, she points out, be a widow before long.

I am not sure I agree with all of this. Cousin Rachel seems so sure of her views; perhaps when I am her age I will come to agree with her, but for now I am afraid I do not.

Saturday, March 26, 1864

I no longer read aloud to Mother, as she cannot stay awake for long. I wish Father were here — I would not be so afraid if he were. Our only hope is in the Lord, though He seems far off.

Wednesday, March 30, 1864

The snow is almost gone. I am worried about Mother — Doctor Harris has been here twice this week.

I am beside myself with fear

Saturday, April 2, 1864

Our troops passed near here today. They looked quite destitute. Many of them had no shoes. For one brief moment I thought I saw Tally among them. But it was only a boy, a young boy. Like Tally he was taller than the others, and he had the same curly brown hair and piercing, sad blue eyes. I was relieved that it was not him, for the boy looked quite forlorn.

Tuesday, April 12, 1864

I have not written for the last two weeks because of Mother's condition. I am beside myself with fear for her and what will become of us.

Doctor Harris is, I am sure, doing his best, but Mother looks more and more tired every day. Doctor Harris said he would be encouraged if Mother would only show a little craving for food, but she hardly takes a nibble, just some tea from time to time. It is more than I can bear to gaze upon her pale countenance. She understands everything and appreciates all we do for her, but somehow it is not enough.

My heart is desolate

Monday, April 18, 1864

Mother died today.

Thursday, April 28, 1864

I have tried not to indulge myself in the dubious luxury of grief — but Mother's leaving has cast a gloomy shroud about the house. It is the saddest event that has yet occurred in my young life. I have tried to behave as Mother would have wanted me to — and, indeed, as she so earnestly requested of me when we last spoke.

I cannot help but remember, with great longing, those glorious days before this horrible war descended upon us and ruined everything. Everything. I cannot help but yearn for a return to that time. Perhaps I will wake one morning and Mother will be busily organizing the servants, going over the chores with Iris, the cooking with Denise, the sewing with Dolphy. O how calmly I write about it.

Mother seemed to spend more and more time confined to bed these past few weeks. That night, Mother was sleeping soundly and I must have dozed off on the sofa, although I was resolved to stay awake. But the next thing I knew someone was gently shaking me and softly calling my name, "Miss Emma, Miss Emma," but the voice seemed far away, like someone calling through a mist, like on the moors in *Wuthering Heights*.

I was afraid to open my eyes, and hoped that the calling would go away and the shaking would stop. But whoever was calling would not stop and the shaking persisted. I willed my eyes to open and perceived Iris, her black face glistening with the tracks of her tears saying, "Miss Emma, your Mother wishes to see you."

I still did not know whether or not I was dreaming. I told Iris that I had to comb my hair first, but Iris said that that would wait, and helped me rise and led me to Mother's bedside.

The room was gray, the morning sun just beginning to cast its light. I placed my hand on Mother's brow, which felt moist, and reached for a cloth that was kept on the night table. Tenderly I wiped the sweat from her forehead and waited for her eyes to open.

Mother looked so serene and regal lying there. A light seemed to frame her beautiful face, and I could see that the pain and suffering were no longer etched there.

It seemed like quite some time before Mother opened her eyes. When she did I could see that her dark brown eyes were telling me to prepare myself. She pulled me near, which must have taken all her strength. "Dearest child," she said, "I fear my health is failing me, and I will not be able to care for you as before." Tears filled her eyes, but none fell. "Be sure to help Aunt Caroline," she continued, her voice almost a whisper, "and spend as little time as possible on tears, for tears will do us all no good. We must trust in the Lord's blessing."

She asked me if I understood and I said that I had, although I must confess that I honestly do not understand.

Suddenly, my body felt chilled to the bone. All I could think about was how well Mother had borne up during her illness and that I now must do the same.

It was only then that I realized Aunt Caroline was there. She put her arm around me and led me to my room, where I clutched the daguerreotype of Mother that I always kept next to my bed and sobbed till somehow I must have fallen asleep.

I was unable to attend Mother's burial in the family graveyard. When I saw the men coming to take her away, my heart stopped beating and I turned from the window and sobbed in my bed, unable to rise. I could not bear it.

Aunt Caroline came to my room later and said I should not be concerned about not attending Mother's burial. She said she would do all she could to give me the love and care she knew I would dearly miss and that,

50

although she knew no one could ever replace Mother, she would do her best to help.

I have tried as best I can to obey Mother's last wish, although, I must confess, I have spent a great deal of time in my room. My heart is desolate.

Although I was ashamed of my selfish behavior, I could not help it. My room provided me with the solitude I needed — at least for the time — and I spent countless hours sitting in my window, watching the negroes come and go.

Friday, April 29, 1864

Aunt Caroline reminds me so much of Mother. Like Mother, she seems resolved to these times and, like Mother, she has an unshakable faith in the Lord. She talks to Cousin Rachel and me about trusting the Lord, but I am not sure I can have the kind of faith that she and Mother have.

Baby Elizabeth is quite pretty, just like her mother. The same sparkling blue eyes. Aunt Caroline allowed me to put her to sleep for the first time. I rocked her and sang "Three Little Kittens" and "Hush-a-Bye, Baby."

Sunday, May 8, 1864

After breakfast we took the carriage into town and attended church for the first time in quite a while. Aunt Caroline said that it was the most wonderful sermon, but I heard little of it, my mind filled with thoughts of Mother. Mrs. Broyles, Mr. and Mrs. Garlington, Cousin Martha, and Mrs. Fellers expressed their greatest sympathy.

Tuesday, May 10, 1864

We received word of the death of Lieutenant Walker.

I must write tonight

Wednesday, May 11, 1864

I took a walk in the garden, which helped soothe me. In the distance the apple orchard was a radiant field of large, white, billowing balls.

How I loved to idle away the hours, walking the garden paths, while Mother tended to her plants, weeding, hoeing, and pruning them with great care and patience, often assisted by Amos, who seemed to care for them almost as much as she did.

Being there reminds me of how much pride Mother took in her garden, especially the rose garden, which was her special joy. It was known throughout Gordonsville, and Mother took great delight in showing guests around it.

I remember one particular day last spring, when Mother and I left the garden, our arms filled with pink and red roses, some of which I took up to my room to dry and some of which Mother gave to Iris, who made them into rosewater.

A rose garden, Mother liked to say, helped remind us that nothing beautiful in life comes without thorns.

I cherished the time I spent in the garden with Mother, and I try to care for the flowers even more now that she is no longer here to tend to them.

Thursday, May 12, 1864

I received a letter from Father today.

My dearest daughter:

I am today in possession of a letter from your Aunt Caroline providing me with the sad intelligence that your precious mother is no longer in this world.

I am certain that her unexpected and lamentable departure has caused you to suffer great sorrow. Words of consolation often fail at times like these. I can only say that it is a great comfort to me to know that your dear, loving mother will abide in heaven, where she will joyously join her precious son in the hollow of His hand. Merciful are the ways of the Lord.

I urge you to take some consolation in that knowledge. Aunt Caroline has kept me informed of your circumstances, which I know are quite difficult to bear. Such is the way throughout much of our hallowed land.

These circumstances have been visited upon us by the Abolitionists from the North, who have in-

vaded our land and forced us to respond with all the means at our command. Please take refuge in knowing, as I do, that our proud Confederacy is watched over by a kind providence and that there will come a time when we will surely return to the life we knew and cherished before the Abolitionists chose this blasphemous and brutal course of action.

It gives me great pain to know that I cannot be with you at this time. I know you must be grieving sorely, feeling the severity of your loss. Although I would dearly like to return home to give you some comfort, my duty is here, with my men.

Trust in the Lord, as I do.
Your Father

Wednesday, May 18, 1864

A week has almost passed since I last wrote in my diary. The negroes seem confused, and I feel it is no wonder. Last night I heard them singing their beautiful songs.

Thursday, May 19, 1864

Cousin Rachel does love to talk. We talked all day about marriage, which appears to be Cousin Rachel's favorite topic. She went on at length about how men are full of deception, and that young girls must take care to protect themselves. Cousin Rachel says it is better if we are cautious in affairs of the heart. I told her I agreed — at least I nodded quite frequently — but in my heart, especially when I think of Tally, I am not quite sure I share her feelings. I look forward to, some day, being married, for I consider that the natural course of life.

Tuesday, May 24, 1864

Cousin Rachel and I talked in my room again this evening.

Saturday, May 28, 1864

Aunt Caroline and I spent the better part of the day preparing bandages that are to be brought to the church. Our sick and wounded soldiers are being cared for there.

I talked to Aunt Caroline for the first time about how frightened I was this past winter while Mother was confined to bed — how diligently I prayed each night that Mother would get well and how disturbed I was that she remained pale, thin, and weak. And how I imagine her still walking about the house, seeing that everything was proceeding smoothly, just the way she always did.

Aunt Caroline has been patient and loving and no one could ask for more. But no one can ever replace Mother. I miss her terribly. O wicked day. Sometimes I feel as if I will be overwhelmed by sadness. But this is no time for tears, as Mother said.

Sunday, May 29, 1864

There is talk of a terrific battle just east of here — near Spotsylvania Courthouse. Terrible casualties are feared on both sides.

Monday, May 30, 1864

I must write tonight. I confess that I do not feel up to the task. I wonder if every Monday will be blue, for that is the day that Mother bid us good-bye forever.

Friday, June 3, 1864

No one dresses prettily any more. I thought about this because I was considering what to wear this morning and saw my white cambric dress, the one with the roses on it, the one I wore when I met Tally.

Monday, June 6, 1864

Reports are that there has been a ferocious battle at Cold Harbor, near Richmond. Although it is thought that the cost was great, General Lee's army has, it is believed, emerged victorious.

Despite the heat I have tried to tend to the garden.

Tuesday, June 7, 1864

Cousin Rachel has a very bad sore throat — perhaps if she talked less her throat would not be under such strain. It is no wonder she has a raging fever. Doctor Harris says there is nothing to be concerned about, but of course Doctor Harris also counseled that Mother would recover with the proper care and rest. Cousin Rachel is miserable, and Aunt Caroline is in and out of her room with tea and honey.

I gave Baby Elizabeth her bath again this evening.

Thursday, June 9, 1864

Mr. and Mrs. Garlington paid a visit. He is very grave, while she says little. They talked in the parlor all morning in hushed tones. It scares me.

58

Tuesday, June 14, 1864

Cousin Rachel lectured me again today about boys. When I brought her breakfast she told me it was important not to be taken in by them, because they are fickle. Cousin Rachel seems old beyond her years, and in some ways bitter.

All the boys are gone now

Thursday, June 16, 1864

A letter from Father.

Aunt Caroline read the letter aloud in the parlor. In attendance were Mr. and Mrs. Garlington, Doctor Harris, and Mrs. Broyles, with Lily and Lucy. Cousin Rachel barely said a word to them, which made me quite unhappy. Cousin Rachel can be quite discourteous at times. They were all very eager for any news about the fighting. Mrs. Broyles is quite concerned about the condition of her sons.

Father says he wishes he could be with us but he does not think that will happen soon. He writes about how important it is to have faith in our just cause and how important it is not to let the Abolitionists subjugate us and take away our country. He says he is on a glorious mission and he will not rest until the vandals are driven from our soil. His spirits are good, for he believes the Lord is with us.

He said it was his painful duty to inform us of the death of Captain Rawlings. They were crossing a river and his horse threw him and, evidently, Mr. Rawlings could not swim. Before Father could offer any assistance, Captain Rawlings had drowned. They did all they could to bring him back to life but it was to no avail. He requested that Aunt Caroline break the news to Mrs. Rawlings and the children. Poor Mrs. Rawlings. I am sure she has only just recovered from the death of her baby girl. The baby was so ill following her premature arrival that Mrs. Rawlings decided not to have the dear, sweet child christened. The baby survived until the third week in February and then was laid in her tiny coffin. Mrs. Rawlings was nearly demented with grief.

Father does not sound as hopeful as he once did, despite his brave words. It seems to me that things have changed. No longer do we turn out waving handkerchiefs and flags, dressed in our finery to bid our brave boys good-bye. All the boys are gone now.

Friday, June 24, 1864

All talk is about Yankees.

There is no more salt, and Dolphy says she hardly has enough needles for sewing. Aunt Caroline says that a barrel of flour costs $70.

Saturday, June 25, 1864

I slept very late this morning and had breakfast in my room. At times the sadness about Mother overwhelms me.

The Broyles brothers continue to suffer terribly from the wounds they received in battle. Tom lost both legs, which were shattered by balls from Yankee rifles and had to be amputated immediately, without the benefit of chloroform or morphine. Robert's wounds are less severe. Needless to say, Mrs. Broyles is quite beside herself.

Lily and Lucy tend to their brothers as best they can.

O what a strange war it is

Tuesday, June 28, 1864

I received a letter from Tally today — dear Tally. I miss him terribly.

He complains that the war is going badly and the men are discouraged and tired of seeing things so unspeakable that he can not commit them to paper. He believes our efforts are futile and curses the politicians who got us into this war — politicians who stay home while his comrades are falling in gruesome sacrifice.

He says it rained most of last week and they had no tents. All around them is mud, mud, mud.

They are hungry and many of the boys are returning home to protect their families. He will continue to fight because he does not want to abandon his comrades.

Tally told about coming upon some Yankees at a place where they were separated only by a creek. They were so close they could holler to each other, and one of the Yankees proposed that they put down their arms and meet midway. They agreed to bargain, and built a raft and met in the middle of the creek, where they traded for canteens, coffee, and tobacco. Tally misses coffee more than anything else, besides sleep.

O what a strange war it is.

Tally asks that we send him clothing — his are in rags. He could use new boots, a hat, some undershirts, and socks. I have not told him about Mother, so he still sends his greetings to her. He signs his letter affectionately yours. I miss him terribly.

Saturday, July 2, 1864

Cousin Rachel was injured yesterday riding Tempest, who, it appears, was frightened by something and threw her ten feet in the air. She fell upon her left side and was knocked insensible. Amos found her and she is now in bed, unable to move. Doctor Harris examined her and she does not have a fracture, which is a relief to us all.

In the morning I brought Cousin Rachel buttermilk and biscuits for breakfast. She did not drink the buttermilk, but did eat one of the biscuits. For lunch I brought ham, green apples, and cheese, although I fear that is the last of the ham.

I asked her if she would like me to stay so we could have a chat and she said she did. I continued to knit the socks and gloves I am going to send Tally.

I am going to bring Cousin Rachel her breakfast each morning and try to cause her to be less gloomy.

She had barely recovered from her sore throat and probably should not have been out riding. Besides, there is too much danger about.

Those eyes haunted me

Monday, July 4, 1864

To celebrate — hardly the word — Aunt Caroline and I brought as much food as we could spare — some apples, nuts, grapes, a bottle of Father's good wine — and roses from Mother's garden to the poor Broyles boys, who have still not recovered from their grievous wounds. You could see that it lifted their hearts, although they looked so wistful and forlorn. Their eyes followed us as we left their house. Those eyes haunted me later, resulting in a restless night.

Aunt Caroline placed a small Confederate flag on the dinner table to mark the day.

Thursday, July 7, 1864

I am trying to be more pleasant in my daily conversations with Cousin Rachel. She can be quite trying at times. Mother always believed it was an art I should practice — not sheer flattery. That is nonsense. But she said I must pay more attention to pleasing people, conversing about the things they wished to converse about. She told me from time to time that I was too willful and that sometimes I should not express my thoughts so freely.

Friday, July 8, 1864

There is talk of the negroes leaving. Mr. Garlington said he overheard Nelson telling one of the younger ones which way to go when they ran off to join the Yankees. Nelson is surely one of the more clever negroes we have ever had. Father believes he requires careful watching.

We have always treated Nelson as one of our family. When he was a little boy Mother nursed him back to health when he was ill with the fever. I am surprised at his ingratitude if indeed Mr. Garlington can be believed. He thinks they have forgotten their place. It is hard for me to judge.

Saturday, July 9, 1864

My watch is broken.

Monday, July 11, 1864

Cousin Martha and Bettie visited today. They have fully recovered from the measles, which plagued the entire family for weeks. Cousin Martha says the Yankees will not rest until they have killed every one of us.

Tuesday, July 12, 1864

Mr. Garlington and his wife visited today. They say the Yankees are different creatures than we are, that they do not worship the same Lord. We are, Mr. Garlington says, like oil and water and will not mix. It is best, he says, we go our separate ways — that is the Lord's will.

Cousin Rachel appears to be recovering from her fall. She is walking about and is able to join Aunt Caroline, Baby Elizabeth, and me for breakfast. The baby is growing each day, and her various utterances are sounding more like words. Today is her first birthday. We celebrated by singing and playing the piano in the parlor.

I pray that the Yankees will soon leave our land

Friday, July 15, 1864

Aunt Caroline, Cousin Rachel, and I have been working all day cutting and sewing shirts and making bandages for our valiant boys. I pray that providence will watch over them. I pray that the Yankees will soon leave our land and allow us to resume our lives.

Wednesday, July 20, 1864

One of the negroes — a little girl named Cinda — has been taken violently ill with scarlet fever.

Saturday, July 23, 1864

Cinda died today.

The moonlight last night reminded me of Tally, the night we met at Aunt Caroline's.

Sunday, July 24, 1864

The weather is quite warm today.

Monday, July 25, 1864

Aunt Caroline, Mrs. Broyles, and Mr. Garlington and his wife talked in hushed tones in the parlor nearly all day. They do not want Cousin Rachel and me to hear, but we slip in unnoticed when the conversation is especially heated and silently settle upon the sofa under the window. The talk is, of course, about the war. There is disagreement about how it is going. Mr. Garlington is certain that we will emerge victorious, but the others are not so optimistic. They fear our boys are tired to the bone. The talk is all dark and dreadful.

Tuesday, July 26, 1864

One of the negroes was run over by a wagon. We expect he will recover.

Wednesday, July 27, 1864

Aunt Caroline and I visited the Broyles boys today. Cousin Rachel declined to accompany us. They are sorely in need of food and are, I fear, doing poorly, especially Tom. It is quite distressing to see those valiant boys lying there in such discomfort.

Tom called out in his delirium that he was going home now, and sat up and began trying to put on his shoes.

The air is filled with restlessness

Thursday, July 28, 1864

Tom Broyles has died. May the Lord protect us. I try to keep my faith in Him.

Friday, July 29, 1864

Bless our negroes for they are very faithful. Everyone is complaining about their negroes, although I cannot see much change in ours. They still appear to me to be cheerful, loyal, and well behaved. Amos still takes me for rides and teaches me all the little tricks he knows. Some of the negroes are lazy — but, then again, I think that was always the case with some. Sometimes I wonder what goes on behind their masks.

Saturday, July 30, 1864

Cousin Rachel and I were excused after dinner. The talk in the parlor seemed particularly heated. The air is filled with restlessness. All we can do is await our fate.

Cousin Rachel talked again, at length, about missing school. She seems quite distressed and talks for hours at a time, and then lapses into silence for days.

Everyone talks as if they were just tables and chairs

Tuesday, August 2, 1864

It is impossible for me to tell if the negroes understand what is taking place — they come and go as usual, serving dinner while everyone talks as if they were just tables and chairs.

I am not sure Mother would permit this if she were here. Mr. Garlington believes they are wiser than we think — "we" means Aunt Caroline, who seems in constant disagreement with him and Doctor Harris. He thinks they are simply biding their time, waiting for the Yankees to set them free.

Wednesday, August 3, 1864

I spend more and more time tending Mother's garden. I picked some red roses to place on the dinner table.

The house is so quiet. It used to be filled with visitors. The second and third floor guest rooms were nearly always occupied. Now the house is empty and we rattle about.

I sat in my window, well after everyone was asleep, dreaming of days gone by and wondering if we will ever laugh again.

Thursday, August 4, 1864

I am reading *Jane Eyre*, which helps occupy my mind. I am enjoying it more than anything in recent memory. Jane Eyre certainly has a sharp eye. Her descriptions of those around her are precise and unforgiving.

Friday, August 5, 1864

Aunt Caroline — with her soft, sweet, soothing voice, her graceful, caring ways, and her bright blue eyes that seem to peer into your very soul — has been a constant comfort to me these past three and a half months. Like Mother she assures me that the Lord will not forsake us. I try to keep my faith.

I have done my best to help her take Mother's place and run the house. I owe her much, and I hope I have not disappointed her. At times I am tempted to sink into melancholy, but then I remember Mother's last words —

tears will do us all no good — and I fight back those tears and help Aunt Caroline with the tasks at hand.

I continue to imagine Mother once again descending the stairs, greeting Iris, dispatching Denise, sitting with Dolphy, and seeing to it that all the little things are set about in an orderly fashion and making sure that everything is just so.

Aunt Caroline and I are doing the best we can. Our servants have, I think, done their share. Especially Iris.

Of all my students, Dinah is the most attentive. She always arrives promptly, eager to begin her lessons. At times I am able to sit with Dinah later in the week and go over her writing and spelling, which she seems most concerned about and, I must confess, I feel most comfortable teaching.

I think a great deal of Dinah's attitude is due to her mother's persistent urging. I am proud of them both. I know Iris appreciates my efforts and that helps me continue.

At times I imagine Mother's happy face beaming down. How I long for her praise. When Mother was pleased I could feel a warm glow about me.

The newspapers are filled with woeful reports

Saturday, August 6, 1864

So much of what is me comes from Mother. Just reading again reminds me of that. Everyone always knew that the best gift to give Mother was a book. One of my lasting images is of Mother peacefully reading her book in the parlor while Father read his papers or played dominoes with Brother Cole.

Like Mother, I too would read during those long, serene evenings. I hope I am thought of like Mother when I have my own family.

This morning I rose at first light, eager to continue the story of Jane Eyre. I feel so badly for her — she seems so lonely, with little to raise her spirits — yet she bears up so well. I have a growing respect for her perseverance in the face of grave adversity.

However, I am trying not to spend too much time reading in my room, as I think it worries Aunt Caroline, who has enough to do taking care of Baby Elizabeth and keeping a watchful eye on Cousin Rachel.

Sunday, August 7, 1864

There are nothing but negroes all around us. All the men, except, of course, Mr. Garlington and Doctor Harris, have gone off to war.

Mr. Garlington thinks our negroes are spoiled, but I think they just have good manners. Maybe it is merely an act and I am being fooled — that is what Cousin Rachel thinks — but I am afraid she always sees the worst in people.

Spent a good portion of the day tending to the horses, who, I fear, have been neglected. Falla's colt is growing quite steadily.

Monday, August 8, 1864

I spent a quiet day reading in my room. Aunt Caroline is in the parlor, and I have not seen Cousin Rachel.

Robert Broyles has disappeared. His mother thinks he may have headed south, but no one knows.

Tuesday, August 9, 1864

I am not recording all the rumors that are about. The newspapers are filled with woeful reports.

Wednesday, August 10, 1864

Last night I stayed up very late reading *Jane Eyre*; although tired, I could not wait to see what the next chapter would bring. Her life, like my own, seems to become more complicated with every turn in the road.

Spent a quiet day sewing shirts with Dolphy, who delights in my progress with needle and thread.

Another week — not a word from Tally.

Friday, August 12, 1864

After breakfast I fixed my hair. It has been such a long time since I did that — I honestly cannot remember when I have spent that much time before the mirror. I fixed it the way Aunt Caroline fixes hers. I plaited it down my back and have worn it that way all day.

I am happy my hair is long.

At dusk I went to the garden and gathered some sweet-smelling roses.

As Jane Eyre says, "Even for me life had its gleams of sunshine."

Sunday, August 14, 1864

Aunt Caroline has suggested that she and Cousin Rachel play together. Cousin Rachel has not played her flute since she arrived, although I know she brought it with her.

Cousin Rachel does not seem to be very happy these days, and we no longer talk as frequently as we did, which, I believe, is largely due to her melancholy moods.

She declined Aunt Caroline's invitation and so Aunt Caroline played in the parlor — she prefers that piano to the others in the house — while I read *Jane Eyre*, which I am liking much more than *Wuthering Heights*.

Aunt Caroline plays beautifully, her long, slender fingers — her pinkie is as long as her ring finger — lightly dancing over the keys, her head bowed in concentration. At times I can hear her humming the tune as she plays.

Monday, August 15, 1864

Cousin Rachel seems to be practicing her flute for the first time. I can hear her in the early evenings, up in her room. She plays quite nicely and I hope she continues, as I believe it will help keep up her spirits.

She has kept much to herself these past few weeks, but yesterday she returned to her former self and is once again speaking from great heights on any number of issues — the war, negroes and especially, marriage.

Her health is suffering once again. She was confined to bed due to a weak stomach and a touch of dysentery. Perhaps it was something she ate.

Tuesday, August 16, 1864

Cousin Rachel dropped her scissors today and they stuck in the floor, which she said is a sign that we would be getting a visitor. She says we all should prepare ourselves.

I think Aunt Caroline is quite concerned about her, although she has not said anything to me.

Wednesday, August 17, 1864

Miss Sally Robbins visited today. It has been a long time since we saw her. She is engaged to Lieutenant Charles Jones and is constantly concerned with his well being. It has been weeks since she's heard from him. Sally Robbins is rather staid, and Cousin Rachel was quite put off by her.

After dinner Cousin Rachel went on — quite at length — lecturing Sally Robbins about her views on marriage, most of which, of course, I am quite familiar with.

Cousin Rachel is quite critical of Sally and states that rushing headlong into marriage is a dreadful path to trod. She spoke at length about the evils of submitting to men and said that it was important for young girls like ourselves to enjoy our lives rather than find ourselves bound to a life of toil and trouble. She says that when we — Sally and me, I suppose — are older we will see that when your heart is broken you will not wish to have it so again.

It was quite a trial for everyone to sit through this discourse politely. Aunt Caroline was so disturbed that she excused herself saying that she wanted to see that the baby was sleeping soundly. The baby had a slight cough all day.

Cousin Rachel's speech was particularly vexing, as she and Sally Robbins are the same age. It was also curious because Cousin Rachel appears to be shielding something from her past. I would have asked her to tell me why she seems so troubled, but it appears that the topic still weighs heavily on her soul so I decided to remain silent.

Thursday, August 18, 1864

While I was working in the garden, Cousin Rachel joined me and continued the conversation of last evening as if we had never parted. She confided that she was becoming quite melancholy and believes she has gone into a steep decline. She says that it is only now and again that she is able to regain her composure. It seems this is not the first time this has happened to her, and it is quite a trial for her.

She said that life is a bitter cup from which we are all forced to drink.

Saturday, August 20, 1864

Another week has passed and still not one word from Tally.

Sunday, August 21, 1864

I must confess that at times I simply wish Cousin Rachel would learn to conduct herself in a more appealing fashion. Her behavior with Sally Robbins was quite embarrassing.

Wednesday, August 24, 1864

I spent the evening alone, reading *Jane Eyre* in my room. Her thoughts eerily mirror my own:

> It is a very strange sensation to inexperienced youth to feel itself quite alone in the world, cut adrift from every connection, uncertain whether the port to which it is bound can be reached, and prevented by many impediments from returning to that it has quitted.
>
> I will do my best: it is a pity that doing one's best does not always answer.

The war is at our door

Thursday, August 25, 1864

All talk is of Atlanta. The Yankees are rumored to be preparing to invade the city. There is an air here of hopelessness. Many of our friends and neighbors are coming to bid us farewell — perhaps forever.

Sunday, August 28, 1864

Last night I looked out my window and saw men in the trees watching the house. I trembled with fear and felt a chill, despite the heat.

The war is at our door.

Monday, August 29, 1864

The Yankees have invaded the Broyles house. When Mrs. Broyles woke, the garden was filled with soldiers, their bayonets glistening in the early morning sunlight. They broke the window, stole food, and within minutes the house was filled with rough men and no officer in attendance.

Then they left just as suddenly as they had come. Mrs. Broyles was too frightened to stay there, and took Lily and Lucy and began the journey to our house. She was fortunate enough, when they were three miles away, to see Amos, who gave them a ride in his cart. Amos was good enough to provide umbrellas so they did not suffer from the intense heat.

Mrs. Broyles says she was so startled by the intrusion that she imagines any noise now to be a recurrence, and she cannot stop her heart from palpitating so fearfully that it frightens her. She said one of the Yankees told her that they were not going to let Rebels sleep comfortably in their homes while their own wounded and sick men suffered.

All of the negroes welcomed the Yankees with open arms. The negroes told the Yankees about the bloodhound Mr. Broyles used to track down runaways and then went with them to shoot him. The negroes whooped and hollered in their quarters when they heard the shots and the dog's pitiful howls.

Tuesday, August 30, 1864

As I read late into the night, once again Jane Eyre uncannily has put my feelings into words I possess not the wisdom to conjure:

> I was in my own room as usual — just myself, without obvious change . . . where was the Jane Eyre of yesterday? Where was her life? Where were her prospects?

This is all some horrible dream

Thursday, September 1, 1864

Early this morning we learned that the Broyles house was taken over by Yankees. A Yankee officer came by and advised us that his troops would not injure anyone but that the house was required for a hospital to tend to his wounded men.

We are all quite startled by this turn of events, but Aunt Caroline has cautioned that we must remain calm. I am doing my utmost to live up to her expectations, although part of me yearns to believe that this is all some horrible dream from which I will soon awake.

Saturday, September 3, 1864

Today, at dawn, a Yankee soldier came to our house and asked me if I would tell him where our troops are. I refused — although, of course, I have no information as to their whereabouts. The soldier said he was tired of the war and wished to go home, and if I would tell him where they could be found, it would help him make his escape. He said he had been willing to fight to save the Union but that now the war was being fought by Abolitionists who want to free the slaves — he wished to fight no more.

I said I knew nothing that could help him, and the man rode off. He seemed quite agitated, and Cousin Rachel says he was drunk. We were all quite shaken by the ordeal. Our troops are nowhere to be seen. It is thought that they have been forced to withdraw in the face of Yankee advances.

When we sat down to breakfast the house was surrounded by Yankees, who threatened to destroy everything if food was not given to them. Cousin Rachel, quite beside herself, ran to lock the front and back doors but they broke down the library door and smashed windows and entered the kitchen and the pantry and carried off all the food they could find.

Monday, September 5, 1864

Everyone is shocked by what is happening to us, but there is little we can do about it.

There are reports that Atlanta is being evacuated and the Yankees are about to capture the city. It is, however, impossible to be certain of anything.

Tuesday, September 6, 1864

One of Mrs. Jane Allen's negroes ran off with her diamond ring and other jewelry. Mrs. Allen was distraught because the ring belonged to her husband's mother. Mr. Allen was killed earlier this year. She reported the theft to one of the Yankee officers, but he said nothing could be done about it.

Nothing seems safe anymore

Friday, September 9, 1864

I have not written for three days because there has been no time and only bad news to report. Wednesday a Yankee officer presented himself to Aunt Caroline and informed her that our house was to be handed over immediately to him so that it could be turned into a headquarters for the federal troops in the area. We were to move all our belongings into the third floor guest rooms or, if we preferred, he would furnish wagons that would carry us wherever we liked.

Aunt Caroline asked him just where he suggested we go. He said he could not help her with that but he was willing to provide conveyances that would carry us, our household articles, and personal possessions.

Aunt Caroline told him we would prefer to stay, and he said he would be returning by midday and to please make sure that everything was attended to. I was so proud of Aunt Caroline. Cousin Rachel burst into tears and ran to her room and locked the door. Mrs. Broyles was not much use either. She simply sat in the kitchen and wept.

Aunt Caroline and I had no other choice but to begin moving everything into the third floor bedrooms.

Iris called Nelson and Amos and somehow they collected most of what had to be moved. Nelson had to break down Cousin Rachel's door so we could move her things. Cousin Rachel and I are in one room, Aunt Caroline and the baby in another, and the Broyles family in a third.

At midday, while the Yankees were elsewhere, we began hiding the silver and Mother's jewelry. Everything was hidden in the garret. We hope they will be safe — although nothing seems safe anymore.

We had to step around Cousin Rachel, who appears quite beside herself and was sitting on the stairs sobbing uncontrollably because she had been deprived of her room.

Monday, September 12, 1864

The news is bad all over. Mrs. Cornelia Finch's house has been set aflame. The Yankees came shortly after breakfast and informed Mrs. Finch that she should remove everything from the house — which she did — although it was quite a chore since she has five small children and all her negroes have run off. There was no one to help her except her invalid brother, who was at least able to hold the baby.

While they were leaving, the Yankees were pouring liquid all over the house, and as they drove away they turned to see the house go up in flames. Amos reports that the house has been burnt to the ground.

Tuesday, September 13, 1864

Finishing *Jane Eyre* has left me breathless and thirsting for more.

Her story relieved me of so many of my current concerns — if only for a brief time. She too seemed to exist in the eye of a storm.

I have developed the highest regard for her character: her steadfastness to principle; her concern for others less fortunate than herself — this despite her own numerous misfortunes; her integrity, even in the face of dire consequences.

I hope someday to be able to emulate these character traits.

I am trying not to feel blue

Wednesday, September 14, 1864

Mrs. Broyles is refusing to eat and is not looking well. She remains in her room, with Lucy, who seems afraid to leave her side. Fortunately, Lily has proved to be a great help. She has grown quite attached to the baby and helps me tend to her, which is something I have done with more frequency in order to help Aunt Caroline. I do enjoy playing with Baby Elizabeth, who grows more responsive to me with each day. I have been applying oil dutifully to her hair on a daily basis, in hopes that it will curl, but to no avail.

At night I hold her in my arms and sing "Hush-a-Bye, Baby," which has become her favorite song. She falls asleep in my arms after a few minutes, and I lay her quietly in her crib, as my thoughts turn to Jane Eyre.

I watched the slumber of childhood, so passionless, so innocent — and waited for the coming of the day.

Friday, September 16, 1864

Aunt Caroline has decided that the silver and the jewelry will not be safe in the garret. Early this morning, after the Yankees had departed, we took everything and put them in holes we dug in the ground behind the garden where the grass slopes down to the pond.

Saturday, September 17, 1864

My birthday.

Aunt Caroline gave me a shawl she had secretly been knitting and a gold thimble and some pins she said belonged to Mother. Denise was able to somehow find enough flour to bake me a cake, and she put a rose on it, because she knew it would remind me of Mother. And Dinah gave me a card she wrote out all by herself. I shall treasure it forever.

I am trying not to feel blue — although it is quite impossible. It is my first birthday without Mother.

I see little hope

Monday, September 19, 1864

A letter from Father.

He says we should not be discouraged, and assures us that the Yankees are an inferior breed, and that the Lord will watch over us and not allow the wicked Abolitionists to prevail. We are locked in what will be a long, valiant struggle but we must have faith in the Lord.

Father maintains that the Abolitionists would like to destroy our country and see the negroes set free so they could live just like white people, and he is certain that that is not the Lord's plan. He is sure that setting them free would ruin their lives as well as ours.

They are about to move camp, although they have no orders yet, because there is a big battle looming, and it is believed that the Yankees are quite near. The men are steadfast in their determination.

He complains that he has not received a letter recently and wonders what is the reason.

I dearly hope that where he is, the situation is better than here, for I see little hope for us.

Wednesday, September 21, 1864

Everywhere there is turmoil. The Yankees are roaming the countryside, at times drunk. Mr. Garlington says that a rowdy band of Yankees — not commanded by any officer — is demanding five hundred dollars or they threaten to set the house on fire. Some families have paid only to find, sometimes just hours later, another wild band right behind them, making the same demands. There is little one can do. I must confess we have been spared great travail because of the troops who now make their headquarters here at our house. Colonel Davenport has done his utmost to maintain order and keep the soldiers behaving properly. Of course, daily life now has become quite a chore. Putting together a meal is a problem not only because of the scarcity of food — I cannot even remember the last time we had beef — but we have to scurry about the pantry before the soldiers are awake and fix breakfast by candlelight and then bring everything upstairs to the third floor.

Aunt Caroline and I see to it that the baby and Mrs. Broyles are fed first. Mrs. Broyles is looking quite poorly and continues to spend all day in her room, attended by Lucy.

I wonder if he and Father are fighting the same war

Saturday, September 24, 1864

A letter from Tally.

O how glorious I feel even in the midst of the trials of our daily life. Just to know that he is alive is enough to fill me with hope.

I wonder if he and Father are fighting the same war. He says he is so tired of marching and fighting that at times he just throws himself on the hard ground. He has never been so exhausted in all his life. The flies swarm like bees and are an abomination.

He writes that he has never seen so many dead, wounded, and broken men, that this war is taking a dreadful toll. The wounded suffer terribly and the doctors kill more men than they cure. Some suffer dreadful complications from their wounds, and he watches helplessly while they endure their private tortures only to die in the end. Many of them are thirsty and their throats are parched and cracked, their faces blackened with smoke and powder, and they are hungry all the time. He longs for something good to eat.

He writes that one of his friends was captured during a recent skirmish but escaped two days later, making his way to a nearby stream. He was able to remain underwater as the Yankees fired all around him. Believing, at last, that he must be dead they left, and he returned to camp wet as a rat and covered with mud.

Tally says he has become hardened to the sight of death — a cornfield where one battle was fought had so many dead bodies that he could have walked over it without stepping on the ground. The Yankees outnumber them and have better rifles, which are treasured when they are captured. During a recent fight the Yankees retreated in such haste that they were unable to bury their dead. He has seen enough of war and hopes never to witness it again.

More and more men are deserting every day. Last week someone in his company was caught and condemned to be executed. Tally was forced to be among those in the firing squad. The wretched man, blindfolded, was marched to the designated place and tied to a stake. Tally does not know if his gun was loaded, as half of the men were given blank charges. The man was trying to return home in order to help his family. The letters they receive from home tell of their families having little to eat. He wonders why we have not written to him, although he says he did receive the clothes we sent.

99

He is of the opinion that they will have another fight soon.

He has changed, he says, although he hopes he is the same Tally I met before he left and the thought of returning home and seeing me is the only thing that keeps him going. He feels fortunate to have escaped injury or worse, or fallen prey to any of the illnesses that are plaguing his comrades, many of whom are suffering from chronic dysentery or typhoid fever.

He says he does not have the words to express his sorrow upon hearing of Mother's passing, but he knows that, in a way, she is still with us. His words are like balm for my soul, and I am relieved that he has received at least one of my letters. He said he never wished to be back home so much in all his life and he wonders if I am receiving his letters. He has not received a letter from me in a long time.

Sunday, September 25, 1864

Cousin Rachel marched down the stairs this morning and demanded to see Colonel Davenport. After much fuss she was admitted into the library, which now serves as his office. She told him she would be unable to enter the house by the front door if he insists on putting up the Union flag. Colonel Davenport said the flag would stand and that this was now federal property. Cousin Rachel said she would enter and leave only by the back door in that case. Colonel Davenport said Cousin Rachel could do as she wished and had his soldiers escort her from the library.

Tuesday, September 27, 1864

Mr. Garlington remains optimistic, although Lord knows it is hard for me to understand his belief that the Confederate troops are about to push back the Yankees.

I am glad Mother is not here to see what has happened

Wednesday, September 28, 1864

I visited the family graveyard today. I am glad Mother is not here to see what has happened. Sometimes I am thrown into a state of melancholy when I think about her and the days that seem gone forever. Mother, reading aloud to me while the fire warmed us. I especially remember the first autumn fires — how brightly they burned. I doubt if they will ever burn quite so brightly again.

Friday, September 30, 1864

We hear that Mrs. Mallard was standing on the porch of her house with her two small boys when a Yankee rode by with chickens tied to his saddle. In a scornful tone he warned her that the war would soon be over. She defiantly told him that Southerners would fight to the death and that her boys would continue the fight when they were grown.

The Yankees found a hog that Mrs. Mallard had buried. One of the soldiers accidentally discovered that the ground under him was hollow and dug through the roof of the hastily constructed hiding place and unearthed the pig. They butchered the animal right there and rode off with the pig tied to the saddle along with the chickens.

The Mallards now have little to eat.

Saturday, October 1, 1864

The Yankees invaded Doctor Harris's house. They took some pieces of the cake that his cook had made and threw some coins into a plate and rode off.

Shortly after, another band of Yankees approached and took the rest of the cake, as well as the coins left by the first bunch, and ordered Doctor Harris's cook to prepare a meal for them, which they found so delicious they decided to make her come with them back to their camp. Doctor Harris's cook is quite fat and they forced her up on a mule — which she has never ridden in her life. The other negroes stood around laughing, although, I must admit, I did not see the humor in any of this.

A few hours later the cook came walking back, saying that she fell off the mule so many times that the soldiers decided to go on without her. She told the Yankees that southern boys would never have taken the money because they were raised with better manners.

Iris said she heard an owl screech near the house, which meant someone would soon die.

Sunday, October 2, 1864

Mr. Garlington has had his negroes dig new gate post holes. When they ceased work for the evening, he put his bags of gold and silver in the holes and barely covered them with dirt, so that in the morning, unbeknownst to them, the negroes put the gate post in place without being any wiser. He is quite pleased with himself.

Yesterday morning the Yankees left hurriedly and when they returned at dusk, they had a wounded man with them. They laid him outside by the trellis fence surrounding the garden. He seemed to be in a woeful state. He looked quite parched and, although I assumed his comrades would tend to him, I decided to bring him some water. I approached with great trepidation — there was no one around. He could barely open his eyes and looked as if he were burning up with fever. He was so young, about Tally's age. I showed him the water pitcher and he nodded, which seemed to be quite an effort. I held it to his lips and carefully tipped it so the water trickled into his mouth. Some ran down his face but he drank heartily. When it seemed that he had drunk his fill I stood up, turned, and walked away. "Thank you Ma'am from a thirsty man," he called out. I nodded and went back into the house.

When I awoke I looked out the window to see if he was still there. He was gone. Later that morning I saw the soldiers placing his limp body on a cart and taking him away.

I am not as frightened as perhaps I should be

Monday, October 3, 1864

Aunt Caroline learned today that Nora Canning was helped by a kind Yankee. A troop of soldiers drove by her house and stopped. Her youngest was crying and the soldier asked why he was crying. Mrs. Canning said it was because he was so hungry — she hadn't been able to give her children anything to eat for two days. The soldier, his eyes filling with tears, said he would come back later with food. He was as good as his word — returning that night with biscuits and hot coffee, which he shared with her and the children.

Unfortunately, this kind of behavior is rare, and there are daily reports of one horror following another. Mrs. Canning's neighbor was set upon by a band of Yankees who wanted to know how long it had been since our troops passed this way. Her boy refused to tell them and the Yankees tied a rope around his neck and swung him from a tree limb until he was nearly dead. Finally, they cut him down and went on their way, laughing at the wretched joke.

Thus far, we have escaped without such incidents, but I cannot help but wonder if our time will come. We remain as much as possible on the third floor. Aunt Caroline and I do our best to stay clear of the soldiers, who swarm about the house throughout the day.

I am surprised that I am not as frightened as perhaps I should be — certainly not considering our present living conditions.

Lily came down with me to care for Baby Elizabeth while I fixed breakfast. Lily is, as I have said, a great help with the baby. Having Elizabeth here provides a ray of hope that better times than these might be on the horizon.

Wednesday, October 5, 1864

The Yankees laugh at our negroes because they have not run off the way so many around here have. They fail to comprehend the reason for their loyalty, which the Yankees consider foolish. Amos replied to one, with the air of dignity he always has about him, that he does not leave because this is his home. He is proud of all we have taught him. Iris told them that if she left there would be nobody to take care of Miss Emma. I have known Iris all my life, and I do not know what I would do if she left.

Thursday, October 6, 1864

Lily has come down with scarlet fever. She was very restless all last night, and the fever continues hot and high today and her throat is generally swollen and sore. She is sitting up and talking, which is a good sign, and she remains quite sensible. Colonel Davenport has been kind enough to have one of the Yankee doctors look at her.

Saturday, October 8, 1864

Lily seems relieved this morning. The fever appears to have subsided, although Aunt Caroline insists she remain in bed. She misses being with Baby Elizabeth, but there is too much risk involved. We are all crowded up here in these rooms and it is quite difficult. I am finding it nearly impossible to find the time required to maintain my diary. I strive to wake at dawn, take my diary from the bottom of the bureau drawer, and write as much as I can before breakfast. I feel fortunate that the soldiers have not chosen to search our rooms. We have so little up here and are so clearly in strained circumstances that I do not think the soldiers pay us any mind.

Cousin Rachel sleeps all day and is up all night,

which was quite disturbing at first, but I have become accustomed to it.

It takes a long time to recover from scarlet fever and Aunt Caroline is giving Lily as much care as possible.

I have not been able to write Tally and, alas, I have not heard from him in quite some time.

Sunday, October 9, 1864

Mrs. Broyles spent most of the morning looking for her hair comb. She is very pale and is losing a great deal of weight.

Doctor Harris's cook was found dead this morning. Presumably, her heart gave out.

Tuesday, October 11, 1864

Lily seems to be responding to treatment and appears to be on the mend. She rested last night and slept soundly for the first time since the fever began, although she still does not have much appetite, which is fortunate because we have so little to eat. Aunt Caroline is fearful that the baby will also fall prey to the fever.

There was death shining in his eyes

Friday, October 14, 1864

Mr. Garlington has been found hanging from his apple tree. We are all horrified.

At first, it was thought to be a suicide, which apparently was the intent. Foul play was suspected because his shirt was so awkwardly buttoned, and the shoes he had on were new with not a scratch or hint of dirt on the soles. It was discovered that he had been smothered in his bed and only then carried and hanged from the apple tree.

All the silver, jewelry, and money — including the gold hidden under the newly placed gate posts — was taken. It appears that they had been planning this insurrection for quite some time. Mrs. Garlington is beside herself with fear and grief. She is fortunate that she too was not slain, for it is known far and wide that she is quick to whip her servants for the slightest indiscretion.

Romeo is believed to have led the plot and he has run off, along with the rest of the negroes. It is said that they rubbed pepper on the soles of their feet, and that is why the dogs cannot locate them.

Mrs. Garlington says she heard nothing.

Father has always disagreed with the way Mr. Garlington treated his negroes. Mr. Garlington claimed that they were obstinate by nature, and it was required that the impudent ones constantly be reminded of his authority by daily corporal punishment. Fear of their master was, according to Mr. Garlington, necessary to get them to work properly.

Mr. Garlington sold Romeo's wife and oldest child three years ago, which was the cause of grave and continuous problems. He steadfastly refused to let Romeo visit his wife, even though he knew the family to whom she was sold. They did not know the whereabouts of the oldest child.

This was, I know, something Father tried successfully to avoid and he counseled Mr. Garlington to reconsider — which he refused to do.

That same year Romeo's baby son died, although I am not sure what was the cause.

Mr. Garlington accused Father of pampering our negroes and warned him that it would lead to their becoming indulgent and spoiled, which would in turn lead to insubordination. Both Father and Mother could be quite firm and strict when it was warranted — Father especially — but I think the wisdom of their way can be readily seen in the continued loyalty of our negroes, while all around us others are running off to join the Yankees or worse, as witness the events at the Garlington house.

Iris has insisted on sleeping outside my room to protect us — which has made her the object of great scorn from the soldiers who are stationed downstairs. They question why she would do this, and Iris tells them that she has nursed me since I was a baby and that she has no intention of abandoning me now. Bless her.

I am proud that our negroes have chosen to remain with us. I have always wondered what they truly thought. We live with them but we know so little about them. I have often made note of the fact that they are one way with us and another with their own color. I would think that this deception is something they have had to adopt.

I must confess that whenever I saw Mr. Garlington I had the eerie feeling that there was death shining in his eyes. Perhaps all of this was written in the book of fate.

Sunday, October 16, 1864

All around us people are leaving. Some heading south, others heading west, taking whatever they can with them. I support Aunt Caroline in her decision to stay. Where would we go, and what would happen to us? We cannot go to Richmond, for all reports are that the situation there is dire. And what would happen to our beautiful home? How would Father and Tally find us?

112

How precious life is

Saturday, October 22, 1864

All hope is slipping away. I pray that God will sustain us, yet, at times, I feel it would be better if we all would die and put an end to this misery. I try not to let thoughts like that enter my mind. I think of seeing Father and Tally again and that gives me strength to continue. I think of how Mother would have liked me to act and that too gives me strength.

Tuesday, October 25, 1864

At night we can hear the guns in the distance breaking the silence, and during the day we fear that Colonel Davenport and his men will leave and abandon us to the lawless soldiers who are roaming the countryside. Having our home taken over by Colonel Davenport has proved to be a blessing. If it were not for his protection I do not know what would become of us.

Saturday, October 29, 1864

My thoughts are of Tally. Is that bad? I wonder if we would be happy as man and wife. Marriage is such a holy state, and I would not want to enter it unless it were to remain so.

This war has made me see how precious life is. Odd when I am surrounded by death and darkness. I fear I have wasted my youth on trivialities where sugar plums and balls achieved a disproportionate importance, along with the craving for useless objects. I was living in a state of ignorant bliss. Well, this is no more.

Tuesday, November 1, 1864

Cousin Rachel continues to be a trial. Aunt Caroline has had to have a stern talk with her about how she acts when she is around the Yankee soldiers. Aunt Caroline is concerned that Cousin Rachel might provoke them to something regrettable. I heartily agree with her, and I am not sure why Cousin Rachel is acting this way.

We no longer talk about anything — although I have tried. Early yesterday morning I heard her softly playing her flute while I was washing. I quietly reentered the room and waited until she had finished the piece. It was quite nice, which I told her. She just stared at me with a faraway look in her eyes and then got back into bed, turning her face to the wall.

Aunt Caroline and I have been appreciative of the manner in which the soldiers who occupy our house have conducted themselves and wish the situation to remain so. We expected the worst after hearing reports from others. We have not been shown any disrespect, and they show much consideration.

Despite their kindness I cannot help but think how long it has been since I lay down in peace at night. I sleep fitfully and wake in the morning just as tired as when I laid my head on the pillow the night before, fearful of what the day will bring.

Why can we not go on living as we did before?

Thursday, November 3, 1864

Cousin Rachel is filled with hatred for the Abolitionist soldiers, and she says the war has turned her heart to stone. She says the Yankee flag is a horrible symbol of this hateful invasion. She has sewn a small Confederate flag inside the folds of her dress. She says this is the true spirit we should show, and she accuses me of putting on a false face when the enemy is all around us. I have always been a very private person and I cannot change my ways now. Cousin Rachel accuses me of superficiality, which, I must confess, offends me. I do have faith — although at times, Lord knows, I waver — that better days are coming. I am sorry this irritates her so, but I could never abide political talk and I am afraid I cannot do so now. Even before the war, when Father and Mr. Garlington and Doctor Harris would talk about politics at the dinner table, I usually found some reason to excuse myself.

I do not know whether secession is the right choice, nor do I know if freeing the negroes will answer all our problems. They seemed so content before all this began that I am unsure as to what all the fury is about. Why can we not go on living as we did before? Is it not enough to believe in the life we had? I do not hate the Yankees as Cousin Rachel does but nor do I understand why they have chosen to come to our land and spread terror, deprivation, and upheaval in their wake.

Friday, November 4, 1864

Cary Baldwin and her children have left.

Mrs. Baldwin heard someone at the front door and before she could put some clothes on, they were thundering at the shutters, demanding entrance and waking the few negroes that remained.

All were ordered to assemble in the dining room. The children, rudely awakened by the commotion, were dumbfounded by all the activity.

She and the children were driven into a state of panic. The Yankees have incited the remaining negroes into a fearful state — employing them to keep watch and let them know of any suspicious activity, such as Confederate soldiers or hidden weapons.

She begged the soldiers to conduct themselves with more consideration, explaining that she had not been well lately and that she feared the excitement might damage her health. One of the Yankees — who appeared to be quite drunk — told Mrs. Baldwin, in a surly tone, that her husband and brothers were killing his countrymen and that they did not care what happened to her.

She was afraid that he would kill her, but he was more interested in food than anything else, and he ransacked her house with the others and took what food they could find, shot all the pigs and fowl, and rode off, carrying them in bags.

I fear my heart will simply break

Monday, November 7, 1864

Colonel Davenport and his soldiers departed, hurriedly, this morning, although we are unsure of the cause.

The house is in a complete shambles.

The downstairs is in wretched condition. It is frightening to see. There is dirt and confusion everywhere. They have broken into everything — chests and bureaus forced open, their contents destroyed or taken, the china and the crystal shattered, and the fruit knives Mother prized gone. The linens and curtains have been torn; the furniture destroyed; the piano in the parlor broken, I fear, beyond repair.

Outside, our lovely lawn is no more — there are ruts made by their wagon wheels crisscrossing every which way, and Mother's garden has been trampled by their horses and mules, who have also stripped the bark from the trees in the apple orchard. Most distressing of all is that they have taken our horses — the stables are empty except for Falla's colt — and have butchered most of the animals and taken them too. The smokehouse lock has been pried open, the door forced in, and the contents emptied. The yard is filled with rotting garbage.

The negroes' houses remain intact.

I immediately began trying to restore order in the pantry and the kitchen, with help from Iris and Denise. It will take days and, I fear, many of the other downstairs rooms are beyond repair. The library remains, oddly, untouched. I think this is due to the fact that Colonel Davenport used the library as his office and also because the Yankees have no interest in books.

I wonder if these few words can convey my despair. I fear that nothing I say can truly express it. For the first time in quite a while I have shed tears. I fear my heart will simply break.

Friday, November 11, 1864

Early yesterday a group of Yankees came by but, much to our relief, passed on without coming into the house.

Saturday, November 12, 1864

Still no Yankees. We do not know what to expect.

Sunday, November 13, 1864

Last night three Yankees came looking for our soldiers and the guns they said they had heard we had hidden. I was awakened by the sound of their horses' hooves on the back porch. They were banging on the back door with their sabers and threatening to break in unless we responded. Fortunately, Aunt Caroline was able to rush downstairs in time to prevent any more damage to the house. She barely had time to put on her night dress and her hair was falling loosely around her shoulders. Aunt Caroline explained that the house had been occupied these past two months by Colonel Davenport, who only recently departed, and that we were sure, therefore, that there were no troops hiding about. This seemed to assure them — although they remained sitting all over the front porch and laughing and joking in the most outrageous manner all night. Finally, at dawn, they rode off.

Thursday, November 17, 1864

Nelson, along with almost all the other negroes except Iris and Amos, has run off. I am sure he convinced the younger ones to go with him. We are all quite dismayed. Fanny, Rosetta, and the children all left with him. I am certain that Nelson convinced them to do that. Nelson's leaving has taken me quite by surprise, I must confess. Amos and Iris remain as faithful as ever.

Sunday, November 20, 1864

We walk about in constant fear of the Yankees, fearing that at any moment we might be invaded. We all feel like prisoners in our own home, although there is no one about. We are afraid to open the windows or step outside. Sometimes I feel so shut up I have to go out for a walk despite the weather and the fear. When I do, Aunt Caroline insists that Amos be nearby.

I am no longer young

Wednesday, November 23, 1864

Sometimes I try to remember what our lives used to be like, but it has been so long I have difficulty conjuring up the images. I can, at times, picture the house when it was alive and full of activity — everyone getting ready for a carriage ride into town or perhaps an excursion into the countryside. Mother giving the servants last minute instructions, Father and Brother Cole seeing to the bags, and me sitting at my vanity for what I am sure must have seemed like endless hours, holding everyone up while I decided how I should wear my hair or which dress would be the most flattering. Those days are gone forever — I am no longer young.

At times I feel like I am a thousand years old — that is what this cruel war has done to me. No matter what the outcome — if peace was declared tomorrow, if the Yankees vanished from our land and allowed us to govern ourselves, if all the negroes were somehow miraculously returned to us and resumed their former roles, if all of this were to occur, I know I have changed forever and there is no going back.

I was at a loss for words

Thursday, December 1, 1864

Cousin Rachel has become impossible to understand. She says she feels like a heroine because of the war and the Yankees, who, she believes, are certain to be driven from our land. She wishes she could play a greater role in their defeat. Women, she says, should be proud of the task that is before them and that in the end we can all be proud that we have stood up to the Yankee invaders. She says she is sorry she does not have a pistol, for if she did, she would shoot some Yankees.

I cannot share her view and wonder if there is something wrong about me. I scold myself for my despair, but I am certain that Cousin Rachel is simply deluding herself. She lives in a world of make-believe.

Friday, December 2, 1864

This morning, while looking out my window, I saw a Yankee soldier standing just behind the oak out by the garden. He stood still, as if he knew I was watching, but I could see the brim of his hat when he made a movement. I was concerned about it all day but nothing ever came of it.

Saturday, December 3, 1864

We wait in breathless anticipation for news.

Sunday, December 4, 1864

Baby Elizabeth is ill.

She has a very high fever and sleeps little, tossing in her crib. She eats nothing, and swallowing seems to cause her great pain.

Aunt Caroline is besides herself with concern. She stayed up with her until early this morning, when I awoke and went in and gently urged my aunt to get some sleep, assuring her that I would wake her if necessary.

The baby slept peacefully for a few precious hours and, at dawn, opened her tiny eyes. I think I could see a questioning look in her eyes, wondering where her mother was. I was at a loss for words to comfort her and had to be satisfied with patting her cheeks.

We both must have fallen back to sleep, for when I awoke I was sitting in the rocker with the baby fast asleep in my arms.

Monday, December 5, 1864

Baby Elizabeth still has a raging fever and shows little appetite. Her throat appears to be swollen and it is quite distressing to see an innocent child suffer so. No matter what kind of nourishment we give her she turns her head aside. It is as if she too has given up hope.

How long O Lord, how long?

Thursday, December 8, 1864

The weather turned quite cold today. O how I long for the time when there was a fire in every hearth shielding us from the cold nights, when the house was such a haven from the harsh winter just outside our door.

The moon always seemed to shine most brilliantly in the winter, hanging in the night sky like a hopeful light among the twinkling stars. At those times it seemed that all was well.

Now the house is constantly damp and cold. There is little firewood and, although Amos has done his best to keep us supplied, he is old and tired and can only do so much. We are huddled in blankets and shawls a great deal of the time.

Friday, December 9, 1864

I scarcely think the baby will live out the night, as her fever is once again making rapid progress. She seems quite ill despite our constant attentions, which I fear are proving futile. I try to keep my faith in the Lord, but I'm afraid not even He can help us.

We are all alone. Thank the Lord for Amos and Iris. Amos has provided enough wood for a fire, which helps keep the baby warm. Without them we would be in an even worse state.

Sunday, December 11, 1864

How long O Lord, how long?

Wednesday, December 21, 1864

I have not written in my diary for the past two weeks, being simply unable to record the tragic death of my dear cousin, who was taken so suddenly from us. We have lost the only ray of light in our dreary existence. This war has torn apart our lives and the pieces have been scattered to the wind. The only thing that keeps me from utter despair is the knowledge that Aunt Caroline needs me in the way that I needed her when Mother left us forever. I cannot fail her and must put my unspeakable grief aside.

Thursday, December 22, 1864

I am growing thin and feeling weak. I can no longer even weep.

There is a black hole
where my heart previously beat

Sunday, December 25, 1864

How many thousands of years ago was it that we all came together to celebrate this most joyous holiday?

But this day is forever cloaked in a black shroud of grief.

There is a black hole where my heart previously beat. Anything would be better than this painful wound — a wound that grows infinitely more acute when it is filled with the uncertainty about Father and Tally. I am unwilling to accept that they, along with Mother, Brother Cole, Uncle Benjamin, and Baby Elizabeth are gone forever — never to return.

I find it impossible to imagine them lying cold upon some battlefield with no one to care for them. I cannot bring myself to believe — as others seem to — that somehow it would be worth it. Is anything worth dying for? Is this awful waste — this painful sacrifice — justified in God's eyes?

Epilogue

Miraculously, Emma's house, although extensively damaged, survived the war. Aunt Caroline and Amos Braxton continued to live there when the war ended. Aunt Caroline, forced to earn a living for the first time, turned the house into an orphanage. Amos, although seventy-one, was an accomplished carpenter and he was able, along with some hired help, to repair the inside of the house. "Aunt Caroline's Home," as it came to be known, functioned from 1865 until 1893, when Aunt Caroline died at the age of 62. Amos died three years later.

Cousin Rachel lived with her Mother at the orphanage, helping occasionally with the children, but only occasionally. Although speculative, it is assumed that Rachel Colsten suffered a nervous breakdown during the war.

In 1867, Aunt Caroline was forced to commit her to the Richmond Lunatic Asylum, where she died a year later when she fell, jumped, or was pushed from the fourth floor of the asylum. Unfortunately, the available information surrounding her death is confusing and, at times, contradictory.

Colonel Robert Stiles Simpson died at the Battle of Cedar Creek on October 19, 1864. Apparently, he had become separated from his regiment, was without a coat in bitter cold weather, and had taken the overcoat of a dead Yankee soldier for warmth. He then attempted to find his way back to his own lines and was accidentally shot and instantly killed by Confederate soldiers, who mistook him for the enemy. He is buried next to his wife, in the Simpson family graveyard, which survives to this day. The house, however, went to ruins after Aunt Caroline's death and was demolished some time after 1893. There is no trace of it today.

Taliaferro "Tally" Mills was wounded twice and taken prisoner on the outskirts of Winchester, Virginia, in September 1864. He was taken to a federal prison in Elmira, New York, in April 1865, when Confederate commander General Robert E. Lee surrendered the Army of Northern Virginia to Union commander General Ulysses S. Grant at Appomattox Courthouse, ending the war.

He was released a month later and made his way back to Virginia and the Simpson home where he was united with a relieved Emma Simpson, who knew nothing of his capture or his fate. They moved to Richmond where they were married. Tally went to work for *The Richmond Examiner*, beginning what was to become a lifelong, successful career as a journalist. In his later years he became well known as the publisher of a small but influential weekly newspaper. They had two children, Robert,

132

born in 1868, and Jane (named after Jane Eyre), born two years later.

During the early years of their marriage, Emma, who was considered quite a beauty, taught piano and volunteered at the Richmond Library. Over the years, as the children grew, she devoted more and more time to working at the library, where she developed a reputation as quite an authority on Charlotte Brontë. Tally died in 1916, at the age of seventy, and Emma died the next year.

Iris, who, with her daughter, Dinah, accompanied Emma and Tally when they moved to Richmond, lived with and worked for them for a number of years. Some time before 1875 Iris married and moved north with her husband and daughter, possibly to Chicago. Their whereabouts after that are unknown.

The ring Tally sent Emma never did quite fit on her finger — she always wore it on a chain around her neck. It has been passed down through the generations and currently is worn on the finger of her forty-five-year-old great-great-granddaughter Emma Clark Broughton, who lives in New York City, where she is a journalist.

Life in America

in 1864

Historical Note

Any understanding of this nation has to be based . . . on an understanding of the Civil War. . . . The Civil War defined us as what we are and it opened us to being what we became, good and bad things. And it is very necessary, if you're going to understand the American character in the twentieth century, to learn about this enormous catastrophe in the nineteenth century. It was the crossroads of our being, and it was a hell of a crossroads: the suffering, the enormous tragedy of the whole thing.

— Shelby Foote

The Civil War, fought between 1861 and 1865, was the darkest and most critical period in American history. It was a bloody, brutal, and bitter war. Three million soldiers fought at a time when the population numbered only thirty-one million. More than six hundred thousand died — nearly as many Americans as died in all other wars combined — two thirds of them from illness and disease. Frequently families were torn apart as brother fought brother.

There were two central issues that divided the nation and caused the war to be fought. One was slavery. The economy of the Southern states was based on slavery. In the 1850's, as the country was rapidly expanding to the

West, the issue of slavery in the new territories became, despite attempts at compromise, an incendiary issue.

Many Northerners were opposed to the expansion of slavery in these new territories. Abolitionists, an extreme but vocal minority in the North, wanted to abolish slavery wherever it existed. They considered it evil and contrary to the ideals of democracy.

Most citizens of the South believed that blacks were biologically inferior to whites and therefore unable to care for themselves. Blacks were better off, they argued, being watched over by their white masters. Northerners, they believed, were out to destroy their way of life both economically and socially. Southern leaders threatened to secede from the Union and form their own country. They claimed that the United States was a voluntary Union of independent states that had a right to withdraw from that Union at any time. The majority of citizens in the North favored preserving the Union. This, along with slavery, became the primary reasons the war was fought.

In 1860 Abraham Lincoln was elected president. He vowed to keep the country united: "A house divided against itself cannot stand. I believe this government cannot endure permanently half slave and half free. I do not expect the Union to be dissolved — I do not expect the house to fall — but I do expect it will cease to be divided. It will become all one thing, or all the other."

For Southern leaders, Lincoln's election signaled that the time had come for drastic action. Eleven Southern states seceded from the Union, creating the Confederate States of America.

In December 1860, Southern forces, supported by artillery, surrounded the tiny federal Fort Sumter, located on an island in Charleston Harbor, South Carolina. By the spring of 1861, Lincoln was forced to send ships to resupply the Union soldiers who had been besieged for over four months. On April 12, 1861, the Confederates opened fire on Fort Sumter and the Civil War began.

Both sides were tragically mistaken in their belief that the war would be brief.

The first major battle took place just twenty-five miles away from Washington, D.C., near a small stream in northern Virginia named Bull Run. Ordinary citizens brought picnic baskets and binoculars and sat down to watch the fight from the sidelines. The Confederate soldiers counterattacked so fiercely that the watching civilians and the inexperienced Union soldiers fled in terror. Almost five thousand soldiers were killed or wounded that day.

For the next four years the war was a series of endless, bloody battles in places like Shiloh, Cold Harbor, and Antietam. In three days of fighting at Gettysburg there were over fifty thousand casualties. Americans were slaughtering each other at a staggering rate and it seemed that the war would never end.

The North and the South were two very different regions. The population in the North was about twenty-two million, while the South had only nine million inhabitants, at least three million of whom were slaves. The North was industrialized and had a well-developed transportation system, while the South was mainly an agricultural society. Three fourths of the world's cotton was grown in the South. It was a vital part of the Southern economy — and cotton picking was dependent on slave labor. The South had a much stronger military tradition than the North, but they were badly outnumbered and outgunned.

Militarily, the South's only goal was to repel what they considered the invasion from the North. They had the advantage of fighting on familiar terrain and the benefit of local support. However, this meant that Southern civilians suffered greatly as the war ravaged their land and destroyed their way of life. The Union Navy's blockade of the coastline resulted in constant shortages of food, clothing, and medical supplies.

Almost every Southern family lost at least one family member during the war.

On the first day of January, 1863, President Lincoln signed the Emancipation Proclamation, which stated that all slaves in the Confederate States were now free. This did not have much practical effect, since the South was not about to pay attention to a document issued by the enemy. But it did have great political impact because it officially declared that the war was being fought to put an end to slavery as well as to preserve the Union.

By 1864 the Confederate army, commanded by General Robert E. Lee, had been weakened by battle losses. General Ulysses S. Grant, who commanded the Union armies, pressed his advantage, attacking Lee in Virginia. Their ensuing battles resulted in massive casualties on both sides. Still, a decisive victory eluded a determined Grant, and Lee maneuvered successfully and continued to rally his troops to fight on.

Hoping to increase the pressure on Southern soldiers and civilians, Grant sent General William T. Sherman's 100,000-man army eastward to Atlanta, Georgia. After seizing Atlanta and leaving it in flames, Sherman began his "March to the Sea." His men burned and destroyed nearly everything in their path as they advanced relentlessly to Savannah, up into North Carolina and on to Virginia to join Grant.

In Virginia, Grant's seige of Petersburg eventually forced the evacuation of Richmond, the Confederate capital. Lee had no choice but to face the military reality that the Southern cause was lost. He surrendered to Grant at Appomattox Courthouse, Virginia, on April 9, 1865.

Tragically, only five days later, President Lincoln was assassinated. He never saw the Thirteenth Amendment, which abolished slavery forever, signed into law.

A typical Southern plantation home.

Slave quarters.

The fashions of the 1860's were very ornate. Dressmakers often copied Parisian designs they found in illustrated magazines such as this one. Southern girls and women wore fanciful silk-and-satin dresses with crinolines (to maintain the full skirt) to balls and other social gatherings.

Girls wore specially designed costumes with narrower skirts for horseback riding. They sat side-saddle, which was considered more ladylike.

The title page from the first edition of Jane Eyre. One of the most popular English writers of the nineteenth century, Charlotte Brontë was also read in America during the Civil War. She published under the pseudonym Currer Bell — a man's name — because at that time in history, critics and readers often dismissed women's writing as inconsequential.

Photographer Alexander Gardner captures a scene of daily life.

Abraham Lincoln was President of the United States from 1861 until his assassination in 1865. His primary concern was the preservation of the Union. Before his inauguration, he said there would be "no bloodshed unless it is forced upon the government."

The second draft of the Gettysburg Address written in Lincoln's own hand. Beginning with the famous words, "Four score and seven years ago, our fathers brought forth on this continent a new nation, conceived in Liberty and dedicated to the proposition that all men are created equal," it is only about 270 words long and captures the reasons the war was being fought.

146

Thousands of boys who fought in the Civil War were between the ages of twelve and sixteen. Many of them recorded their experiences in journals and diaries.

The Civil War was the first American war to be documented with photography. When pictures of the dead at Antietam Battlefield, like the one shown here, first arrived at Mathew Brady's New York City studio, The New York Times reported, "Mr. Brady has done something to bring home to us the terrible reality and earnestness of war. If he has not brought bodies and laid them on our dooryards and along the streets, he has done something very like it. . . ."

Telegraph battery wagons such as this one near Petersburg, Virginia, made it possible for journalists to report on the war. It was not uncommon for people to learn about the deaths of loved ones from the newspapers.

Weeping Sad and Lonely (When This Cruel War Is Over)

Words by Charles C. Sawyer. Music by Henry Tucker

CHORUS
Weeping sad and lonely,
Hopes and fears how vain!
(Yet praying,)
When this cruel war is over,
Praying that we meet again!

VERSE 2.
When the summer breeze
is sighing
Mournfully along;
Or when autumn leaves
are falling,
Sadly breathes the song.
Oft in dreams I see thee lying
On the battle plain,
Lonely, wounded, even dying,
Calling but in vain. (Chorus)

VERSE 3.
If amid the din of battle,
Nobly you should fall,
Far away from those
who love you,
None to hear you call,
Who would whisper
words of comfort,
Who would soothe your pain?
Ah! the many cruel fancies
Ever in my brain. (Chorus)

VERSE 4.
But our country called you, darling,
Angels cheer your way;
While our nation's sons are fighting,
We can only pray.
Nobly strike for God and liberty,
Let all nations see,
How we love the starry banner,
Emblem of the free. (Chorus)

Though this song originated as a Union lament, the sorrow expressed in the lyrics was felt by people on both sides. The South soon adopted it and altered it to say, "Oh! how proud you stood before me / In your suit of gray, / when you vowed to me and country / Ne'er to go astray."

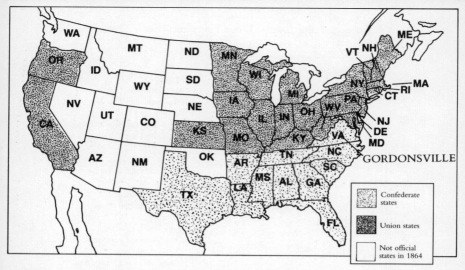

Modern map of the continental United States, showing the approximate location of Gordonsville. This map also shows which were Union states and which were Confederate.

This detail of the South indicates the important battles of the Civil War.

150

About the Author

BARRY DENENBERG is an acclaimed nonfiction writer whose main interest is American history. Writing for the *Dear America* series was compelling to him because, "It allowed me to write history from the perspective of those who experienced it. Not the history made by politicians, but the history made by ordinary people during extraordinary times. History from the bottom up, not the top down." Denenberg immersed himself in a wealth of material, concentrating on the diaries and letters of the time, sources not generally available to middle-grade readers.

"The Civil War was a pivotal event in the history of the United States. It was the only war where Americans fought each other. Because the military activity took place overwhelmingly in the South, I decided to tell the story from the Southern perspective, a perspective that asks the question — as moving today as it was then — What is it like to have your world torn apart while war rages at your doorstep?" Setting the diary in Gordonsville, a small town in Virginia, enabled him to show the grave effects of the war on ordinary civilians.

"While doing the research for *When Will This Cruel War Be Over?*" he says, "I found I could, after a while, *al-*

most feel what it was like to be Emma Simpson. It is that experience that I hope comes through in her diary."

Mr. Denenberg's nonfiction books include *An American Hero: The True Story of Charles A. Lindbergh*; *Voices from Vietnam*, a *Booklist* Editor's Choice Book and an ALA Best Book for Young Adults; *The True Story of J. Edgar Hoover and the FBI*, a Junior Library Guild Selection; and *Nelson Mandela: "No Easy Walk to Freedom,"* all published by Scholastic. *When Will This Cruel War Be Over?* is his first work of fiction for middle-grade readers. He lives in Bedford, New York, with his wife Jean and their daughter, Emma.

For my own lovely Emma

Acknowledgments

The author would like to thank the editorial, production, and design staffs at Scholastic for their painstaking efforts on his behalf. In particular, Tracy Mack, whose caring shines through on every page.

Grateful acknowledgment is made for permission to reprint the following:

Cover portrait: *Mary Cadwalader Rawle* by William Oliver Stone, 1868. Oil on canvas. The Metropolitan Museum of Art. Gift of Mrs. Max Farrand and Mrs. Cadwalader Jones, 1953.

Cover background: *A Planter's House in Georgia*. Colored engraving. 19th Century. The Granger Collection, New York.

Page 143 (top): *The Old Westover Mansion* by Henry Edward Lamson, The Corcoran Gallery of Art, Washington, DC.

Page 143 (bottom): Slave quarters, The New York Historical Society, New York.

Page 144 (top): Ball dresses, March 1862, The Irene Lewisohn Costume Reference Library, The Metropolitan Museum of Art, New York.

Page 144 (bottom): Horseback riders, from *Peterson's Magazine,* June, 1864, ibid.

Page 145 (bottom): The house of Mrs. Lee in Pleasant Valley,

Maryland, *Gardner's Photographic Sketch Book of the Civil War,* Dover Publications, Inc., New York.

Page 146 (top): Abraham Lincoln, photographed by Matthew B. Brady, from *Mr. Lincoln's Cameraman: Matthew B. Brady,* Dover Publications, Inc., New York.

Page 146 (bottom): The Gettysburg Address, The Library of Congress.

Page 147: Edwin Francis Jennison, private in a Georgia infantry regiment, The Library of Congress.

Page 148 (top): Dead soldiers in front of Dunker Church at Antietam, The Library of Congress.

Page 148 (bottom): U.S. telegraph battery wagon, The Library of Congress.

Page 149: Music and lyrics to "Weeping Sad and Lonely" ("When This Cruel War Is Over"), from *Songs of the Civil War,* Dover Publications, Inc., New York.

Page 150: Maps by Heather Saunders.

156

While the events described and some of the characters in this book may be based on actual historical events and real people, Emma Simpson is a fictional character, created by the author, and her diary is a work of fiction.

Copyright © 1996 by Barry Denenberg.

All rights reserved. Published by Scholastic Inc.
557 Broadway, New York, New York 10012.
DEAR AMERICA®, SCHOLASTIC, and associated logos
are trademarks and/or registered trademarks of Scholastic Inc.

No part of this publication may be reproduced, or stored in a retrieval system, or transmitted in any form or by any means, electronic, mechanical, photocopying, recording, or otherwise, without written permission of the publisher.
For information regarding permissions, write to Scholastic Inc., Attention: Permissions Department, 557 Broadway, New York, NY 10012.

Library of Congress Cataloging-in-Publication Data available.

ISBN 0-590-22862-5;
ISBN 0-439-44558-2 (pbk.)

10 9 8 7 6 5 4 3 2   02 03 04 05 06

The text type in this book was set in Bembo Roman.
The display type was set in Ovidius Demi.
Book design by Elizabeth B. Parisi

Printed in the U.S.A. 23
First paperback printing, October 2002

My Name Is America

The Journal of James Edmond Pease

A Civil War Union Soldier

by Jim Murphy

Scholastic Inc. New York

Virginia, 1863

I have been told to keep a record of what we do, tho I do not know why I was picked. I am not the best at spelling. Coreper — Corporal Bell is. I am not the smartest, either. Osgood Tracy is the smartest in the Company. That is why we call him the Little Profeser. And we are doing exactly what we have been doing for some days now — marching around and getting nowhere! Besides, keeping this record has already been the death of two good men and I don't need more bad luck on my head! Well, you have read it all.

Luten — Lieutenant Toms looked over what I wrote and said I had got it all wrong and to do it again. "Put in details," he said, so I will. Lieutenant Alexander Toms has ordered me to keep "an accurate and honest account" of G Company of the 122nd Regiment, New York Volunteers, from Onondaga County in New York State. Lt. Toms is keeping his own account and will combine it with this at the end of the war to make "a true and fair history of our brave men and their core — courageous deeds." That is exactly his words.

I still do not see why I have to keep this record when I know it will be my death.

Lt. Toms said to stop complaining like a greenhorn recruit. He said I was chosen because he can read my handwriting easier than most. He also said there is no curse to keeping this journal and that he is pretty certain I will last to the end of this war to finish it — unlike the first two. "You are not one of those crazy patriot fools who sticks his head up high to show how brave you are," he said. "When we come under fire, you hug the ground like a baby hugs its mother's teat." I want it clear that I am as good a soldier as any in G Company and have a torn-up arm and a black tooth to prove it!

Lt. Toms said what I wrote was better, but was still missing some important details. When I talked back fresh and said, "But I put your name in as many times as I could, sir," he said I could sit apart and miss dinner til I know what I left out. This is hard to do because we had scared up some hens who are now in a pot with some turnips and an onion and the smell makes my head swim.

What I remember is that last month — which was October — we left Warrenton Junction and went north to Bristoe Station, then on to Centerville — all in Virginia — to head off the Rebs, who was trying to get at the National Capital in Washington. The fighting was hot but we saw little of it, as we was assigned to protect the rear of the supply train as usual. Our army pushed the Rebs back and back and then we followed them south and are today close by Rappahannock Station — still in the Secessia land of Virginia. So marching has been our work and entertainment now for almost twenty days. I will add only that the first keeper of this journal was killed on the march to Gettysburg by a runaway wagon; the second died at the hands of a sharpshooter on a very peaceful Sabbath — the only shot fired that day that I recall and the only man killed in the army. What else is there to say?

Lt. Toms said there was more to say and that I should "think carefully and fully." But how can I when all around me is the smell of chicken and the sound of smacking lips? I will try this: G Company is forty-two strong today, plus one three-legged dog and one Negro camp servant. We have had nine desertions since Gettysburg, so tomorrow there may be fewer. It is November 5, 1863.

I did not show this to the Lt. Instead I asked the Little Profeser to read it and he did, but he could not talk because his mouth was full. He did point to a written "I" and when I looked puzzled he pointed to me. I am not as bright as some, but I am not an empty barrel, either. So I will write: *My name is James Edmond Pease.* I am a private in the United States

Army of the Potomac, which is under the command of General George Meade, and I am sixteen years old, I think, or thereabouts.

I showed this to Lt. Toms and he smiled and said, "Pull up a log, Private Pease. While you sup, I will tell you some other things I would like in the journal." And that is what I am going to do — tho there is mighty little chicken left to "sup" on!

November 6

Lt. Toms's first bit of advice was "start with the date and the rest will follow naturally." So I have given the date and will add that we was up at five this morning, marching by six, with only hardtack biscuits and a tin of coffee in between. The coffee had to be as old as Colonel Titus himself and tasted like the inside of a boot with the foot still inside. But since it was an improvement over yesterday's coffee, I am not complaining.

Once again our orders from regimental head-quarters are to guard the rear of the supply train. This is as good a job as any to me, but does not sit well with the rest of the men, who are eager to see some fighting. And once again Lt. Toms has sent Willie Dodd and his dog Spirit with a request that we be allowed to join up with the rest of the 122nd — at the forward line of battle!

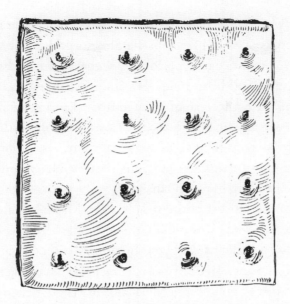

Decided to draw our ever-present "friend" and, after several attempts, managed to produce this version of a hardtack biscuit. Johnny Henderson said it looked like a real tooth-breaker to him — which I take to be a compliment.

At noon of the same day: The answer to Lt. Toms's request was no — as it has been every day since Gettysburg. I did sigh with relief when I heard this, but I also know that my bad luck can follow me into a church if it wants, so there is no relaxing for me.

After this, we marched along for four miles in a cold drizzle that has left us damp and cranky, me especially since I am sure every Reb sharpshooter has me as a target. Even Johnny Henderson — who usually has a smile painted on his face —

said he would bite the ear off of any man or beast who looked cross-eyed at him. Charlie Shelp said Johnny was just missing his mama again, so Johnny went at him and the two rolled around on the ground, fists and mud flying and cussing and such, with the rest of the Company and several of the mule-drivers looking on. I may be mistaken, but I believe the Company's sentiment was with Johnny, as Charlie has offended about everyone with his mouth. He did me when he started calling me Orphan Boy.

One of the officers of the supply train, Major Mitchell, rode up just as Lt. Toms was pulling the two apart. The Major told Johnny and Charlie to "save your fight for the Rebels," but it was Lt. Toms who answered: "We are saving it, but guarding a mule's ass is not our notion of a fight." Major Mitchell looked as if he had drunk bad milk and said, "Lieutenant Toms, if anyone would have you, I would be happy to see you get your wish," and then rode off. How is it that when Lt. Toms talks back nothing happens to him, but when I do I get to sit aside and watch everyone else eat? And he did not even say "sir," that I heard.

3 o'clock: The supply train has been stopped a-while, so I will do some writing, as instructed. Lt. Toms wants me to do a list of all the men in our company, being careful to give their proper ages and spell all names correctly. This is not such a hard task since our Company is down considerable from its original 97 men and 3 officers. Here are those left:

8

Lieutenant Alexander Toms 43
Sergeant Robert Donoghue 26
Corporal John Bell 21   Corporal Philip Drake 22
Private James Pease 16   Pte. David Bernard 20
Pte. John Keller 22   Pte. Charles Stevens 31
Pte. Develois Stevens 17   Pte. William Kittler 26
Pte. Philo Olmstead 35   Pte. James Crozier 21
Pte. Charles Holman 37   Pte. Benjamin Breed 21
Pte. William Bateman 18   Pte. Niles Rogers 34
Pte. Charlie Shelp 25   Pte. Theodore Stevens 16
Pte. Lyman Swim 17   Pte. Osgood Tracy 21
Pte. Hiram Wicks 29   Pte. William Zellers 30
Pte. Chester Youngs 21   Pte. Jehial Lamphier 44
Pte. Cornelius Mahar 20   Pte. Peter McQuade 17
Pte. Miles McGough 22   Pte. Sanford Van Dyke 18
Pte. John Williams 31   Pte. Henry Wyatt 17
Pte. Henry Clements 18   Pte. Hiram Woolsey 20
Pte. George Chittenden 29 Pte. James Wyatt 20
Pte. Alonzo Clute 20   Pte. Brower Davis 19
Pte. John Doty 35   Pte. John Farner 44
Pte. Miles Gorham 21   Pte. Boswell Grant 38
Pte. Will Hammond 17   Pte. Johnny Henderson 19
Pte. Joseph Landphier 34
Pte. Willie Dodd 16   Spirit 3

We have no capt. since Lt. Toms was reduced in rank, no
second lt. since Harrison Jilson died of typhus fever, and no

9

third lt. since Ernst Altgelt was transferred to K Company after all their officers was killed. Lt. Toms has a Negro servant named Caesar, who was freed from a house here in Virginia and works for his keep. He does not know how old he is, but Lt. Toms guesses he might be as old as 50. That is all of them every one, unless one is in the woods on a call of nature and I have forgotten him.

Same day near dark: Skirmish fire off to our right a mile or so. Firing came on very suddenly and is very hot. We are so used to hearing cannon and musket fire that we hardly notice it any-more, but this time it sounded sharper to me and I got gooseflesh when I knew it was getting closer. Lt. Toms thinks the Rebs are driving in our guard pickets and told us to load our muskets and form a line along the road to face the oncoming sound.

Everyone — including Lt. Toms — looks nervous. "Hold your fire, boys. Hold your fire," Lt. Toms is barking out louder than he needs to. "Hold your fire til I give the command." The Lt. and some others may be recalling Gettysburg, but I think most of the men are nervous because we was issued only five rounds of ammunition today — ammunition being in short supply — and five rounds will not last but a breath or two in a good fight. Lt. Toms has just screamed, "What the Devil are you doing, Pease?" and I told him I was making "an accurate and honest account of the

10

fight, as ordered, sir." "Load your damned musket and find a place in line!" he ordered very loudly, which I will do now.

Later: It turned out to be all noise and excitement and nothing more for us — which is fine, since I am not eager to add my blood to the cover of this book. Not for $13 a month, which we haven't seen in three months any-way!

The fighting came very close — maybe a half mile off — and went on for several minutes. We could hear the *pop, pop, popping* of muskets talking to each other and even smell the burnt-up powder drifting through the trees, but it is very hilly in here so we did not see anything at all even with most of the leaves gone.

Major Mitchell rode up and told Lt. Toms to take us out a quarter of a mile from the road and form another line of defense there. We was to hold off the enemy while he moved his wagons to a safer spot. We responded instantly, but had got only a few steps when Major Mitchell called out, "And, Lt. Toms. Do not fire til you see the enemy clearly, do you understand?" Lt. Toms said, "Yes, sir," but I could see he wanted to say more. And so did the rest of us.

What happened at Gettysburg was a mistake. A terrible mistake, but an honest one. The smoke from thousands of muskets and the hours-long cannon duel was choking thick and blinding. I know, because I was behind our breastworks of cut saplings, and I saw those hazy sillouet — silhouettes of

11

men coming up the hill — dark, ghostlike shapes without definition and, I might add, without a regimental flag either. What I did see plainly was that they was firing at us — just like any good Reb would.

I hadn't been in many fights before Gettysburg — none of us had — and I wasn't a very good shot either. I just pulled the trigger and hoped to hit a tree or something close enough to a Reb to scare him off. They was the enemy, but I figured that if they didn't try to hurt me, I didn't have to hurt them. But something happened at Gettysburg that changed that.

First, like a fool I stuck my head up to see what the Rebs was up to and saw those soldiers coming at us. Before I had a chance to get down behind cover, a minié ball ripped into my arm. It wasn't bad — just a grazing — but it burned as hot as a poker. Then while I was sitting there looking at my arm and the little bit of blood that was oozing out, a shell exploded above us and I got hit in the mouth by a piece of flying iron. I was so mad I jumped up and fired back — this time taking better aim. The rest of the Company fired at those advancing figures too, til we had silenced those guns, every one of them. It was what we had been told and taught to do, after all, and no one who was there would have ever blamed us. We never knew they was Union soldiers til it was all over!

Only, the officers at head-quarters wasn't there and did not understand how we could fire at our own men when they was so close. They said our Company had panicked because it was our first real fight and that Lt. Toms had failed to control us — which is just not true, neither one. No one believed Lt. Toms's story, and all the other officers who had been near us and could have told the truth was either dead or wounded. Of course, I blamed myself some for what happened to the Lt., me being unlucky and all from birth.

That is why we all wanted to say something to Major Mitchell, but no one did. We know better than to do that when there is a real fight going on. Instead we went out to welcome the Rebs, and I think we was all in a mood for a good fight. Even me! But before we got very far, there was a ferocious volley of musketry up ahead, followed by a loud cheer.

"Those will be our reinforcements," Lt. Toms said, and I believe he was disappointed that we had not been there to help. The fighting was pretty fierce for a few minutes; then, very quickly, it began to let up and started drifting away from us til we was standing in a quiet patch of woods with nothing but the smell of the powder to remind us why we was there. Lt. Toms had us form a defensive line any-way and we stayed like that in the empty woods, mostly watching Spirit chase after tossed sticks. Major Mitchell remembered us three hours later and sent word that we could come back in, which we did promptly.

Lt. Toms saw me writing and asked to see it. He said I got it pretty much right except that he had not been nervous and had not been thinking about Gettysburg at all til the Major

13

said what he said. He added that for someone who did not want to keep the Company journal I was certainly scribbling an awful lot down, so maybe I enjoyed this more than I let on. He is right about this last, any-way.

November 7

Received our orders this morning: Guard rear of supply train, et cetera, et cetera and so forth. Lt. Toms accepted the orders as he always does, with a crisp salute to the delivering captain and a polite "Yes, sir." But when the Capt. was gone, Lt. Toms let out such a blast of cussing and yelling and stomping about that even the mule-drivers nearby was greatly impressed. Heavy artillery duel way off and exchanges of musket fire. Some are in the middle of it today, but not us.

The Lt. said that when things are quiet, I am to write "brief histories of each of the men." A battle is going on, but the supply wagons hardly move during a fight, so there is not much to do. The Lt. also said I should start with myself, and I will do as ordered and be done with it.

I have no recollection of my parents, not one, tho Uncle often complained that the Angel of Death had freed them of their burden and saddled him with it instead, so I guess they both died of fever or some such. I was brought up by Uncle and Aunt — they did not like me using their given names and so I don't — on their farm near the town of Warners, which is not near anything at all, and my earliest recollection is of clearing rocks from the field while Uncle plowed. "Prayer will bring you to Heaven's path and work will guide your footsteps" was a favorite phrase of Uncle, and he practiced what he preached seven days a week, taking but a few minutes off to pray on the Sabbath. When we wasn't doing chores, I copied or read passages from the Bible, old newspapers, and the three books we had. Of my Aunt, I do not remember much other than she rarely left the house, rarely spoke — and when she did, her voice was as frail as a flower's petal — and seemed to be always nervous.

I guess I would be there still except that the rain did not fall as expected in the summer of 1862 and we seemed to produce more rocks than vegetables. Uncle began quoting the Bible more and more and Aunt seemed even more uneasy — if that is possible — and both of them turned cold eyes on me as less and less food made its way to the table. They never did say it, but I think they blamed me for holding back the rain! Maybe they was right. I mean, I was bad luck for my parents, so who knows about such things?

So one morning, to escape the stares, I went out and sat in the woods by the edge of the field. My thought was to join Uncle when he came out to work, only a strange thing happened. As I sat there, Uncle and Aunt began doing their usual chores — milking the goat, feeding the few chickens left, repairing a broken fence and so forth — and neither so much as looked up for me or called my name. All day I watched and all day they went about their business. I was hungry at lunch

15

and hungrier still at supper, but I did not budge. And they did not call for me or in any way seem to miss me. Even then I kept hoping for some sort of sign from them. The sun went down, and a while after this the yellow light from the house candles was snuffed out and it was clear they had gone to sleep. Which was sign enough for me. So I started walking down the road, taking away the one burden of theirs that I could. I continued walking til the day, three months later, when I saw a call to a war meeting and signed on as part of G Company. And that is my story told in more words than it deserves.

Later: A surprise. We was ordered forward in the afternoon to support the actions of the rest of the 122nd. Lt. Toms and some others looked happy with this, but I am not alone when I say that I was content to guard the supply train, as there is little to dodge back there but mule droppings.

We was issued three days' rations and forty rounds of ammunition — so we knew we would be very close to the fighting — then off we marched, joining up with several other companies along the way. My knapsack never felt so heavy as on that short walk.

We followed the road for five miles or so, but as we got close to the sounds of fighting, we went to the right and crossed a field with a sorry-looking farmhouse sitting in the middle. The owners — a sour old man and his sour old wife — stood in the doorway watching us file by. She was

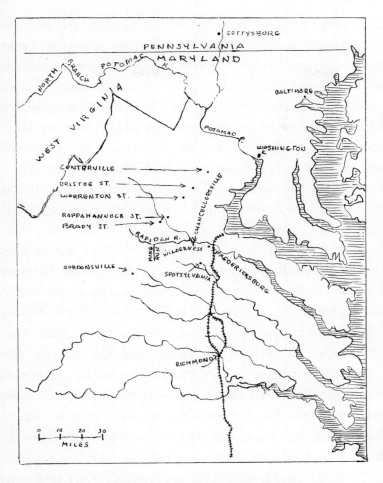

Drew this map of some of the places we have visited or might visit — according to Sgt. Donoghue. Johnny said I should have put little waves where the water is instead of straight lines; the Little Profeser said I should have put in the locations of mountains and lakes; the Lt. thought it nice, but said that Baltimore was closer to Washington than I have shown. I think some-one else should draw the map next time!

saying over and over, "Yank murd'rers. Yu'll burn 'n Hell," tho she changed it every so often to "Thivin' murd'rin' Yanks. Burn 'n Hell, all a ya!" The man just glowered at us and spit wads of drippy brown tobacca juice in our direction. Charlie Shelp talked back to them mean, but such comes natural to Charlie. The rest of us was just happy to get to the woods so those two ancients could not put the evil-eye on our backs. I certainly did not need any more of that trailing after me!

It didn't take long before I saw signs of the fight — trees with their sides chewed at by musket balls, chunks of earth ripped up by ten-pound Parrott shells. On a little, we passed some trees that had been cut in half, as if a giant clumsy hand had snapped off the tops and tossed them aside. Then we came to the first dead soldier — a Reb in a crisp new butternut uniform.

He was sitting on the ground, leaning back against a tree, and seemed to be in a comfortable position with his eyes closed and his hands clasped together on his lap. Any other time, I would have thought him asleep and dreaming of home and peach pie, but out here that thought does not scour. Besides, his face was already the color of yellow clay and the front of his new uniform was stained dark with blood.

"Shot thru the heart clean," the Little Profeser said as he stood over the body. "Dead since morning by his looks." "Not dead soon enough for me," Shelp added, and then he turned to me and said, "Hey, Orphan Boy. This one here looks like you. Got a cowlick the same as you too." And he was right.

The dead soldier even looked to be my age, which did not help my confidence any. "Move along. Move along," Lt. Toms ordered us. "There are plenty more Rebels up ahead and they'll be alive to shoot back."

We didn't see any more bodies, ours or theirs, so I guess both sides had time to haul away their dead and wounded. Except the boy, that is. Up ahead was a wide-open field where we formed a line of battle along one side after leaving our knapsacks and Spirit in the care of Caesar. Across the field from us — maybe 300 yards away — was another thick, dark woods in which the Rebs was supposed to be hiding. The field was pretty well churned up by the earlier fighting, with the stiff bodies of fifteen or twenty horses and a lot of equipment scattered all about. So we stayed there — 500 soldiers shoulder to shoulder with muskets cocked and at the ready — waiting and waiting for their charge.

For the better part of the day we was on that cold ground, muskets aimed at the invisible enemy, and listening to the real battle going on somewhere far away to our left. Some of the boys wanted to get the fight going and called out to the Rebs to come on and such, which is a silly thing to do as far as I am concerned. If a fight is going to happen, it will happen and doesn't need me to hurry it along. It wasn't long before the cold got into my bones and set me off shivering, so I put my hands in my pockets and prayed that this would not mean another round of my ague. The last time I had those shivering night-sweats, I thought I might die I was so weak and tired. After the sun set, a courier appeared with fresh orders, and a few minutes later Lt. Toms said, "Okay, boys, we are going back."

The Reb boy was still there, leaning back and, like a good soldier, waiting his turn to be collected. And the sour old man and sour old woman was there waiting for us. Everybody waits in a war.

Charlie Shelp on a day when he seemed unusually pleasant and cheerful — for him! Lt. Toms said the drawing wasn't bad and that I could include others if I had time.

November 8

Today's orders: guard the rear of the wagons — so I guess yesterday was a real emergency and no one will have us yet. Lt. Toms did not get upset today and he did not send Willie and Spirit out with his usual request. "It would be kinder for them to shoot me and be done with it," he said quietly, and I think he meant it. He went on to say that he couldn't go home with this disgrace on his head, and since they wouldn't let him fight he could never prove himself in battle. It did not help that Lt. Clapp from A Company visited this morning at breakfast and told Lt. Toms about the fighting they had done yesterday while we was guarding an empty field.

Later: I asked Sgt. Donoghue what I should write down as his history and he gave me the queerest look. When I said it was an order from the Lt., he shook his head and said it was all non-sense, this writing down what happened and who was there and such. But then he said, "My father was in the regular army when I was born, and my mother and I and later my two younger brothers, we all followed him when he moved from place to place. He was a cooper by trade, and a fine one, too, but no one outside would hire the Irish, so that is how he came to the army. His name was Flann, and hers was Mary. Have you got all of this, because I don't want to say it again. When I could, I joined the army, which is why I am here. Is that enough?" I said yes and he walked away muttering, "Non-sense, that is all it is," and I was happy to have gotten what I did from him. I will add that the Sgt. is married and has three children, all girls.

I am still free of the ague, so I guess it has passed me by this time.

November 9

Much the same "excitement" as yesterday — following the wagons. When we stopped, I was sent out with some others to watch for enemy raiders who might sneak up on our wagons. Spent most of the time wrapped up in my poncho facing away from an icy wind and thinking about that dead Reb boy. I wondered if he would get a proper burial or whether he would just sit out there til some hungry pig found him. And I wondered if his friends missed him or if his parents was somewhere thinking about him and worrying. Then I thought, at least he had someone to worry after him, which made the wind feel even sharper and me feel very lonely indeed.

7 o'clock: Talk tonight at supper was about the elections and my curse. I am too young to vote, so I did not listen closely to what was said about the election. I do know that all who could voted against Copperhead candidates, who are

22

for the secession of the South. My curse was another story.

Most — the Little Profeser among them — said such things do not exist, except in the mind of the unlucky, and Charlie Shelp added that I was as dumb as a fence post for believing such things. Everyone laughed at that and I felt my face flush red, but Johnny Henderson jumped in then and said it was dangerous to make fun of a curse. He said his uncle once spit down a neighbor's well and the next day his uncle drowned while fishing. "He'd fished that pond for thirty, forty years," Johnny said, "but he'd put bad luck on himself by spitting down that well, and the water got him!"

Shelp said Johnny was as stupid as me, and that together we had as much sense as a drum. But I wasn't listening to Shelp; I was smiling at Johnny, because I knew he had made up the story so Shelp wouldn't pick on me alone. It didn't even bother me much when Shelp made up a song about me and sang it over and over:

Good people, I will sing you a ditty,
And hope that it doesn't annoy;
I make an appeal to your pity,
For I'm an unfortunate boy.
'Twas under an unlucky planet
That I was born one night;
My life since first I began it
Has been cursed in dark and light.

So do not make sport of my troubles,
But pity one who feels no joy,
For I'm an uncomfortable, horrible, terrible,
  inconsolable Jonah Boy.

November 10

Crossed the Rappahannock on a pontoon bridge at the tail end of the wagon train. Since there must be 500 wagons in the train, we did not get to cross til it was nearly dark. It is a good thing we didn't have to wait for the cattle to cross too! Lt. Toms seems all in and is not his usual self, which might have something to do with the official report that was circulated yesterday. It congratulated the 122nd for charging and carrying a strong enemy position during the battle of the seventh, and for taking 1,600 prisoners, plus small arms and three cannons. It also said that Lt. Clapp had been promoted to the rank of captain because of his valor and leadership in the field. Some of the Company have been trying to think of a way to cheer up Lt. Toms, but so far we have had no good ideas.

November 11

Today the trampling of thousands of cavalry horses, followed by tens of thousands of foot soldiers, followed by thousands of mules and hundreds of wagons, churned the road into a mud-pike. Spent too much time hauling stuck wagons from the thick soup.

At one point we came to a wagon whose six mules had gotten tired and stopped to rest. The driver was heaping one cuss after another on them, along with some fierce blows from his whip, but they just stood there with heads bowed. Willie — who has a tender spot for all dumb creatures, not just three-legged ones — told the driver to stop what he was doing, which the driver did, but only so he could turn his mortar-gun mouth on Willie and the rest of us nearby.

While the driver's back was turned, the mules ended their rest break and began walking forward very slowly. The driver never even heard them — not with his mouth firing cusses, Willie answering back and Spirit dancing around barking. And, of course, no one — not even his fellow drivers! — bothered to tell him what was happening. It wasn't til an officer from the supply train asked the driver where his wagon was that he realized it was gone. At least twenty wagons had already passed by, so the driver raced off after his own, slipping and sliding in the mud while throwing more cusses back at us. It was a fine spectacle to watch and gave the boys a needed laugh.

Several of the boys are sick with the ague and flux and had to report to the doctors, but so far I am fine. There is a rumor that the paymaster is near and this has raised the hopes of some — including me — who wish to visit the sutler for supplies. We have had nothing but shelled corn, a little meat, hardtack and coffee for three days now.

Later: Lt. Toms very quiet today and no one bothered him with talk. So when Henry Wyatt wanted to know where we was headed, he asked his brother James — Henry being shy always. James asked Corp. Bell, who asked Sgt. Donoghue, who, after some thought and hesitation, went to Lt. Toms and stated Henry's question. "Where are we going!" Lt. Toms shouted. "How in the name of Hell would I know? They don't tell me any-thing any-more! The damned mules know more than I do! Ask them!" Lt. Toms fell quiet again, and Sgt. Donoghue came over to us and said we could ask our own damned questions after this. The rumor about the paymaster turned out to be just that. No pay — no trip to the sutler.

November 12

We are headed for Brandy Station, where the army will spend the winter. This information was gotten from one of the mule-drivers. Johnny Henderson thinks this is about as close to actually talking to a mule as you can get, a mule being a rather more reliable source of information than a dri-ver. The rest of the day had us marching, hauling stuck wag-ons, marching, hauling, marching, hauling — and a sorry, muddy bunch we were by night.

I have a case of the shakes, which may be the ague or something worse, and have been having trouble sleeping. I have also had a hard time forgetting that dead Reb boy. I am going to take quinine and hope this will drive off the ague and the boy.

November 19

We have been in camp this week, getting ready for winter. By the time we got here, most of the men had already chosen their tent-mates for the cold months ahead. Only Johnny Henderson, Charlie Shelp, and myself was left, and I was glad to be with Johnny since he is as near a friend as I have. We was also joined by a new man from Syracuse — Washington Evans.

Washington said his father is a carpenter and that after the war he would be too, and it turned out to be a great fortune to have him when we built our stockade tent. Ours is sturdier than most, with a tightly constructed stone-and-stick chimney topped by a handsome pork barrel. Inside, Washington put together furniture, including a barrel table and four stools. We are the envy of the Company and even Lt. Toms came out of his tent to inspect our work and said it was the coziest he had ever seen. Eight new men have joined G Company, tho none are as welcome as our Washington.

Had the shakes for five days, but not bad enough to visit a doctor — thank Heavens! That Reb boy came back a few

27

times in my dreams, but has faded away again. The only thing we lack now is food — or rather a variety of it, corn being plentiful. It is hard to believe how many ways we can cook our corn: We have parched corn, boiled-corn dough mush, corn coffee and the latest invention to make it go down good is to half-parch it and then grind it coarse — like hominy — and then boil it with a small piece of pork as a season. This last is the best by far.

View of our stockade tent. That is Washington Evans sitting in the doorway talking with Johnny.

November 20

Very cold, with our day used up stacking boxes and barrels near the commissary depot. Lt. Toms gave instructions and then stood off by himself. He is about as downhearted as a man can get. Lt. Toms was a schoolteacher in a tiny town near Syracuse before the war, but hoped to have a military career after. Now he is certain he will never be allowed to rise above a lieutenancy and that he will always be given the worst assignments. I think he may be right.

The new men are all sick with bowel complaints, tho none are serious cases so far. The good news today is that the boxes and barrels we wrestled contain soft bread and desiccated vegetables, so we will have something to go with our corn!

Later: Johnny and Charlie Shelp have been at it again, and this time Shelp landed several good punches and Johnny's face is swelling up and raw. I wasn't there or I would have stepped between them to spare Johnny some. By the time I heard about the fight and got to our tent, Sgt. Donoghue was telling Shelp to leave Johnny alone from then on. Shelp did not take the Sgt.'s words well and said this was none of his affair, so Sgt. Donoghue — who is a very big man, but of a calm and peaceful nature — usually — hit Shelp so hard his feet left the ground.

When Shelp recovered enough to sit up, Sgt. Donoghue told him to get his equipment and move to the last tent in our row, which is closest to the swamp and not very well made, either. "You can't order me to move!" Shelp shouted. "Only the Lt. can!" "If you want," Sgt. Donoghue said in a low, menacing way, "I will move you myself with this," and he held a fist in Shelp's face. The Sgt. looked around and said,

29

"Williams and Davis, help this man up and to his new home. Wyatt and Doty, get his things out of here. Have one of the new men move into this tent. And Shelp, if you bother Pte. Henderson again, you will answer to me. Now *move!*"

The new man's name is Charlie Buell, so we still have a Charlie among us. He is 30, I would guess, or around there, and he carries himself well, being tall and fit looking, and speaking in a clear, precise voice. Like just about every other man who has the ability, Charles has a mustache, tho his is very neatly trimmed. He said he was a lawyer in his home town of Manlius and joined after helping several escaped slaves get to Canada. He seems a good exchange for Shelp and our winter should be more pleasant for it. Johnny is being treated like a wounded hero for having freed us of the enemy. I certainly think he did.

November 23

Capt. Clapp came this morning, and after a brief visit, Lt. Toms was as happy as he has been in a long time. I was glad to see this change in the Lt., but I knew it meant trouble for me and I was right. There is to be some sort of "surprise action" soon and Capt. Clapp wants G Company to be a part of his command. So I will not have a quiet — and safe — winter after all!!

Lt. Toms called the men together to tell us what he knew, which was not much other than we would leave in a few days and be close to the Mine Run River. "We have a chance to prove ourselves," he told us. "Maybe our only chance. I want this Company to be the best in the 122nd." He even asked about the Company journal, which he has not shown interest in for many days. He glanced through it and seemed pleased, but he did say, "Pease, why are you still going on about your bad luck? Didn't your people teach you any better?" I was going to say, "I was brought up on the Bible, which is full of magic and miracles, and even a story about Jonah and his bad luck with the whale. So why is being cursed so strange?" But I didn't because I didn't want to sound like a blasphemer — and I didn't want to miss supper again! "Well, just keep your head down and do what you have always done, and you will be fine, do you hear?" "Yes, sir," I answered, but I can't say that I was much reassured. His only other comment about the journal was that I should list the new men, but I don't want to use up the space til we see who deserts.

The Lt. then sent Caesar to the sutler for some provisions and we are to have a special meal tonight! I was happy then that I had held my tongue. "A Thanksgiving meal," Lt. Toms told us, "for our deliverance."

November 24

Lt. Toms is quite happy today, but the rest of us are feeling stuffed and sluggish because of our meal — which consisted

31

of real eggs, soft bread, butter that was not more than a week or two old, beef stew with real potatoes, dried peaches and coffee and sugar. After dinner Lt. Toms brought out eight bottles of whiskey — which must have cost a great deal, since we have not seen this in over two months! — and Sgt. Donoghue gave each of us a share in our coffee. It was a fine feast and enjoyable, tho Shelp seems to have turned his mouth on me, repeating often that he did not want to stand near an unlucky Jonah Boy. We will see where this leads.

Asked Corp. Bell, Jehial Lamphier and the Wyatt boys about their pasts, but no one is in a mood to talk, which is just as well because I am in no mood to write.

November 26

Sgt. Donoghue woke us this morning before sunrise with "Happy Thanksgiving. Prepare to march in twenty minutes," and we did, this time as part of Capt. Clapp's unit.

4 o'clock: Crossed the Rapidan River just above the Mine Run River at ten and was immediately given a Reb salute of flying minié balls. Our Company got sent out, along with K Company, to shoo our Secesh friends away while the army marched on.

The woods and underbrush was something thick, so we did not move in any particular order. Crouching low, we went from tree to tree, trying to avoid the hot metal coming at us while working our way toward the sound and smoke of the firing.

I have to admit to being very nervous as we entered the woods. I even started to have trouble breathing and had to take in little gulps of air, but I kept moving forward by watching the man in front of me — who happened to be Johnny Henderson — and dashed ahead whenever he did. My breathing settled down some and was almost normal when I saw something move out of the corner of my eye.

I was sure I had a Reb located — maybe 400 feet away — and I pointed my musket at the tree near his position. I was holding steady, aiming, finger on the trigger, when I heard the loud crack of a shot out of the many that was crackling around me and then the whooshing sound of the ball coming at me.

I know this does not seem possible, but stranger things have happened in this strange war and I know what I heard, so I ducked — and just then the ball sent my forage cap sailing. I was so startled I just sat there on the ground, staring at my cap with its new ventilation hole thru the band and wondering what that ball would have done to my head if I hadn't moved.

"You O.K.? You O.K.?" Johnny screamed in my ear all excited, and I nodded. "Let's go, then! Come on!" he yelled, pulling me to my feet. "Lt. Toms has ordered a bayonet charge and we are lagging."

33

Johnny started dragging me along, and I stumbled, then righted myself and began to run on my own, fumbling to put on my bayonet as I did. I hardly had a chance to look where I was going before I plunged through a tangle of leaves and branches and followed the others, who was forty feet in front and plunging through leaves and branches too. Suddenly I found myself very mad at what had almost happened to my head and I wanted to get the Reb who had fired at me, whoever he might be. Lt. Toms was way out in front, maybe 100 feet from me, his sword raised high in his right hand, and shouting "Come on, boys, come on! This way!" and I thought what a fool he was to be out there like that, all alone, and at the same time my legs began moving faster and I made up the ground between myself and the rest of the Company.

I was just a few steps behind one of the new men, with the rest of the Company spread out on either side. I didn't notice anyone else, but I am sure Willie Dodd was near because Spirit, who hadn't been tied up, was to my left and weaving this way and that way through holes in the underbrush and barking madly.

The Rebs was still firing on us and the hissing of lead was all around. Just then the new man went down in a heap ahead of me. That ball was meant for me, I thought, which made me madder still, and then I realized he had just gotten his bayonet snagged on some vines and tripped over his own clumsy feet. But that didn't make me any less mad at the

34

Rebs. I leaped over the new man and a second later I was right next to the Lt. and heading into the smoke of a recently fired Reb gun.

I saw a shadow move up ahead and thought about stopping to fire, when I remembered those shadows coming at us at Gettysburg and thought better of it. I did not want to cause the Lt. any more trouble. So I ran at it, musket lowered now and my bayonet aimed at its center — its stomach — and let out a howling scream that startled even me. Just then the woods in front of me began to crackle like popping corn tossed into a hot fire and the air around me vibrated and whizzed as the miniés flew over, around and near me.

I had not one thought in my silly head as I ran at the enemy, except that I was going to get the one who shot at me. I did have this strange feeling at the same moment — just a feeling, not any words — that I needed to protect the Lt. — tho why he would need *me* to protect him I wouldn't know.

The smoke from the volley rolled out to meet me and a thought *did* enter my head then. The thought was — on the other side of that smoke are a whole lot of Rebs with muskets and bayonets waiting for you. But by the time that thought was all strung together I was in the smoke and knew it was too late to do anything else, so I screamed again and lunged forward, bayonet extended.

Which is when Lt. Toms's voice broke through clearly: "Pease, what the Hell are you doing? Get back here!" which was also when I came through the wall of smoke and discovered —

35

well, nothing. The Rebs was gone and the only trace of them was their backs as they skedaddled through the trees.

I guess I should have fired on such easy butternut targets, but I was breathing so hard I probably wouldn't have held my musket too steady. Besides I didn't see the point. We had driven them away from the rest of the army, which is what our orders had been.

Lt. Toms and the other men came up then, and everyone started talking at once — the Lt. wanting to know why I'd charged so far ahead by myself and saying I could have been killed, the others patting me on the back and making all kinds of noise about how I'd driven off General Robert E. Lee's army single-handed, that I was a regular hero and so forth. But the only thing I could say between gasps of breathing was "Where is my cap," which Johnny dashed off to retrieve.

That's when Sgt. Donoghue said, "Look at that," and pointed to my stomach. There was a ragged hole in my uniform. I unbuttoned my shirt and pulled out this journal, which I keep in there whenever we leave camp so I will not lose it and so no one else will steal it. The cover, which is of hard board, had a clean hole in it and the ball itself was lodged inside, having made a journey all the way to the entries about Gettysburg.

"Lord," Johnny exclaimed when he came back and examined the hole in my cap and the ball in the journal, "you are one lucky soldier for sure." But I didn't see it that way. As far as I was concerned, the lead was getting closer and closer and

36

it was only a matter of time before it hit its mark.

Only three wounded in our Company — Corp. J. Bell was shot in the leg and the doctor says the bone is broken; W. Zellers was hit in the shoulder, tho the injury is not bad; and W. Bateman had his left eye nearly poked out by a branch he ran into, but he says he aims with the other so he will be okay. Assorted other bruises and sprains and cuts, all minor.

November 27

After our skirmish yesterday, we marched double time til we caught up with the rest of the 122nd. Lt. Toms received a personal "Well done" from Capt. Clapp and some other officers after K Company's capt. related what took place in the woods. This cheered all of us who want to see our Lt. Toms restored in rank someday. There was nice words for me, too, but by this time I had found my tongue and said I was just following Lt. Toms's orders and had gotten confused in the smoke, which is true, I think. The boys have been studying the recovered ball very carefully and say it is a lucky charm and that I should keep it in my pocket. I said I did not want anything to do with it because metal attracts more metal, so now the boys are going to pass it around among themselves, each one getting to hold it for a day.

November 28

Woke to heavy rain and grumbling thunder. The 122nd was ordered to join up with Gen. Warren's Second Corps, so we and thousands of other soldiers spent the day clomping thru mud. Everyone fears another "mud march" such as we had last January, but that would not bother me. Mud is a lot safer than fighting. Besides, every time I think about what a fool thing I did in those woods and what could have happened, I become very excited and then, afterwards, I get sleepy and want to find a warm blanket. So I am marching with my eyes half open.

November 30

Yesterday we worked like beavers throwing up protective breastworks and preparing to charge the Rebs. The enemy had a strong position, with swamps and gullies behind and to the sides, so any run at them would have been straight on across a wide-open field 1000 yards long. For some reason I continued to be exhausted and fell asleep often, but at least this prevented me from worrying. Even the occasional shots exchanged did not disturb my rest.

Sgt. Donoghue said I might sleep the war away if I wasn't careful and so I did this self-portrait.

At nightfall the order to charge was revoked and we withdrew. Lt. Toms said it was smart to call off the charge since not enough of us would have been left alive to bury the dead. Henry Wyatt called out, "I would have," because he was the holder that day of Lucky Minié, as the ball is now called. "Just stay clear of Jonah Boy," Shelp said. "He is marked, no doubt about it, and so is anyone around him." Sgt. Donoghue went to say something to Shelp, but I said not to and that he didn't bother me, which wasn't true, but I did not need Shelp to be even angrier at me than he already seems to be.

We are at the Rapidan River today and will cross tomorrow. Lt. Toms thinks our fighting is finished for the year — finally! — and I, for one, will be happy to be back at Brandy Station and in our safe, warm home.

December 2

Arrived in camp to find our tent filled with six loafers! They left very quickly — at our request and Sgt. Donoghue's urging — but it took my tent-mates and me quite a while to clean the mess they left. These loafers was so lazy as to chop up our bench, barrel table and stools for firewood! They was from a Maine regiment and we somehow would have expected better of them than we got!

I was so tired, I thought I would fall asleep the minute I pulled the covers over me, but I stayed awake a very long time instead, thinking of this and that, but mostly seeing myself running at the enemy and screaming and seeing muskets flashing in my direction. And the dead Reb boy. He had come back too. I have been in fighting before, but this is the first time a memory has followed me so long after. Is this another part of my bad luck — to remember?

December 3

We built ourselves a bench and more stools, but barrels are scarce, so we have no table yet. Drilled, helped unload wagons and cleared a section of brush behind the sutler.

I asked Henry Clements about his life and it was as if the Heavens had opened up and a great rain had begun to fall. He talked and talked and talked — a deluge of words — and told me how his great-great-great-*great* grandparents had settled in New England and raised seven children. Then he told me what happened to each of these children, and their children and *theirs!* It was like all the begats in the Bible — how Cain begat Enoch, who begat Irad, who begat Me-hu'ja-el and on and on — til my head was spinning. If I have this correct, Henry (ours) was born to Henry (the fourth or fifth Henry Clements to appear) and to Henrietta Clark (who was a second cousin of this Henry and who bore a strong resemblance to some other Henry's mother, which created "talk" in the family, it appears). Any-way, Henry (our Henry's father) ran a dry-goods store and livery service and Henrietta gave piano lessons and played the organ in church. They was fairly

well off and well connected and had even tried to keep
Henry (ours) from having to go into the war by buying a sub-
stitute for him, but Henry (ours) did not think it an honorable thing to do, so he enlisted. Henry said he was given a
very good education, and even went away to Harvard
College, which is a good thing, I think, just to keep all of his
relatives straight in his head. I think I will not add another
history to this journal for some time.

Johnny is writing home for some herbs to put in a con-
coction that will, in his words, "let you sleep like a baby even
under the barrels of the big guns." I am almost afraid to say
it — since I worry that some of my bad luck might rub off on
him — but he is as close to a friend as I have ever had.

December 4

Two from our Company deserted last night, and another
would have, but a sentry spotted him and brought him in. One
of those who got away was our tent-mate Charles Buell. I guess
helping a few Negroes get to Canada is a lot different than getting shot at for them! Several men have the bloody flux and
are in the hospital, which was a barn before we got here.

Later: The man caught deserting was sentenced to stand on
a platform in the middle of camp for twenty-four hours
without coat or hat. After this, he will clean out the horse

41

and mule corrals by himself til Lt. Toms says other-wise. Most of us think this a fine enough punishment because he did not run off during a battle. But others — especially his fellow greenhorns — think he deserves something more severe. It is true that in some brigades he could be tried by court-martial, and sentenced to be shot, but Col. Titus has a more lenient attitude with his men.

Of course, a discussion developed over this — soldiers are always scouting for something to yap about — and this discussion boiled up into a little argument when talk got around to the best reason to fight in this war. Sgt. Donoghue said he was part of the regular military before the war and would be after, and following orders, especially to fight, is how you advance in rank and pay. John Farmer said he was a good Christian and that "the bondage of slavery had to be broken once and for all time." George Chittenden said he was also a good Christian but did not care one bit about the Negroes and that they could all go back to Africa as far as he was concerned. He joined because the rebellious states had committed treason and had to be taught a powerful lesson. Lyman Swim came because two of his friends did and he did not want to be seen as a coward or a Copperhead.

I was asked why I had put my neck at risk, and when I said, "Because I needed a pair of boots and dinner," everybody laughed. But that is the truth. And when the Sgt. asked why I didn't leave after I had got my feet covered and belly full, I got an even bigger laugh when I answered, "Because the boots fit perfect and the dinner tasted good." Which is also the truth. At the time I signed my papers I had been on my own for three months, and while happy to have freed Uncle and Aunt of my bad luck, I have to admit there was too many quiet, hungry nights.

December 5

Drilled in the morning, chopped wood in the afternoon. Lt. Toms was beaming — that is how the Little Profeser described his smile — as he read the part of the official report saying: "Special note is made of the distinguished actions of Cos. K, Lieut. Wooster, and G, Lieut. Toms, who engaged a superior number of enemy skirmishers threatening our line of march and subsequently drove them off." The Lt. was not made a capt., but this recognition pleased us anyway. Of course, Shelp had to say, "Hey, Jonah Boy, they didn't mention you or your hero's charge," and this bothered me more than it should have because I really did not want to be mentioned. Or did not think I did.

Four more men have come down with the bloody flux, so seven are in the hospital now. We also have two cases of the ague — tho I am not one if you do not count waking in the middle of the night with the cold sweats and troubled thoughts.

December 6

Drilled, chopped, ate, looked at the newspaper and avoided Shelp. That was my day. And wrote this.

December 7

Same as yesterday, tho we did not drill or chop today. Lt. Toms said I might want to add the names of the six new men still here, so I will:

Pte. Washington Evans 19   Pte. John Robinson 35
Pte. Asa Rich 21   Pte. Otto Parrisen 33
Pte. Hudson Marsh 22
and the near deserter, Pte. Theron Chrisler 19

No one will have Chrisler in their tent so he is in a wedge tent by himself near the swamp. Despite his isolation we know when he is near because of the high stink he trails wherever he goes.

Also, I was appointed temporary corp. — because Corp. Bell has been sent north for his broken leg and Corp. Drake has been added to the numbers in the hospital. I tried to say I did not want to be corp., but Sgt. Donoghue said it was not like an invitation to a dance, but an order, and Sgt. Donoghue can be very convincing. I am not the praying sort — not since leaving Uncle's — but I did pray that Bell's leg and Drake's stomach get better fast so I would not be corp. very long. What happened in the woods was an accident and I do not want others to think it will ever happen again.

December 8

Same as above with chopping, but without drilling, tho I did not get to relax with the other men because I had to carry messages for Lt. Toms and Sgt. Donoghue and fill out the roster. Two of my new duties!! The big excitement was the disbursement of a ration of Army whiskey — four spoonsful each carefully dealt out by Sgt. Donoghue. Now, was that not a big drink! I think the Sgt. got the best of this arrangement, as he had a chance to smell the whiskey before we got it.

Decided to try another history and approached William Kittler. But Kittler said he did not want to talk, and when I said it was an order, he said he had no recollection of his parents or where he was from or even of enlisting. Johnny thinks Kittler may be hiding some kind of sordid past. Kittler is always unusually quiet and often goes off by himself, but he has also been an honest enough soldier to date. Johnny joked that I get a history from Shelp, but I am not that brave yet. So I told Johnny it was his turn instead.

Johnny told me his father died when he was young and that his mother raised him and his three sisters on the family farm.

"She would get us up and fed, then go out and plow the field or hire a crew to harvest the crops, and then come back and bake pies for the church dinner and such. She has more energy than all of G Company put together." Johnny intends to take up farming too, and thinks he will marry a girl he knows in a nearby town when the war ends.

This drawing is called "All in a Day's Work."

December 9

A quiet Sunday at home. The Christian Commission and a pack of preachers descended on the camp and went to every tent looking for like-thinkers. A meeting was to be held on the drill field, with promise of a "free package of useful articles" for those who attend. Some went along to the meeting, but most stayed inside out of the cold, writing letters, reading, playing cards, smoking and such. I have noticed that in warm weather when we are fighting, many of the men are pious followers, but during the winter when things are quiet and shooting is rare, few respond to the call — unless offered a package. I thought about going myself — to avoid having to deliver messages and for the package — except that the first thing the preacher who came by did was quote the Bible and this reminded me too much of Uncle. So I stayed in our tent and joined pieces of broken candles together to make one good one. Every so often, when the wind shifted, I could hear the sweet sounds of hymn singing and then I listened to the words very carefully.

Sleep still restless but hope for better tonight.

December 10

Very cold during the night and a young snow fell — very unusual this time of the year according to those who know — which has turned everything white and covered many undesirable flaws in the camp — such as our trench latrine. B and H Companies staged a snowball battle, with B Company taking the part of the Rebs. B Company seemed to be getting a thorough drubbing when one of our boys shouted, "Here comes old J.E.B. Stuart and his boys," and we dashed in, scooping up snow and throwing it just as fast as we could til it was H Company's turn to back up. Other companies joined the fight and even some officers, and pretty soon we had a fine battle going with 600 hundred "soldiers" at least. I took a ball of packed ice in the back of the head, but when I turned I couldn't see who had thrown it. I have my suspicions, however.

December 11

Drilled a little, but not with much enthusiasm. The weather is so cold that our hands are numb and there are many long faces in camp. Johnny put together a fine-smelling stew for the tent, but when I put my spoon in for a taste, the pot fell from the pole and most everything was lost in the fire. There was some grumbling about my heavy-handed spooning, but Johnny said it wasn't my fault. He is a steady friend. Had hardtack and what we could salvage from the fire — which was a few potatoes and gritty chicken — as dinner. Word about my accident spread thru camp quickly, because later when out walking, Shelp said, "Hold on to your cooking pots, boys! G Company's Jonah is coming."

Fewer responded to sick call today, tho several — including Corp. Drake — remain in the hospital and are not better despite repeated doses of quinine.

December 15

Boiled our clothes this day and then assembled a nice stew — which did not fall into the fire! Unlike some tents, we *did*

48

clean our pot before going from one activity to the other. The stew was an interesting mix of real and desiccated vegetables and beans, but would have been better if we had added an onion, in my opinion.

December 16

Lt. Toms read this journal and said, "Good God, Corp., next you'll be putting in recipes for pie!" He then said I did not have to write so much and that when I did it should be something "truly interesting or significant, and generally of a military nature." I guess that means I should not mention the outbreak of lice that has laid siege to two tents and threatens the rest!

December 25

Christmas Day began with the delivery of mail and packages. Johnny received a box filled with newspapers, letters, sweets and canned food. I think he saw that I was all alone in my bed, so he made me help him open all of the little boxes and tins, so that we could sample the gifts. Then he glanced thru a batch of letters and said, "Jim, this one is for you." At first I thought he was joking and I felt embarrassed that I was the only one in the Company with no family outside, but he saw this and added, "I am not joking, Jim. This letter has your name on it. Here," and he handed it to me. I looked at it and could hardly believe what I saw:

49

Private James Edmond Pease
Company G, 122nd (Third Onondaga) Regiment
New York Volunteers
Army of the Potomac
Brandy Station, Va.

This was the first letter I had ever received in my life and I was so stunned I looked at Johnny, then at the letter, then back at Johnny. "Close your mouth and open the letter," he said. "It's from Sarah. I can tell her handwriting any-where."

Sarah is Johnny's sister, who is 14, and her handwriting is so small and so finely drawn that I thought it might break into a hundred pieces if I handled the envelope too roughly. But I did manage to close my mouth and open the letter and read it, too, after which Johnny said, "Well, what does it say?" so I read it to him. It was short and I am not sure Lt. Toms would think it "truly interesting and significant," but I certainly do, so I will copy it here:

Dear Private James Edmond Pease,

Our brother Johnny wrote to us about your courageous actions last month, and about the way you charged ahead of the Company to face the enemy alone. We were all very impressed by this, and moved by your valor and bravery, and I wanted to write to tell you that you are in our prayers and thoughts every day. Mother said that Johnny is certainly lucky to have a companion and friend like you, and I agree with her.

With all sincere wishes for your continued health,

Miss Sarah Rebecca Henderson

Johnny grabbed the letter from my hands and looked at it. "If you write back to her," he said, "she will answer you, and I guarantee she will say much more. She is a chatterbox in person *and* in letters usually." I will write her back just as soon as I can think of what to say.

Among the articles Johnny got was a bag of sleeping herbs that his grandmother put together. They looked like twigs, roots and leaves to me, but when I boiled them up, the smell was very sweet. Johnny has no idea what is in it. "She goes thru the woods near her house gathering this and that" was all he could say. It tasted just fine. Not strong or bitter. Right now, I feel very sleepy, but I made myself write this so I would not forget the details. Later, in my bunk, I will read my letter one more time and then pull my blanket around me snug. I must say this is the nicest Christmas that I can remember.

January 1, 1864

The Army welcomed the New Year with a cannon salute and the firing of muskets, accompanied by much singing and a tin or two of whiskey. Before going off to be with the officers, Lt. Toms raised his cup and said, "To the best, the most loyal Company in the Army of the Potomac. May we be the first to enter Richmond!" Sgt. Donoghue stood then and said, "To you, sir. The best any Company *or* any Army can hope to have!" And we all cheered and drank to this because we all believe it to be true.

I am sleeping much better and have not had a visit from my dead Reb friend in days, thanks to the sleeping herbs.

January 2

Began a letter to Miss Sarah Henderson, but after the "Dear Miss Henderson" I did not know what to say. And this was my third attempt to write her! I am not sure what will interest her. I do not think she wants to hear about chimney fires, freezing nights or the way the measles have the doctors very busy. I will have to think very carefully on this.

January 14

Lt. Toms had me come to his tent this afternoon with the journal. The only other people there was Sgt. Donoghue and Caesar, who unfolded a map of the region on a small table. "Corp. Pease," the Lt. began, "I want you to take careful notes of what is said here."

It seems that come spring there will be a major offensive — which is not a surprise since there is always some sort of big action every spring. There would be two parts to this action. One to draw out Gen. Robert E. Lee's army or some part of it — the next to strike at the left flank of his army and get between it and Richmond.

While Lt. Toms explained this, Caesar showed us the most likely route this force would take. At first I was startled to see him do this and not the Lt., since servants — especially Negro ones — are never allowed to be a part of such conversations. I must have looked odd or some such, because Lt. Toms stopped what he was saying and explained that in the past Caesar had been rented out by his master to work on various plantations near Gordonsville. "He knows the roads better than any regular Army scout, so listen when he says something about the terrain or trails or people." I said, "Yes, sir," tho I still found it strange to follow Caesar's dark finger as it moved about the map.

"We have been selected for a special assignment," the Lt. continued. Sgt. Donoghue let out a little groan. The last time we had been given a "special assignment," we trailed along after the supply train. "Don't worry, Sgt.," the Lt. said. "We will be in the thick of it. Capt. Clapp has told me we will support Maj. Pettit's artillery."

When Lt. Toms said this, he was smiling and so was Sgt. Donoghue and so was Caesar. Maj. Pettit is always in the

53

fiercest part of any battle and he is often referred to —
behind his back, of course — as "The Merry Widow Maker,"
because he will hold his guns in place at any cost and seems
to enjoy the added excitement. I did not like the sound of
this springtime job, and if I smiled it was probably a thin one.

"Needless to say," Lt. Toms said, "this is to be kept secret.
Not a word — not a hint — to anyone, not even to those at
home. I want you to know because we will begin training
with Maj. Pettit, and the men need to learn their tasks perfectly. Maj. Pettit does not tolerate mistakes. And Corp.
Pease." The Lt. turned to face me directly and he looked
extremely serious. "Keep that journal on your person at all
times. I don't want anyone to know what is going to happen."

"Uh . . . y-y-yes, sir," I said, a bit startled. You see, my mind
had wandered a little. Cannons are the prime targets in any
battle and I was picturing what it would be like being near
them during an all-out shelling. "It will never leave me, sir."

"Good," he said. Then, from the table drawer, he took two
small pieces of fabric that turned out to be sgt.'s chevrons
and handed them to me. "You will be needing these from
now on." I looked at what he placed in the palm of my hand,
blinked and must have looked confused. He broke into
another broad smile and said, "Congratulations, Sgt. Pease."

He shook my hand, and so did Sgt. Donoghue and Caesar.
"But what about Corp. Drake, sir?" I asked. "He is in line next."
"He is also being promoted, but he is still too weak from his
illness. Besides, we will need three sgts. when we begin this

54

training." "But there are other men, sir, who are older and deserve to — " But he waved my objections aside and said, "I gave this a lot of thought, Sgt. You are the best man to be third sgt. now. Sgt. Donoghue needs help, especially with the record-keeping chores. He will explain what your new duties will be." "Ah, yes, sir," I stammered again. "Ah, thank you, sir." "No need to thank me, Sgt. You earned those." He paused here, then added, "But do me a favor, Sgt. No more charging the enemy on your own. You make the rest of us seem like laggards." He and the other men laughed very loudly at his joke, and I did too. A little. Then Caesar produced a bottle of whiskey and four glasses and we all had a drink.

I was still stunned at my promotion, happy about it and a little scared by the new responsibilities, and occasionally — in my head, not out loud — saying the words "Sgt. James Edmond Pease" to hear how it sounded. Then a troubling thought entered my head. One important duty of a sgt. is to be the first to stand when a charge is called to urge the rest of the men on. It is a little like wearing a red shirt with a great white X drawn across the chest for all of those Reb sharp-shooters to see.

January 15

Took some good-natured kidding about being made sgt. from the rest of the boys last night, but most seemed happy for me. This morning was my first real test.

I called roll, which was not very hard because I know the men. When I said, "Shelp," he did not answer at all, but stood there in the front row with his arms folded across his chest, acting bored. I called his name again and there was still no answer. Some of the boys giggled, thinking it good sport to play with a new sgt., but the look on Shelp's face said he was not playing.

I tried his name a third time, and got an answer, but from another man who said "Here" in a very high voice. This produced a great roll of laughter from the Company and I felt my face flush red. I was about to shout something at the one who had answered and at Shelp when I remembered Sgt. Donoghue's words: "Don't let them get under your hide. If they see they can upset you, they will never let you alone."

So instead I looked at the roster and said, "Pte. Shelp is not here, I guess, and is absent without permission." Everyone knew what that would mean. Anyone reported absent without permission would be put in the cold stockade for a day or two with little to drink or eat, and might possibly be given an aromatic chore such as the one given Theron Chrisler.

Brower Davis said, "But he is right in front of you. Umm, Sgt."

"I did not hear him answer when I called his name," I said. "So he is not here as far as I am concerned. And I don't want to hear any more comments, either." I went to mark Shelp absent when I heard his voice. "Here," he said in a very sullen way, then added, "Sgt. Jonah Boy."

56

"You will call me Sgt. Pease, Pte. Or do you want to be on report for that too?"

There was a low murmur from the Company, I think because they felt I was being too harsh on Shelp for such a little thing. But it was not a little thing — not to me — and I wanted Shelp to know it right off. After a moment of silence, Shelp replied, "No, Sgt. Pease, I don't." His voice did not have a minié ball's weight of respect to it, but I had gotten him to answer, so I went on with roll call. Later I noticed that back in our tent Johnny and Washington was both unusually quiet and uneasy around me, so I was glad when Lt. Toms told me that there was to be a meeting with Maj. Pettit.

7 o'clock: We spent the day with Maj. Pettit and his aides learning how he wants his batteries supported by soldiers. He had a battery of light artillery — six cannons in all — set out in the drill field fully manned, with K, A and C Companies in support. Usually this kind of instruction would be carried out by one of Maj. Pettit's aides, but there he was in person with his aides looking on. We stood with them on a nearby hill, so we had a clear view of the men's movements.

"Watch how and where they move," Maj. Pettit instructed us. "In battle, there will be fifty to seventy-five guns under my command, but you will be assigned to support just six. Tell your men to stay low when they are in front of my guns or they will lose their heads. And be quick when you move. My

57

guns fire to a rapid count — sometimes every thirty counts — and if you are not down when the count is ended we will not halt the firing, do you understand?" We did.

He was also very particular that we cover his flanks and rear carefully as it is difficult to move hot guns and he did not want to redirect fire unless it was absolutely necessary. "The Rebels lost more men than they could replace last year, so they will not be making so many costly head-on charges."

"That was some show," Lt. Toms commented afterwards as we went back to our tents. "What did you learn from it?" "To move quickly and without hesitation," Sgt. Donoghue said. "To stay low," I answered. "Very low."

I am going to end this now and write a letter to Miss Sarah Henderson so I can share my good news with someone who does not wear a uniform and who is not angry with me. I have not been very successful in writing her before, but now I have something real to say. And I think I will tell her that I have kept her letter in my vest pocket ever since I received it.

January 22

Things still seem strained with the Company. I asked Sgt. Donoghue about this and he said some are probably angry because they was not made sgt., some probably think I am acting high and mighty when I give an order and some just don't like anyone who is not a pte. "Don't worry about those people," he told me. "They are not worth a bit of thought.

Your real friends will always be there." Sometimes, he added, the men do not know how to act, so they become quiet around anyone who has gotten a promotion. "They need to see how you act with them before they can feel comfortable." So I will try to remain calm and see what happens.

Drilling with the artillery battery has begun and Lt. Toms seemed pleased, so I guess we are doing the job — tho it all looks very confused from where I am. The only unusual incident came when Maj. Pettit reviewed his batteries and support and said, "Lt. Toms, your Company is the shabbiest I have seen in a while." Lt. Toms stood tall and said, "It has never gotten in the way of their fighting, sir." And then he added, "We have not been on the receiving end of such supplies since Gettysburg, sir." "Oh, that," Maj. Pettit said, looking annoyed. He turned to one of his aides and said, "Capt., these men are under our care now. See that they are outfitted properly." The next day, like magic, a supply wagon rolled up to our tents with fresh uniforms and boots. I will be glad to be rid of both my old uniform and hat, as the bullet holes are sore reminders of a close call. Too bad I can't get a new book to replace this one. It has more history about it than I want to recall.

February 2

Decided to begin again with the brief histories, hoping this would put the men at ease. I began with Osgood Tracy

59

because I knew he had a birthday coming up. Osgood said he was born during a terrible blizzard and that his father, who is a surgeon, delivered him and took care of his mother, who had been in labor a long time. Osgood never went to school, except for a few years early on and a year in medical college, but was taught at home by his father and his mother, who spoke six languages between them, including Greek and Latin. He said that they spoke a different language at every meal and that, as far as he is concerned, chicken tastes best in French. When the call came to enlist, his father signed on as a surgeon and is now the brigade surgeon for the 1st New York light artillery; Osgood left school when he heard about his father's enlistment and signed on himself, but as a regular soldier. Osgood also told me that most of the doctors he has encountered in the army — excepting his father, of course — are not fit to lance a boil, let alone treat someone seriously hurt, and that most men die from the "care" that they get and not their wounds. This is something most soldiers already know and is why we avoid the doctors at all costs. But Osgood said I should write it into our Company history so everyone will know.

February 12

Maj. Pettit has us drilling just about every day, with the cannons often firing blank cartridges and other companies playing the Rebs. Some of our Company are beginning to complain, saying they already know how to fight. But fighting under the barrels of cannons with the deafening noise and blinding smoke is a different sort of fighting. Altho not dangerous in the least while they are firing, I can assure you it is very disagreeable, for the concussion of the air almost crushes a person to the ground. So we needed to be out there to get used to the feeling and learn to hear and obey orders.

I said all this to the men and Shelp had to answer back: "And how did you come to know this and the rest of us not?" I felt instantly annoyed by his words — probably more so than I should have — and I was recalling Sgt. Donoghue's advice not to respond too quickly to a taunt when another man — William Zellers, who was not a grumbler — said, "He has seen as many fights as you, Charlie. And been wounded too." "And," another pointed out, "he has meetings with the Maj. and Lt." "That don't make him an expert," Shelp said. "I didn't say I was an expert," I said in a matter-of-fact way. "But this isn't charging the enemy head on or sniping at him from behind trees. We need to move around more quickly to protect the guns." "It is all a lot of dancing to me," Shelp said, but he wasn't challenging me directly, I think because most of the men, even the grumblers, knew I was right about this. "Give me a good old fight any-time," Shelp added. I knew that our generals aim to give him his wish, but I could not say so.

Received a second letter from Miss Sarah Henderson!!! In my letter to her I had mentioned my unease at keeping the Company journal and in reply Sarah — for she told me I should call her Sarah — sent a silver coin that her great-grandfather had carried during the War of Independence. He was only fifteen when he joined the state militia and in six years of fighting he never received even a scratch. I am not sure about the value of good-luck charms, but I think I will keep this letter and its coin with the other. That way I will not disappoint Sarah.

February 14

Many of the boys in the Company are rereading letters and heaving deep sighs. I began to write to Sarah, and Johnny saw what I was doing and said, "Sarah will think you are in love with her," but he was laughing, so I know he did not intend it in a mean way. Even so I felt myself blushing and had to play with the fire til this passed.

The day was not so cold, so we all spent time out in the sun. Johnny sat on a log for a long time trying to write a letter to his mother.

Sgt. Drake has returned to the Company, and Miles Gorham will replace him as corp.

February 22

I am not sure what to make of this day. We had been running mock battles all day, with K and E Companies charging from various positions. I was running back and forth between Lt. Toms and our men with orders and changes in orders when a spark from the hot guns must have gotten into a caisson because it suddenly exploded and I was the nearest to it. I pulled up straight — I did not even have enough wits about me to duck down! — and one of the wheels flew by my head not more than two feet away, followed by bits of wood and metal and such. I did kiss the ground about then, helped by a rush of hot air, and received a pelting of dirt, rocks and other pieces of the caisson.

I glanced up, amazed that I still had my head on my shoulders, and I noticed that a few of the men had paused in what they was doing to look in my direction, but not many, and not any of the men at the guns, which still fired away even tho two of the cannoneers had been hit by parts of the caisson too. The men still played their parts as if nothing unusual had happened.

"Move, Sgt. Pease. If you are not dead — move!" That was Lt. Toms screaming at me. I jumped up and ran as if the Devil himself was chasing me, and I must have been a sight, because I was covered with debris and spitting out dirt. But the orders was delivered and our Company responded. A few minutes passed during which I contained my curiosity, but eventually I had to glance around. Where there had once been a caisson was now a large hole — big enough to bury a man in! — and not much else. When I looked to where Maj. Pettit was, he was still seated on his horse, observing the action. I would wager any amount that he did not even blink when the caisson went up.

Later, back at camp, I heard Shelp's voice, "I tell you, bad things follow him everywhere." He did not use my name, but I don't think he had to. Johnny said I was certainly the luckiest man in the Army. So there are two views of me. Sgt. Donoghue said I had acted well considering what had happened, and I told him I had just jumped at the sound of Lt. Toms's voice. "That is what any good soldier does. He moves when ordered. That's what the men will do for you too." I wish I could believe what the Sgt. said, but I am not sure many of the men will ever jump at my voice — or that I will live long enough to give many orders.

The only bright spot is that today I received a third letter from Sarah, and Johnny said, "She is sweet on you, Jim. I can tell." I would write her a letter about my day, but my head hurts painfully, so I will boil up the last of my sleeping herbs and try to rest instead. But I will keep the words "she is sweet on you" in my head.

64

February 25

Maj. Pettit has us learning how to load, aim, fire and maneuver the light artillery, as well as all commands. "You should know the procedures," he explained, "so you can fill in when any of my men are wounded or killed." The Little Profeser noted that the use of the word "if" would have suggested that something *might* happen, while the word "when" means it will *certainly* happen. It is sometimes hard for me to recall that I joined this army to get a pair of boots and dinner! Now look where I am! Head no longer hurts, tho I am still wary around the caissons when the guns are hot. A sound sleep is once again hard to find.

Approached Niles Rogers about a brief history, but he said his throat hurt and I should ask his tent-mate Philo Olmstead. Philo grew up in Belvedere, New Jersey, where his father was an undertaker. "One summer we had a fever that carried off a lot of folk and we buried a good part of the town. When the fever passed, the town was mostly young, and then there wasn't much business for my father and we had to leave. So we traveled into New York and didn't stop til we came to a town with a lot of old people. Business has been good ever since!" Despite his background, Philo is a very merry soul and is always ready to laugh. When I asked him why he didn't go into the burying business, he said, "It's usually steady work, but I prefer to deal with my neighbors when they can talk back, so I became a carriage maker."

Sent a brief letter to Sarah telling her about my "near miss." Johnny said he was going to write Sarah and say that I "pined" for her so much that the earth shook and exploded under my feet. I then "ordered" Johnny not to write about the incident — so being a sgt. has some advantages.

March 7

Spring must be near because enemy skirmishers have been hitting and jabbing at us at various places for the past week or so, and we have been doing the same for them. Lt. Toms says that Gen. Lee and the Rebs are probably cooking up their own spring plans and he just hopes we can get ours going before they do theirs. Accompanied Maj. Pettit's guns to meet Rebs wandering nearby, but they skedaddle whenever artillery arrives. The Maj.'s men can unhitch, load and fire so quickly that most of the time the Rebs are not out of range and it is always a lively sight to see them dance from the shells.

I have been looking for a letter from Sarah these past days now, but there is never mail for me. Has she forgotten me already? I asked Johnny if he had gotten any mail and he said no, but he did say he had "disobeyed orders" and written Sarah about the caisson exploding — he said because he knew I would not say enough about it — tho he swore he did not put in anything about my pining away.

March 11

We have just learned that there is a new commander of the National Army, Lt.-General Ulysses S. Grant. Everyone was happy that Gen. Meade will stay to command the Army of the Potomac, since he is well liked by the boys and officers alike. Sgt. Donoghue said we should stop worrying about Gen. Meade and start worrying about our skins, since a new commander will always try to prove he deserved his promotion with a victory — and guess who will have to do the fighting.

Still no letter.

March 16

It happened very quickly. Yesterday Lt. Toms was called to a meeting and immediately after he issued orders to pull down our winter homes and be ready to march. We are now moving along the pike road at a leisurely pace in the general direction of Jefferson. Winter is over officially, I guess, and now the fun begins. No more time to write.

March 17

Have begun a letter to Sarah, but don't know when I will be able to send it out. We are in a wooded section about three miles from main roads, so little mail comes in or goes out. I will continue writing day after day til I can mail it, which will give me something to do besides worry. One good thing about keeping busy — I am so tired at night that I drop off to sleep as if I had not a care in the world.

William Kittler off by himself as usual. When I showed this to Johnny, he said, "He is a strange one, now isn't he?"

March 23

We have been skirmishing regularly with the Rebs, tho we have had only one wounded seriously — H. Clements — and the boys seem eager to meet the enemy more. Sgt. Donoghue said, "Even Spirit seems more feisty than usual." So far, the heaviest fighting has been over who should be carrying Lucky Minié, which resulted in a flattened nose and a black eye and some hard feelings. There is now an official list which is kept by Corp. Gorham.

The only other "action" to report was my three skirmishes with Shelp, all very minor, but still annoying. I took the "high road" in all three by letting pass some remarks that could have gotten him time in the stockade, but this did not seem to lessen his anger with me. When I asked Johnny why he thought Shelp acted this way, Johnny said, "Some people are born mean and that is the way they live and there is no explaining it." I guess that is as good an explanation as any.

March 24

Chased the Rebs most of the day, but to little purpose. Our line of march has been altered and we seem to be heading back toward Brandy Station. Lt. Toms told Sgt. Donoghue, Sgt. Drake and me that 30,000 troops have left and are headed south. "Let's hope Uncle Robert bites at the apple," he said. "Then we will take a bite out of him."

It has been over a month since I last heard from Sarah. Johnny has received only one letter from his mother and none from his sisters or other relatives in this time, and thinks there is mail for us sitting in a wagon in some farmer's pasture. Sent off my last letter to Sarah and will start another.

March 25

Rested today and so did the Rebs, so it was quiet and peaceful. The rain that has fallen all night and today probably has something to do with this. Have lived on hardtack, salt pork and corn meal for a week now, so I traded two pounds of tobacca for a chicken — a steep price — and boiled it up in a coffeepot with some root vegetables and salt. Drank the soup from the spout and found it very good, and Johnny agreed.

Some letters and packages caught up with us in the afternoon, but none for me. Three months ago I would not have even given it a thought. Was able to finish my letter to Sarah and mail it out. Once it was gone, I wondered if writing before she has replied to my other letters will offend her as too forward. Johnny said, "At least you're not thinking on being bad luck and such any-more." Which is not true, not exactly any-way, but I did not confess this to Johnny. He then added, "She loves to get letters, especially from you, so don't worry about writing too much."

March 26

Have not moved and all remains quiet and wet. Rumors drift thru camp about what is happening and where we will be headed next and some of the boys even say we are going to try to get between Gen. Lee's army and Richmond — tho I never say yes or no. Pete McQuade asked if I knew something I wasn't telling and when I said no, he became upset, wanting to know why I wouldn't tell him. He says he needs to know if we are going to fight in a day or two days or a week or two weeks, that he feels that something bad will happen to him and he wants to be prepared. It seems that his turn with

Lucky Minié was two days ago and will not come up again for nearly a month, so he is nervous. I was not sure what to say or do, and he seemed very serious, so I gave him the silver coin Sarah sent me and told him its story. I hope Sarah will understand why I did this.

Received back pay today!!! Many of the boys have set to gambling it away, but I put my money in a sock and will hold it til I know what to do with it. Johnny said that since our pay is here, our mail will probably follow — on July 4th!

Later: At dinner, Willie Dodd asked that Spirit be given a regular turn with Lucky Minié, saying he was as much a part of G Company as any of the rest, but the boys voted this down. Willie was upset, of course, but he seemed better when I asked him for some history. His mother died when he was just five, and his father was — and still is — an engineer for the New York Central Railroad, so Willie has spent most of his life on trains going from one town to another. He came by Spirit after the dog was hit by a train — not his father's — and lost its front leg. "But don't feel sorry for him," Willie said. "He can outrun most any animal and I can't think of anything he can't do that a dog with four legs can — except lift his leg to pee." Willie was just fourteen when he enlisted, and when I asked how he had managed to pass — him being four years under the legal age to enlist then — he said he guessed he got in on his length. Willie is tall for any age. He said that after the war he intends to join the railroad and maybe be an engineer himself someday, which I think will suit him as he is always on the move whether in camp or not. Willie wanted to know how I had managed to enlist, and I had to admit I had lied my way in. I signed Uncle's full name to the paper saying CONSENT IN CASE OF MINOR, and when questioned about it said, "You can check with him yourself if you don't believe me," but the recruiter only grunted and then went on to the next man in line.

April 2

Broke camp and did more marching. I am not sure how all this helps us to beat the Rebs, but we have seen a great deal of Virginia and its people. Not many are openly hostile toward us, tho a few — mostly the old people — tell us we are trespassers and robbers and Yankee trash. The rest just stare at us when we pass thru a town and keep their thoughts inside — which is wise when there are so many soldiers near who want a fight. The Negroes give us very little response, tho now and then one or another will nod as we go past or tip their hat if no Secesh white man is around to see them. Several have run off from their owners and joined our march as camp servants. So far no Southern owners have come asking after them — and I doubt many will!

April 9

Well, after more marching and no fighting we have settled down in a grassy spot and pitched our tents. We have been put in reserve and Lt. Toms said, "Enjoy this while you can." The newspapers are full of stories about the action south of here and "hints" of what might follow. These hints sound as if the writers were in the tent with Lt. Toms and the rest of us last January! I wonder if Uncle Robert reads the same newspapers as we do!!!

Later: Mail has arrived — with three letters for me!!! Johnny saw me reading them and said, "I think I will have a sgt. for a brother-in-law any day now!" I took a good deal of ribbing from the other men after this but managed to give some of it back, as almost everyone has letters today.

April 12

This spot filled up pretty fast and soldiers are now camped in a farmer's field and orchard. Most are Gen. Warren's men — our own 122nd is not in sight — and more are expected every day. A long line of wagons went by today and we even saw some familiar faces among the mules and drivers.

The only thing of note today is that I had another skirmish with Shelp. He and some other men were playing cards when a dispute broke out and Theron Chrisler called Shelp a cheat and Shelp called Theron a whiny coward and threw over the table to get at him. I got between them and some other men grabbed hold of Shelp — which was lucky for me because I think he would have hit me just as well as Theron. I told Theron that he had better have proof of what he said and when it was clear he had none — other than that Shelp had won about all of his money! — I told him that I had never known Shelp to cheat and that if he didn't watch out — but I never got to finish because Shelp started yelling, "I don't need your help! I can take care of him!" And he tried to get at Theron again, but the men held him back. I ordered the men holding Shelp to take him off somewhere to settle down and he went off with some very hot words for Theron and me! Next, I told Theron that I did not want to see him gambling again — ever — since he did not know how to lose and that he should get to his tent fast before I got angry. I have a feeling that I will hear from Shelp again, even tho I did stick up for him.

April 22

Have not had time to write in this journal what with filling out the roster reports for the paymaster and other sgt. chores. I have only found time to write Sarah two very brief letters since her three arrived, but I will try tonight after final roll call. I asked Johnny if Sarah's hair was a little or a lot curly and he responded by telling me he was tired of telling me this detail and that about her and having to tell her this detail and that about me. "Go get your picture taken and have her send you one of her and be done with it!" I think this is a very good idea.

April 24

Went to town to have a picture taken but no one there has a camera — or if they do they don't want to take a picture of a Yankee. Sgt. Donoghue said there is a newspaper photographer somewhere in camp and he might take my photograph, so I am going out now to find him.

Later: I hunted and hunted all over the camp, but it is not easy to find one man among 3000! Finally I came on Mr. Thom. Roche and his photographic wagon and he made a carte-de-visite photograph of me in my uniform for one dollar. I thought the price a little steep — especially since it did not take more than a few moments to take the picture — but Mr. Roche said that chemicals are dear down here, especially since every officer in camp wants to sit for a picture. Now to finish my letter and send it — and me — off. I wonder what Sarah will think.

April 30

Lt. Toms said to be ready to move in the morning. I guess our little rest is at an end.

May 2

We have been marching, sometimes double-time. Covered fifteen miles yesterday despite poor roads and heat, leaving behind extra clothes, books and whatever else was not absolutely necessary. Lt. Toms did not say much to me all day other than "Keep them moving, Sgt. If the Maj. can keep his guns moving, we can keep our men moving." At one river crossing, one man — George Chittenden — was swept down water, but we managed to drag him to shore before he went under. We heard later that two men was not so lucky when their wagon overturned.

Today we covered eighteen hard miles and the men are exhausted. Several of them are missing tonight due to straggling. Sgt. Donoghue is doing paperwork and Sgt. Drake is no-where to be found, so I am going back for the missing men on my own.

George Chittenden drying his shoes after his morning swim.

Later: Went back a mile or two and found four of our men off to the side of the road in a cozy glen with men from other companies who had also dropped out of the line of march. There was a fire and a pot of coffee and a kettle with some sort of bean stew boiling away — a pleasant domestic scene, I thought.

When I entered, most of our men seemed embarrassed — at not having kept up with the rest of the Company and at having been sought out like schoolchildren — but they was nice enough and even offered me a cup of coffee. Charlie Shelp was there and was not happy to see me.

I told our men that Lt. Toms wanted them back in camp and Shelp said, "I am not leaving til I eat." The men not from G Company encouraged Shelp, and one said, "You can't order an injured man to march and this man is injured. I saw him limping myself. It's against the rules." Shelp looked pleased that he had such loyal supporters and shook his head in agreement. I may be mistaken, but I believe Shelp's courage was bolstered some by the whiskey the men was passing around. "Yes, it's against the rules," he agreed.

If I was Sgt. Donoghue, I would have made Shelp and the others obey with my fists, but I am a full head shorter than the Sgt. and a lot lighter. There was not much I had to use against them except my words, and I wasn't sure they would work. "If you are really injured," I said to Shelp, "you should report to the doctors. But you don't look injured to me, Pte., just hungry. Have your dinner and then find us up the road a ways."

The men from our Company seemed happy with this

77

solution and even some of the other men — the ones who had backed Shelp — looked satisfied. But Shelp said, "You can't make me go to the doctors. You can't make me do any-thing!"

"I am not going to make you do any-thing, Pte. But I will tell you that when final roll call is taken tonight, you had better be in camp or at the doctors and not in between."

Shelp began to say more, but I turned from him, wished the rest of the men a fine meal and said good night. Sgt. Donoghue would have had those men marching back with him and no back talk either, so I felt very much alone as I walked to where we had camped. I am not at all sure I am up to this business of being a sgt.

10 o'clock: Final roll call taken. All but C. Shelp are in camp.

May 3

Shelp still absent, and the assistant surgeon in charge of the field hospital says no Charlie Shelp is in their care. We are to march at any moment, so there is no time to look for him, or to write about it.

May 4

We have met up with the rest of the 122nd — and the rest of the Army as well! — and crossed the Rapidan at Germanna

Ford. We was near the head of the march and among the first across with orders to go up the Culpepper Plank Road a mile and hold the area til the rest of the army could get across. A force of Sheridan's cavalry has already swept ahead to clear the roads, and we are to follow them as closely as possible to rid the surrounding woods of Reb skirmishers.

The land is fairly open and rolling here, with stands of trees and some burned-out houses about, but mostly unplowed fields. A dark line of the woods is up ahead to greet us and is why the area beyond is referred to as the Old Wilderness on most maps. Lt. Toms said that we might have 80,000 to 100,000 troops behind us by tomorrow night.

Noon: We was ordered forward again and told to secure another mile of the road. There are about 400 soldiers in this group, plus a number of Maj. Pettit's light artillery and some cavalry. Behind us we can see the landscape already swarming with troops and wagons and ambulances and other equipment. I am not happy to be showing myself so clearly to the Rebs, but I must admit to a proud feeling when I see so many fellow soldiers.

We had just begun to move when Charlie Shelp suddenly appeared, panting heavily and covered with leaves and dirt and looking as if he hadn't slept a wink. The others greeted him warmly and he was smiling when he joined the march, and I might have let him alone and been done with it, but I couldn't.

If I didn't say something to him, then I would not be doing my job and who knows what he or someone else would do next. So I called out, "Pte. Shelp, you will step out of the line."

I admit that I was about as scared as when we go into a fight, but I went over to where he was by the side of the road any-way. "You did not report for roll call last night or this morning. Do you have a reason for being absent?" "I was at the doctors," he said, "having my injury treated." "Then you have your discharge orders from the doctor," I said. He looked startled for a second, then felt his vest pockets and said, "I guess I dropped them. When I was running to get back here." "You weren't with the doctors, Pte. I checked. You are on report, and when we are finished out here, you will be dealt with, do you understand? Now get back in line." Shelp stood quiet for a few seconds and I could tell he wanted to hit me, only too many was around to see and his punishment would be even more severe if he did that. But as he walked past me he mumbled, "We will see who gets back, Sgt."

If I was scared before, now I was stunned. A few moments ago, I had to worry about the enemy I might have to face. Now I have to worry about the one who is marching along with me as well.

6 o'clock: At around 2 o'clock the woods closed in on both sides of the road, a scraggly collection of oak and pine trees — alive and dead, standing up and falling over — with vines and ill-formed shrubs all around. The road is about twenty or thirty feet wide, so we had to march shoulder to shoulder, and what a tight feeling that gave us all.

A little on and we halted and sat by the side of the road, having a hardtack "meal." The officers had a meeting and then we sgts. met with our lts. — and they told us to be alert and that we might run into the enemy at any moment. Both things we all already knew, but the officers, being mostly lawyers, probably thought it best to hand down this "information" officially.

When I got back to the men, I found Johnny writing to his mother and sisters. I told myself that I should write Sarah just as soon as my sgt. duties allow, which might be a while. I noticed how steady Johnny's hand was and commented on how calm he seemed. He said he is all excited inside but does not see the point of showing it. "I will either survive a fight or not and it isn't in my hands any-way," he said, and looked up. "He knows what will happen to me and that is good enough for me."

Most of the men believe similarly, while a few believe there is no Divine hand involved in any of this. When I was with Uncle and Aunt, they said God rewarded us according to our thoughts and deeds. I can understand that I have been bad enough to wind up here, but I cannot believe that Johnny has done anything to deserve being shot at or killed! And if he hasn't, then why is he here? I am not smart enough to see what the grand scheme is, but these thoughts rattle around in my head and I try to make some sense of them.

The bugle has sounded and we are about to march on. I glanced up and saw our men getting ready to march. Then I spotted Shelp. He is on the other side of the road staring right at me now — right through me! — his eyes as dark and as menacing as any stormy night. I am telling myself to be calm and finish up this entry, but a cold shiver goes thru me any-way.

9 o'clock: After our stop we went another mile more along the plank road, then took a smaller road — more like a rough path — that went off to the right into the thickest sort of woods imaginable. This path is not much wider than a wagon and in bad condition with no bridges over streams, so our progress has been slow. We have stopped so the officers can talk over the latest scouting reports.

Lt. Toms told Sgt. Donoghue, Sgt. Drake and me that Lee's army is five or ten miles from here and headed our way. Fast, according to the scouts. "They aim to catch us in these woods," the Lt. said, "so we can't maneuver and use our numbers to full advantage. I don't think they'll do anything tonight, but we have to get the men ready for a real fight." So I guess Uncle Robert was not fooled a bit by the first soldiers that went out.

We are to move ahead another half mile or so, then put up

breastworks for tomorrow's fight. The only other thing we know for sure is that we will be on the extreme right flank of our line of battle.

May 5

This is the wildest mess of woods I have ever been in and believe it is correctly named the Old Wilderness. We happen to be near a substantial clearing in the woods — a very rare thing as far as I can tell — with our cannons on a slight rise with a good view to the other side. Maj. Pettit has left twenty cannons here at the clearing, back a little in the woods and concealed by leaves, so they are not easily seen.

This open section appears to have been an expanse of swamp or bog that dried up years ago and left a scattering of dead and collapsed trees, a shaggy grass covering and some exposed boulders and rocks. The Lt. told us that our line of battle runs for almost two miles to our left, in the general direction of Spotsylvania Court House, tho the trees and shrubs are so thick that you can't tell if a line exists. The rest of Maj. Pettit's guns are scattered along this line, and he is as agitated as a thunderstorm because the trees will make it hard to use his artillery to best effect any-where but in the few open sections. We have been listening to the sound of heavy fighting since the sun came up, so the cannons have not been totally silenced.

It is quiet here — or I would not be writing this! — and we feel quite isolated, but this has given the men a chance to make coffee and breakfast, and speculate on what might be going on.

I have the new men to watch over, including Theron Chrisler. Also Johnny Henderson, Boswell Grant, Niles Rogers and Willie Dodd are with me, and of course, Spirit is too. Sgt. Donoghue said to keep a sharp eye on Chrisler, and to shoot him — in the back, if need be! — if he tries to run off again. I am not sure I will do this, since I share his fear, if not his inclination to run. That is my group and I am happy with them — and happy that I do not have Shelp to deal with.

Our job is very simple. Last night we took down a line of trees to one side of the clearing for some 300 feet and removed brush in front as best as possible. Now my men are positioned every twenty or thirty feet along this rough breastwork. Out in front of us are C, A and K Companies. If the enemy tries to get around our flank, they will hold them back out there. If they can't, we are back here to give them covering fire til they reach us. Maj. Pettit sent word that we are not to surrender this spot *on any account*, so this could become a very hot place if the men out in front can't hold them. There are more reserves behind us on the path in case they are needed along the line of battle, and I think there are other companies out in the woods, but who can tell?

84

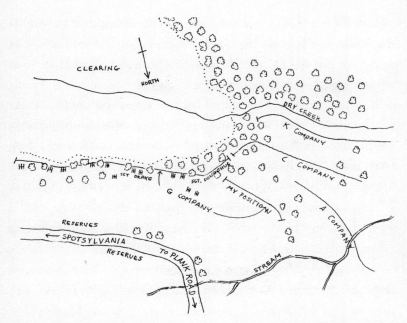

Johnny thinks this map is accurate, but he says my trees look like heads of broccoli. I would "plant" even more — since the woods are very thick in here — but my hand is tired.

Later: We was just beginning to enjoy a restful morning when the first Rebs struck, at around 11 o'clock. The fighting from earlier seemed to be coming down along the line of battle, getting closer and closer, but very slowly so it was not at all alarming. We heard bugles and the report of a cannon from the other side of the clearing after 10 o'clock, but then the sound died away and we settled back again, supposing that they had decided to make a fight somewhere else. Some men even began making plans for dinner!

Sgt. Drake thinks it was a trick of the wind, that the fighting was actually close by, but the sounds got lost in the woods and did not reach us. Whatever the truth, suddenly our advance pickets began speaking in the woods across the way, which was followed by a stern volley from the enemy. Then our pickets came across the clearing on the double-quick, calling that the Rebs was on their heels — which any fool with ears and a brain already knew.

I did not have the best view of any of this, being 200 feet from the closest gun with my back to the clearing, tho I turned often to see what was happening. I was watching when our pickets reached the breastworks and threw themselves over. A scattering of Rebs had entered the clearing by this time, some firing our way, others kneeling to reload, the rest coming on. Around this time, Maj. Pettit nodded to one of his aides, who gave the order and one cannon fired canister at the enemy — which sent a hail of metal pieces into the faces of the closest Rebs. This seemed to cool the fighting spirit of them all because they stopped what they was doing and dove for the ground — and I would have done the exact same! — and the attack ceased right there. Maj. Pettit did not have his other guns fire at the enemy as they dashed back into the woods, which seemed odd, but at least the few Rebs we saw are gone.

Fighting continues in the distance to our left — tho few messages have been received today and the path behind us is still jammed with soldiers, so there is little traffic along it. We may be so far out here that no one cares about us or this patch of dirt. Let's hope so.

In the evening: They came on at dusk — something Lt. Toms suggested they might do. So I guess they care. The shadows was beginning to lengthen when first one Reb soldier, then two, three, four and more scurried from the far woods, bent low and searching for what little cover there was. These advance pickets had been sent out to see what we would do.

Naturally, our men opened fire on the shadowy targets and may have picked off one or two. It was hard to tell. Ten more entered the clearing in the meantime, moved forward 100 feet, dodging and ducking, and went to ground when they found shelter. Pretty soon this small group had miniés whistling thru the spring leaves at us and it was our turn to duck.

"Find your targets before you shoot," I heard Sgt. Donoghue order, as he moved among his group. "Make your shots count. Don't waste a single shot." Which was good advice, so I went along my little line and told the same to my ten men. We had been issued sixty rounds yesterday, but getting resupplied in this tangle of trees will be hard. Our sixty shots might have to last all night and tomorrow.

Sgt. Donoghue appeared at my side. "Listen for our pickets out there," he instructed me, tho he really didn't need to. I had no intention of being caught "napping" and then have to

87

answer later to him, Lt. Toms and Maj. Pettit! He had just finished speaking when — *whiz*! *bang*!! — a shell burst over our heads and — *fiz*! *whiz*!! *rattle*!!! — the fragments came tearing thru the treetops above us, which made us duck even lower and grab hold of our forage caps. When the metal stopped falling, the Sgt. looked up at the leaves above, which had been clearly punctured in many places by the metal, smiled and said, "I guess it wasn't our time. Good luck, Pease," then hurried off.

We went back to our work then, which became real when the advance pickets from K Company began to be heard. My breathing got faster and I had an odd sense that things was beginning to happen too quickly around me to see.

There are two kinds of charges that I know of. In one, everybody jumps up right away and runs at you, that is, after the cannons have softened up the other side. This is the sort of charge that the Reb Gen. Pickett made at Gettysburg. The second begins slowly, with little groups of men moving forward, poking and probing in various places to find the softest spot to charge. So in a little while, if they think ours is the easiest to get thru, the charge will come — and it was this that had me edgy.

"Steady! Steady!" I yelled at my group, but I was really yelling at myself not to think too much. If you don't do much thinking, but watch instead and then let your feet and body react, you can keep the creeping shakes under control. "Keep those fingers off the trigger," I added, just in case any of the new boys was feeling as jumpy as me and might twitch their trigger finger by accident.

All around us it seemed that muskets was barking and chattering away, punctuated every so often by the sound of a cannon and the *whooosh* of a shell overhead followed by its explosion — tho we still couldn't see what was happening.

"Look, Sgt.," Boswell — who was closest to me — shouted, pointing to the clearing. I glanced around and saw a line of butternut uniforms break from cover and begin running across that open space toward our line. Then I heard the sound — a steady wave of it, like the scream of 1000 wounded animals gone crazy with pain. I'd heard it before, but every time they let out their Reb Yell, I have to admit it chills me to the bone. Every so often one of these charging men would be hit by a bullet and fall, opening a gap in their line. Pretty soon this first line looked like a mouth of rotten teeth — tho none of those still running seemed inclined to turn back!

When the first group had come about 100 feet, their advance pickets stood and joined the charge, while behind them a second line of men emerged from the woods. They was shoulder to shoulder, almost touching each other they was so close, and screaming as loud as the first line. Thinking back, I guess that somewhere between 300 or 400 men was charging toward our guns, maybe more.

That is when I realized what had happened. Earlier, Maj. Pettit had fired only one gun, which was enough to warn off the enemy. But they was back now and eager to get that

89

gun — not realizing that a lot of others waited also. The Rebs was about halfway across when the trap — for that was what it was — was sprung and the entire battery fired with an unholy explosion that made the ground and trees quiver. A wall of smoke was instantly created, making seeing even worse, but I saw enough to know that the metal pieces ran across the clearing like a hot scythe, cutting down men, grass and any-thing else standing.

The damage to the enemy line was severe and their screams terrible, but it did not stop their charge or our work. I turned my attention to the woods down in front of us, where the fighting was getting louder, and I noticed that some of A Company's men was moving forward. I shouted to my group to be alert and to stop watching the clearing.

Another volley from our cannons erupted, followed by more screams and the rapid *snap-crackle* of both sides' muskets. The breeze shifted, pushing smoke over us and filling up the woods around us. It had already gotten pretty dim, but now the smoke made seeing impossible. In front of us smoke and shadows and more smoke and shadows drifted thru, with an occasional flash of yellow-blue to indicate the position of a musket. I was already nervous enough, but not being able to see made my stomach jump. That's when I decided to make some quick visits — as much to distract myself as to make sure my men was okay.

Boswell was first and I told him to watch the clearing and shout if anything happened there. Then I hurried on. Not much

90

fire was being directed at my group, but miniés sailed over our heads any-way, so I was bent over low when I ran to the next man. That was Theron Chisler, and he was peering ahead so intently that he jumped a little when I threw myself down beside him. "You O.K., Theron?" I asked, and he nodded yes. His eyes was big and round and I thought I should say something to put him at ease. "Good," I said, and added, "but I can tell you that I wish those fellows would go home for the night so I can get something to eat." Theron cracked a smile and said he agreed. Then I told him, "Stay low, hear? I'm going to check on the others now. And don't shoot unless you know what you're shooting at, okay?" He nodded again, and then I moved on, going from man to man, and saying much the same to each.

When I got to Johnny, he seemed very snug and not at all concerned. He was at a spot where three trees had come down, and he had piled up bits of wood and rocks to either side of his position so he could see thru a tiny slit between the trees. If an enemy minié ball was looking for him, it would have to have very sharp eyes. The last one on my line was Willie Dodd, who was tucked in behind a thick section of tree trunk and happily feeding Spirit hardtack. "Evening, Sgt.," he said as if nothing unusual was happening around him. "Care for dinner?" I patted Spirit and took a cracker, only when I bit into it my mouth was so dry it just sat in there like chalk.

I looked around quickly, making a real show of studying what was going on in front of us, but of course, I couldn't see any-thing at all. There was shadows moving around out

91

there, but nothing that suggested the Rebs had broken thru, no shouted warnings or urgent bugle notes. The heaviest fighting was still coming from the clearing, which was now way off to my left. Just then, our cannons roared again and I pulled my head back behind the tree and gulped that wad of dry hardtack down, but it got stuck in my throat.

"That was something, wasn't it, Sgt.?" Willie said.

I nodded, forcing the hardtack the rest of the way down, then managed to say, "Almighty fierce. Sounds like Maj. Pettit has added some guns over there."

A moment later, a cheer rose from those very guns and told us the Rebs had given up the charge across the clearing and was withdrawing. The firing continued for fifteen or twenty minutes, then died away very quickly. There was a series of shouted commands — to stop shooting, to move this company or that one here or there, to see who had been wounded — and then things quieted down. The only sounds left now was the moans and cries of the wounded, most of whom was lying in the clearing.

I went back along my line and did another check of my men. A number of men from K and one or two or three from A and C Companies were being helped to the path where they would wait for the ambulances, but I think it safe to say that we did not suffer many losses or serious injuries tonight. Lt. Toms said the Rebs was "stubborn in their fight, but not dogged" — which may mean that we are not very important to their plans. Time will tell.

Sgt. Donoghue came over to see how we had done and said that no one from our Company had been killed, tho three had been hit by exploding shells: T. Stevens, D. Bernard and C. Mahar. Fighting up the line had sounded very heavy — heavy enough to have most of the reserves on the path behind us moved up the line away from us — but there is no way to tell what has happened.

10 o'clock: When things settled down, a flag of truce appeared from across the clearing and after some talk the Rebs came out to collect their dead and wounded. The wounded was easy to locate because of their moans and cries for help and water, but it took some time to find all the dead. Ten or more men with torches roamed here and there to search in every dark spot. I remembered the dead Reb boy we'd seen in the woods and thought it a shame that he hadn't been found like these fellows here.

Some friendly chatter was exchanged with the searchers and one Reb — who was forty feet from our breastwork — said, "See you in the morning, Yanks." But he made a mistake in addressing his comments near Shelp, who responded, "We will see you dead and in Hell, Johnny." I believe that Reb was genuinely surprised by Shelp's tone and thought him rude — and so did I.

I have to do a report on my men and then Sgt. Donoghue, Sgt. Drake and I are to meet with Lt. Toms. I am going to write a quick letter to Sarah and have decided to send all of my money to her for safekeeping. Later, I will get someone heading to the rear to take my letter back. This will take most of the night but I am glad for the distractions.

May 6

Did my report, had my meeting, wrote my letter and even found someone to take my letter out — for $1! — and then had to stand guard between 2 and 3 o'clock A.M. Nothing unusual moving "out there" except a thick, damp fog. After this, managed to close my eyes — for ten minutes, I think! — and then it was 5 o'clock and time to get up and get ready to greet the Rebs.

K Company — who felt the hardest fighting yesterday — was replaced by reserves. C and A Companies both asked to be left in place, and three other companies was moved up to add to their numbers. There are now over 200 blue uniforms positioned down in front of me and many more around the clearing. There is a feeling among the officers that they might try to get around us here and then move up our line of battle along the narrow path.

Maj. Pettit relocated his guns — which was hard work in the tangled undergrowth — and four now stand near the middle of my little line.

Had breakfast this morning to the sound of distant fighting. Fog has lifted some and the Lt. said it will burn off by eight, but that we should keep the men alert since our "friends over there" might like to fight with it as cover. I know something is going to happen because couriers have been flying up and down the path since 5:30 A.M., and the officers have had many meetings.

Someone also thought it important that we receive a supply of ammunition — but no food, so we have only one day's rations left. Pete McQuade joked that the gens. probably don't think many of us will be needing to eat if the Reb forces are as persistent today as they was yesterday. McQuade patted the shirt pocket that held the coin I'd given him and added, "But I'm not worried. Not a bit." This prompted a review of the Lucky Minié list and it turns out that Willie Dodd is to have it today.

One of Maj. Pettit's aides scouting Reb positions. Johnny said I was getting better at drawing trees.

Have visited my men many times already. Johnny is in very good spirits despite not having Lucky Minié. He has made his position even snugger with additional piles of wood, and when I greeted him, he asked me how I liked "Fort Henderson." I told him then that I had sent my money to Sarah for safekeeping and he said, "That is almost like a marriage propos

dark it is dark. what time is it? no strength

will try to write — but it is still dark and tired Head hurts and hurts and tired where are my men and the sgt, and Lt.?
can hardly see beyond this tree with the dark or is it my eyes? Voices talking — heard barking — will check. Can feel pencil — can feel myself writing — must be alive. Voices all around

Dark still. and head is throbbing still knock I took not so serious, but every thing is spinning —
Must find a safe place away from here — Rebs moving everywhere. A voice is talking over and over in my head — "The way of the wicked is like deep darkness; they do not know over what they stumble." Familiar voice — Uncle's? who is the wicked? Foolish to be huddled here and writing. where are the others?

later: Sun is just up and I have stopped to rest my leg — suppose it is may 7 or maybe May 8. I could have lost a day, I guess. Can see the woods better, but this doesn't tell me where I am.

Head still hurts, there is a dull pounding behind my left eye and the rest of my body is sore, especially my left shoulder and wrist. Hand numb but nothing broken that I can tell so I count myself lucky — a funny word for me to use — Someone coming

Another Reb patrol. Squads of cavalry and companies have been going by since my eyes first opened after the explosion. Fighting far off, tho where is hard to tell. I don't even know where I am exactly — maybe a mile from where the fight was. Uncle's voice still making visits! No food and need to close my eyes again — will write more later.

Somewhere sometime later: I have found a hollowed-out hole in the side of a hill with shrubs and saplings all around — a good snug place to fit my body. This seems a quiet enough spot, but the Rebs have men roaming about looking for us, so no place is safe for long. Will write what I can remember about yesterday's battle and then sleep. Must travel at night.

Here is what I remember — but I may not recall it all. I was writing in this journal when a bugle sounded and someone off in the woods to my left yelled, "Here they come! Here they come!" Lt. Toms and the other officers was instantly alert and issuing orders; men started running here and there and a scattering of musket fire erupted. The cannoneers all leaped into position, officers ready. Not more than a few moments had passed and the fight was in full swing.

I tucked the journal in my shirt, took up my musket — which I had loaded with dry powder earlier — and turned, ready to fire, when there was a succession of booms from across the way, answered immediately by a full volley from our cannons. Just the thought of the sound made by all the cannons and the way the earth shook makes my head throb even now!

A second later, the ground all around began to erupt as shells hit and exploded and dirt and debris began flying. A shell ripped into the breastworks and instantly killed Niles Rogers and injured Otto Parrisen. Good soldiers both. Another of my charges — Hudson Marsh — cried out, "I am killed, I am killed," and I went over and saw that he had been hit in the shoulder and was bleeding some. "You're not dead yet," I yelled in his ear. "Get yourself back to the ambulances if you have to," but then he realized there was so much metal flying that it was safer to stay put.

I wish my head was clearer. Even now, sitting here in my quiet nest, what happened is still murky. I know our cannons was firing as quickly as they could be loaded, so the ground was in constant motion and dust was jumping up with one and then another and another *Boom*!!! I heard Sgt. Donoghue and Sgt. Drake shouting orders and so I did the same, tho what I said is lost to me.

A shell hit one of the cannons on my line and pieces of it — and the men around it — went flying. I remember thinking, "They have our range now," and seeing Lt. Toms moving among the men, his right arm dangling as if he'd been hit, with Caesar at his side holding him up. I saw men from C Company rushing forward, then almost immediately they was running back, along with some from A Company. A wagon rumbling toward the cannons with fresh ammunition hit the side of a tree and flipped onto its side. I heard shouted orders and the screams of the wounded, ours and theirs — I yelled to my group to be ready to cover our retreating soldiers — there was the sharp blasts of bugle commands and the guns, of course, big and small, popping and booming everywhere. I was disoriented and confused —

Must stop for a moment — to rest and let my thoughts calm down. Can't remember what happened next any-way. The voice — Uncle's I'm sure — is back — "The shield of his mighty men is red, his soldiers are clothed in scarlet. The chariots flash like flame when mustered in array; the chargers prance." How many times did I copy these lines? How many times did Uncle read and mark my mistakes and make me copy them again?

Later: I was sleeping peacefully with no dreams in my head at all when suddenly I heard a voice shouting in my ear — a new voice — Corp. Gorham's. I woke up and blinked, looking around quickly to see what the Corp. wanted. But I was alone, of course, and still in my hole in the side of the hill. It is too light to travel, so I will write instead. The Corp.'s voice has helped me remember more.

The battle was going on all around and I was confused when suddenly Gorham was next to me yelling: "Sgt., the Lt. has been taken away injured and Sgt. Donoghue is hit too. He said to get you."

I didn't respond to him at all. Instead, I looked to see if we had any reserves on the path to help out, but there was none. Then I counted my men to see how many of them was still there. Aside from Parrisen and Marsh, everyone was okay. "Sgt.," Corp. Gorham said, and that brought me back full to the situation.

"I'm leaving you here in charge of these men, Corp. Tell them to stay low and give our men out there good cover," I said, and then asked, "Where is Sgt. Drake? Is he O.K.?" "He is up the line and was fine when I left." "Good," I answered — because Sgt. Drake was second sgt. and would take over for Sgt. Donoghue. I went to the clearing.

Here it was a mess — blasted holes in the breastworks, our dead and wounded, pieces of artillery here and there, shouting and cries of pain. Shelp was standing up, screaming at the top of his lungs, challenging the Rebs to come and get him and cussing at them. The rest of our men was shooting and reloading as quickly as they could and looking very grim.

Sgt. Donoghue was sitting with his back against the breast-works, shot thru the bowels, holding his guts in his hands and bleeding badly. "Pease," he said clearly, but weakly, "they are going to get thru unless we get help. Keep them . . . the men . . . keep them together. Pull them in . . . close to the guns, hear? Drake is . . ." He winced and looked down at his wound, then looked up at me with an odd little smile on his face. "Doesn't hurt but a little. Strange. Very strange." He was already pale from lost blood, so I told him I would take care of everything and then tried to convince him to go back to the ambulances, but he said no. "Do your work, Pease. Just do your work. Don't worry . . . about me. I will be fine."

I didn't have any idea what to do next, but I thought it couldn't hurt to order Shelp to get down and shoot at the Rebs. "You haven't killed one with your cussing, Charlie." He looked at me with about the same amount of hate he did the Rebs, growled something at me, but then he ducked down and started shooting. I ran past Shelp and up the line, look-ing for Sgt. Drake to tell him what had happened to Sgt. Donoghue and Lt. Toms and to see if he had any other instructions for me. I probably should have sent another man and gone back to my position, but I was nervous about doing something wrong while waiting for an answer.

I tossed my musket aside as too heavy, so there I was a per-fect running target for the Rebs and that thought made me pick up my feet even quicker, I think. Another of our cannons

101

was destroyed and Maj. Pettit's horse was hit. It went down on its front knees and the Maj. had to leap clear before it rolled over on him.

"They are thru on the left!" I heard someone shout from up ahead of me. If that was true, it meant that we was cut off from the rest of the army and any possible help. We was an island surrounded by waves of angry butternut.

I found Drake, who was already responding to Maj. Pettit's orders to relocate his guns. I relayed my information, but all I recall him saying was "Good luck, Sgt. And watch yourself."

The Rebs was coming across the clearing, but their charge was irregular. Beyond Sgt. Drake's position they had gotten very close to our breastworks; where we was and below they hadn't gotten halfway yet. But they still came on.

I ran down along our line again, shouting, "Aim and shoot! Aim and shoot, fellows!"

The men at the breastworks at the clearing seemed to have settled into a regular pattern of shooting and then I realized we might need cartridges pretty quickly, so I had Sanford Van Dyke — who had been hit in the hand, but not so bad — see how much ammunition the men really had. If they ran out, there would be nothing left to do but retreat. At the clearing, the men were down to ten or fifteen rounds each, so we didn't have much time. I sent Develois Stevens scampering to find ammunition.

Next I went back to where my men was and checked to see how much ammunition they had. Forty to fifty rounds

102

each, I discovered. I also found that the forward lines had begun to fall back and I assumed they was running short of ammunition. Just then I remembered something Sgt. Donoghue had told me at Gettysburg and I said to Asa Rich, "Go around to the dead and wounded and gather up their ammunition and give it out over at the clearing."

After this my recollection becomes somewhat of a swirl with a lot of blank spaces. I was told that Maj. Pettit was killed somewhere up the line, cut in half by a shell. His aides was barking out the orders in his place — but I was wondering when they would realize this spot was lost — because without a lot more ammunition and reserves it was most certainly lost — and hoping they wouldn't wait so long that we couldn't get out and back to the rest of the army — wherever it was. Of course, this was Maj. Pettit's group and they didn't like to leave a fight.

I also remember seeing the men in front still coming back to us. That's about when I noticed that one of the cannons on my line was shorthanded and I started toward it, thinking to help out — and then the earth around me opened up with a deafening roar. I felt myself lifted into the air and tumbling over and over and when I came down everything went black and quiet for me — tho I don't remember hitting the ground at all.

That is all I remember of the fight. I guess I was knocked out by the explosion or by landing on my head and it was a while — hours maybe — before I am sure I heard a noise behind me — the rumble of cavalry, most likely. Far off but

103

clear enough to freeze my hand til the danger passed. Since I was ordered to keep a record of what happened — and since there is nothing else to do while I wait — I will continue my story where I stopped: After being tossed around by the explosion it was a good deal of time before I became aware of anything. First came the horrible, strangled braying of a wounded mule, calling and calling and calling — then I heard the moans of the wounded and the sounds of fighting — far, far away and nothing but a distant grumble. And barking. I heard barking and knew Spirit was near.

My face was mashed into the ground and when I blinked my eyes open I found myself staring at leaves and twigs and clots of dirt. It was dark by this time, but I could see enough to know that the fight was over here — the ground had that chewed-up look and there was some bodies near, just shapes so I didn't know who they was. Then came the voices — real ones — so I stayed still and listened.

Turned out to be a couple of Rebs searching the bodies for boots, food and cartridges. They was whispering — which told me they was on the sneak and should be somewhere else, probably where the fight was. I played dead, as they went on whispering and shopping. Spirit barked and barked and then he set to growling. I wanted to look to see what was happening, but didn't. Next I heard a yelp and I supposed one of the Rebs kicked Spirit. When they had found all that they needed, they drifted off and the area around me was still except for the groans of the wounded and the cries of that mule.

That is when I moved my legs to see if they worked and got my left arm out from under my body, tho I moved slowly and quietly in case other Rebs was near. I could hear cavalry going up the path and some wagons and assumed they was Rebs — but it was dark enough and I was far enough away that if I was careful, I could slip away and avoid being taken prisoner.

I rolled onto my side next and pushed myself into a kneeling position. My head and arm and chest was on fire with pain but my legs seemed fine enough. I knew I could get clear as long as my legs held out. When I stood, I was so dizzy I swayed and had to lean against a tree for a while. This gave me a chance to glance all around.

I could just see the clearing thru the tree branches and bushes, not clearly. Just a lighter patch of gray. And the breastworks — solid and straight in places, ripped up in others. And some bodies and twisted up pieces of artillery. One soldier was on his back, his arm frozen as it was reaching up. For what? Help?

I didn't see any movement anywhere. The moans was away from me, in the clearing mostly. I thought about going around to see who was injured and who was killed — Lt. Toms wants a careful record of such. Then I thought better. The section was empty now, but it might take a while to find them, and the Rebs might be back any minute. And what could I do to help them? I didn't even have any water. I had to get away and do it while my legs had strength to carry me and my brain still worked. But which way?

The path was out of the question — too busy with enemy patrols. Our Army — if it still existed — was up toward Chancellorsville or thereabouts, but since the Rebs had broken thru the line, that way would be swarming with them. So I had to go in the safest direction — which was across where the Rebs had been when the fight started and deeper south into the woods.

Before setting off, I looked up and down my line as quickly as I could. I thought about Johnny then, so I went — hobbled, really — to where he had been. "Fort Henderson" was empty, and when I felt around I didn't find any signs of blood. Johnny might be a prisoner or he might have made it back to the main army, but at least he wasn't dead and that would please Sarah and her mother and sisters. That got me thinking about Sarah, wishing I had a picture of her — and it was then I noticed a strange shape down the line.

What I found was like a vicious punch to the stomach. Thinking about it even now makes me feel sick. Willie Dodd — who was the last holder of Lucky Minié — was sprawled on the ground, arms flung out, his right leg bent up at an awkward angle under his body. And on his chest was Spirit — dead, run thru with a bayonet by one of the Reb looters I'd heard prowling about earlier.

I wanted do so something for Willie and Spirit — take care of them somehow, maybe bury them proper or say some prayers. Maybe go look for those Rebs and — But I suddenly

106

felt weak and lightheaded, and my legs seemed as if they might buckle under me. Besides, a cavalry unit was thundering along the path in my direction.

I climbed over our breastworks and wandered toward the dark woods, past where A and C Companies had made their fight, past where the Rebs had had their advance pickets. There was dead soldiers to step over in these woods, some I could see was ours, some theirs.

I made a frightful amount of noise for someone trying to sneak away, but the cries of the wounded and that mule covered my clumsiness. I stopped to rest when the woods suddenly got thicker and turned to look back over the battlefield — and found it swallowed up by the black of night, still and sad. I couldn't see anything, not really, but it was all there in my head any-way. What was it Lt. Toms had said after Capt. Clapp had visited him that day last November — that this would be our deliverance?

My legs felt heavy and then I tripped and fell, and it took a time before I could push myself up. When I looked, I saw that I'd tripped over a severed leg.

And a voice started in — not Uncle's this time, but mine. It was another Bible line, one that I'd liked the sound of and wrote often, trying to picture the brave soldiers doing their noble work. I'm not sure how much I like those words now, but they seem to fit what happened. "Horsemen charging, flashing sword and glittering spear, hosts of slain, heaps of corpses, dead bodies without end — they stumble over the bodies!"

107

I was half a mile out and already feeling lost when I remembered seeing Spirit's body lying across Willie and I thought: They didn't have to kill that little dog. He didn't do anything to them but bark. He didn't have to die, and my eyes clouded up some as I left my friend and his dog and all the others behind and limped deeper into the Old Wilderness.

Later: I had just finished the last entry when a bunch of Rebs rode up and dismounted on the hill behind me. I thought they had sniffed me out, but then they commenced to jabbering away and laughing about how the Federals had run. Can't be talking about *our* Company — no one ran that I saw. Not even Theron Chrisler. They didn't seem to be nosing around for strays like me, so I relaxed some — til I smelled the coffee.

My stomach began growling then and reminding me it hadn't been fed in — who knows? Pulled leaves from the bush covering my little space and stuffed them in my mouth — bitter but got the juices going and the growling simmered down. Closed my eyes and chewed — thinking about poor Willie and Spirit, and Sgt. Donoghue, who must be dead too, and Johnny and the others. I even thought about Shelp and hoped he'd gotten away.

I wanted to read Sarah's letters, but I didn't dare take them from my pocket because of the noise they would make. So instead I thought about Sarah and wondered if she was thinking about me.

108

That's what I did til the Rebs finished their coffee — probably got the coffee from us! — and packed up and rode away. Must leave. This section is as busy as the plank road.

Night: Dark. So dark can't see what I write, but am wide awake and will write any-way. Left last "home" when sun went down — moved deeper into Reb country. Clouds covered the moon and stars, so I walked where the walking seemed easiest. Went on — became confused — went on some more. Stepped into a stream — stopped to drink. Continued journey, slipping several times and getting caught in a sticker bush that scratched my hands, neck and face. Headache not as bad but it is still with me and wrist and leg are sore. Now at edge of field and will bed here — with biting bugs as company. Peaceful except for insect noise and some animal calls in the dark and my thoughts. Where is everyone I know? How are the Lt. and Caesar? Who else was hurt — or killed? How is William Kittler? I did not recall seeing him at all during the fight, but he must have been there. What is Sarah doing now? Sleeping peacefully most likely, with no idea at all of what has happened to us.

May 8 ?

Woke to sound of men working in the field. I counted four Negroes and thought to approach them — Caesar said they was all "kindly disposed to the Federal soldiers and would be truthful about roads and trails." But then I saw a white girl, riding toward them, cradling a musket, and I changed plans. They was far off, so I moved along the edge of the field unseen. But to where?

Tried to orient myself according to sun and thought about battle map and Caesar's finger moving across it. Head is still foggy and map remains unclear — but Caesar did say over here we would find "poor soil, poor farms, poor and mean white folk."

Stomach gave a shout about then, but all I could feed it was thoughts about my last real meal. A bit of hardtack would be a welcome feast just now, but gnawing on a stick is all I can do. Good thing there are so many streams in here or I would have no hope of escaping.

Can barely read last night's scribble. Wonder if the Lt. would change his mind about me keeping the journal if he ever saw that?

Later: Walked a little and find myself very nervous every time I come to a path or trail. Have heard patrols roaming the woods, thankfully far off. One time I came very close to two men arguing over who had eaten the most chicken and assumed they was a Reb patrol. No one else argues so loudly about food as soldiers do.

My head spins from hunger while my stomach agrees with growls. Kicked over a rotted log and saw it swarm with crawling creatures — a fine meal for some. Thought about it for myself, but then I gagged and so I guess I am not *that* hungry. Not yet any-way.

Skirted two fields after the first, both empty. Then I smelled food — close by and inviting — a stew with beef and potatoes my nose told me — and when my stomach learned this it set to churning and complaining! So I went toward the smell just to see.

What I found was a small cabin surrounded by a neat little garden that was just beginning to turn green. Smoke from the cook fire was pouring from the stone chimney and bringing me that delicious smell. I was standing there breathing in "dinner" when the door opened and a white woman came out. I ducked when I saw her, not knowing what to expect, and she went right to her garden, where she cut some greens and then went back inside.

"There is food in there," I told myself, "and a bed." These thoughts made my legs tremble — I was only 200 feet away — so close I could imagine the food, feel the soft mattress. Surely she would not refuse me. Besides, there did not

111

seem to be a man around — with so many gone to fight, this is a land without a lot of grown men — so I could always take what I wanted, even without a weapon.

Very tempting. But then a voice in my head — yes, *another* voice not my own — said, "Think it thru first." It might have been the Little Profeser who said this to me long ago — who can remember? Any-way, the voice added, "You don't want to act too quickly, especially when there are people around who want to do you harm." And she might be one — probably is one.

So I started wandering away — still taking in the smell — when there was a familiar loud report of a musket behind me and a second later a ball sailed over my head and took a bite from the side of a tree. I didn't hesitate, but started to run — only my sleeve got snagged on a branch and I couldn't get it free at first. I tugged hard, snapped off the branch and tore my uniform and started to run — tho I am not sure most folks would see it as running I was so clumsy and tired.

It was the white woman who shot at me and it was her who commenced shouting — cussing me to get off her land, calling me all kinds of terrible names and hollering that she'd seen a Yankee and so forth. But I didn't mind her yelling. As long as she was yelling, she wasn't reloading.

When I was out of her sight, I stopped to catch my breath, leaning heavily against a tree. Then I heard a second shot fired, followed a little time later by another — signal shots to alert her neighbors about trouble, I guessed. I pushed myself away from the tree and headed down a rocky hill. When I reached the bottom, I heard another alarm gun to my right answer the woman's, soon followed by another from over here, and then another from over there, and another and another. A number of dogs started in barking too. All around me it seemed. I have heard musket fire many times since becoming a soldier, but I must say I have never felt as small and as helpless as I did just then. Hurried on, listening and looking and nervous every step.

It is now late in the day and I am near a small clearing with two log shacks in it — tobacca drying shacks, I think, because they are so tall, with some smoke seeping from the cracks near the roof of one. A while back, the door opened and an ancient Negro woman came out to gather up dead sticks. She's in there now, alone I think, and I am here writing this, waiting for darkness and asking myself silly questions — will she be "kindly disposed" toward me or will she turn me in? Will she have any food to spare? They are silly questions because I know I can't delay. I need food and I need rest and I need them now. I hope this will not be my last entry in this journal!

May 9

Yes, it is another day. Sunrise to be exact, and I have just opened my eyes from a sweet, long sleep. I intend to write a little and then be on my way. About last night — I put away

113

the journal and began inching toward the shack, every step slow and deliberate, my heart thumping nervously.

At the edge of the clearing I paused to look and listen carefully. I'd made some sort of mistake with that white woman — a noise, a movement — and it nearly cost me my life. I didn't want to do the same here. The woods was empty and quiet and so was the clearing. No one was moving around in the dark.

I found a small pebble and tossed it at the door. It struck with a soft crack. Since I had heard it, someone inside should have too, only there was no answer. I threw another pebble, this time a little harder.

The woman replied in a language I didn't understand — other than it was a question of some sort. Not angry, tho. More like a cautious, "Who's there?" "A friend," I answered in a whisper. "Come out, please."

The door creaked open a bit and the woman peered out. I had moved out of the woods and closer to the door so she could see me full. "I'll not harm you," I said, taking a step toward her. "I need help." The door opened more — enough that I could see her face — hard and questioning — and her eyes — dark and suspicious. I could also see a small knife clutched in her hand, ready to go to work on me if I turned out to be unfriendly.

"I am unarmed," I said, and raised my hands so there was no mistake about this and even turned around once. "Food. All I need is some food. A little. Any you can spare."

114

She looked me up and down several times and I guess I must have presented a pathetic sight when I think on it — blown up in a bloody battle, dirt and powder burns on my face and clothes, two days strolling thru the woods, hiding in dirty holes, no food and only a little restless sleep. She shook her head several times and said something to me, tho what it was I do not know. She spoke French with a heavy Southern accent and seasoned with only a bit of American. When I asked her to repeat what she said, she waved her hands toward the woods as if to tell me to go away. If I had any doubts about what she meant, she made herself clear when she closed the door firmly.

I should have left her alone — I had no right to put her in danger. But I had no choice either, so I said, "Food is all I need. I'll lick the pot if that is all you have." And I would have, happily, I was so hungry and desperate. When she did not reappear, I said a little more loudly, "Please, I won't stay long."

That door stayed shut, and I did consider leaving. But when I looked around, the woods was so dark and deep that I went straight to the door and knocked several times. "Please, open up. I have some coins — not much, but they are silver." I fished in my pockets for the coins, but couldn't find them. I was getting impatient and maybe a little louder than I should have been, considering. I know I wished Osgood Tracy was there to use some of that French he knows to get me in. "They are here . . . somewhere. If I can't find them, maybe buttons from my uniform — "

Suddenly the door opened again and the woman stuck her head out, shushing me to be quiet and not looking happy at all. After glancing around, I think she said, "Step up, step up. Hurry!" But for some reason I hesitated, so she backed into the shack and waved with her hand that I should come in.

I went inside and was happy to see no one else in there. A tiny fire burning on the dirt floor in one corner gave off some welcome warmth and a layer of thin smoke — tho no worse than the smoke in one of our stockade tents. I hardly noticed the smoke smell to be honest. I was taking in another smell — food!

The woman rummaged thru a burlap sack and came out with a stump of a candle that she lit and stuck into a potato on a tiny table. She spoke to me — again, I had no idea what she was trying to say — but then she patted a little bed next to the table and gestured that I should sit. When I had settled onto the bed — and, oh, didn't it feel comfortable! — she handed me a ladle of water, which was room warm, but tasted fine. Then she deposited a small kettle on the table and handed me a wooden spoon.

I had no idea what was in that kettle — maybe hen or rabbit or even squirrel — and I didn't care. I ate it and made as much noise as any table of ten soldiers gobbling down a home-cooked meal.

The candle didn't throw much light, but enough that I saw into every corner of the room and its contents, which was not much. This rickety bed I was on, the table and a wooden

116

chair — which the woman was sitting in — plus a few small sacks and barrels scattered around the dirt floor. While I ate and studied the room, the woman talked on and on.

A little I figured out, most I did not, so I just nodded and smiled — that is, between bites of food. At one point I thought, what a crazy loon she is for talking away when she knows I don't understand her. Then I remembered the many voices I'd had in my head and decided that if she was crazy, then I certainly was too, and probably more so.

I finished up what was in the kettle and then my manners began to return. "Thank you," I said. "That was good. Thank you." She had never taken her dark eyes off me while I was eating — and her eyes were curious and nervous mixed. I knew she was scared. Not of me, but of being found hiding and feeding me, the enemy.

I stood up, prepared to leave. "I have to go now," I said. I pointed to the door. "Go. I have to go to my people. Can you point me to the Rapidan — " and then I must have wobbled some because she came over and made me sit again and even indicated that I should lay down and sleep. It would be all-right.

I did not fight her. I could not. I lay back and put my head on a thin pillow that smelled of body oil and wild herbs and leaves and felt as heavenly as any hotel pillow could. She sat down again and blew out the candle.

"My name is James," I said. "James Edmond Pease. Tomorrow I have to get back to my company." She said something but I

117

had to ask her to repeat it. She said firmly, "Sally, boy. Coll me Sally."

"Good night, Sally," I said. She didn't answer. Instead, she leaned back in the chair, staring at the fire that was more glowing embers than flame now. She was deep in thought. A few minutes later a faint smile creased her lips and she nodded several times and mumbled. "Yes, yes, yes." At least I think she said that, tho why I don't know. Then she began singing very softly. The words was foreign to me — French, I guess — but they was soothing and gentle and made me feel safe. I wanted to say something, ask her some questions — like, if she was a slave, why was it she lived out here by herself? — but I didn't. I didn't want to interrupt her. It was the first time I remember ever being sung to sleep.

Tobacca shacks — Sally's is the one closest. No matter how much I tried, I could not make them look as worn out as they really are.

Later: When I finished writing last time, I sat back — I was outside leaning against the shack. Just then, there was the rumble of horses moving fast and coming closer. A Reb patrol? I wondered. I stood up, not sure what to do. I could scamper into the woods, but how far could I hope to get?

It was Sally who grabbed me by the arm and pulled me back inside the shack, where she motioned that I should stay in the corner behind the door. She made it clear that I was to sit there and be quiet. Then she started fussing over the kettle of corn mush she had sitting in the fire.

I had no choice but to obey, so I sat with my knees drawn up and my arms wrapped around them, making myself as small as possible. When the horsemen rode up just a few seconds later, Sally went to the door to talk to them.

There was six or eight of them I guessed and they was so close to the door that they nearly blocked out the light. The one I took to be the group's leader said, "Benjamin, you check that other shack there for signs of the Yank while I talk to Sally here." "Yes, Grandpa," the one named Benjamin answered in a squeaky, little-boy voice. This was no Reb cavalry unit. The old man said good morning to Sally in French, his voice a little breathless, but pleasant enough other-wise.

He and Sally started chatting away, him asking her questions and her answering. I had some notion about what was being said because the man used the word "Yankee" several times. At one point the leader's horse poked its nose in the door and nudged Sally, and I tensed up, expecting the animal

119

to betray me somehow. Sally just patted the animal casually and spoke to it in a friendly manner.

I could hear the other horses snorting and tapping restlessly at the ground with their hooves, hear the squeak of the saddles, hear the riders talking. Most of the voices sounded young, like school boys out playing. "Nothing there, Grandpa," Benjamin said at last. "What's she saying, Bill?" another one of the group — an adult this time — asked after a while, obviously impatient with the conversation. "She says she ain't seen the Yank or heard any strange noises." "Do you trust her?" the man asked. "As much as you can trust any of 'm," Grandpa replied, and the group of riders all laughed. "Anything else? That was a lot of talking for so little information, Bill." "Well," Grandpa said, "she did wonder if we'd like to take breakfast with her. Corn mush." "Breakfast!" the man said with obvious disgust. "Let's get out of here. This place stinks God-awful." Stinks? I inhaled — quietly — but all I smelled was smoke and corn mush.

Sally and Grandpa talked some more briefly — all very pleasant and matter-of-fact — and then I heard the riders turn and hurry off. They had not even bothered to check inside her shack — maybe because the door was wide open and she had been so calm and casual. I let out a sigh, while Sally went back to the kettle of corn mush.

"Thank you. For what you told those men," I said, but Sally shook her head as if to say it was nothing unusual and handed me a bowl of mush and pan bread with honey. We did not talk much while we ate, but when I finished I said, "Well, I should go now." I tucked this journal inside my shirt. "Is there a safe place in the woods where I can wait for dark?" — and after listening and checking carefully, I went outside and reckoned which way was north by the position of the sun. "If I go that way, will I come to the Rapidan?"

Sally stared at me a second — she seemed almost frozen — so I thanked her again and took a step away from her shack. That set her moving, because she flew out of that shack and was on me in a second, talking fast and shaking her head no and holding tight to my arm. I shook her off — I had never been held by a Negro before and I think it scared me some — but she latched on again and seemed even more upset. And this time I didn't shake her off.

I tried to ask her a question or two — what was the matter? Why couldn't I go? "Is it that old man?" I asked. "Those fellows on the horses?" I pointed to the hoof marks in the dirt around us. That gave me a pause, remembering all of the alarm fire that trailed me from that woman's home. Sally shook her head no and started talking again, all the while gesturing with her hands.

Of course, I didn't understand her, which made her impatient, but that was okay because I was impatient too. I tried to leave again, but Sally held tight. Then she stopped talking and I could see her puzzling out how to tell me what she wanted to say. I knew she'd hit on something when her face lit up with a smile and she went and broke off a small, dead branch from a nearby tree.

121

The next thing I knew, she was drawing a big rectangle in the dirt and filling it in with the stars and bars. It wasn't the prettiest drawing I ever saw, but I could tell it was the Reb flag. "Rebs? Reb soldiers? Is that what you mean? There are soldiers around. Where?" She waved her hand in a wide arc that said they was every-where and then drew a map of the area.

The Lt. was right. She knew the surrounding land pretty well and even put in the location of big and small farms and buildings. At first I thought she was going to show me a trail out of there, and I was excited at the notion of getting back to the boys. But then she pointed to the Reb flag and started making Xs in various places. One. Two. Three. Four, et cetera, et cetera.

If I felt the alarm shots had nearly surrounded me, those Xs told me something even worse. Except for a few isolated fields like this one, Rebs was camped all around us. And there would be patrols and messengers and such traveling all over the place too. I'd been lucky yesterday — very lucky! — to stumble thru and find Sally's. I wasn't sure I had enough luck in me to slip back thru again, especially during the daylight.

Sally must have seen how upset I was, because she began talking in an animated way — something about night and someone called Davie. "Who is this Davie?" I asked. "Will you take me to him?" It took some time to make myself under-stood, and some more time for me to understand that no, I wasn't going to Davie, he was coming to me. And that was all Sally would say.

122

After we scuffed out the drawings of the map and flag —
and I have to say I liked kicking at that flag — Sally led me
deep into the woods and pointed to a spot that would be my
"home" for the day. She had put together a little sack of
food — cheese, a good hunk of pan bread, a small cask of
water, several turnips and her knife. Then she left to work on
the farm of the people who owned her. She made me to
understand this with another map and by making believe she
was scrubbing down a floor.

With Sally gone and us not trying to "talk," it is suddenly
very quiet and still. So here I am, back in the woods and
alone. Waiting.

Later, around 12 noon: Dozed off several times today with all
sorts of people and thoughts and worries swimming around
in my head. Woke when horses came thundering by on what
I guess is a nearby road. I made myself as small as possible,
expecting those riders to come charging into the clearing
again.

When I heard the distinct sound of shouted orders, I knew
it was soldiers. My first thought was, If I don't run and make
them angry, they won't shoot me outright. But when they
came into the clearing and approached the tobacca shacks,
my second thought was, Stay calm, Pease. They don't know
you're here, so don't do anything foolish. I pressed myself as
flat as I could to that damp ground.

123

Sally had chosen this spot well. She had planted me some 400 feet from the clearing, in a section filled with rocks, fallen, rotting trees, nasty sticker bushes and underbrush, plus a healthy stand of young and old trees. And everything was leafing out. Unless someone stumbled over me, I might be taken for a rock if I just held still.

It didn't take long for the patrol to reach the shacks. They was far away and the leaves made seeing difficult, but that was fine with me. I did hear the officer in charge say "Search 'm," tho his voice was very faint and had no urgency to it. I decided then that I was being too curious, so I put my head down among the carpet of leaves, closed my eyes and listened as each door was thrown open and the soldiers reported.

"Empty, sir," the first shouted, "a few barrels and such. Big hole in the roof too." Another voice said, "Someone's livin' in here, Lt. A nigger by the looks of it. No sign of the Yank, tho."

Knowing that they was searching for me made the hairs on the back of my head tingle and I wanted very much to open my eyes just then — to see if they had any notion where I was. But I pressed my eyes closed even harder and told myself to lie as still as a stump. It was quiet again and I had the feeling that there was a lot of Reb eyes scanning the woods for me. Don't move, I told myself. Don't even breathe hard. Then, after what seemed like a long time, I heard that Lt. say, "They said she was crazy scared. Bet she just saw one of the field hands wandering past and thought she'd seen the whole Federal Army."

The men all laughed at that and a little while later they

124

withdrew and I opened my eyes. The last thing I heard one of them say was, "They oughta burn those shacks down."

Later: Dark clouds have moved in and the air feels heavy. Rain is on the way. At least my achy head and sore body think so. An hour or so ago a pair of riders entered the clearing and slowly rode up to the shacks. Both boys carrying very tall muskets. Was one of them Benjamin? I stayed low again, but watched as they circled the buildings, obviously looking for something. Me? At each door one dismounted and checked inside. Then they left.

Have eaten all of the food Sally provided. She has been as generous as she could be with the little she has, but my stomach still complains. Read my letters several times, listened to riders moving along the road and fretted. Set to dozing and had a remarkable dream. I pictured myself on leave going to visit Sarah and her family and heard myself asking her to marry me!!! That "little" idea startled me awake. I wondered what right had I to think Sarah would want to marry someone like me and, if she did, how I could provide for her and children. I wanted a number of children because being an only one can be a very lonesome thing. Suddenly I had a lot of mouths to feed and no land or skill to do it with — which was even more worrisome. Then I thought, Well, James, you have survived a number of fights and even been made a sgt. over others, so maybe you are ready to be wed. Many

125

older men have done a lot less with their lives and it didn't stop them.

Still later: The sky is darkening and a cold mist is falling. Where is Sally? Will she be back soon with Davie? Will she be back at all? Should I think about striking out on my own? A wet night would be good cover for my journey, but it is bad for my spirits. Uncertainty, doubt, fear, hope, impatience and misgivings are my companions now.

Night: Sally came home at last! — and with her she brought more rain. She did not come out to me right away, and I did not approach the shack — even tho I was soaked thru and shivering. She left the door open, so I could see her light the fire and begin putting together a meal as if I did not even exist. I could not help but think about that last day at Uncle and Aunt's farm and feel very blue. Then I told myself what I already suspected — she is just waiting to see if anyone has followed her before bringing me in. Besides no one who sings you to sleep would just forget about you.

A few minutes later she came to the entrance and stood there, checking all around and listening. Then she looked right to where I was and waved that I should come in.

When I got there, a little stew was just beginning to bubble and the smell was wonderful — and my stomach said so! — but that was not what was on my mind just then. "Where is Davie?" I asked. "Will he be here soon? I have to leave, Sally. Tonight."

Sally put a potato she was peeling — the one that held the candle — into the kettle and said something to calm me down. But I just kept asking her about Davie and saying I had to leave and such til she said something sharp and pointed to the table. I may be the one wearing a sgt.'s chevrons, but Sally is the one with an officer's command!

So I sat down and waited while the stew cooked up, and then we ate it and not many words was passed between us. I was beginning to think I would finish my stew and just leave, when Sally got up and began putting what little food she had in a sack. So I was leaving after all.

I decided to write in the journal til Davie appeared and I was at this work when — without sound or announcement — a man stepped into the shack — followed by four other people — a woman and three children!

The man and the woman glanced at me, then commenced talking with Sally — and I could not figure out any of it — and all the while the three children looked me up and down suspiciously. At one point the man — who I took to be Davie — began studying me especially hard. He is an impressive man — I guess he might be thirty or thirty-five years old and over six feet tall and very strong looking, even fierce. But it is his eyes that speak loudest — they are dark, almost black, intelligent and move so quickly that I am sure there is nothing that escapes his attention.

The woman was younger than the man while the children looked to range in age from five or six all the way up to ten. Suddenly everyone fell silent. "Am I going with him now?" I asked Sally, pointing to the man and then to myself. I assumed no one spoke American because the man said something to Sally in French and she said something back. He then turned to me and announced, "I am Davie, Sally's nephew. This is my wife, Martha, and these are our children." He spoke American with a southern accent, with some French there, too, but not so thick as to make understanding hard. "Sally says we will all be leaving just as soon as she speaks with the children." "We *all* will be leaving?" I asked. "All of us," Davie said gravely, pointing to the children, his wife, Sally and himself. "We are all that is left of our family. Now come here, please, young sir. We have to prepare for the journey."

May 10, near dawn

It is hard to tell about last night, so many things happened. While Sally talked with Martha and the children, Davie got me ready by mixing up a fine batch of mud right there in Sally's floor and rubbing it all over my face and hands and even the brass buttons of my uniform. "Won't it be hard to get thru with all of them?" I asked Davie at one point. "Sally is telling them now what they must do," he said. "They will listen to her. And the rain will help."

That was true, about the rain. It was a cold, steady shower now — the kind of weather that drives most soldiers to find shelter. Still, trying to slip seven people past the Rebs would be pretty hard to do. And then there was Sally. "Will Sally be okay?" I asked. "Will she be able to make the journey? Those woods are fierce and — " Davie waved the questions away. "If any of us make it out, it will be Sally. Don't you go worrying about her, Sgt. Worry about yourself."

Sally finished talking with Martha and the children, then she turned to us and let out a soft laugh when she saw me. She said something to Davie, who also laughed. "She says the mud makes you look like her husband, who is gone ten years now. But she thinks you might be even scrawnier."

We left right after this, with Davie leading. The oldest child — who was a girl — was right behind her father. Behind the girl came Martha, who was holding the hand of a boy, while Sally followed them with the other child — a girl — in tow. I came last in our little parade.

"Come along," Davie said as he entered the woods by way of a tiny trail. I thought we would be in for a bad trip when the little girl became afraid and started whining and struggling to avoid entering the dark woods. That kind of action was okay here near the empty clearing, but if we was close to Reb soldiers, it could cost us dearly. Fortunately Sally gave the little girl's arm a hard tug and said something in her ear, and then we went on without a peep from either child.

Davie had moved ahead of us — about thirty or forty

129

feet — so we could barely see him. He told us before leaving that we was to watch him carefully and to move when he moved, stop when he stopped.

He seemed to have a purpose for every step he took — at least I hoped so. The woods all looked the same to me, and without a moon or stars I had no idea what direction we was headed. Sally was right to make me wait — without a guide I would have been lost in no time or been scooped up by the Rebs.

If I had any doubts about this, they disappeared when we was about a half mile from the clearing. Davie suddenly stopped and did not move for a very long time. I could see him leaning forward, listening and searching the woods. He heard or saw something, I was sure. But what?

Time dragged along while we waited, and the two littlest began pulling this way and that. Both Sally and Martha knelt beside the children, holding them tight and whispering to them.

At last Davie came back to us and whispered first to Sally and then to me that there was a small fire in the woods off to the right about 200 feet. Guards for the pasture where a sizable number of Rebs was camped, Davie guessed. If that was true, I told Davie, it meant that there was other guards positioned all around the field at regular intervals. "Is there another way?" I asked. Davie shook his head no and said this was the best route — there was another Reb camp to the left and the land to the right was too rough. We needed to get

130

beyond the pasture ahead but he did not seem to know what to do next and commenced whispering with Sally and his wife.

"They will likely have little fires," I said, interrupting their talk. "On a rainy night, the officers will let them have fires to drive off the cold. And they will give a signal to say everything is O.K. Probably every fifteen minutes. That is how our guards work, any-way."

Davie told this to the others, then said we would wait for the next signal and if he felt it safe we would move ahead. Otherwise, we would have to go back and try another night. I was to carry the little girl, while he would carry the small boy — that way, there would be fewer feet to cause noise. I also told Davie that once we was past the ring of guards, we should angle to the left and then stop to listen again. There might be a second line of guards posted and they would signal at a different time than the first. "Sally was right," Davie whispered as he shouldered one of his children. "She said a sgt. in the army would know things that would help us. Even so young a sgt. She knew that the moment she saw you."

I must have looked startled by his words — I mean I don't believe I present a very military appearance just now — but Davie added, "It was in your eyes, sgt. Sally can tell a lot by the eyes."

I picked up the girl and she immediately began reaching toward Sally, whimpering to be in her arms. My shoulder and arm hurt some where I'd landed on them, but that wasn't

131

what bothered me most. I was thinking: This could be very bad for us, especially if the girl got loud. Fortunately Sally was right there, soothing and hushing her gently, so the girl did not struggle hard to get free of my arms.

What Sally said, I do not know. But I did hear the name Harriet several times, so I commenced whispering in Harriet's other ear and saying her name often, til she turned her big eyes on me and even reached out to touch my face and whisper something back to me. It was while we was whispering back and forth that I realized how light she was — a good gust could have sent her sailing like a leaf — and how thin her arms and legs really was.

Pretty soon, Harriet grabbed hold of my uniform and held tight. Around then, I heard a distant shout, and immediately it was repeated and repeated and repeated down the line of guards. The voices got louder and clearer as they approached, til we could hear the guards singing out, "All is quiet!" one after another. The call was sounded just to our right, where Davie had seen the fire, and then — not more than 100 feet away! — it came again on our left. Then the call continued its journey, fading away to nothing as it went around the rest of the pasture.

Davie did not hesitate, but moved forward very slowly. Now was a time to be thankful for a rainy, moonless night, as we was as silent and as invisible as tiny night creatures trying to avoid the eyes of the owl. After we passed the first line of guards and went to the left, we halted again to listen. Not long after this, the same shouted signal could be heard sweeping around the pasture. Fortunately, the inside line was not spaced so tightly together, so it was easy to slip between the nearest guards.

We was now between the guards and the main camp, circling around the pasture in a bit of woods I would guess was 300 feet from the camp — enough that I could see where the woods gave way to open pasture, but could not see any tents or other army equipment. During all of the waiting Harriet fell fast asleep on my shoulder, her breath coming regular and warm, as if nothing in the world was wrong — and I was happy to have it so.

We traveled like this all the way around the pasture — a half a mile at least — and eventually we came to the spot where Davie wanted to cut off into the woods again. Which meant we had to go back thru the lines of guards once more.

This time we was aided not only by the regular call, but by the fact that a guard change took place just then. There was all sorts of commands being issued, men talking — mostly complaining that the change of guards was late, as usual! — and a general stomping and crashing thru the underbrush with some cussing. So we hunched down low and was past all of them in just a few minutes.

Davie picked up the pace a mite then and I assumed that meant there was no Rebs camped over here. So on we went — over fallen-down trees, around rocks, across little streams. In some sections the walking was easy, but just when

133

I relaxed a little, some sticker bush would jab at me to remind me I wasn't safe yet. The sleeping Harriet had pulled her legs up and made her body into a ball, so carrying her even in the rough terrain was easy.

The land was thickly wooded and generally flat for nearly an hour, but then we came on a series of steep hills with lots of slippery rocks to climb. At one point Davie decided to walk up the middle of a cold, fast-moving stream, and we followed.

All of this was beginning to wear me down, my leg and arm being banged up as they was, and Harriet suddenly seeming to grow heavier. I started to breathe hard. How was Sally holding up? I wondered. How was Martha and the oldest girl doing? But they all seemed fine. Fortunately for me, Davie stopped often to listen and to peer ahead into the darkness, which gave me time to rest. He seemed to be choosing particularly rough terrain for our travel, to avoid Reb patrols, I guessed. There was hardly any other life in here, for that matter. Even the animals stayed clear of these places.

We came to a narrow road and stopped to rest and taste some of Sally's food. Harriet and her brother slept on, while Sally, Martha and the older girl looked as exhausted as I felt. "Are we far?" I asked. I did not want to walk another step if I did not have to, and besides, we had used up just about all of the night already.

Davie was working on some corn bread and looking up the road. "Far?" he said. "Not very far, I think." But he did not seem very sure of this. "Do you know where this road leads?" I asked. "North," Davie said, "I think it leads North." "You think?" I asked, and I am certain my voice sounded alarmed. "You mean you're not sure if this road goes North?"

Sally must have heard my upset because she and Davie and Martha began talking back and forth among themselves, pointing this way and that, sometimes up the road, sometimes into the woods behind us. Then Davie said, "Sally says the road goes North to a bigger road. She says if we follow the big road a few miles it will take us to a place where we can cross the river."

I thought about this a moment. The road was temptingly flat and I know my feet would welcome a few miles that did not include tree roots, large rocks and streams. Then I thought better. "If the Rebs control the land above here," I said, "they will have guards posted in places. We should stick to the woods."

A heartbeat later — as if to prove me correct — we heard a rumbling that was already mighty close on us. I rolled over and partly covered the sleeping children. "Get down and stay still," I hissed, and soon we was all no more than lumps on the ground. And good thing too. The rumbling — the sound of hooves, I now realized — was accompanied by the clink of metal on metal. Then the cavalry — Reb, I could just see — began going past our position, one after another after another, on and on, without end. 100. Maybe 200. Maybe more. After a while, I gave up looking at them and closed my eyes.

We was not more than fifteen feet from them, but Davie

had selected a spot deep in shadow and the riders swept past us. If any glanced our way, they probably thought we was rocks or logs. Even after the line of horses ended and everything grew quiet again, we stayed on the ground without moving.

"That was close," I said when I finally got up and had Harriet in my arms again. "Come along," was all Davie said. "No time to waste."

We was across the road — and we ran very quickly to the cover of the other side — and plunged into the woods. A little beyond the road we came to an empty field. "I think this is good," I said. I was remembering Caesar's finger moving over the map in Lt. Toms's tent and how he said there was more farmland along the Rapidan. We skirted this field and soon came to another and another. Then there was another section of woods and not long after this we came to a wide body of water — the Rapidan.

Davie took us up along the river several miles to where the ford was. Which army controls this area? I wondered. Fortunately, I heard a series of orders issued — all in a very comforting Northern accent.

At the ford, the guard challenged me just as soon as he heard us, telling me to halt and say the password. I answered by telling him who I was and what company I was a part of. "I have been lost in the woods since the 6th," I told him. "Come forward slowly with your hands raised," he ordered, and I did as ordered. "I would raise my hands," I said as I stepped from the woods, "but I have a child in my

136

arms. And there are more with me. Five more."

He had his musket pointed at me as we approached, and his eyes opened wide when he took in my appearance and then saw Sally and the others. "Damn if you don't look just like one of these niggers here," the guard said. I moved a few steps closer and turned to the side so he could see my sgt.'s chevrons. "These are my friends, Pte., and they saved my life. You will treat them with respect, do you hear?" "I didn't mean nothin' by it, Sgt.," he sputtered. "It's just that you look . . . well, you look — " "Never mind how I look, Pte. Take me to the officer in charge and be quick about it."

We was brought into camp then and left at the guard's tent with warm blankets to wrap ourselves in. I handed Harriet over to Sally — tho Harriet actually clung to me so it took some doing to pry her fingers loose. Next some tins of Army coffee appeared. Just as thick and old as any I have ever had — and just as delicious!

A bucket of water was produced and I washed as much of the mud from my face and hands as I could. The others was now huddled on a cot, wrapped tight in their blankets and sinking fast into needed sleep. Except Sally, that is. Harriet had gotten fretful, and Sally had her on her lap and was stroking her hair and humming.

After this an officer came to question me and I was happy to tell him about the Reb troops I'd seen near Sally's and the cavalry headed along the road. I tried to find out about the 122nd and my Company, but this officer was sour at being called out so late, and any-way he did not have much information about them. He did say that the fight in the woods had gone back and forth — first they looked to take the day and then us. He couldn't have meant where we was, since it was clear they had beat us badly there! The fighting swung to our favor after their Gen. Longstreet was wounded and had to leave the battle, but then Gen. Lee managed to get his army over to Spotsylvania before we did and was still there and still fighting. He didn't know exactly where our regiment was. They could be any-where between the Old Wilderness and Spotsylvania, or they could have even been pulled from the fight and put in reserve.

"You should get some rest, Sgt. And report to the adjutant's tent for duty in the afternoon." Report for what? I wondered. But that wasn't the most important thing on my mind just then. "What about these people, sir?" I asked. "They helped me escape." "We'll see about them tomorrow, Sgt. There are some empty tents over by the sutler's shanty you can use. The sgt. of the guard will show you where they are."

I thanked him, and then the sgt. came in and took us to our tents for the night. I was so tired, I do not even remember saying good night or thank you to Davie or Sally or any of her family. But there will be tomorrow for that. Tonight I am to sleep on a soft cot under a warm blanket — but first I will reread Sarah's letters one more time and pray for peaceful dreams.

138

May 11

Spoke with a Capt. Riskind around noon. He told me there was no way to know where G Company was at present and that til this was known I would be assigned to help unload ambulances. In the past this would have been just fine with me, being a safe occupation, but I protested this time — only the Capt. did not want to hear any of it.

I also told the Capt. about what Sally and Davie had done for me, and asked if they could get help from anyone. "There is a new group running around camp these days — the Union Commission, from up in St. Louis or there-abouts. I'll ask them what can be done." I thanked him and then took lunch — a mighty heap of it — and wrote Sarah a brief letter to tell her I am very much alive, and that I was sure Johnny was too. After, I went to the field hospital to help with arriving ambulances.

The ambulances stream into camp day and night fully loaded. Most of the wounded are being transferred from regimental hospitals close to the fighting and have already been treated. Many others have been wandering about for days and have only now found their way to the surgeons. The surgeons here are very busy — prying pieces of metal from torn-up flesh and sawing off mangled bone.

I ask about the 122nd and G Company whenever I can, but no one — not the ambulance drivers, surgeons, nurses, litter carriers or wounded — has any news of them. When he heard me asking these things, one of the other litter carriers said, "If you ask too often, you'll find them for sure, and then you will be back in it. I have been here four weeks and expect that I can stay, as long as I don't make too much noise."

I thought about what this soldier said all day. They certainly need help here, as the ambulances keep arriving. But the number of wounded tells me that they need help out there too and maybe more so.

Ambulance arriving with wounded.

7 o'clock: When my day was over, I went hunting for Sally and Davie and their family. It took a while, but I found them with some officers, all of them working at cleaning clothes and cooking and such. I arrived just as Sally was lecturing a capt. about leaving his clothes all about his tent, and the capt., who did not understand a word she was saying, just stood there nodding his head while his friends laughed at the scene. Davie said they had traded one dirty house for another, but at least here they can leave when they want. And it seems they will be doing just that in two or three weeks, according to Davie. A representative from the Union Commission said a train would take them to St. Louis, where the group has its head-quarters and is helping the refugees from the South.

Sally brought us bowls of potatoes, carrots and beef — much different food from what we had just a day ago! While we ate, I asked Davie and Sally some of the questions that had come into my head — like where Sally had come from that she speaks French and not American? Davie told me, "Sally is from an island off the coast of South America. She and her sister was taken and sold to people living outside of New Orleans when Sally was seven. It was a big place and the white folk was decent enough, but then Yellow Jack fever came and lots of people died. My mother and father and brother's family. Sally's husband too. Even our master's wife — that was when he decided to leave, so his two children would be safe from Yellow Jack — and Sally raised such a fuss til he brought us all to Virginia. We was in Virginia ten years when you come along." I asked if they had ever considered running North before now, and Davie said, "We considered it every day — even before the war — but Sally said no, we had to wait for the right time. Sally said you wanted to get back to your soldier friends something bad and knew you

141

would too. And so would we if we went along. She could tell you did not give up easy."

We talked more, mostly about what they did — which sounded a lot like what I did on Uncle and Aunt's farm! Except that I was never beat, no matter how bad things got, and I could leave and not worry that any-one would hunt me down.

Seems that Sally was such a talker and so stubborn that her owner thought the house might be quieter — and the other Negroes less "agitated" — if she wasn't around all the time — which is why he let her live apart in the abandoned tobacca shack. I told them that I had included them in my journal and I took it out to show them. Sally spotted the minié-ball hole and touched it, looking from it to me. Then her face brightened and she spoke to Davie. "Sally says she is proud to be in your book. She said your words must be very strong to stop a musket ball like that."

May 12

I think some would call it a miracle. Today I was helping with the wounded when I heard a voice say, "Sgt. Pease, we all thought you dead and gone!" It was Pete McQuade, who had bandages on both his hands, his right leg and parts of his face, and he looked to be thinner besides.

He told me that after I was "killed" — because that is what everyone thought — wave after wave of Rebs came over and

Maj. Pettit's men finally called retreat. Most of those who could move themselves made it back to the main road, where the officers rallied them. They went up the road and joined the fight again, but then the woods caught fire and forced them to retire a second time. That is where Pete got shot in the leg and then the fire burned him as he was crawling off. "The Company's been shot up bad, Sgt.," he added, tho he didn't remember exactly who had been killed or wounded. I asked about Johnny, and Pete thought him fine the last he remembered seeing him. "But the fighting has moved over near Spotsylvania and is very hot, I heard. They was headed for the Ny River, last I saw them."

I told Pete I would be going over there myself just as soon as I could break free from my duties here. Pete said he thought they could use my help, and then he told me to fetch something from his vest pocket that I should keep. It was a coin — the silver coin Sarah had sent me for good luck and which I gave to Pete a while back. "This didn't do you much good, Pete," I said. "Oh, but it did," Pete replied. "I count myself lucky to have gotten out at all. A lot didn't."

I tucked the coin into the pocket with Sarah's letters, thanked Pete and went back to my work. Later I found the officer in charge and told him I knew where my Company was and wanted to go back to them, but he said I would have to wait til orders was issued officially. I said it was important that I get back to them, but he said it was important to wait for the signed papers to come thru. "Otherwise we will both

143

be in trouble, Sgt.," he explained. "Gen. Grant is cracking down on stragglers and such, and he is a man who means business."

I thought about what this officer said while I helped move the wounded from the ambulances to the surgeon's tent. Sgt. Donoghue always said, "An order is an order, and it isn't our job to go question them either." That is true, I believe, but I do not recall the officer "ordering" me to stay in camp, and I have certainly not heard from Gen. Grant directly. So I have decided to leave — before anyone gets around to ordering me not to!

May 13

Said a tearful good-bye to Sally and Davie and the others, and thanked them over and over for helping me and wished them well in St. Louis. Next I found Pete McQuade and told him what I was doing. Then I hitched a ride out of camp on an ambulance, which took me up the road several miles. Have walked ever since — the roads being less congested at night, tho still busy with supply wagons going and coming, cattle being taken to the army for food, and ambulances, of course. The ambulances never seem to rest.

Came upon some soldiers having breakfast at sunrise and was invited to join them — for $1! These fellows had been near the center of the line of battle on the morning of May 6 and had been pretty well licked by the Rebs too. When I asked one of them which was the fastest way to Spotsylvania Court House, he just shook his head and said, "Take my word for it, Sgt. You don't want to go over there. It is a living Hell." When I said I did, he handed me his musket and cartridge box and said, "You will need these more than me then. I am going home!"

His rifle felt heavy to me, not having held one in many days — heavier than I remember and much heavier than little Harriet. I had to smile when he wished me "good shooting."

Later: I am down to the last pages of this journal — who would have believed I would be alive to say that — and so I must choose my words carefully. The road has been very busy as I get closer and closer to the fighting. Early in the afternoon I heard the rumble of the big siege guns in the distance. The sound of artillery grew louder and stronger, booming and booming away, and when I pictured them — and what they could accomplish! — my legs wobbled some.

Came to several cutoffs in the road, with streams of men and wagons heading up them and away from the fighting. The crackle of musket fire could be heard now too, mingling with the rumbling thunder of the cannons. I have to admit that I thought a second or two about turning up one of those roads and disappearing into the crowd. Most everyone thinks me dead, so I probably wouldn't be missed.

But then I thought about Sally — who helped me when she really did not have to and put herself at risk. And Harriet. How many other Harriets are there waiting still for our help? And I thought about Johnny — who is like a brother to me — and Lt. Toms and the rest of the boys. I even thought about Charlie Shelp, who is as cussed as they come and no friend of mine, but I think I can handle him just as I can handle Reb sharpshooters, my curse, and Army coffee. And there is Sarah too — who I never want to disappoint. Ever.

Which got me to thinking. When I left Uncle and Aunt, I left nothing and headed toward nothing. Now I am heading toward people who count on me and need me, even if just a little. I will probably never be a very brave soldier, but I think I can do my job and do it in an honorable way. And after this war is over? Who knows?

I looked up just then, and there, not many feet in front of me, was a capt. on horseback staring right at me. He had a crisp uniform, a perfectly clipped mustache, sat very straight on his horse — and seemed to be the sort who did not take much none-sense. When I was closer, he called out to me in a sharp voice, "Where are you going, Sgt?"

I will tell you that my heart jumped a beat and my blood ran cold, thinking I had been caught absent without permission and would have to pay the price. But then I gave the Capt. a sharp salute like those the Lt. gave to the Capt. delivering our orders each morning. "I have deserted my post at the field hospital, sir," I said, "and I'm heading to Spotsylvania and the fighting." The Capt. looked at me a moment, trying to figure out if I was lying or just crazy. "What is your name, Sgt.?" he asked. "I am Sgt. James Edmond Pease, G Company, the 122nd Regiment, New York Volunteers, from Onondaga County, sir. But I did not volunteer to carry stretchers."

The good Capt. looked at me closely, and I am certain he decided then I was indeed crazy. But he just smiled at me and said, "Then you had better hurry along, Sgt. They will be needing you about now." "Yes, sir," I said. I then turned to go on my way when the Capt. called out, "Oh, and Sgt., good luck to you." "Thank you, sir," I replied, "But I believe I have all the luck I will need."

Epilogue

James located what remained of G Company near Spotsylvania Court House late in the day of May 13. He was warmly greeted and happy to be among familiar faces, but sad to see so many fewer of them. He learned then that the recent fighting had taken the lives of four of his comrades besides Willie Dodd and Spirit: Sgt. Donoghue, Niles Rogers, Lyman Swim, and Cornelius Mahar. Another twelve had been wounded, though only six had serious injuries: Lieutenant Toms, Otto Parrisen, Hudson Marsh, Benjamin Breed, Pete McQuade, and James Wyatt.

James had little time to mourn the loss of his friends. Confederate General Robert E. Lee had control of the land around Spotsylvania, and Union General Ulysses S. Grant was determined to have it — at any cost. By the time James arrived, Union forces had already spent several brutal days attacking strong Rebel defensive positions, but had failed to break through Lee's lines. James and G Company were in the thick of it every day until May 23 — with James recording what happened in a brand new journal — when they were finally given two weeks' furlough.

Free to do what he wanted, James accompanied Johnny to

the Henderson farm in New York State. "We had a needed rest," James wrote, "and I was able to meet many of Johnny's friends and relatives, as well as Sarah." The young couple's meeting went extremely well for both of them, and on June 4, James and Sarah were wed in the local Episcopal church.

The celebration had barely ended when James and Johnny found themselves back in Virginia and in the middle of the fighting once again. G Company would take part in several maj. battles before the end of the war, including action at Cold Harbor, Petersburg, Cedar Creek and Appomattox Courthouse. When Robert E. Lee finally surrendered his army, on April 9, 1865, James's Company had been reduced to just twenty men, the rest either dead, wounded or taken prisoner. At the time he left the Army, James was seventeen years old and had risen in rank to second Lieutenant.

It was during these final months of fighting that a sketch artist from *Frank Leslie's Illustrated Newspaper*, Francis Schell, spotted James drawing in his journal. Schell thought James's work showed great promise and suggested he send samples to his boss. Soon James began submitting sketches of soldiers in camp, on the march and in battle, several of which were reproduced in *Leslie's*. He became a staff artist for *Leslie's* at the close of the war and covered such important stories as the building of the transcontinental railroad, the exploration and settlement of the West and the Indian Wars. Sarah accompanied James on these assignments and eventually wrote articles of her own. Sarah and James had one child, Kate.

As for the veterans of G Company, they met every year at the reunion of the 122nd New York Volunteers, where they exchanged recollections of the war and brought each other up-to-date on their lives. Johnny Henderson did indeed marry the girl from the neighboring town and became a successful farmer, but he was best remembered for spinning tall tales about the Civil War. His favorite was about the time James charged ahead of everyone else and drove off several hundred Confederate soldiers singlehandedly.

Osgood "Little Profeser" Tracy went back to medical school and became a doctor with a successful practice in Albany, New York, while Washington Evans became a skilled carpenter and helped to construct some of the most beautiful mansions in Syracuse. Charlie Shelp took his fiery, no-nonsense personality west, first as a foreman on Union Pacific Railroad work gangs and later as manager of a fur-importing company in San Francisco

But of all the personal stories, the most intriguing was that of the notoriously shy William Kittler. William was wounded in the leg by an exploding shell at Cold Harbor, but he refused medical treatment for several days despite the obvious pain. Infection set in, followed by a high fever, during which William became unconscious and was finally rushed to the surgeons. It was there, while having his uniform cut from his body, that William's secret was revealed — William Kittler was in fact a woman! Her real name was Gabrina Sales, and she had cut her hair short and joined the army in the same patriotic fervor that had gripped most of the men and boys. She was discharged from the Army and shipped North to recover and no one from G Company ever heard from her again. Rumor had it, however, that a soldier looking remarkably like William Kittler — and limping noticeably — had been spotted during the fighting at Appomattox.

As for Lt. Toms, he recovered from his wounds and returned to lead G Company in January 1865, when the Army laid seige to Petersburg, Virginia. He was repeatedly passed over for promotion during the rest of the war, despite a clean record and many heroic acts. After being severely wounded at Fisher's Hill, Virginia, he was discharged from the Army still with the rank of lieutenant. He returned to his hometown and family, where he took up his old position as schoolteacher.

James made several attempts to find out what had happened to Sally and her family, but was never successful. He did, however, receive a letter from a former volunteer for the Union Commission, the civilian organization in St. Louis that helped relocate many refugees from the war. While there were no records of where individuals had been sent, the volunteer recalled that a number of former slaves had been given farmland in the Dakota Territory near the Canadian border. Letters to the area received no reply.

James returned to the United States briefly in 1910 to attend the forty-fifth anniversary celebration of the end of the Civil War. Many of his comrades from G Company had passed on by then, leaving just a handful to remember the men and boys who had fought to preserve the Union. James died of a heart attack four years later while staying on Palawan Island in the Philippines; Sarah died ten years after James while on assignment for *National Geographic* in New Zealand.

Almost a year after the death of her mother, a steamer trunk was delivered to Kate Pease's home in Montana. Inside were the personal effects of her parents. At the bottom, carefully wrapped in a hotel towel were her father's Civil War journals. The final entry in the second journal reads:

"June 5, 1865: Well, the war is over and we have made it thru alive! Johnny and I will walk home tomorrow, but today will be spent in saying good-bye to friends and having our last — I hope! — Army supper. Because Lt. Toms is at home recovering, I will take these journals with me and hold them til he decides to write his history of G Company. I only hope that something I say here will be of use to him, tho I don't see how the words of a scared boy could interest him — or anyone else — very much. As I end this entry I believe I can truly say that *now you have read it all.*"

Stuck in the back of the journal was a small, yellowing envelope with a tarnished silver coin inside. On the envelope was written: "Luck is measured by the friends you make and the people you love."

Life in America
in 1863

Historical Note

On April 12, 1861, Confederate cannons under the command of General Pierre G.T. Beauregard opened fire on Federal forces at Fort Sumter. With this act, the Confederate States of America — which would number eleven states from the South after the fall of Fort Sumter — declared war on its Northern counterpart. The war (referred to as a revolution in the South and a rebellion in the North) would last four bloody years and cost the lives of an estimated 600,000 soldiers.

At the heart of the Civil War was the issue of slavery and whether each state had the right to decide for itself if slavery would be permitted within its borders. To white Southerners, slavery — and control of its 3,860,000 black slaves — was crucial both economically and culturally. They insisted that their farming economy could not survive and prosper without the cheap labor provided by slaves. Besides, they claimed, blacks were inferior and needed to be watched over and cared for by their white masters.

Most Northern states had already banished slavery and were pressing for its abolition in the rest of the United States and in the two million square miles of land west of the Mississippi. White Southerners viewed abolition as arrogant and a direct threat to their traditions and way of life. After decades of political wrangling, court cases and compromises, the issue came to a head with the election of Abraham Lincoln as President in 1860.

Lincoln had declared himself firmly opposed to slavery and its introduction in the western territories, but he was willing to let it exist and die a natural death in states that already sanctioned it. His position did not appease Southerners, especially since a majority of the newly elected Congress was firmly antislavery. It would not be long, proslavery advocates warned, before the new President and his Congress flexed their political muscles and placed more and more restrictions on slavery. They had to act quickly before it was too late. And so, on December 20, 1860, South Carolina passed an ordinance of secession, proclaiming that the union previously existing between it and the other states was dissolved. Within weeks, six other Southern states adopted their own ordinances of secession.

This move took Lincoln and most Northerners by complete surprise; the bombardment of Fort Sumter three and a half months later sent them into action. Lincoln put out an urgent call for 75,000 volunteers — the first of many such calls — to defend and maintain the Union. Meanwhile, a second wave of secession strengthened the Confederacy, and broadsides and newspaper ads proclaimed the need for able-bodied soldiers.

Men on both sides rushed to sign up. Would-be soldiers crowded the recruitment centers in large cities or signed on with locally organized units. Emotions ran so high that enlistment quotas were surpassed everywhere. Caught up in the fervor of the moment were boys from both the North and the South.

No one actually knows how many boys were able to join their side's army. Record keeping (when it existed at all) was extremely sloppy at the time, and enlistment procedures were so lax that most boys who claimed to be eighteen — which was the legal age of enlistment at the opening of the war — were allowed to sign up unchallenged. One study made by the U.S. War Department at the close of the nineteenth century estimated that of the 2,100,000 who served in the Union Army, over 800,000 were seventeen years old or younger. Of the 850,000 soldiers the Confederacy sent into battle, between twenty and thirty percent were underage.

Why these boys were so eager to join varied a great deal. Of course, many boys knew what the issues were and willingly put their lives at risk for their beliefs. But a surprising number had little notion or understanding of the political and social implications of the war. They had simply been caught up in the "war fever" that swept the country and wanted to be a part of what they thought would be a brief but glorious adventure. Others enlisted hoping army life would be an exciting alternative to the routine of endless farm chores back home. Still others signed on for no better reason than because their friends had, or because they didn't want to appear cowardly or sympathetic to the enemy.

While their motives for enlisting differed, these boys did have one thing in common: They loved to write. Almost every soldier sent letters home, and a surprising number kept detailed journals of their experiences. Usually, their writing styles were direct and simple, and their spelling was often highly creative. What is more, they tended to focus on the everyday events of army life — the bad coffee and lack of food, the tedious daily routine, the hours of marching and their actions in battle. Yet it is through this intense focus on details that they are able to bring this war so fully alive for us today.

After four years of civil war, after the loss of hundreds of thousands of lives and a massive destruction of property, the Union was indeed restored and the slaves were freed from their bondage. Gone, too, was the idea that any state or collection of states could decide to break free of the others or that the federal government was subservient to the states. In its place emerged a stronger central government, one that would orchestrate the taming and settling of the vast West, become a majority world power and play a larger and larger role in the lives of its citizens.

The Civil War also changed the boys who fought in it. It robbed them of their childhoods, forcing them to confront a hateful and violent adult world. But like the Union they fought for, those who survived came out stronger for their scars and wiser for their experiences.

The Civil War began on April 12, 1861, when the Confederate army opened fire on Union forces at Fort Sumter in South Carolina. Early in the war, volunteers on both sides rushed to join up, for reasons ranging from the defense of their homelands to the assurance of a pair of boots and dinner. The Union soldiers often wore kepi hats, with flat, round tops and stiff visors, like the ones worn by French soldiers.

To reinforce the regular army, President Lincoln asked for 75,000 volunteers to enlist for three months' service, as advertised in this recruiting poster. Few were prepared for the ensuing four-year conflict.

VOLUNTEER ENLISTMENT.

STATE OF   TOWN OF

I,   born in
in the State of   aged   years,
and by occupation a   Do HEREBY ACKNOWLEDGE to have
volunteered this   day of   18 ,
to serve as a Soldier in the Army of the United States of America, for
the period of *THREE YEARS*, unless sooner discharged by proper
authority: Do also agree to accept such bounty, pay, rations, and
clothing, as are, or may be, established by law for volunteers. And
I,   do solemnly swear, that I will bear
true faith and allegiance to the United States of America,
and that I will serve them honestly and faithfully against all their
enemies or opposers whomsoever; and that I will observe and
obey the orders of the President of the United States, and the
orders of the officers appointed over me, according to the Rules
and Articles of War.

Sworn and subscribed to, at
this   day of   18 ,
BEFORE

I CERTIFY, ON HONOR, That I have carefully examined the above
named Volunteer, agreeably to the General Regulations of the Army, and
that in my opinion he is free from all bodily defects and mental infirmity,
which would, in any way, disqualify him from performing the duties of a
soldier.

EXAMINING SURGEON.

I CERTIFY, ON HONOR, That I have minutely inspected the Volunteer,   previously to his enlistment, and that he was
entirely sober when enlisted; that, to the best of my judgment and
belief, he is of lawful age; and that, in accepting him as duly qualified to
perform the duties of an able-bodied soldier, I have strictly observed the
Regulations which govern the recruiting service. This soldier has
eyes,   hair,   complexion, is   feet   inches high.

Regiment of   Volunteers.
RECRUITING OFFICER.

No._____

*Volunteered at*_____

_____18 ,

*By*_____

_____ *Regiment of*_____

_____ *enlistment; last served in Company* ( )

_____ *Reg't of*_____ .

*Discharged*_____18 .

CONSENT IN CASE OF MINOR.

I,   Do CERTIFY, That I am the father of
that the said   is   years of age: and I do hereby freely
give my CONSENT to his volunteering as a SOLDIER IN THE ARMY OF THE UNITED
STATES for the period of THREE YEARS.
GIVEN at   the
Witness: day of   186 .

DECLARATION OF RECRUIT.

I,   desiring
to VOLUNTEER as a Soldier in the Army of the United States, for the term of
THREE YEARS, Do Declare, That I am   years and
of age; That I have never been discharged from the United States service on account of
disability or by sentence of a court-martial, or by order before the expiration of a term
of enlistment; and I know of no impediment to my serving honestly and faithfully as a
soldier for three years.

GIVEN at
The   day of
Witness:

Each volunteer for the Union army completed an enlistment form, top, and a Declaration of Recruit form, bottom. The legal age for soldiers was eighteen, but some as young as ten years old lied about their ages in order to be allowed to fight.

After individual companies learned drills, commanders held mass drills to teach maneuvers within larger units of regiments and brigades.

In its exposed position, the Gettysburg headquarters of Major General George Meade became the center of a terrible artillery fire on July 2, 1863. Several soldiers were killed, forcing Meade, the Commander of the Army of the Potomac, to abandon the building.

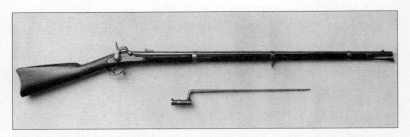

The Springfield musket was the preferred weapon of most soldiers, but it was long (58 inches), heavy (almost 10 pounds), and difficult to use. Even the best soldiers could not load and fire more than three shots per minute. The development of the rifle, pictured here, allowed for more shots and a farther range, which forced the offense to a longer charge subject to heavier fire and, therefore, greater losses.

The eight days of fighting during the battles of the Wilderness and Spotsylvania cost both sides dearly. More than 35,000 Union soldiers were killed, wounded, or missing. Confederate losses were estimated at about 18,000. J. Becker's sketch shows Union troops during the Battle of the Wilderness.

Union soldiers used mortars to bombard the Confederate lines. The largest of these guns could hurl a 220-pound missile larger than a basketball a distance of two and a half miles.

Breastworks made of stone or timber were sometimes constructed to protect soldiers from incoming fire. This sketch by Edward Forbes shows Union soldiers behind breastworks during the Battle of the Wilderness, May 5–7, 1864.

Surprisingly, Union and Confederate soldiers often gathered together after a day of battle. Soldiers traded food, coffee, tobacco, and other useful items between the lines.

Every week, thousands of letters passed through the post office at the Headquarters of the Army of the Potomac, top. *The U.S. Mail Service,* bottom, *which served the Union Army, was reliable; the Confederate Postal Department, however, was sometimes a source of great frustration to Confederate soldiers and their families.*

Almost every soldier sent letters home. The letters tended to focus on the daily routine of army life, with its endless hours of marching and drilling. Here, Union soldiers read letters and play cards to pass the time during the siege of Petersburg, Virginia.

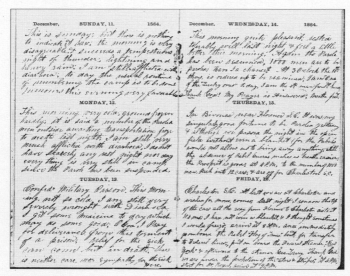

Some soldiers recorded their experiences in journals. These pages from a Union soldier's journal describe time spent in a Confederate military prison.

166

A jonah, the ill-fated fumbler found in every company, angers his fellow soldiers by spilling their coffee, dousing their fire, and wasting their meager rations.

Bad coffee and lack of food were common complaints among the soldiers. Here, a group of Union soldiers lines up for a serving of soup.

About 600,000 Union and Confederate soldiers lost their lives in the Civil War, which resulted in the end of slavery and a more powerful Federal government.

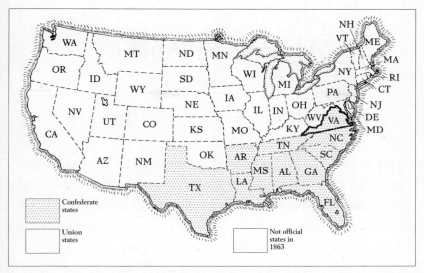

Modern map of the United States, showing the location of Virginia, as well as which states were Union and which were Confederate in 1863.

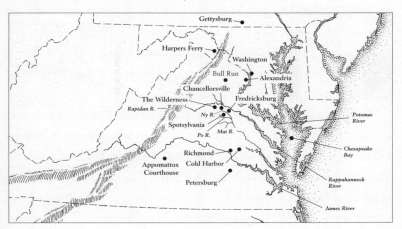

This map includes the sites of several significant Civil War battles, including Gettysburg, Petersburg, Bull Run, and Cold Harbor.

169

About the Author

JIM MURPHY confesses that he never found the Civil War very interesting when he was in school. "The politicians and generals all seemed to write in the same stiff, florid style, and the war was always described in overly complex military terms. Then one day, while researching another book, I came across the diary of a soldier, Elisha Stockwell, Jr.

"My first surprise was to learn that he had enlisted when he was just fifteen. Until then I had never realized that someone so young had been a part of such an important event in American history. My next surprise was how much I enjoyed his writing. He was direct, honest, wonderfully detailed and very, very funny. Even at the worst of times, he always seemed to find something humorous about the situation.

"In preparation for writing this journal, I went back and reread Elisha's diary. I also read the journals of Thomas Galway, who enlisted in the Union Army when he was fifteen and rose in rank to first lieutenant, and Benjamin C. Rawlings, who was the first Virginia volunteer for the Confederacy, at age fifteen, and had been promoted to the rank of captain by the time of Appomattox. Each of these boys had unique and exciting Civil War experiences and were witnesses to many unusual events on and off the battlefield. In addition, each lived through the frightening experience of being routed by an enemy charge and finding himself trapped behind enemy lines. Inspiration for James Pease's encounter with Sally and subsequent escape through enemy lines are based on a real incident involving a nineteen-year-old lieutenant from Missouri, George W. Bailey."

Jim Murphy is the author of over twenty-five award-winning books for children. *The Great Fire* was a Newbery Honor Book, an NCTE Orbis Pictus Award winner, and a *Boston Globe–Horn Book* Honor Book. In addition, *The Boys' War* and *The Long Road to Gettysburg* were both SCBWI Golden Kite Award winners; *Across America on an Emigrant Train* received an Orbis Pictus Award; and *A Young Patriot* was given special recognition by the Sons of the Revolution, with the Fraunces Tavern Museum Book Award. Mr. Murphy has written one other book for the Dear America series, *West to a Land of Plenty: The Diary of Teresa Angelino Viscardi*. He lives in Maplewood, New Jersey, with his family.

Acknowledgments

Grateful acknowledgment is made for permission to reprint the following:

Cover portrait: A detail from Winslow Homer's *Young Soldier: Separate Study of a Soldier Giving Water to a Wounded Companion*, 1861. Oil, gouache, black crayon on canvas. Cooper Hewitt Museum, Smithsonian Institution / Art Resource, New York.

Cover background: Peter R. Rothermel's *Battle of Gettysburg: Pickett's Charge*, The State Museum of Pennsylvania, Pennsylvania Historical and Museum Commission.

Interior illustrations copyright © 1998 by Jim Murphy.
Page 159 (top): Union soldier, Library of Congress.
Page 159 (bottom): Recruiting poster, ibid.
Page 161 (top): Mass drill, Library of Congress.
Page 161 (bottom): Meade's Gettysburg headquarters,
    Gardner's Photographic Sketch Book of the Civil War,
    Dover Publications, Inc., New York.
Page 162 (top): Springfield musket, Smithsonian Institution

Photo No. 37692-C.

Page 162 (bottom): Sketch of the Battle of the Wilderness, *Frank Leslie's Illustrated Newspaper*.

Page 163: Union soldiers with mortar, Library of Congress.

Page 164 (top): Breastworks, *Frank Leslie's Illustrated Newspaper*.

Page 164 (bottom): Union and Confederate soldiers, National Archives.

Page 165 (top): Post office, Army of the Potomac, *Gardner's Photographic Sketch Book of the Civil War*, Dover Publications, Inc., New York.

Page 165 (bottom): U.S. Mail Service, Library of Congress.

Page 166 (top): Union soldiers, ibid.

Page 166 (bottom): Union soldier's journal, ibid.

Page 167: Jonah drawings, *Hardtack and Coffee or The Unwritten Story of Army Life*, by John D. Billings, George Smith & Co., Boston.

Page 168 (top): Union soldiers lining up for soup, Library of Congress.

Page 168 (bottom): Dead soldier, *Gardner's Photographic Sketch Book of the Civil War*, Dover Publications, Inc., New York.

Page 169: Maps by Heather Saunders.

To Dianne Hess — with appreciation and love

While the events described and some of the characters in this book may be based on actual historical events and real people, James Edmond Pease is a fictional character, created by the author, and his journal is a work of fiction.

Copyright © 1998 by Jim Murphy.

All rights reserved. Published by Scholastic Inc.
557 Broadway, New York, New York 10012.
MY NAME IS AMERICA®, SCHOLASTIC, and associated logos are trademarks and/or registered trademarks of Scholastic Inc.

No part of this publication may be reproduced, or stored in a retrieval system, or transmitted in any form or by any means, electronic, mechanical, photocopying, recording, or otherwise, without written permission of the publisher.
For information regarding permissions, write to Scholastic Inc., Attention: Permissions Department, 557 Broadway, New York, NY 10012.

Library of Congress Cataloging-in-Publication Data available.

ISBN 0-439-43814-X;
ISBN 0-439-44560-4 (pbk.)

10 9 8 7 6 5 4 3 2   02 03 04 05 06

The display type was set in Caslon Antique.
The text type was set in Berlinger.
Book design by Pauline Neuwirth.

Printed in the U.S.A. 23
First paperback printing, October 2002

A Picture of Freedom

—

The Diary of Clotee, a Slave Girl

by Patricia C. McKissack

Scholastic Inc. New York

Belmont Plantation

Virginia 1859

March 1859

The spring blooms are comin' and the sky is a sure blue. March never knows if it wants to be a spring month or a winter month. The heat's come early to Virginia this year. That's fine with me though. As long as it's hot I have to fan young mas' William and Miz Lilly, my mistress, during their study time. This mornin' was the first day of my third learnin' season. For now on three years, I been fannin' them, liftin' and lowerin' the big fan made of woven Carolina sweet grass — up and down, up and down. The fan stirs the thick air — up and down, up and down — and chases away worrisome horse flies and eye gnats. It may seem like a silly job. But, I don't mind one bit, 'cause while William is learnin', so am I.

Standin' there fannin' — up and down, up and down — I come to know my ABCs and the sounds the letters make. I teached myself how to read words. Now, I can pick through things I find to read — like throwed away newspapers, letters in the trash, and books I slip off Mas' Henley's shelf. It scares me to know what I know sometimes.

Slaves aine s'posed to know how to read and write, but I do. Miz Lilly would fall down in a fit if she knew I had made myself a diary like the one she's got on her bed

3

table. It don't matter to me that hers is all wrapped in fine satin and got ribbons and beads on it and mine is just made up of papers I found in the trash and keeps tied together with a measure of yarn. It's a diary just the same. Mine. And I aim to write in it whenever I get a chance.

I got to be real particular and make sure nobody finds out though, 'cause if my mas'er finds out I would fall under the whip. Time and time again I done heard Mas' Henley swear that if he catches his slaves with learnin' he'll beat the skin off us, then sell our hides to slavers from the Deep South. He got the law on his side, too. Anybody found teachin' a slave in the state of Virginia can be sent to jail. Sure! Wonder why the white folks is so determined to keep us from knowin' things? What are they scared of?

Cain't help but laugh a little bit when I think of what Mas' Henley would think if he knew I could read better than his boy — and that it was his own wife that had teached me!

It's near dark. Pray Lord, don't let nobody find my diary hid behind the loose brick in the outside chimney wall, back of the kitchen. Hope it can stay dry and safe until I can sneak away to write again.

Next mornin', first light

I got up extra early and churned the butter for breakfast and helped out in the kitchen the way Aunt Tee

4

'spects me to every mornin'. That give me a little time to practice my writin' at my spot by the big tree out behind the kitchen. Sunrise is a good writin' hour — when all is still and quiet.

I want to tell somebody 'bout all the things I done learned for the past three years. Words got magic. Every time I read or write a word it puts a picture in my head.

Like when I write H-O-M-E I sees Belmont Plantation and all the people that live here. I sees the Big House where Mas' Henley, Miz Lilly, and William stay, livin' easy. I sees the separate kitchen with the attic above it where I sleep along with Aunt Tee, Uncle Heb, and Hince. I sees the Quarters where my friends live, and beyond their cabins, the fields and orchards where they work. I sees Aunt Tee cookin' at the fireplace, and the stables where Hince takes care of Mas' Henley's prize racin' horses, and the gardens and grounds that Uncle Heb makes pretty. Home. That one li'l word shows me all of that.

Mas' Henley thinks he owns everything here at Belmont, but he don't own all of me — not really. I know, he can tell me to come and I got to come. When he say do this, I better do it or he'll put the whip to my back. But I done learned that he cain't tell me what to think — and feel — and know. He look at me every day but he cain't see what's in my head. He cain't own what's inside me. Nobody can.

Few days later

It rained all the long, long day. Everything is dampish and sticky. I wondered if my diary stayed dry in its hidin' place. No need to worry, the stone covered it well.

Next day

It rained again today. When it rains hard, the field slaves don't have to work. But our work in the kitchen goes on all the time — no days off.

Aunt Tee say I'm lucky, gettin' picked to work in the Big House. I aine so sure. Livin' right under Mas' Henley and Miz Lilly aine so easy to me. We got to do their biddin' all hours of the night and day. But field work is hard — hard on your back, and in the summer, the heat is smothery. I guess what it comes to is bein' a slave aine no good no matter where they got you workin'.

Next day

I just wrote T-R-E-E. I see my tree — the live oak behind the kitchen where I come to write whenever I can slip away. I put a "s" on tree and now the word is trees. The picture in my head turns to the apple orchards. In spring, the apple trees are filled with bright, white blossoms. I close my eyes and see the same trees in the green of summer, and full of good-tastin' apples in the fall. I love playin' with words — puttin' letters in and takin' letters out and lettin' the pictures change.

Monday

I know it's Monday, 'cause Miz Lilly comes to the kitchen every Monday mornin' to pass out the flour, sugar, and meal.

It's so hard keepin' secrets from the people I live with. Sometimes when I'm helpin' Aunt Tee in the kitchen, I want to tell her 'bout my learnin' so bad. But I cain't, even though she's 'bout the closest thing to a mama I got since my own mama died five years ago. I don't think she'd do a thing to hurt me, but she been real close with Mas' Henley all his life. Been his cook — since before he got married to Miz Lilly. Cain't take the chance.

I want to tell Uncle Heb how I used his whittlin' knife to make a writin' pen out of a turkey quill. He'd be right proud of his Sunflower Girl, that's what he calls me. But he's old now, forgetful. He might just slip up and tell the wrong person, who'd tell Mas' Henley on me just to win a favor.

What I wouldn't give to tell Hince how, whilst I'm dustin', I slip ink out of Mas' Henley's study in a glass bottle. I can see him laughin' so his eyes would water up. I'd come more close to tellin' Hince my secret than anybody — him bein' like a big brother to me, always teasin' and funnin'. Hince say I study on things all the time — off by myself too much. He don't understand I aine off to myself 'cause I want to be. I'm just bein' careful-like, not wantin' to be caught practicin' my writin' and readin'.

If Mama was alive I could tell her. But Mama is gone, gone forever. Dead. So there's nobody I trust enough to tell.

Two days later

It aine even summer yet, and William is fussin' 'bout the heat. I am twelve and he is, too. But he seems so much younger. Maybe it's 'cause William is forever whinin' 'bout something — 'specially at study time. I just stay quiet and listen, fannin' — up and down, up and down. Aunt Tee say William is spoiled to a stink. Mas' Henley thinks his son is a little piece of heaven here on earth. 'Course, nobody else shares that notion, not even the boy's mama.

Next day

There's goin' to be a dinner party in the Big House tonight. Aunt Tee sent me down to the Quarters to get Aggie and Eva Mae to help out in the kitchen. Whenever I write F-R-I-E-N-D, I always put a "s" on it, 'cause I have two friends — Eva Mae's daughter, Missy. She's fifteen. And Aggie's daughter, Wook. She's sixteen. They all growed up now, but we still be friends. Known them all my life. Cain't even remember a time when I didn't know them.

I've always been a little jealous 'cause Wook and Missy be closer to each other than they's to me. And they each got their mamas with them. Missy's daddy was Mas' Henley's best jockey, but he was throwed from his horse and killed a year or so back. Now Hince do all the ridin'. Eva Mae is still grievin' and Missy misses her daddy much as I miss my mama.

Wook is lucky to have a daddy like Rufus. Anybody who knows Rufus and Aggie likes them. Rufus came to Belmont 'bout two years ago from over in Hampton. He's a strong man, big, but not fat — not tall either. Uncle Heb say he's a God-fearin' man. Mas' must have seen that Rufus was a natural-born leader, so he made Rufus the field boss.

A lot of women had their eyes on Rufus when he came, but he married Aggie, a big fine woman who had a daughter, but Rufus took Wook to be his very own daughter.

Aggie is goin' to have a baby real soon. When her time come, Aunt Tee will do the birthin'. Aunt Tee is the plantation midwife — birthed Hince, Wook, Missy, and even birthed me. She look out after all the 'spectin' women. She's showed me the secrets to all her medicine recipes, but she will not let me go to a birthin' with her. I want to know 'bout such things, but Aunt Tee say, it's not for me. How do she know it's not for me, if she aine never let me go?

Next day

Even though we don't live but a short walk from each other, Wook and Missy and I don't get to visit much durin' the week — just on Saturday nights and Sunday. I got to 'fess, I likes Wook better than Missy. Missy always pushed and hit us when she was young. Now that she's a big girl, she push and hit with words. Just yesterday she come sayin' I thought I was somebody, 'cause I work in the Big House. Aggie and Wook work in the fields, hunched over all day in the hot sun. Aunt Tee say that's enough to make a body mean.

Friday

Fear of another frost is over, and the moon is full. Aunt Tee said it was time to plant the house garden behind the kitchen. The family will eat out of it all summer and well into fall. Put in greens, goobers, cabbage, okra — all we could plant on that one spot. Takin' care of the house garden is one job I don't mind doin'. Its fun workin' with the plants, watchin' them grow and make food.

10

Next night

It stormed earlier tonight. Flashes of lightnin' lit up the attic room. I tried not to be scared. Lord, I miss Mama. When I was little and it would storm, me and Mama would hug up close and I wouldn't be scared.

The rain has finally stopped, but it is still, hot, and muggy — cain't sleep. Besides, I woke up dreamin' 'bout Mama again. I slipped quiet-like out of the kitchen, careful not to wake nobody, so I could come write.

I am here at the live oak, my spot. Here I can let my tears drop like the rain and tell the moon 'bout my sadness. Writin' 'bout my dream helps the hurt go away.

In my dream, I touched Mama's round, brown face. Like she used to do, she wet the tip of her apron and dabbed away the sweat over my upper lip and on my forehead. I saw myself readin' to her. She smiled and clapped her hands. I heared her soft voice praise me the way Mas' Henley do William when he gets the least li'l thing right.

"I knows so much more, Mama. Let me show you." The soft in her face changed and her eyes held a warnin' I couldn't understand. "What's wrong, Mama?" She wanted to say somethin', but she was pulled away into the dark by some powerful big hand. "Mama, wait." She was gone, and I woke up to the cold, hurtin' truth. Mama is dead.

11

Next day

I slipped off to visit with Missy and Wook today. I found them 'mongst the young tobacco plants, 'longside Rufus. I was so glad to see them. We used to have a great time together, playin' games. Then Mas' put Missy and Wook to work in the fields, and I got put to work in the Big House. Wook's face looks tired and drawn. All Missy wanted to talk 'bout was how cute she thought Hince was. Cute? Hince? Missy got eyes for Hince? She did say somethin' that made good since. She say that Rufus had asked Mas' Henley if he could hold a service at Eastertime. I'm surprised. Mas' aine in the habit of doin' things nice for nobody less'n it serves him.

Easter Sunday

After breakfast, we all gathered in the Quarters for the Easter meetin'. Most times all of us be so tired, we just fall out on Sunday. Try to rest. Be ready for sunrise bell come Monday. But Rufus lifted everybody's spirits today.

Mas' Henley came to the service to see what we was doin' — come talkin' 'bout how he didn't want no shoutin' and carryin' on 'bout fredum. He told us to pray for good weather and a big harvest. Sing 'bout joy and happiness. No sad songs. I wonder does he really believe we'll pray for his good fortune and not our own? He say if we do like he say, then he'll let us have more meetin's on Sunday.

Anyhow, Mas' Henley sat down, and Rufus took over. Wook tol' me once that Rufus had been the slave of a preachin' man before bein' sold to Mas' Henley. Uncle Heb say Rufus had learned the Bible from cover to cover — and know all the stories by heart. One day, I want to read the Bible for myself. There's a Bible that stays on Mas' Henley's readin' table. I've looked at it many times, but I've never touched it. I think he'd know if I did.

Rufus began the meetin' by askin' Uncle Heb to speak a prayer. Then he called on Aggie to sing. Then Rufus told us a story 'bout a brave man named Daniel who stood down lions with just his faith.

When we find ourselves in the lion's den, Rufus say that we should be like Daniel and believe that God will deliver us from all harm. Everybody shouted amen to that, even me. But, I'm not so sure 'bout facin' a lion. What a scary thing . . . facin' a lion.

Monday evenin'

The last meal of the day is over and all the dishes is washed. I'm so tired! "You don't know what tired is," Aunt Tee told me. "Be glad you aine got to work the fields." I cain't demagine bein' tireder than I am now. I wondered did Wook and Aggie go to bed feelin' sick-tired like me?

Day or two later

There's just enough light to practice my writin'.

Freedom is one of the first words I teached myself to write. Down in the Quarters people pray for freedom — they sing 'bout freedom, but to keep Mas' Henley from knowin' their true feelings, they call freedom "heaven." Everybody's mind is on freedom.

But it is a word that aine never showed me no picture. While fannin' this afternoon, my eyes fell on "freedom" in a book William was readin'. No wonder I don't see nothin'. I been spellin' it F-R-E-D-U-M.

I put the right letters in my head to make sure I remembered their place. F-R-E-E-D-O-M. I just now wrote it. Still no picture. Nothin'. The letters just sit there on the page. Spelled right or wrong, freedom got no picture, no magic. Freedom is just a word.

Friday

Whenever I dust Mas' Henley's study I look at his calendar and get the date. Today is Friday, April 1, 1859.

First Sunday in April

'Round here, they don't work the field hands on Sunday, but us who works in the kitchen and Big House, don't get but a few hours off on Sunday mornin' and in the evenin' after the last meal is served. We didn't even get that much time off today.

A new girl named Spicy come to the kitchen today. She's got 'bout fifteen years. Miz Lilly bought her from the Ambrose Plantation. S'posed to help Aunt Tee and me with the cookin' and cleanin'. I'm glad she's here. We need all the help we can get. But Aunt Tee aine so happy. She thinks Spicy is a spy for Miz Lilly.

"Clotee, make sure you don't give Spicy no bones to take to the Big House."

It's a fair warnin'. Mas' Henley and Miz Lilly promise us extra clothin' and sweets if we tell them things. The Missus promised to give me a handkerchief with yellow and purple pansies at each corner if I told her things 'bout what went on here in the kitchen. I wouldn't tell her nothin' if she promised me a box full of handkerchief. None of us in the kitchen are tattlers. I hope Spicy aine one either.

Later the same day

Spicy seems nice enough. Quiet though. We got her settled in and ready to start work come daybreak Monday, here in Aunt Tee's kitchen.

"Our day starts when the roosters crow," say Aunt Tee.

It made me dizzy listenin' to her put to words all the things we do 'round here. We fix three meals every day — take the food up to the Big House and serve it. Miz Lilly likes her food served on time. First meal is on the table at 8 o'clock. Midday meal is served up at noon. Dinner is at 6:30 o'clock. Then we clean up and get ready for the next day. In between, we do general house cleanin' — dustin'. Miz Lilly wants a clean house, but she aine willin' to help keep it clean — throw stuff all 'round in her room, dresser all messy. We wash on Monday and iron on Tuesday. Eva Mae and Aggie come up from the Quarters to help out on those days.

"William don't eat at the table with his folks," Aunt Tee say. "He eats at a smaller table to the side an hour 'fore his folks. You'll serve him. You understand, girl?"

Spicy shook her head yes. I aine never seen nobody with eyes that look like big pools of sorryness. I wonder what's done happened to Spicy to make her look so sad?

Monday

It's Monday again. Miz Lilly come swishin' to the kitchen first thing this mornin', measurin' out the flour, sugar, and so on. Actin' like she know what's goin' on.

16

"That woman don't know salt from sugar," Aunt Tee chuckled under her breath, "let alone how to cook with it." But the Missus likes to pr'tend that she's in charge of the kitchen, but we all know better. Ask anybody and they'll tell you Aunt Tee is the mistress of Belmont's kitchen.

Miz Lilly counts the cans of perserves and the dried vegetables 'gainst the recipes, makin' sure we don't eat extra food or give it away to the people in the Quarters. In the Quarters, they don't never get enough to eat or enough time to eat it.

But Aunt Tee been cookin' here at Belmont since Mas' Henley married Miz Lilly sixteen years ago. She was the onlyest slave he owned when he come here. Everybody else b'longed to Miz Lilly's family. They was the one's rich. Mas'er come from Tennessee, po' as a church mouse, but he wooed the widow Lilly until she married him. Aunt Tee say Mas'er married the money and not Miz Lilly. He was hopin' that if'n he owned Belmont it would make him a gentleman. He aine no gentleman though, no matter how much money he got.

Aunt Tee got her own way of doin' things in the kitchen, and it makes Miz Lilly mad. "I aine 'bout to cook and not eat," say Aunt Tee, laughin'. She knows how to pinch and save back, so we most times got

17

a-plenty to eat. Sometime, she skims off enough to slip food to a sick child or a nursin' mother in the Quarters. What we're all hopin' is that Spicy can be trusted not to tattle.

I don't know for sure, but I don't think Spicy is a tattler. She aine talkin' much to nobody. So we just been leavin' her be.

Monday again

Spicy been here a week, already. She's as big as a man and just 'bout as strong. But Lord that girl is clumbsy. She's forever stumblin' over things, droppin' things, and knockin' over things.

"She been used to hard work," Aunt Tee say, with a little less suspicion in her voice. Spicy got on the good side of Aunt Tee when she helped wring the water out of big ol' heavy sheets like they was just hand towels and never once complained — even when her hands was all red and sore. Spicy can lift hot pots and even chop wood. Her hands is rough, but even so, she's right pretty. Hard to get a look at her square on, — 'cause she holds her head down all the time.

She's older than me and bigger than me. For some reason, though, I feel like she needs takin' care of. Maybe it's her sad eyes that make me feel that way.

18

Later

"That gal b'longs in the fields," say Mas' Henley when he saw Spicy servin' the table with me.

"She'll be a great help here in the house," say Miz Lilly. Say she bought her for a little of nothin'.

Spicy don't know it yet, but she's in the middle of a big mess here at Belmont. Mas' Henley and Miz Lilly always be on the two ends of a stick. One say up — the other is bound to say down. Miz Lilly bought Spicy, so Mas' Henley is sure to find fault with her.

It goes like that all the time — them two havin' silly fights 'bout one thing or another. Miz Lilly say Aunt Tee is uppity and needs a good beatin'. Mas' don't like Uncle Heb. Say he's useless. "Diggin' 'round out there in them roses don't put meat in my storehouse." He cain't see that Belmont is a pretty place 'cause Uncle Heb cares so much 'bout the flowers. Mas' Henley cain't see pretty 'cause he's too mean inside.

If mean was a tree, it would grow tall here at Belmont.

Tuesday

Durin' lesson time, the Missus gave William a smack on his ear. "And you, Clotee! Come closer," she snapped at me, as if I had somethin' to do with the heat.

"Move that fan faster." But that's 'xactly what I wanted her to say. *Move closer*. Standin' directly behind William, I can look over his shoulder and see the words in his book.

Sometimes when I'm fannin', I make out like I done fell asleep — I let my arms drop. Then when Miz Lilly yells at me, I jump like I'm wakin' up. This makes her think I'm not interested in what's goin' on.

I have to be careful doin' that though. I don't want to get caught learnin', but I don't want to lose my job neither.

Next day

The noon meal was broke up when twenty riders stopped by Belmont lookin' for a man what they say is a northern abo — somethin' I aine never heared before. The compression on Mas' Henley's face say to me that whatever he is, the man is in deep trouble.

Mas' Henley sent Hince to ring the plantation bell, callin' everybody to the front of the house. Mas' counted heads to make sure all twenty-seven of us was there. He showed 'round a drawin' of a white man with a tangle of dark hair. He had a patch over his left eye.

"You ever see this man, you come straight and tell me. I'll make it sweet for whoever helps us catch him." He looked at the picture, spat, then crumpled it into a ball and throwed it away. Again, he called the man an abo-abolistine, I think.

When no one was lookin' I picked up the crumpled-up piece of paper and hid it under my dress. I want to know what this abolistine is.

Thursday

Spicy and I helped Aunt Tee make ginger cakes. Spicy spilled more than she got in the bowl. She's just natural-born clumbsy. Right after the last meal, Hince and Uncle Heb come to the kitchen for dinner.

Aunt Tee had fixed a two layer cake with strawberry perserves in the middle for Mas' Henley, or at least he thought it was for him. Aunt Tee had saved out just enough batter to make me a little cake 'bout the size of my hand. She say, "A bird flew by and told me there's a girl livin' 'round here who's been in this world near 'bout twelve years."

Nobody knows the real day I was borned, but Aunt Tee say, "You come here when the dogwoods bloomed."

"Yo' mama loved the very breath you took. All us did," say Uncle Heb. He handed me a doll he'd carved out of hardwood, no larger than two thumbs.

I've named her Little Bit, 'cause she so small. Mama knew Aunt Tee and Uncle Heb. In fact when she got sent away, she put me in their care. That all happened when I

21

had just come to the age of rememberin'.

Hince made me a sun hat out of field grasses, and put it on my head. He had to tease me 'bout it, sayin', "If you lose it, I'm gon' bus' yo' head."

These words seemed to upset Spicy somethin' fierce. She snatched off her apron and ran out the door. I started to go after her — tell her Hince didn't mean it. He wouldn't hit me. "Let her be," said Aunt Tee. So we did.

Spicy is totin' a basket full of sorrow on her head. Been beat down so much, I 'spect. When somebody raise they hand, she covers her head. Mostly I been lettin' her be. She don't say much, so I don't say much back to her. At night when we lay side by side on our sleepin' pallets, I can hear her cryin'. I wonder can she hear me cryin' sometime, too?

Friday

Seen Mas' Henley's calendar today. It's Friday, April 15, 1859. Been practicin' my writin', too. I just wrote R-I-V-E-R. I sees the James River out in front of the Big House. Wonder what's down that ol' lazy, movin' river? I aine never been away from Belmont. Maybe one day Miz Lilly will take me 'long with her when she goes to Richmond to shop and visit.

22

Saturday

This mornin' Hince and Spicy got into the worse spat. She's real touch-ous 'bout her name being Spicy. Hince found out, and that was good for a tease. He asked if Spicy was more cinnamon or more nutmeg? Lord, what did he say that for! Spicy hauled off and whacked him right in the mouth. "You half-white dog," she screamed at him. Hince went sprawlin' out on the ground.

"You addled, girl?" he shouted back. Hurt took over his face. None of us ever say much 'bout the way he looks. Spicy's eyes filled with tears and she stomped off in a huff, sayin', "You might look like ol' mas'er, but you aine really white. And I aine got to put up with you devilin' me!"

Words said cain't be taken back — even if they is true. Hince could pass for anybody's ordinary white boy — a member of the Big House family. He's got grayish-lookin' cat eyes, and curly, sandy hair. There's talk in the Quarters that his daddy is a white man — Mas' Henley's brother, maybe, or even Mas' Henley, hisself. I don't care who his daddy is. Hince is like my brother and I know it bothers him that he looks white, but he is black.

Later

Whenever I'm troubled 'bout somethin', I go find Uncle Heb in the roses and help him weed. 'Fore I know it, the troubles don't seem so bad.

I told Uncle Heb 'bout what Spicy said. "Color of yo' skin don't matter when you're a slave," Uncle Heb s'plained to me real easy-like. "Virginia law say, if the mama be black, then her chir'ren be black. If the mama be a slave, then her chir'ren be a slave. Hince looks white but he's black 'cause his mama Ola was black. Never mind who his daddy be."

Aunt Tee never say who Hince's daddy is, and I dare not ask. Cain't help but wonder though. Does Hince know who his daddy really is? And if it is Mas' Henley, then, how do it make him feel, bein' the slave of his own daddy? There's somethin' deep down wrong 'bout such a thing. But it go on all the time. Lots of white-lookin' black folks live in the Quarters. They's daddys be white, but they mamas be slaves. So they be slaves, too. Aine right!

I aine never seen my daddy. Mama told me his name was Bob Coleman. He drowned in the river 'fore I was borned. We all live right here on the river, but caint none of us swim. Mas' won't 'llow it — say we run away. Thinkin' 'bout my daddy makes me think 'bout my mama. I miss Mama so bad it hurts 'cause I knew her, touched her face, seen her smile. But in a strange way I miss my daddy, too, even though I aine never, ever saw him.

24

Midweek

Sunshine skies, blue skies so far this week. Spicy and me been piecin' a quilt 'bout a hour or two every night — patches from old rags the Missus throwed away. Aunt Tee is always busy scrubbin' old pots with river sand, or shellin' or snappin' some kind of bean. If Uncle Heb aine down in the stables with Hince or drivin' the family to or from somewhere, he sits with us. We tell stories to pass the time.

My favorite story is how Uncle Heb and Aunt Tee got married.

Uncle Heb starts the tale, but Aunt Tee puts in along the way. When Aunt Tee got to Belmont, Uncle Heb was livin' here over the kitchen where she was put to live. She caught his eye right away, she bein' so fine-lookin' and all. "She put me in the mind of you, Spicy, but she was real skinny. Didn't weigh more than one hundred pounds soakin' wet. I says to her for fun one day, 'How can you be a good cook thin as you is?'"

Aunt Tee took one look at Heb, and says to Mas' Henley, "I aine gon' live in sin with no man, never-you-mind how old he is." And she just wouldn't cook for a day or two.

Uncle Heb picks up the story again. Miz Lilly was put out. In her mind, slaves stayed where they was put, and that was that. Left up to her, Aunt Tee woulda got a good beatin' for havin' the nerve to rebel. But Mas' Henley is particular 'bout who fixes his food. Aunt Tee done been

25

with him for years. When Miz Lilly tried to get one of the women from the Quarters to cook, he wouldn't 'llow it.

Finally, Mas' come upon a perfect salvation that was good for everybody — 'specially Uncle Heb. One Sunday mornin' durin' the Christmas Big Times, the preacher man come to Belmont. "Mas' announced that Aunt Tee and me was to jump the broom."

"Didn't ask us. Just told us," said Aunt Tee. "I wouldn't have chose this old man, myself," she always say, smilin'. "But over time, I done warmed to the idea of havin' him 'round though."

"Come Christmas it will be our sixteenth year together," Uncle Heb say. At that point, Aunt Tee always pats him on the back of his hand. That's the way the story always ends, everybody smilin'. Them smilin' at each other. I love that story and the way they tell it. It makes me feel good all the way through and through.

Friday

The days is gettin' longer, and that means we have to work longer, too. In the summer, Miz Lilly bath almost every day. This evenin', Spicy and me carried water up the steps in buckets and poured it in Miz Lilly's bathin' tub. Then when she got through, we had to drain the water into buckets and take them down the steps and dump it. Spicy spilled water all up and down the steps comin' and goin'. I got tickled at her, and she got tickled at her-self. 'Fore you know it, we was laughin' so hard. It felt fine to laugh. And it felt even finer to see Spicy laughin'. I didn't think she knew how.

Next night

It's a clear night. Good moon. Good night to write.

The upper room was too stuffy to sleep, so I brought my mat outside. We sometimes do that. Spicy followed me. It was just the two of us girls. We just laid there, lookin' up at the stars. We had laughed together, so it was easier for us to talk together.

Come to find out, Spicy is motherless, too. And, just as I thought, she been mistreated somethin' awful — beaten and yelled at by her ol' mas'. Say he's meaner than Mas' Henley. I cain't demagine.

"If I could, I'd run away from this place so far they'd never fine me," she blurted out, lookin' like a cornered cat. "You won't tell on me, will you?"

"None of us is tattlers," I told her.

"I aine either," she said. I believe her.

Fourth Sunday in April

Sunrise will be here soon, but before startin' the day, I want to write "freedom" again. It is such a strong word to so many people. F-R-E-E-D-O-M. Freedom. No picture

27

comes to my mind. It just aine got the magic. It shows me nothin'.

I've looked at the drawin' of the one-eyed man over and over. His face don't show me nothin' neither. One thing for sure — if the one-eyed man is doin' somethin' that makes Mas' Henley mad, then I figure he cain't be all that bad.

Monday

Miz Lilly favors her daughter Clarissa and I see why. She's all growed up and married with children of her own near 'bout the same age as William. Aunt Tee say Miz Lilly thought she was through havin' babies, when along come William. She almost up and died tryin' to get him borned. If it hadn't been for Aunt Tee they say Miz Lilly would have done died. The fancy doctors from over in Richmond had done everythin', but Aunt Tee fixed up a potion and the next mornin', little William come into this world feet first.

"The tree with all its won-won-won . . . " William was tryin' to read a poem and got stuck on a easy word. His face turned all red. "What's it say, Mama?"

Miz Lilly is short tempered and quick to hit in good times. Today wasn't one of her better days. She whacked William's knuckles with a stick. "Wonderful!" she shouted. "Wonderful. That's a plain English word used by millions of people. Wonderful. Look at it. Say it. Won-der-ful!"

William threw the book over his shoulder and stomped away. Miz Lilly followed close behind, threatenin' to skin him alive. The lessons ended on that sour note.

I looked in the hedges and found the book William had tossed away. I'll give it back to the Missus in a bit, but not before I've had a chance to finish readin' the rest of that poem.

Tuesday

Wonder what a new pair of shoes feels like? It's warm enough to go barefooted now. My feet are glad to be out of William's old throwed away shoes. The ground feels good comin' up through my toes all soft and cushy-like. Maybe that's how new shoes feel.

Wednesday

Mr. Ben Tomson's Betty came to Belmont to finish fit-tin' a dress for the Missus. Betty is a good seamstress. Her mas'er hires her out to make clothes for people far away. Makes weddin' dresses, fancy party dresses — every-thin'. Good as she is, though, Betty cain't hold a candle to my mama when she was the seamstress. Here at Belmont. Everybody say so.

The ugliest dress in Virginia is bein' made right here at

Belmont for Miz Lilly. It is a shade of light green that looks washed out — no color. I'd rather wear this little plain cotton shirt I got on, with nothin' underneath it, than all that grand mess she's havin' made.

After Betty finished in the Big House, she stopped by to speak to Aunt Tee in the kitchen. I listened, careful not to jump into grown folk's talk.

Betty say Jasper and Naomi from over at the Teasdale Plantation runned away several weeks ago! The dogs was on they cents, when all of a sudden, they got all befuddled — went to howlin' and carryin' on.

"Heared red pepper will do that," say Aunt Tee.

Then Betty say somethin' that make me listen real close. "Word tell, it was a white man that helped them get 'way on a railroad what runs under the ground — a one-eyed white man, they says."

That set me to thinkin'. If the one-eyed man helped Jasper and Naomi run 'way then he must be what they calls a abolistine.

Day later

I cain't stop thinkin' 'bout the abolistines. Seems some white folks don't want slavery. They be the abolistines. I can hardly demagine that — but it makes me happy to know that them kind of people is out there somewhere. The white folks that is mas'ers wants to keep slavery. I know 'bout them. I want to know more 'bout the abolistines. Where do they live? How many is it? Do they all wear patches over their eyes? Are they all men? One thing for sure is that the abolistines is helpin' slaves to get to freedom, and knowin' that is good for now.

Friday evenin', April 29, 1859 (I think)

Spicy and I was dustin' the large parlor. Spicy broke a vase and Miz Lilly gave her a bad whuppin' — ten hard swats across the back with a switch — look more like a tree limb to me.

Aunt Tee rubbed her wounds with a paste made from powdered oak leaves and rain water. Takes the sting out and keeps the sores from festerin'. It almost made me sick when I saw Spicy's back. It wasn't the new cuts, but the old scars. She done been beat many, many times before — and hard, too. Now, I see why Spicy is so deep down hurt — been beat on so much. I aine never come under the lash like that, and I don't want to either. Miz Lilly beat Spicy bad just for breakin' a vase. What would she do to me if she knew I could read and write? The idea makes me tremble.

Sunday — after last meal

I almost died of fear when Spicy spilled gravy on a guest's dress, broke a plate, and chipped a cup while servin' dinner. I thought Miz Lilly was goin' to kill her. Miz Lilly promised her guests: "She's goin' straight to the tobacco fields tomorrow." I saw Spicy smile. She wanted to get sent to the fields — to get away from bein' 'round Mas' Henley and Miz Lilly. That was a silly way to go 'bout it, and I told her so, later on. Anyway, Spicy's plan didn't work. 'Cause just to spite his wife, Mas' Henley took sides with Spicy. Say all Spicy needs is to be trained.

"Why do you care what happens to me?" Spicy asked me later.

"I saw your back and I wouldn't want that to happen to you again — not to nobody! And I like you —" Spicy looked real surprised — like nobody had ever said that to her before.

So for now, Spicy stays with us in the kitchen. And I'm glad. I think she might be, too.

First Sunday in May

Cooked and served three meals. Two house guests. Toted waters for baths. Helped with the clean up. I am so tired. No spirit to write. I've still got to wash out my dress, so I'll start the week clean.

Monday night

Aunt Tee sent me down to the Quarters to take a ointment to Aggie. Spicy went 'long. Wook tries to be nice.

But for some reason, Missy done took a dislikin' to Spicy. That Missy is really changin'. I showed her Little Bit, and she laughed at me 'bout still playin' with dolls. Later, Spicy told me not to worry 'bout what Missy say. "People teases you sometimes 'cause they know it'll make you mad."

I asked her why she let Hince's teasin' make her so mad then?

"I hate my name," she say. "Spicy! Whoever heared of such a silly name? My mama was all set to call me Rose. But our ol' mistress say no, and named me Spicy. Mama had to do it — couldn't say nothin' 'bout it."

The more I learn 'bout Spicy the more I like her, but the more I hurt deep down for her, too.

Day later

Hince hardly ever comes to the kitchen since he and Spicy had that bad fallin' out. So, I been goin' to the stables whenever I get a chance. "Is Spicy mean to you?" Hince asked me.

"Not at all." I told him Spicy is just totin' a lot of hurt from the way she been treated. He nodded a understandin'. I really do like her a lot. I think she might be my friend. I wrote F-R-I-E-N-D-S. This time I seen Hince, Wook, and now Spicy. Missy aine even now in the picture.

33

Wednesday

Hince and Mas' Henley been goin' to horse races most every week. They rode off last night, on the way to Southampton. Hince is a mighty fine jockey — wins a heap of money for Mas' Henley.

Wednesday evenin'

I can smell the word K-I-T-C-H-E-N and see it, too. It always smells good — herbs hangin' from the eaves, dryin'. Hickory chips slow-burnin' on the back fire. A pot bubblin' or boilin'. Aunt Tee loves her big, four-hip fireplace where four grown women can stand side by side and cook together. She's truly the mistress of Belmont's kitchen.

Miz Lilly was in the kitchen today chatterin' on 'bout what she wanted fixed for a special dinner. Aunt Tee just say, "Yes, Miz Lilly," but in the end, Aunt Tee cooked what she always fixes on Wednesday.

I had to tell Spicy how Aunt Tee and Mas' Henley get along. Mas' Henley be real particular 'bout what goes in his mouth. He don't trust nobody but Aunt Tee to fix his food. I once heared him say, he wouldn't eat behind a cook he had to beat — scared of bein' poisoned, I s'pose. Aunt Tee know just who she cooks for, and it aine Miz Lilly. "Mas' 'spects to have fried chicken and whipped potatoes on Wednesdays and that's what I fixed." And that's what we served to the guests tonight.

Next day

Tellin' Spicy the way things work here at Belmont is fun. Last night I 'splained to her why Mas' Henley favors Aunt Tee, but all the time 'gainst Uncle Heb. The best way for her to get an understandin' was to start at the beginnin' — back when Mas' Henley first come to Belmont.

Uncle Heb was here at Belmont when Mas' Henley married Miz Lilly who was a widow-woman with one child. Uncle Heb ran the place, keepin' the orchards goin' and all.

Word tell, Uncle Heb was once a tall, handsome man. Even now, all crippled from hard work and age, he still look good. First thing when he got here, Mas' Henley wanted to sell Uncle Heb. Miz Lilly wouldn't have it. Uncle Heb had been born here at Belmont. Him and Miz Lilly's daddy, David Monroe, was boys together. Miz Lilly likes to brag that presidents and governors have ate here at Belmont.

Uncle Heb loves to brag, too. "Been all over this 'Merican land," he say, callin' up memories of when he traveled 'round with David Monroe. He say he been everywhere. "Take the time me and the Mas'er went to

35

Richmond . . . Norfolk . . . Jamestown . . . even been to Mount Vernon. Been everywhere, all over this big 'Merican country." I would give anythin' to see just one of them places.

Hince is the onlyest one of us who done traveled further than Uncle Heb. I remember once, William told me there were ghosts in the woods and a big snake lived there. It ate up all slaves who dared to leave Belmont. It was Uncle Heb who taught me better. Everybody young and old loves the old man — everybody 'cept'n Mas' Henley — and that's 'cause he's part of Miz Lilly's family. "Mas' Henley aine nothin' but white trash who married into a fine Virginia family," say Uncle Heb. He's never had no use for his new master.

Saturday

There was a gatherin' down in the barn tonight, 'cause Wook jumped the broom with Lee — a man from the Teasdale Plantation — near 'bout twice Wook's age. Mas' Henley came down to the party and said a few words 'bout wantin' them to have lots and lots of babies.

I cain't believe Wook is married. She's only a few years older than me — and I aine near 'bout ready to be married. And by the look on Wook's face she aine ready neither. I didn't even know she was lookin' at boys. Now,

36

she's married — and I didn't even know it. Why didn't she tell me?

All of us from the kitchen were there. Spicy came, even though she didn't want to. Uncle Heb cut roses for each one of us to put in our hair. I took the red one, and Spicy liked the yellow one. She looks happier than when she came here, but her eyes still hold a lot of sorry.

Hince got back. He was there, dancin' with all the girls. The only man that aine married here at Belmont is Hince. Everybody's wonderin' who will Hince jump the broom with? The way Missy been lookin' at him, I think she'd say yes to him today. But Hince can do better than Missy. I sure hope so.

Hince does know how to have a good time. Ever since I can remember he's danced with me first. Tonight, he passed right by and asked Spicy to dance first. I was surprised and a bit put-out. I 'spose it was his way of makin' up to her. I didn't think Spicy would dance with him — but I was wrong.

When she stood up, everybody started gigglin'. Everybody knows how clumbsy Spicy can be. But she fooled us all, kickin' up her heels and pattin' the juba better than anybody 'round here had seen before.

I saw a side of Spicy I didn't know was there. She was happy, smilin' big, light-footed, free as a bird. Spicy wasn't clumbsy at all when she was dancin'. Lookin' at

Hince and her turnin' together, made me forget that I was mad at Hince for not dancin' with me first. It was all right.

After that dance, everybody was askin' Spicy to cut a pigeon wing, or shoo fly. Nobody asked me to dance. Even if they did, Aunt Tee wouldn't let me, 'cause she say I'm not courtin' age yet. Just Hince, 'cause he's like a brother.

It was such a good party — but I don't think Wook enjoyed one minute of it. She just sat with her arms folded, lookin' sad. If she didn't want to get married, why did she?

Sunday

Hince came to worship service for the first time this mornin'. Only 'cause Aunt Tee made him. He sat between Spicy and me and made faces, tryin' to make us laugh. Aunt Tee pinched me on the arm to make me behave. All the time Missy rolled her eyes at us. Then afterwards, we all had to hurry back to get supper on the table. But Missy jumped in front of Spicy. "Jus' 'cause you up in the Big House with the white folks, don't mean you gon' get to marry Hince. He gon' jump the broom with me, so don't you be lookin' at him, you hear?" And she strutted away.

Hince aine thinkin' 'bout jumpin' the broom with nobody. Missy just wanted to say somethin' mean to Spicy.

38

But I cain't help but think — Spicy and Hince? Now that's a match I wouldn't have put together. But the more I think 'bout it, and remember them dancin' together — the better I like the idea. Spicy and Hince.

Monday

I been learnin' a lot durin' study time. I know the seasons, the days of the week, the months and the order they come in. Mostly, we tell time by the sun, the moon, and what's happenin' on that day. The rains have set in and it's hard to tell one day from the next — just grayness. No sun. Everythin' I touch feels dampish.

Tuesday

Wook waved at me from the fields. I waved back. Aunt Tee say I cain't keep company with Wook any more, 'cause she's a married woman. "Girls and women ought not to mingle."

When I write Wook's name, I sees her bein' a growed-up woman with a husband. A part of me wants to be round and full like Wook, or maybe a little bit wild and pretty like Missy, or even tall and strong-lookin' like Spicy. But I aine none of those things. But if I could be — I'd like to be just a little bit pretty.

I've looked at myself in Miz Lilly's mirror before. I aine what you call homely, but I'd like for my teeth not to

39

be so big. My head sits square on my shoulders, but I'd like to be taller — stronger. I guess I'm all right, but I don't feel all right.

Wednesday

It was durin' the dark of night when Rufus came knockin' at the kitchen door, hollerin' and all in a sweat. Aggie was 'bout to give birth. I begged Aunt Tee to let me go with her durin' the birthin', but she aine never let me go and she didn't this time neither. She took Spicy. I was mad and sat in a huff. Big girls got to do all kinds of things. I wasn't little any more and I wasn't a growed up woman. I was somethin' in between.

I fumed and fussed until they got back, and I made Spicy tell me everythin' — everythin'. Aunt Tee was right. Mid-wifein' aine for me. I don't think I ever want to see a baby bein' birthed — not after what Spicy say went on. But I looked close at the smile on Spicy's face while she was tellin' me that Rufus and Aggie had a big, healthy boy. "And I helped to get him here," she say real excited-like. Spicy had light in her eyes. I heard happy in her voice, and I knew Aunt Tee was right to take Spicy along.

Next day

All I can think 'bout today is that Aggie and Rufus have now made Mas' Henley the owner of twenty-eight

40

slaves. Their little baby don't belong to them — he belongs to Mas' Henley.

Followin' day

I went to see the new baby today. I picked a bunch of wildflowers to take to Aggie. Aunt Tee sent a basket of good things she had been holdin' back for Aggie to eat 'cause she's nursin' and needs the nourishmentation.

Wook showed me her new baby brother. It felt so good to hold him — so soft. Aggie and Rufus be so proud. I see why. Their baby boy is so beautiful. Aunt Tee seen to it that Mas' Henley 'llows new mothers a week free from the fields after havin' a baby. Aggie will get to be with her son for a whole week — just him and her.

I finally got a chance to talk to Wook and I found out about her gettin' married. Like I suspicioned, Wook hates bein' married. But Mas' Henley made her marry Lee. See, Miz Lilly keeps up with the girls who come of age, and she tells Mas' Henley. When Wook turned fifteen, he told her to choose a husband. When she didn't, he picked out Lee — said they'd make strong babies. "Lee don't love me," she said. "And I don't love him. This aine no marriage."

"Aunt Tee and Uncle Heb didn't love each other when they got married, but they grew to, later on. Maybe you and Lee will come to care 'bout each other." I didn't be-

41

lieve what I was sayin' and neither did Wook. How can they, when they don't even-now live together? Lee can only get passes once in a while.

Is that goin' to happen to me? When I come of age, is Mas' Henley gon' make me marry somebody just so I can have babies for him to own? I won't let that happen to me. I won't.

Saturday

All week we been busy cleanin' the Big House. Winter dirt been scrubbed away to make room for summer dust. We've all worked until our hands be raw and our backs ache. Aunt Tee made a salve to help the soreness. She makes me watch when she's makin' up stuff. I know the recipes to all kinds of salves and potions, but she done forbidden me to tell anyone her secrets. It makes me feel bad sometimes that Aunt Tee tells me her secrets, 'cause I'm scared to tell her mine.

Later on

An old gamblin' friend of Mas' Henley's, Stanley Graves, been here for a day or so. Miz Lilly been takin' her meals with William. Not that she wanted to, but to spite Mas' Henley. She don't 'prove of his gamblin'.

While Spicy and me was a-servin' dessert, we over-

42

heard Graves and Mas' talkin' about abolistines. I listened to as much as I dared. Graves say they think the abolistines might run a man for president of the United States. I know 'bout the president from study time. He's the mas'er of all the other mas'ers. If the president is a abolistine, then he can do 'way with slavery and the mas'ers can't stop him.

I heared a new word. Cecession. I'm gon' add it to my list of words to know.

Third Sunday in May

I read the calendar on Mas' Henley's desk. It is Sunday, May 22, 1859. Rufus talked 'bout the Garden of Eden this mornin'. God's garden, filled with peace, love, no hurt, no sufferin' and no slavery. There aine no such place 'round here and that's for sure. All through service we could hear Mas' Henley and Miz Lilly fightin' again — shoutin' mean words, flyin' every which way. That means it's gon' be hard on Spicy and me when we have to 'tend her. She just as soon slap us for bein' in the room as to not.

After Sunday late meal, I came here to write in my special spot. I just wrote B-O-A-T, and I sees a boat full of people sailin' past Belmont on their way somewhere. I wave at them. They wave back. Wonder are they thinkin' 'bout me the way I'm thinkin' 'bout them? Wonder are there any abolistines on that boat?

Days later

Rained all yesterday and today — no scary thunder and lightnin' — just a steady drip, drip, drop. Been so damp, mold is creepin' up the side of the kitchen walls. We spent the mornin' scrubbin' the walls down with vinegar water.

After last meal, Aunt Tee sent Spicy down to the stables with Hince's dinner. She come back just a-smilin'. "Well, I do declare," say Aunt Tee, lookin' real surprised. "I b'lieve Spicy is sweet on Hince."

Aunt Tee is 'bout the last one to catch on. Everybody's talkin' 'bout how the two of them been lookin' at each other in that special way. I knew it since the party. Spicy and Hince. Spicy is a different person from when she come here. Different in a good way. Spicy and Hince. That Missy is 'bout to have a cat fit. Good.

Next afternoon

It's Thursday. I shall never forget this day. William almost caught me readin'. Lordy, I got to be more careful. I was dustin' Mas' Henley's study where there are all manner of books. I found one called an Atlas. I was so excited to find out it was a book filled with maps. I was lookin' for Virginia, when, all at once, the door flew open, and William walked in.

44

William laughed real wicked-like. "I know what you were doin'," he said. "You was readin' that book!"

I thought I would die when he called his mama. My tongue got thick and my throat felt dry when I thought 'bout what was goin' to happen to me. Miz Lilly came runnin' from the large parlor, answerin' William's call. "Mother, Clotee was readin'," William said. "She was in here with the door shut. I caught her readin'," and he laughed and laughed.

I stood there with my head down, lookin' as blank-faced as I could. Miz Lilly made William stop tormentin' me. "I thought you called me about somethin' serious. Where would Clotee learn how to read?" she said. Her petticoats swished as she walked away. "Keep the door open, Clotee," say Miz Lilly, turnin' to look back at me, real curious-like. William had been just funnin'. He went on laughin', but my knees was still shakin'.

Saturday

Aunt Tee said her elbow hurt all night, so it was goin' to rain 'fore nightfall. I don't know why it should surprise me. Aunt Tee's elbow is good at callin' the weather. But, the almanack I seen in Mas' Henleys study said the May of 1859 was goin' to be wet.

I found out 'bout an almanack the same way I found

out 'bout the Atlas, just by dustin' the bookshelves in Mas' Henley's study.

At first, I couldn't believe that somebody could know ahead when the moon was goin' to be full. But, sure enough, the moon was full on the very day the almanack say it would be.

Now, I've got to be very careful lookin' through Mas' Henley's books, gettin' answers to my questions. After almost gettin' caught, I'm real nervous-like.

Monday

The sun is still up, even though the time of day is late. Miz Lilly has changed the study time to early in the mornin' when it's cool. I'm still s'posed to fan.

Hince and William went for a mornin' ride, makin' William late. Miz Lilly pitched a fit. Sooner or later all of us gets on the bad side of Miz Lilly, but Hince can't do nothin' to please her. Good thing Hince comes under Mas' Henley's say so. Hince would have it hard if he had to work with Miz Lilly. He knows it and stays 'way from her most of the time, too. Word tell, Miz Lilly hates Hince on account of his mama Ola and the talk that goes on 'bout Mas' Henley bein' the boy's father.

Aunt Tee is real closed-mouthed 'bout it all. But from what I can pick up here and there from the women in the Quarters, Miz Lilly wouldn't rest 'till Hince's mama was

46

sold. Say Ola was just too pretty. Miz Lilly would-a sold
Hince, too, but Mas' Henley put his foot down on that.
Say a male slave would bring more money when he got
older and been trained. Mas' Henley promised Miz Lilly
he would keep Hince 'til he was at least sixteen.

At first frost, Hince will come into his sixteenth year.
Wonder will Miz Lilly 'member the promise? I hope not.
I wouldn't want nothin' bad to happen to my brother-
friend Hince.

Tuesday

Thinkin' 'bout Hince's mama always puts me to
thinkin' 'bout my own, 'cause they was sold one shortly
after the other. Longer days allow me more chances to
write. I just wrote M-A-M-A. Mama. I see her the way I
seen her last — a dark-faced woman with joyedly eyes.
Then the bad lonesome feelin' comes into my heart —
memories that sour in my heart. No more writin' this
night.

Wednesday

I didn't know I was walkin' 'round lookin' so sad, 'til
Spicy said somethin'. While pluckin' chickens for the
dinner meal, I told her 'bout Mama.

I told her 'bout how my mama got caught in the never-

47

endin' fight that goes on in the Big House 'tween Mas' Henley and Miz Lilly.

Soon after Ola was sold, Mas' Henley gave Mama 'way to his sister and brother-in-law, Amelia and Wallace Morgan, as a weddenin' present. Since Mama was a good dressmaker, she could bring good money into their house. I was a baby and not part of the deal. Aunt Tee say Miz Lilly was so mad, when she found out Mama had been gave 'way. Say she turned purple — no doubt worried 'bout who was gon' make her dresses.

The madder Miz Lilly got, the more set in his way Mas' Henley got. "You made me get rid of Ola, now you've got to let Rissa go." That brought 'bout a faintin' spell, the kind Miz Lilly gets when she's tryin' to win a point. All her fallin' out couldn't save Mama. She had to go to Richmond.

Later

The night before Mama was taken away, she gave me to Aunt Tee and Uncle Heb. When Uncle Heb retells it, he say it was right after the Big Times — the first of the year. "Clotee is yours now. Take care of her, love her if you can," she tol' them.

I only got to see Mama, a few times after that — once when Wallace and Amelia come to Belmont and brought her 'long to take care of their baby. Then durin' the

48

Christmas holiday she got a pass to come visit. Each time she came, we laughed and talked, cried and held each other. She always waited 'til I fell asleep, then she'd leave. When I woke up, Mama would be gone . . . just gone.

Five winters ago, a rider come to Belmont. Wasn't long 'fore Mas' Henley come to the kitchen with the news. "Rissa is dead," he said, his voice soundin' flat like unleavened bread. Didn't take long for the words to take hold. Mama was gone on to glory — just gone.

I remember hearin' the people in the Quarters singin' all through the night —

Crossin' over, crossin' over,
Crossin' over into Zion.
Crossin' over, crossin' over,
The beautiful city of God.

When I finished my story, Spicy said, "Your story is my story." Then we both cried. After talkin' to Spicy I felt lots better. Spicy and I have laughed together, cried together, and shared each other's hurts. We're becomin' good friends. I like that.

Monday

Mas' Henley and Hince have gone to a race over in Chester. Miz Lilly been into it with William all mornin'.

49

He stormed out of the house and spent the mornin' with Uncle Heb at the stables. There was no lesson today.

Tuesday

Durin' study time, the Missus turned to figurin' numbers — and numbers don't come to me quick like the letters and words do. But even as bad as I am, William is still worse.

Wednesday, June 1, 1859

There was a meetin' at Belmont this evenin'. While I was servin' up sweets and coffee, I overheard Mas' Henley say he's supportin' a Cleophus Tucker who is runnin' for congress. Mas' Henley is plannin' to put on a big party in his honor on the 4th of July.

"Tucker's the man we need in Washington," Mas' Henley told members of the group.

They left a newspaper on the table, so when I was cleanin' up, I hid it under my dress to read later.

Next day

I read as much of the newspaper as I could, pickin' out words I know. It's still a heap of words I don't know. But I did find out abolistines are A-B-O-L-I-T-I-O-N-I-S-T-S. I know the right spellin' of the words now. I also found

50

out that abolitionists live in places called the New York, the Boston, and the Philadelphia. Then there's somethin' called a underground railroad that slaves ride on to get away to freedom. I really want to know more 'bout that. I wrote all these names on a piece of paper. I'll bind my time. When the chance comes, I'll try to find these things on Mas' Henley's book of maps.

Friday

The rains have finally stopped. No rain all this week. Now the long heat sets in. Mosquitoes are busy, but we've burned rags almost every night to keep them away.

Saturday

Mas' Henley and Hince went to a horse race, and Uncle Heb drove Miz Lilly and William to a neighbor lady's house for the day. So, that meant I could slip into Mas' Henley's study to see the map without gettin' caught. I found the same names I'd written down — the places where abolitionists live. First, there was the Philadelphia, then the New York, and the Boston. I found the Richmond and lots of other places I heared Uncle Heb and Hince talk 'bout. But that's all I can understand 'bout the map. All the lines stand for somethin' I know, but I don't know yet what they stand for. I wrote down as many names off that map as I could get on a sheet of paper, so

51

when I write the names they will be spelled right. All these words got to do with freedom, so I'm hopin' all over myself that they will give me a picture of freedom.

Sunday

The river is high, and the lowlands are flooded. Rufus talked about the Great Flood. Noah and his family went inside the ark and God, himself, locked the door. Noah and all the animals were safe inside the ark. Then the rain started fallin'. And the waters came a-gushin' up out of the ground and everythin' and everybody was drowned. All 'cept'n, Noah, his family, and the animals.

Everybody say, Amen. I really didn't understand the story. I couldn't see in my mind the world all under water. It's like this. I read the words over William's shoulder sometimes, but I don't all the time get what the words mean.

Then Rufus told us his new little son was named Noah, 'cause God saved Noah from the drownin' waters. "God's gon' save us one day, too — but I'm talkin' 'bout bein' saved in the Biblistic way," he said. "Amen."

Monday

I just got one thing to ask — Why did God let mosquitoes get on the ark?

52

Sunday week — second Sunday in June

All week we worked and waited for Sunday. June heat feels hotter than the same heat in May. It was hard to sit still while Rufus told the story of David. When David was 'bout my age, he was a shepherd boy. He stood down a giant named Goliath with a slingshot and five smooth stones. "We must be like David," Rufus told us. "When we find ourselves facin' a giant, we must not run, but face the monster with the courage of David." Everybody said "Amen," even me. But, I didn't feel strong enough to beat up on a giant. Rufus tells good stories, but I just don't understand what makes them so great.

First thing afterwards, Missy come switchin' up to Hince grinnin'. I don't like Missy much any more — and I don't think it has a thing to do with Spicy. I just don't like the way she is.

Monday

It's June 17, 1859. I know 'cause I slipped ink out of Mas' Henley's study today — and a newspaper that was in the trash. Sometimes I surprise myself at the things I do just so I can keep learnin'.

Followin' Saturday

I am writin' by the light of a full moon. There was a lot of excitement today. Mas' Henley and Hince rode in

53

from Fredericksburg. Been gone all week. They brought back a beautiful stallion named Dancer, a gift for William. "He's all yours," the mas'er told his son.

Everybody knew Mas' Henley was just showin' off. The horse was really a racehorse and Hince would be the one who would ride and care for it. But to keep Miz Lilly from fussin' 'bout turnin' Belmont into "a gamblin' den," Mas' Henley pretended he bought the horse for William.

It was so good to see Hince. As soon as he could get away from the stables, he came to the kitchen to speak. He was full of Dancer talk — went on and on 'bout how he was goin' to win a hundred races ridin' him.

Third Sunday in June

Uncle Heb left early this mornin', takin' the Missus to visit the Ambrose Plantation. They'll be gone all day. Rufus talked on Jonah. I liked that story, but I think it would be scary livin' in the belly of a big fish for three days and nights.

"We might find ourselves in the belly of a big fish at any time — but we must not be afraid. We must stay prayed up. Stay strong. Our faith will turn sour on the fish's stomach and it will have to deliver us — free us . . . Let us pray."

I got on to Rufus's Bible stories today. All the weeks he

been leadin' us in service, he been tellin' us two stories in one. His stories are 'bout Bible times, but they is 'bout our times, too. Jonah in the belly of a big fish, Daniel and the lions, and David and the giant is like us bein' in slavery, facin' the mas'ers. But God delivered Daniel, David, and Jonah and he'll deliver us one day. Rufus can't say all that right out or Mas' Henley will make us stop havin' service. But Rufus tells us that in other ways. I didn't understand the stories at first, but now I do. For the first time, I said "Amen" and knew why I was sayin' it.

Monday

I went to the stables to visit Hince for a few minutes and to take a closer look at Dancer. The horse is every bit as fine as Hince said — not like any other. It would take a good rider like Hince to hold him steady though.

"A sure winner!" Hince say real proud-like.

"And he's mine," said William comin' through the door, dressed to ride. "Saddle him up."

William has been ridin' since he could straddle a horse. But anybody can see that Dancer is too much horse for him.

"William," said Hince, patient-like. "Dancer is not ready for you yet. Let me work with him a little 'fore you take him out."

The boy whined and fretted, but at last, he went on

and rode Diamond. Still there was somethin' in the boy's voice that let us know he was bent, bound, and sure to ride Dancer.

Last week in June

There won't be any more lessons until after the 4th of July holiday.

I hate holidays.

Every day there is somethin' for us to do. We're either cleanin' the house, fixin' the meals, servin' the meals, cleanin' up after the meals. No sooner than we're finished, it's time to start all over again.

When guests come, it's double work. We have to tote hot water for the guest's baths, empty the water after the baths, and don't forget cleanin' chamber pots and makin' beds at first light in the mornin'. That's why I hate holidays.

Friday, July 1

Today Spicy and I were scrubbin' floors, gettin' ready for the 4th, but movin' like inch worms creepin' along. All of a sudden, Hince hopped up on the window sill from the porch side. Almost scared us to death. "Okay, girls, why you movin' so slow? Get busy."

"When did we get a new mas'er?" Spicy said, bein' sassy.

"I'd be a poor mas'er to own the two of you," he said with that devilish look in his eyes. "Clotee, you aine big as a chickadee. So, I wouldn't sell you." He turned to Spicy. "And you there, gal, with the dark eyes. I wouldn't sell you either!" Then he added, "I'd just keep you for myself."

I could feel Spicy bein' happy, even though she held her head down.

"You like my brother-friend, don't you?" I asked Spicy when Hince was gone.

"He's not so bad," she say, and went back to scrubbin' the floors. This time she was a-movin' along faster, and hummin'.

July 2

Hince brought Spicy a handful of flowers this mornin'. He shoved them at her from the kitchen door. He aine never done nothin' like that 'fore. "For you," he said. 'Fore Spicy could answer, he ducked away and was gone. He missed seein' the big grin that lit up her whole face.

Aunt Tee just shook her head and poured some water in a cup and handed it to Spicy for the flowers. We both been teasin' her all day, 'bout bein' courted.

July 4

Sunday rest was canceled for everybody. Too much work to do to get ready for the 4th.

I'm so tired. We got our regular work to do and some more — I don't know what day it was. I was up all night yesterday, workin' in the kitchen with Aunt Tee. Aggie and Wook came to help. Missy sees after the baby and helped out, too, when he was asleep. I did all the fetchin' — runnin' from the springhouse to the smokehouse, to the Big House, to the house garden, to the barn and back. "Get me this" and "Get me that." I am writin' this late at night. Ready to crawl into a hole and sleep, but I cain't. Now its time to start cleanin' up.

July 6

Things are finally gettin' back to normal. It will take me days to write 'bout all that happened on the 4th.

Guests started comin' to Belmont early Monday mornin', campin' out on the grounds. Miz Lilly's daughter Clarissa and family were the first to arrive.

Clarissa's husband is Mr. Richard Davies, a lawyer with a fine firm in the city. He's full of seriousness and she's a ball of nerves. I like her though. Maybe it's 'cause she's like a scared rabbit, 'bout ready to run for cover. Not at all like her mama. I can't say much for Miz Clarissa's two sons. Richard, Jr., and Wilbur, who are close to the same age as William, keep somethin' goin' all the time. When William gets with them, they spell T-R-O-U-B-L-E. Trouble.

Soon as Richard and Wilbur set first foot out of the carriage, William came tearin' out of the house like it was on fire. Then all three of them began runnin' through the house, screamin' and yellin', out the back door, leapin' over the hedges, trampin' in the flower beds. Their mama just looked on like it's as natural as the risin' sun. Nobody 'spects better of 'em, so they act that way.

By mid-mornin' on the 4th, many more guests had come. Mas' Henley tried to be real gentleman-like, greetin' people, welcomin' them, shakin' hands. But no matter how much he tries to look the part of a real gentleman, he's still seen as a gambler who got lucky enough to marry a woman with money.

Miz Lilly, on the other hand, was like a fly, flutterin' 'bout in that ugly green dress. She was lightin' just long enough to say a few words then off to another guest. At times like these it's hard to see her slappin' us or yellin' at us 'til the veins in her neck bulge out like she'd been doin' all mornin'. My face is still stingin' where she slapped me for walkin' too slow. Walkin' too slow. I was so tired I was glad to be walkin' at all.

Everybody ate like dogs, gobblin' up pots of smoked ham and beans, fresh greens, smothered chicken, gravy, and rice, and all kinds of pies and cakes. Nobody ever thought 'bout how hard we'd all had to work to fix it. They just ate.

On full stomachs, Mas' Henley didn't have no more sense than to call everybody together to hear Cleophus

59

Tucker, the man who Mas' Henley wanted people to vote for. Mr. Tucker's talk was full of too many words, but people were nice 'bout pretendin' to listen. I was half asleep, until I heard the word abolitionist, then I listened real close.

"I, for one, am tired of abolitionists tellin' me what I should do with my slaves. I'm tired of lawless meddlers comin' into our communities and spiritin' away our nigras on this so-called Underground Railroad."

It felt good to know these words, but I still didn't get a full understandin' of what they meant.

July 7

Pickin' up from yesterday . . .

Hince was set to ride Dancer against a horse named Wind Away, brought up from Atlanta, that was supposed to be the fastest horse on four feet. Just 'bout everybody bet on the Atlanta mount.

I overheared Mas' Henley whisper to Hince, "You'd better ride him to win, boy, or else." Hince laughed in a devil-may-care way and spurred Dancer onto the field.

"Come on, Hince," I shouted, knowin' that if he lost, he'd have Mas' Henley to reckon with. All the folks from the Quarters was pullin' for him to win, includin' Missy. Aunt Tee screamed so, she plum lost her voice. But it was Spicy — Spicy who out-shouted us all! I wasn't the only one to notice it either. I caught Missy givin' Spicy a mean, mean look.

Hince didn't need our cheerin', 'cause he won with room to spare. Mas' Henley carried on so, braggin' and all, folks started findin' excuses to leave.

In the far away I just heard the sound of a train. I wonder is it on the Underground Railroad. I could see in my head slaves on the train headin' for the Philadelphia, the New York, and the Boston. The picture made me smile. One day I want to ride that train.

July 10

Clarissa and the boys have been here since the 4th. They go home today. Nobody will be unhappy to see the backs of their heads. While I served breakfast to William and his nephews, I heard William talkin' 'bout ridin' Dancer by himself. "When you ride up in front of our house in Richmond, then we'll believe he's your horse," said Richard.

I hope William is not goin' to be silly enough to ride Dancer that far by himself. Should I tell Miz Lilly, so maybe she'll speak to him 'bout it?

Second Monday in July

All of the guests are gone home now. We spent the mornin' straightenin' up the guest rooms. It's sick hot,

61

but no matter, I have to weed the house garden. The hat Hince gave me really helps. I hardly ever take it off.

Somethin' was eatin' up my tomato vines. Uncle Heb say put tobacco juice on the leaves. I'd seen him use it before on his roses. So I bit off a piece of tobacco and chewed it to make the juice. Lord, I swallowed some. My head started swimmin', and my stomeck heaved up everythin' I had eaten for breakfast — two days ago.

I've never been so sick in my whole life. Thought for a minute, I was dyin'. How can anybody chew tobacco? I won't ever again. The worms can have the tomatoes.

Tuesday

I saw William down at the stables. He was talkin' to some of the hands. I thought maybe I should tell Miz Lilly what I overheared.

"I think he may try to ride Dancer over to Richmond," I told her.

"Don't be foolish, Clotee. William wouldn't try to do a dangerous thing like that." She made me brush her hair before she sent me away. Maybe she's right. But some-how I don't think so.

Early Thursday mornin'

We polished silver all day. Miz Lilly went over every tray, pitcher, bowl, and candlestick. She found one little spot on a silver tray that I had cleaned and she slapped me so hard I saw stars. I don't get hit often, but when I do, I try to be like Spicy and not let her see me cry. "Spicy is bein' a bad inflewance on you," she said, and slapped Spicy, too. Miz Lilly is awful 'cause she know we cain't hit her back. If one of us whacked her back across her face, I bet she wouldn't be so quick to hit. I got to be careful not to put ideas like hittin' the Missus in my head. Aunt Tee say if you think 'bout hittin' back, you'll soon strike-out, hit back. And to fight a missus or a mas'er means death for sure.

Next evenin'

Durin' dinner, Spicy and I served hot bread and poured water for the Henleys. We came in on Mas' Henley and Miz Lilly fussin' 'bout William gettin' somethin' called a tooter. When Mas' Henley said no, Miz Lilly would not let it be.

As the word-fight 'tween them heated up, Spicy took off the soup bowls, and I served the fried chicken. Miz Lilly won that battle.

Later, the three of us — Spicy, Aunt Tee, and me had our supper together. Whenever Aunt Tee fries chicken for the Henleys, she fries the chicken neck, gizzard, liver, and the-last-part that goes over the fence, and makes a thick brown gravy for us. Eat that with some biscuits and honey — good eatin'.

Spicy and me had Aunt Tee bent over laughin,' pokin' fun at Miz Lilly's faked faintin' spells. Spicy did a perfect Miz Lilly swoon. "Ohhhh, he'll be the first Monroe not to get into Overton School!"

I played the Mas'er. "My mind is made up — William will not have a tooter." Then I belched, and raised up a hip and pretended to pass gas.

"You girls is a mess," Aunt Tee say, hangin' up the dish towel and blowin' out the kitchen candles. I stretched out on my straw-filled pallet next to Spicy.

"Anybody know what a tooter is?" I had been waitin' for the right moment to ask. Nobody knew. I'll add it to my list of words. I figured it had somethin' to do with William's schoolin'. Wonder will it mean I cain't get no more learnin'?

Day later

Spicy and I spent the evenin' workin' in the house garden with Uncle Heb. We helped him tie strips of old rags on a measure of line to shoo the critters away. He told us stories 'bout a spider-man that could talk. Uncle Heb say his mama told him these old spider stories. He say his mama come from Afric. Say white men fell upon them one day and threw nets over her and some other girls. Then they put them on a boat and brought them 'cross

64

the big water. Say that's how all our peoples got here. We come here from Afric on white men's boats.

I once heared Aunt Tee talk 'bout the Afric woman named Belle who taught her 'bout root doctorin' and birthin'. I aine never seen nobody that was natural-born Afric. I'd like to though.

Monday, July 18, 1859

I found out what a tooter is. It is a tutor. Miz Lilly wrote it for William. He's a teacher. Heared Miz Lilly tellin' William durin' lesson that his name is Ely Harms. And he's comin' here in August. He's comin' from a place called Washington, D.C. I know from lessons that's where the President of the land lives in a big white house. Reckon does this Mr. Harms know the President?

Miz Lilly say the tutor will stay here on the place and his only job will be to teach William. I hope I'll get to fan them durin' their lessons, so I can go on learnin'.

Wednesday

The Missus has had Spicy and me busy for the past few days cleanin' her own personal room. We stayed busy for hours, scrubbin' the floors, beatin' rugs, airin' mattresses, and restuffin' pillows.

At the end of the day, Missus called me to her side.

65

"You know that your mama and I were the best of friends?" she said. "You're smart, just like her."

"Why'd you let her go?" I don't know what come over me. Aunt Tee is right. If you think on a thing, you'll end up doin' it. How many times had I thought about askin' her that question? Now I'd dared to ask it. The words just popped right out of my mouth. It's a wonder she didn't slap me. Instead she just gave me a warnin'. "Must not be sassy, Clotee." Then she studied my face. I was sure my eyes had turned into windows and she could see all the letters and words tumblin' 'round in my brain. So I closed my eyes, too scared to move.

"Yes. You're different from the others. I never know quite what's goin' on inside that little head of yours. But it makes me wonder."

Miz Lilly is scary like a bad dream.

Later

Come to find out, Miz Lilly promised to give Spicy the same white handkerchief with purple and yellow pansies on each corner if she brought her things 'bout me.

"I'm not a tattler," she said. "Besides that's the ugliest handkerchief I ever seen!"

So Miz Lilly is lookin' for somethin' on me, now. I trust Spicy not to tell. But who else has she tempted? I got to be

66

so careful. I just wrote D-A-N-G-E-R. I see Miz Lilly's face.

Thursday

At least I'm learnin' from Miz Lilly. I learned today that there's no such word as knowed. It's knew. I never knew that. I do now.

Fourth Saturday in July

Somethin' awful done happened. I knew it. Knew it. William has left here, ridin' Dancer over to Richmond — showin' off.

It started when Hince and Mas' Henley were gone 'way to a race. William went to Uncle Heb, sayin' his daddy had said he could ride Dancer. I told Miz Lilly he'd do it, but she didn't b'lieve me. So, Uncle Heb saddled up Dancer. Last we seen of the boy, he shot out of the stables and down the drive. I got a real bad feelin' aine nothin' good comin' out of this for nobody.

Early the next mornin'

Miz Lilly sent Rufus and other riders out to follow William, but couldn't no horse in the county catch Dancer. All we could do was wait. Not long, the horse came trottin' back up the drive, draggin' William's body like a sack of rags. It was clear the boy had fallen off, but his foot had gotten caught.

Everythin' that happened next is a blur. Somebody went to fetch Dr. Lamb — but it took over two hours for him to get to Belmont. Meanwhile, Aunt Tee did everything she could to help. Spicy and I stood in the shadows of William's room, ready to fetch and hold whatever the doctor needed.

I heard Miz Lilly ask, "Will he live?" I prayed that William would live. I hope God will forgive my selfish reason. I prayed William would live 'cause I knew Mas' Henley would make our lives miserable if his son died.

"Oh, yes," the doctor said, pattin' Miz Lilly on her arm. "He'll live. William's a tough little character." I felt better. Miz Lilly's shoulders relaxed, too. She looked at me and for a second I looked straight into her eyes. I dropped my eyes quickly, 'cause we aine s'posed to look Mas'er and Missus in the eye. But for that quick second I seen somethin'. I seen that she knew that I knew that I had warned her 'bout this, and she had not listened. She was thinkin' 'bout it, too.

"But," added Dr. Lamb. We all listened to what was comin' next. Sadness clouded the doctor's face. "I'm not so sure William will ever walk again."

Miz Lilly really did faint. All I can think 'bout is that it's gon' be awful when Mas' Henley gets home.

Day later — Monday, July 25, 1859

When Mas' Henley heared 'bout William, he went straight 'way to the barn and shot Dancer, a single bullet in the horse's head — like that was gon' make William well again. We could hear Hince cryin' over that horse most of the night.

Then Mas'er come lookin' for Uncle Heb — got it in his head that Uncle Heb was to blame for what happened to William, so he came to kill him — just like the horse. Me and Spicy done learned that in times like these it is best to stay out of the way. We watched everythin' from the room over the kitchen — holdin' one another, tremblin', tryin' not to cry out.

Po' Uncle Heb tried to say what happened, but Mas' Henley went to beatin' him with the barrel of the gun — beatin' him all in the head. I heard the licks — hard licks over Aunt Tee's screamin'. Uncle Heb fell down, and Mas' Henley kicked him and pointed the gun at the ol' man's head.

"Don't kill him, please," Aunt Tee begged for her husband's life. For some reason he didn't pull the trigger. He might as well have though, 'cause Uncle Heb died in Aunt Tee's arms a hour or so later. His big heart just stopped.

Later

Mas' Henley come to the kitchen to see Aunt Tee when they told him 'bout Uncle Heb dyin' and all. He come sayin', "I lost my temper a bit. I wasn't really goin' to kill the old man. You've got to believe that."

When Aunt Tee didn't say nothin', he raised his voice in an angry way. "My boy is up there, unable to walk 'cause that old man let him ride Dancer. He's to blame. He should have known better."

Blame? Mas' Henley don't care nothin' 'bout the real truth. He just make the truth what he wants it to be. The truth is, Mas' was the one who brung Dancer to Belmont and gave him to William. Mas'ers can do that. But Mas' Henley will never make me b'lieve what I know aine so.

"Now, you listen to me," he say, pointin' his finger in Aunt Tee's face. "I don't want you holdin' what happened to Uncle Heb against me, you hear? That old man just died. I didn't kill him."

Aunt Tee looked at her master long and hard — like she was lookin' at him for the first time. "You aine got to worry, I won't poison you. I aine that low-down and ornery."

Rufus tells us to hate the sin and not the sinner. I hate slavery so bad, it's mighty hard sometimes not to hate the slave masters — men like Mas' Henley.

70

Sunrise Tuesday

We held Uncle Heb's funeral this mornin' when it was mornin' but not yet day. 'Fore we had to go to the fields and to the kitchen, we stopped to say farewell to Uncle Heb. He was like a lovin' grandfather to me.

Women from the Quarters came last night and helped Aunt Tee get Uncle Heb's body ready for burial. The men folk went to the cemetery to dig the grave. All the folks from the Quarters came and we sat and sang and prayed. Rufus talked 'bout the peace of death — no more sufferin' — no more pain. I fanned Uncle Heb's body, keepin' the flies away — up and down, up and down. Then I dared to touch him. I'd never touched a dead person 'fore and I knew it would be scary, but it wasn't. Po' Uncle Heb. He felt hard and cold. Not like him. The him that used to be Uncle Heb had flew up to heaven.

At the time when Aunt Tee say she was ready, we wrapped him in a clean white sheet and put him in a cart and carried him to the plantation cemetery where all Miz Lilly's people are buried — her father and mother and grandfather. Miz Lilly came — had nerve enough to cry. Mas' Henley didn't even bother to show up. How could anybody think we were lucky livin' close to people like them?

One sweet song —

71

Still by the river
Waitin' for my Savior
To come for me.
Goin' home, goin' home
To be with God.

Rufus spoke kindly over Uncle Heb, sayin' how good he was and how he had lived. I could feel the hot tears behind my eyes, thinkin' all the while that Uncle Heb would still be alive if Mas' Henley hadn't killed him.

Aunt Tee just looked off into space — thinkin' her own thoughts — never once cryin'. She had cried dry. Hince took it real hard. Uncle Heb had been like a grandfather to him, too — all of us, really. Spicy did what she could to comfort us, even though she had her own sorrow to bear.

Everybody kept sayin' Uncle Heb was free at last. Why do we have to die to be free? Why can't we be free and live?

Wednesday

For the first time as long as I can remember, Aunt Tee didn't fix fried chicken and whipped potatoes today. I wasn't the onlyest person to notice it, either.

Thursday

I've been tryin' to piece together all that's done went on for the last few days. No time to grieve, 'cause our work aine never stopped. Mas' Henley wants his food served on time and the Missus wants her house cleaned, her bed made, her water brought up for baths, and on and on and on — no end to the work she thinks up for us to do.

Aunt Tee misses Uncle Heb so much, she just shakes with hurt. Then she sings a lot —

> *Help me, help me, help me, Jesus.*
> *Help me, help me, help me, Lord.*
> *Father, you know that I'm not able*
> *To climb this mountain by myself.*
> *Help me, help me, help me, Jesus.*
> *Help me, help me, help me, Lord.*

Nobody should have to live as a slave. If a slave can be an abolitionist, then I want to be one, 'cause I hate slavery and I want it to end.

Friday

Whenever I write the word F-L-O-W-E-R I will think of that kindly old man who grew beautiful roses and told the best stories ever.

After the dinner meal, Spicy and I walked through Uncle Heb's flower beds all the way down to the river. The sunflowers were turned toward the evenin' sun. I remembered Uncle Heb called me his little Sunflower Girl. He said my face always looked like it was facin' the sun — full of brightness. I squeezed Little Bit, my birthday doll, which I've come to carryin' 'round in my apron pocket. I like the feel of the smooth wood on my hand. That would please Uncle Heb. My thoughts made me smile. Spicy found a four-leafed clover. It's s'posed to bring good luck. We sure could use some 'round this place.

Saturday

Spicy and me took Miz Lilly's bath water up to her room. She sent Spicy out, but she asked me to stay and fan her for a while. I obeyed.

"Clotee, things are goin' to change 'round here. But, I'm takin' care of you. Don't you worry. Just promise me you won't say a word 'bout your talk with me 'bout William. I never dreamed that he would do somethin' so stupid. STUPID!"

I think Miz Lilly is worried that if Mas' Henley finds out I had warned her 'bout William's plan to ride Dancer, and she'd done nothin' to stop him, he would be really, really mad with her. Now she's tryin' to still my mouth with favors. What is gettin' ready to change 'round here?

74

And how is Miz Lilly gon' help me? None of this makes me feel very good in the stomeck.

Two weeks later

I saw the calendar in Mas' Henley's office. We in August already. August 10, 1859. So much has happened since last I wrote in my diary. I knew somethin' was comin', but didn't know what. Mas' Henley done changed everythin' — everythin'. Nothin's the same.

First, he moved Aunt Tee out of the kitchen. Say he cain't trust her to cook for him no more, 'cause of what happened to Uncle Heb. He put her down in the Quarters to look after the babies. Then to make it worse, he done brung Eva Mae up to the kitchen to be his new cook.

There's more. Missy is takin' Spicy's place, 'cause Spicy's been sent to the fields. I get to stay in the kitchen, doin' what I been doin'. I guess that's what Miz Lilly meant when she say she was gon' take care of me. I'd just as soon go to the Quarters with Aunt Tee than to stay near Miz Lilly.

Spicy aine sorry to be goin' to the fields. She say she'll miss talkin' to me all hours of the night. I will miss spendin' hours talkin' to her under the stars. I will miss her stumblin' and fallin', then laughin' 'bout it. Things will not be the same up here in the Big House without her.

75

Aunt Tee is who I worry 'bout. This is the thanks she gets after all those years of service. Mas'ers don't care how long and hard we work for them. They own us, so they can do whatever they want to us. That's the worse part of bein' a slave. Never havin' a say in what happens to yourself.

Third Monday in August

Everybody knows that Eva Mae aine half the cook Aunt Tee is. But she likes to think that she is.

It hurt me when Miz Lilly wouldn't let Aunt Tee take the old iron bed she and Uncle Heb had slept in for years. The bed had been a gift from Miz Lilly's grandfather to Uncle Heb for his years of service. Now Miz Lilly done gave it to Eva Mae and Missy to sleep in. It's not right that Aunt Tee should have to sleep on a pallet at her age. When we abolitionists end slavery, everybody will have a bed to sleep in. Wonder will I ever get to meet a real abolitionist?

Next day

A horse and buggy turned into the front gate, gallopin' at full speed. Whenever I write the word S-T-R-A-N-G-E, I will remember seein' Mr. Ely Harms bouncin' 'round in that buggy, comin' up the drive. The tutor is here and I can't wait to find out 'bout him.

76

Monday again

The tutor's been here a week. He's a little freckled-faced man with a shock of red hair that sticks out of the side of his hat. He looks like he's been pieced together from parts took from other folks. His teeth got a big gap in the middle, and his legs and arms seem a bit too long and too thin for the rest of hisself. I can't guess his years, but he's got young eyes that look at you over cloudy glasses that sits on the tip of his nose. I'll guess and give him 'bout twenty-five years — give or take one or two.

Miz Lilly fluttered on and on 'bout how sorry she was that nobody — nobody — had told Mr. Harms not to come 'cause of William's bad fall. Mr. Harms used a lot of fast words — real fancy-like. And by the end of supper, he had Mas' Henley and Miz Lilly set on him stayin' on here at Belmont.

I was glad, 'cause if William's studies stop, then so would mine. Trouble is, what sort of tutor was Mr. Harms gon' be?

After the dinner meal that same day

Things in the kitchen be a big mess! Eva Mae got her own way of doin', her own recipes. When I try to show her somethin' she tells me to shut up. "I'm the mistress of the kitchen, now." So, I decided to just let her alone —

77

do what I'm s'posed to do, and keep my mouth shut —
just like she say.

Week later

Dr. Lamb came by — say William was well enough to
start studyin' — an hour or so a day, and added it would
be good for the boy. The first lesson time with Mr. Harms
was today in William's bedroom. I was standin' in my
place ready to fan.

"Why are you here?" Mr. Harms asked, lookin' at me
over the top of his glasses.

William s'plained that I was a fanner. Mr. Harms say
they didn't need a fanner. My heart sunk down to my
toes. My learnin' would have ended right then, too, if
William hadn't gone to whinin' 'bout how it was too hot.
He let me stay. I never thought I'd be glad to hear
William's whinin'.

Few days later

I went down to Aunt Tee's cabin in the Quarters after
the last meal. That gave me a chance to visit with her and
Spicy. She's holdin' her own, but it's got to be hard on
Aunt Tee, losin' first Uncle Heb and then her job.

They live in a real small cabin now with a dirt floor —
no windows, only a door that don't shut all the way. Yet,
everybody in the Quarters is seein' after Aunt Tee. All

them years Aunt Tee took care of them and they children, now they payin' her back with love and kindness. Aine none of them got much, but what they got, they's willin' to share.

I slipped out a piece or two of day-old bread and a few leftovers for her to fill out their meal. I told them how Missy and Eva Mae had changed. They are thick with Miz Lilly, grinnin' and smilin', gettin' in with her. Before I left, I told Aunt Tee 'bout my warnin' Miz Lilly 'bout William and her not listenin'. "She's scared I'll tell Mas' Henley." Aunt Tee agreed. She took me to her heart. "Be careful, chile. Miz Lilly aine gon' stand for you to have nothin' over her head. She'll keep on 'til she find somethin' on you to use — to get rid of you — to keep you down. She'll use them two in the kitchen to help her. To win favors, Eva Mae and Missy will tell everythin' they know and then make up some. Be particular, and watch as well as pray."

Now I've got to be very, very careful, 'bout my readin' and writin' 'cause now Miz Lilly is lookin' for somethin'. Now I know how Daniel must have felt in the lion's den.

Thursday night

Woke up after dreamin' 'bout Mama — all in a sweat. It was unlike any dream I've ever had 'bout her. She was standin' beside Mr. Harms. He was smilin' at me, all the

79

while Mama was sayin', "It's gon' be jus' fine, baby girl. It's gon' be jus' fine."

Rufus say, God talks to us in dreams. If that's so, then I wonder what God is tryin' to tell me?

Last Monday in August

Calendar say it's August 29, 1859.

Mr. Harms brought a book to study time. William wouldn't read it. Mr. Harms never said a word. He opened the book and he started to read. "Long ago, in a far away place called Greze there lived a great hero named Herquelez."

I knew Mas'er John Hamby's slave named Herquelez who lived on a nearby plantation. He was powerful strong, too. But this was not a story 'bout him.

Mr. Harms told us how the long-ago Herquelez killed a big serpent. Then the teacher-man stopped, closed the book, and walked away without sayin' another word.

"There's more, right?" William called out.

"Tomorrow," said Mr. Harms.

I can't wait to find out more, too.

First day of September

There was a big race up in Winchester last week, and Hince won. Soon as he got back, he came to the kitchen to see me and to tell me all 'bout his win. First thing,

Missy come sidin' up to him — like he came there to see her. He asked where Spicy was, right in front of her. I gladly told him.

Monday

Mr. Harms starts each day by sayin' the day, month, and year. Today is Monday, September 5, 1859. So, now I can keep better track of time.

Tuesday, September 6, 1859

William has taken to Mr. Harms like a bird to berries. I declare, the boy is reading now and liking it. I'm learning a lot, too. I'm adding "ing" to my words now, 'cause Mr. Harms made William stop saying, "talkin'," and "walkin'," and "singin'." It is talk*ing*, walk*ing*, and sing*ing*. I remember to write my *ings*, but I still forget to say my *ings*.

Wednesday, September 7, 1859

Mr. Harms has taken charge of William's days. Two men from down in the Quarters comes up every morning and helps William get bathed and dressed. One brings William down for breakfast in his rolling chair. Afterwards, we have our study time — in the cool of the morning — just hot enough to need a fanner, which is still me.

Then it's time for lunch. William eats with Mr. Harms most of the time. The rest of the day William listens to Mr. Harms read to him, or they play card games, or a game called chess. William spends the evenin' with his mother and father — but most time they spat 'bout one thing or another, so he goes off to bed.

Thursday, September 8, 1859

I slipped out late last night. Came out to write in my diary. I heard a twig snap. Someone was coming. I called to see who it was. Missy answered, asking, "What you doing out here?"

I was sitting on my diary. I told her it was too hot to sleep, so I'd come out to look at the stars.

"Why do you always come back here behind the kitchen?"

She was digging for a bone. "I like it back here. I can see the river and the stars."

My hiding place behind the kitchen is no longer safe. I have to find a new place, safer, and real soon.

Friday, September 9, 1859

Since Uncle Heb's been dead, the garden's been looking real pitiful. I pulled a few weeds from 'round the roses. But it just aine the same. I miss him and sometimes turn 'round to say something to him, but he's not there. He never will be there, just like Mama.

Oh, yes, I learned from Mr. Harms that it's around and not 'round. It's something and not somethin'. I've got more out of Mr. Harms' lesson than I ever did from Miz Lilly.

But there's something real different about Mr. Harms, and I cain't put it to words yet. He never even looks at me. Treats me like I'm not there.

Saturday, September 10, 1859

I was digging through some of the trash in Mas' Henley's study, looking for things about abolitionists, and the Underground Railroad. Nothing. I cain't find a thing to help me understand my list of words better. So, when I just wrote F-R-E-E-D-O-M, it still don't show me no picture. But I'm keeping my eyes open.

Sunday, September 11, 1859

Aunt Tee been so sad since she been turned out of the kitchen. I would do anything to help make her laugh and be happy again. I guess that's why I did a very foolish thing. I went down to her cabin to visit. After we'd talked, I used a stick to scratch writing on the dirt floor. *C is for CAT.*

Before I could blink my eye, Aunt Tee had slapped me so hard I had to hold on to the table to keep from tobbling over. Miz Lilly aine never hit me that hard. She rubbed out the letters with her foot. At last, my head stopped swimming and the spots before my eyes cleared up. There wasn't no anger in Aunt Tee's eyes, only fear.

"Do you know what happen to slaves the mas'er finds out got learnin'?" she whispered sternly.

I knew they got beaten, or much worse they got sold to the Deep South. I couldn't make her understand that I was trusting her. I knew she wouldn't tell on me.

"I don't wanna be trusted," Aunt Tee say, near tears. "Look at what trust got me. I b'lieved Mas' Henley would do right by me, 'cause I'd done right by him. Not so. Look at me now. Trusting got me here. Who teached you, chile?"

I was scared to say — and real sorry I'd told her about any of it. I decided to hold back on all the truth. "I teached myself just a few words."

Aunt Tee sucked in her breath and clicked her teeth. Her face was clouded over with worry. "Don't bring trouble to yo' own front door," she say, biting her lip, the way she did when she was real worried. "Don't you tell another living soul that you got this little piece of knowing. You hear me?"

Never have I been more sure of anything. I will not tell another person my secret ever.

84

After study time — Monday, September 12, 1859

Now Mr. Harms is on to something! And I brought the trouble to my own front door.

He and William was reading a play together. As usual I was standing behind them, fanning — up and down, up and down — and reading over their shoulders. William got stuck on the word "circumstances." I was so taken by the story, I plum forgot where I was. Suddenly, my mouth got ahead of my thoughts and I blurted out the first part of the word. "Cir —" I caught myself, but not soon enough.

Mr. Harms jerked around and looked at me — his mouth dropped open a little, like he was surprised. "What did you say?"

"Cir — yes, sir? Yes. *Sir* is what I said. Sir. Sir? May I go, please?" I was thinking fast — Lord let me get out of this.

Mr. Harms looked down at the book, then he looked back up at me and where I was standing. He told me I could go, but asked my name. He knows — he knows! Lord! Lord! What's going to happen to me?

Wednesday, September 14, 1859

I guess I was wrong about Mr. Harms being on to me. He aine said a thing, and I'm still fanning during lessons.

I let up writing for a few days, 'cause I've been too scared to go near the hiding spot, what with Missy slipping around, and maybe Mr. Harms is on to something.

Thursday, September 15, 1859

Spicy looks tired when she comes in from the fields. But she says the tobacco don't slap you in the face, and call you all hours of the night, and send you to do this or that. Spicy likes the fields better than working in the Big House.

Missy likes the Big House. She's struck by all the sparkle and pretty of the Mas'er's house. She go around touching things, and oohing and aahing over it all. She so busy looking at stuff, she gets careless. I have to redo some of her work sometimes to keep us both out of trouble.

When I show her where she's made a mistake, Missy gets mad and starts yelling at me all hateful. "You just think you cute. Make me sick — all the time trying to talk all proper-like. You're just a skinny, little thing, so don't come trying to say I'm stupid." I never say she's stupid, even though I think it. And I don't try to talk proper-like.

Then before the evening is over good, she's back trying to be friends with me again. She always asking me a lot of questions about Hince. I know how to get back at

86

Missy, though. I say, "Why don't you ask Spicy." It's hard to b'lieve we was ever friends. Missy bears watching.

Monday, September 19, 1859

Apple harvest time is almost over. The tall men been knocking apples and then we gathered them. I got to sort with the grown women this year — putting the big, the middle, and the little apples in barrels. It aine the work I like — but I love to hear the women telling stories, remembering. I really like it when they tell a story 'bout my mama.

Tuesday, September 20, 1859

I've found a good hiding place for my diary in the hollow of a tree, just beyond the orchard. I feel safer coming here. My hiding place behind the kitchen was getting too dangerous. I sure miss the way things used to be when Uncle Heb was alive and Aunt Tee ran the kitchen. They were far less troublesome times than these are now.

Later the same day

After the last meal, Missy said to me all syrupy sweet, "We been friends for a long, long time, but I don't know you."

What was that supposed to mean? She knew me, sure.

"I know your name," she say, "and that you favor corn-bread over biscuits. You'll take red color over green color, and you like being off by yourself. But I don't know you, Clotee. Like what makes you happy or what makes you cry? You're not like the others. You're different. What makes you different?"

I'd heard those words before. Miz Lilly had told me I was different, and she'd sent Missy digging for a bone.

"Friends share secrets," she say all friendly and nice. "Do you have one you want to share with me?"

"No," I said and got away from her as fast as I could. Missy is a tattler, sent straight from Miz Lilly. I know it.

Wednesday, September 21, 1859

I wish I could read Mr. Harms as easy as I can read Missy and Eva Mae. There's something 'bout Mr. Harms that sets me to wondering. He looks perculiar, and he acts perculiar, so people don't pay close attention to him. They don't see him all the time watching, taking in everything that's being said and done. But I do.

Just a minute ago, I saw Mr. Harms standing at the edge of the orchard, looking toward the woods and beyond the river. Just looking. Made me nervous — my diary being just a few feet from where he was standing. Maybe I need to move it again.

Aunt Tee and I have not spoke about my learning

since I told her. Spicy put in that she'd seen Mr. Harms watching them working in the fields. Just looking, saying nothing, just watching them work.

Monday, September 26, 1859

I brought my pallet to sleep outside. The stars are so bright, I can almost hear them tinkling. But tonight I heard Rufus singing — his beautiful voice riding on the night wind.

> *Steal away*
> *Steal away*
> *Steal away home . . .*

Was that Mr. Harms I just seen heading for the Quarters? I wonder who he be visiting this hour of the night? Oh well, white men sometimes visit the Quarters in the dark of night, when their wives and mothers aine watching. I'm surprised. Mr. Harms don't 'pear to be that kind of man.

Tuesday, September 27, 1859

Miz Lilly left this morning to visit her daughter Clarissa in Richmond. She goes every September. She'll be gone for several good weeks. These are always happy days for us who work in the Big House.

She usually takes William. And she'd promised to take me this year. But William flat wouldn't go this time. And for some reason, she took Missy instead. Good. I'll get a rest from the both of them. I'm staying with Spicy and Aunt Tee the whole time, even though Eva Mae promises to tell when Miz Lilly gets back.

Friday, September 30, 1859

Miz Lilly's gon'. Mas'er went sporting — will be gone until Monday. William is home, but he's in his room sleeping. Mr. Harms is asleep, too. Belmont is a big play house when everybody's gone.

Spicy and me slipped up to Miz Lilly's bedroom. We put on her jewelry and scarves and hats. We sat at her desk where there is all kinds of pretty paper, and pens and ink a-plenty. I took enough to last me a good while.

We heard a noise outside in the yard. At first I thought it might be one of the dogs or a raccoon. We quick-like jumped out of the bed and ran to the window.

We seen Rufus come slipping from tree to tree then turn toward the Quarters. We figured he'd been out possum hunting. But, a little later, I seen Mr. Harms creeping out from the other side of the woods. We watched as he stole from shadow to shadow until he reached the house and stepped inside. We held our breath until we heard his footsteps pass the door and go down the hall to his room.

We quietly cleaned up, put everything in its place, and left Miz Lilly's bedroom just the way we found it.

What were Mr. Harms and Rufus doing out in the woods together so late at night?

Monday, October 3, 1859

I've been staying with Aunt Tee down in the Quarters. She takes care of Baby Noah and the other children that cain't work yet. When Wook came to get the baby, we got a chance to visit. She aine seen her husband but twice since they got married. Seems he loved another girl from his own plantation and wanted to marry her. Wook has changed a lot. She looks so sad all the time.

I told her how Missy was acting, and she said she wasn't surprised. "Missy has always been for Missy — selfish." When we was growing up, I never knew that side of her, but Wook did. "If I got something, she wanted it, no matter how small it was. She's put out at me 'cause I got married first. She coulda got married ahead of me and I wouldn't a-cared at all."

Later, it was like old times in Aunt Tee's cabin. We sang, told stories, and Spicy and me even got to work on our quilt.

91

Tuesday, October 4, 1859

Mr. Harms fussed at William about saying 'cause instead of *be*cause. I learned it, too.

Later I took Hince his meal down at the stables. We talked for a good while. Him and me talking is fun. The words just pop right out of my head without me thinking on them long. "You ever think of running away?"

He studied on that for a spell. "Sometimes."

"What would you do if you was free?"

"I figures, if I be a free man, I could hire myself out as a jockey. I'd bet on myself and win and win and win, 'til I had 'nuf money to buy all of y'als freedom — Spicy, Aunt Tee, you, Clotee. That's what I would do."

When nobody was looking I wrote F-R-E-E-D-O-M in flour. It still don't show me no picture.

Later the same day

True to her word, Eva Mae told Mas' Henley that I'd been staying in the Quarters with Aunt Tee instead of in the kitchen. He spoke to me about it when we served him the last meal.

"Aunt Tee is like my mama," I said. "I'd like to stay with her."

"You want to stay down in the Quarters with Aunt Tee? Well, what does your mistress say about this?"

"I haven't asked her."

"When she comes home, ask her. See what she says. I'll go along with what she says. You're one of her favorites."

Me? I never thought of myself as being favored by Miz Lilly, unless she wanted something from me.

Wednesday, October 5, 1859

Mas' Henley pitched a red-in-the-face fit 'bout Eva Mae's fried chicken. He called it tasteless slop! Serves him right.

Thursday, October 6, 1859

Tonight Spicy took me by the hand and led me to a hollowed out tree. My heart sank when I realized that it was the tree where my diary was hid. Had she found my diary? All of a sudden, Spicy blurted out that she had a book. To prove it, she reached in and pulled out a Bible. My diary was just inches away. "I've wanted to tell you this forever, but I been scared," she said.

Spicy had a Bible that had been her mama's. "My mama could read and write," said Spicy. Then she told me her mama's story. It was like others I'd heard. Spicy's mama tried to run away, but each time she got caught and beat bad. Finally her mas'er say if she ran away she was

93

gon' get sold. Spicy's mama learned how to write — took her a while. Spicy was borned and still she kept learning. Then one day, she wrote herself a pass and tried to run again. But a slave who worked in the Big House told the mistress and she got caught. Before they sent Spicy's mama to the Deep South, she slipped Spicy the Bible.

"I done kept it all these years," Spicy said. "I cain't read a word that's in it, not yet. One day I will. But even if I don't ever read, I'll keep this Bible forever. It is all I have that b'longed to my mama."

Spicy hugged the book to her chest. "Nobody in the world knows about this book 'cept'n you. And I trust you won't tell, 'cause we're good friends."

Should I share my secret with Spicy? Good sense tells me that I shouldn't. But I want to so, so bad.

Monday, October 10, 1859

Mr. Harms came storming into the kitchen, sputtering and making a grand fuss. He made Eva Mae and me stop what we was doing and listen to him.

"This has come to my attention," he said, holding up Spicy's Bible. "If it belongs to one of you, I want to know, now!" His eyes moved from face to face. "Speak," he shouted.

He could have saved his breath. Neither one of us owned it.

"I'm going to report this to Miz Lilly when she returns," he said.

"Yes, Mas' Harms," said Eva Mae.

The tutor tucked Spicy's Bible under his arm. "Come with me, Clotee," he said. Outside the kitchen, he whispered matter-of-factly. "The view from my room is interesting." What did he mean by that?

Tuesday, October 11, 1859

After breakfast, I slipped into Mr. Harms' bedroom. Standing in the side window, I got a clear view of the woods and especially the tree where my diary and Spicy's Bible were hidden. Thanks be there were no other bedroom windows at that end of the house.

What is going on? Mr. Harms knows my secret for sure. He must have seen Spicy and me at the tree when she showed me her Bible. But why didn't he tell Miz Lilly or Mas' Henley? I'm beginning to think there is more to this strange man than any of us really knows.

Later that same night

My suspicions are right. Mr. Harms is not who he seems to be. When I went to move my diary from the hollow of the tree, there was a note fixed to it.

I know you can read and write.
Please be careful. I will speak to you soon.

The note was signed "H" for Harms.

I hid my diary under my dress and hurried to find Spicy. I didn't want to put her in the heat of things, but she already was. It broke my heart to tell her that Mr. Harms had found her Bible. But it hurt even worser for Spicy to think I'd tattled on her. Even when I showed her how easy it was for him to see us through his window, she still didn't b'lieve me. "If that's true, then why didn't he tell Mas' Henley?"

I had no choice at that point but to 'fess everything. I took a deep breath and showed her my diary and the note Mr. Harms had left. Spicy took me straight to Aunt Tee.

Daybreak Sunday, October 16, 1859

The roosters just crowed. Thank God it's Sunday and not a full workday. Aunt Tee, Spicy and me sat up all night talking. There are no secrets between us now. I'm glad in a way. In fact, I am writing in my diary right here in Aunt Tee's cabin. At first, she was 'gainst my learning — but she say now that she was just scared — didn't want me beaten or sold away. "I will not stand in the way of what might be the Lord's work being done through you, chile."

She even said for me to hide my papers in her cabin. My diary will be safe with her. I worry that I've made life unsure for Aunt Tee and Spicy. If they get caught with my papers, we could all be in sinking sand. Maybe Mr. Harms will be able to help. But who is he, really? I got some ideas, but I dare not put voice to them yet.

Later

Aunt Tee and Spicy don't think I should trust Mr. Harms all the way. But he hasn't done nothing to make me not trust him.

I have looked at the one-eyed man's picture over and over. He don't look at all like Mr. Harms, but for after all that's been happening, I think Mr. Harms might know the one-eyed man. Mr. Harms isn't from the Philadelphia, the New York, or the Boston. He's from Virginia. Can a southern mas'er be an abolitionist? Mr. Harms said in his note that he would speak to me. Maybe I'll get answers to some of these questions then.

Monday, October 17, 1859

"Will you teach me to write my name?" Spicy asked.

I've never really thought about teaching anybody else how to write. I've always been the one learning. I used the poker to write letters in the ashes. Spicy and Aunt Tee looked on with wondering eyes. For the first time I

97

been able to share my secret with somebody. I love seeing them smiling at the letters that makes up their names. I feel warm and good inside. What good is knowing if I cain't never use it to do some good. Spicy made an S. And Aunt Tee made a T. We've had our first lesson.

Tuesday, October 18, 1859

Mr. Harms knows that I know that he knows I can read and write. But he has not said a word to me about it. Treats me the same as always. When will he speak to me?

Meanwhile, Miz Lilly aine back yet, so our housework is not as hard, but Mas' Henley's been around all week in his study. I couldn't get ink out. But Aunt Tee helped me make a mixture of charcoal ash and blackberry wine. It makes a good ink until I can do better.

Wednesday, October 19, 1859

The days are getting shorter, and it's cool in the mornings during study time. Today Mr. Harms changed the study time to early afternoon when it is still hot enough to need a fanner. I would say thank you, but I dare not. He say he will speak to me, so I got to wait.

Sunday, October 23, 1859

Mas' went to fetch Miz Lilly from Richmond. We had the whole day to ourselves again. Trouble is, William wanted to come down to the Quarters to the meeting. Mr. Harms thought it was a good idea. 'Course, we didn't, but what could we say?

At the meeting, Rufus talked about the three boys in the fiery furnace: Shadrach, Meshach, Abedego. Then Rufus sang a song. We all joined in. I looked over at William and Mr. Harms and they were singing and clapping their hands, too.

> *My God's a good God. It is so.*
> *I woke up this morning and by God's pure grace I go.*
> *Yes, God is a great God, this I know.*

We shared a table the way we always do after service. Mr. Harms took William back to the house in his rolling chair. I stayed to be with Wook for a little while longer. All the smile is gone out of her eyes. I rubbed her feet, because they were so swollen. That's when she broke down and cried, saying she hated her husband, Lee. He had got a pass to visit, but came just to say he didn't love her. Lee wants to marry somebody else.

Monday, October 24, 1859

Miz Lilly is home. Lord have mercy. Mas' and Hince left the same day for races in Charleston. We all been busy washing and ironing her travel clothes — scrubbing, scrubbing. Nothing suits her. And she aine stopped going on about how filthy the house is.

Tuesday, October 25, 1859

I caught Miz Lilly in her room at a good time, and asked her if I could stay with Aunt Tee in the Quarters 'stead of in the kitchen.

I knew just how to get what I wanted out of her. I say to her, "Miz Lilly, I was thinking if you let me stay with Aunt Tee down in the Quarters, I can watch and know if somebody's talking runaway talk."

She studied on that notion. "You've never told me one thing about anybody. Why now, Clotee?"

I had to think fast and talk straight. "I figure if I help you, then you'll give me nice things like you do Missy."

That fooled her good! She let me stay in Aunt Tee's cabin, but I still got to work with Eva Mae in the kitchen and help Missy with the housework. It's a little bit like the way it used to be — Aunt Tee and Spicy and me talking all hours of the night. Now, I'll be able to write more often and not cause suspicion. It's no where near as warm or as nice as the kitchen. When I write H-O-M-E, I see here in the cabin. Home aine a place — it's a feeling of being loved and wanted. Wherever Aunt Tee and Spicy are that's home to me.

Friday, October 28, 1859

Been working all week. Today is the first time I've had a minute to write. Most nights I just fall asleep on my pallet, next to Spicy. We all too tired to talk, but it's so good being back together again under the same roof — even though it leaks.

Saturday, October 29, 1859

Aunt Tee has found a way to be useful again. She made herself a job. All the hands in the Quarters work so hard, they be too tired to cook in the evening. So, she's done started cooking for everybody. Whatever the folk can rake together, they bring it to Aunt Tee. She adds it together to make a bigger pot. They come home in the evening to a big pot. Today they had rabbit stew, wild turnips, and ho'cakes fixed by the best cook in Virginia.

After last meal the same day

I picked up pieces of talk at dinner. Mr. Harms was telling Miz Lilly about the Bible he'd found, but he said he found it down by the river. "Yes, Eva Mae told me you'd found a Bible and that you were trying to say it belonged to her or Clotee. Why would you think it belonged to one of the slaves and not a member of the Big House?"

"Slaves steal so badly," said Mr. Harms. "When anything is missing or lost, I always begin with the house slaves. They are the ones most likely guilty."

Mr. Harms was sounding like a mas'er. But when I looked closer, the Bible he showed Miz Lilly wasn't Spicy's at all. Mr. Harms was helping Spicy and me, but at the same time finding favor with Miz Lilly. I felt myself smile inside.

Then Mr. Harms asked if Miz Lilly knew that William has some feeling in his toes? She didn't know — she never takes time to know about such things. Mr. Harms asked if he could use hot water treatments on William's legs. Say he'd learned the treatment from a doctor over in Washington.

"Only if Dr. Lamb says it is all right."

Then, he asked for Missy to help him with the treatments. "No," said Miz Lilly, "Missy is attending to me. Use Clotee."

Mr. Harms knew just how to charm Miz Lilly. If he had asked for me, she never would have let me help. What is Mr. Harms up to?

Monday, October 31, 1859

It's shoe-wearing time again. I hate putting on William's old hard shoes.

Eva Mae, Missy, and me just about harvested everything from the house garden and preserved, pickled, or

102

dried it. The collards are ready to be picked, but Aunt Tee say wait til' the frost hits them, first. This is my favorite time of the year, when the summer heat gives way to fall coolness. I can finally get a good sleep.

Wednesday, November 2, 1859

Hince and Mas' Henley came back home winners. They also had a fine new horse, a beauty named Canterbury's Watch. He's not as spirited as Dancer, but Hince says he's a strong runner — steady. Hince calls him "Can," because he "can run." Miz Lilly came out on the porch, took one look at the horse, stepped back inside and slammed the door.

It was good to have Hince home. Although he spends most of his time with the horses, I miss hearing him laughing and how the sound floats up to the kitchen from the stables.

I told him I was staying in Aunt Tee's cabin down in the Quarters, but I still work up in the kitchen and Big House. "I'm glad you with Aunt Tee," he said. "Somebody to see after her."

Then Hince s'prised me with a piece of red satin ribbon. It was as grand as anything Miz Lilly owned. And it was all mine. Didn't have to slip and play with it. Hince say he had bought it with money he won, betting on himself.

103

"I was going to wait until the Big Times to give it to you, but I couldn't wait. How do you like it?"

The word came straight from my heart and burst out of my mouth. "Beautiful!" Whenever I write B-E-A-U-T-I-F-U-L, I will see my red ribbon. It makes me feel pretty and like I want to dance and dance.

Sunday, November 6, 1859

Hince bought Spicy a measure of cloth and Aunt Tee a comb for her hair. All three of us wore our gifts to meeting. All the women in the Quarters was jealous — but Missy was so mad, she didn't stay through the whole service. Rufus talked on love.

"Love is not jealous," he said, winking at the three of us. I should have been ashamed of being so proud of my red ribbon, but I wasn't. I just held my head higher.

Monday, November 7, 1859

Missy come in the kitchen waving a white handkerchief with purple and yellow pansies on each corner. Lord, who has that girl gone and told on?

Tuesday, November 8, 1859

Missy told Miz Lilly all about the gifts Hince had bought us — mad because he didn't bring her nothing back. Miz Lilly took it straight to Mas' Henley.

Mas' Henley rang the plantation bell. All of us come running to the front of the house. Mas' Henley lead us to the stables. Oh, no. Somebody was getting ready to get a beating.

When Mas' grabbed Hince, my breath cut short.

"How'd you get money to buy gifts?" he asked Hince.

"I used the eating money you gives me to bet on myself to win — and I winned," he say, not feeling like he'd done no wrong.

Mas' Henley reached and got a buggy whip. "Where'd you get the idea that you could slip behind my back and place bets?" He told Hince to lean over and hold on to the wagon wheel. Hince couldn't b'lieve he was getting a whupping. Neither could I.

"But Mas', I didn't slip. I placed the bet, free and open."

Mas' Henley beat Hince. Gave him ten hard licks while we all was made to watch. I closed my eyes and balled my hands in a fist so tight my fingernails dug in the heel of my hand. I wanted to holler out when I heard the swish of the whip hitting my brother-friend's back.

Everybody knew Hince was Mas' Henley's bread and butter — filled his pockets. If Hince got a beating, then what would ol' Mas' do if we got caught doing anything — anything. It didn't have to be wrong — just something he didn't like. Mas' Henley promised never to give Hince eating money when they was out on a trip. Say he could starve to death.

105

Wonder how Missy feels about herself, now? Was getting Hince a whupping worth that ugly handkerchief? We used to let Missy get away with fighting and hitting, because we thought she was pretty and all. I even wanted to be like her. But if being pretty means being that ugly inside, then Lord let me stay plain. Aunt Tee always say what go around, come around. Missy got it coming for what she did.

Wednesday, November 9, 1859

Aunt Tee took care of Hince's wounds. The buggy whip cut his skin, but not as deep as a cat-o'-nine. Hince was shamed, at first — shame of being whupped in front of everybody. Being a winning jockey didn't help him none. Mas' Henley beat him just the same.

Spicy and me tried to cheer him up by talking about Mas' Henley in the worse way. He felt some better. I could see it in his face.

One day when the abolitionists come they will stop all this beating. I wonder how far off that day is?

Friday, November 11, 1859

It rained all day — a slow rain. Turned cold afterwards. Miz Lilly called me to her room. Then we went up in the attic. There were all kinds of boxes up there — things I'd

106

never seen before. Dresses, coats, hats. It smelled of ol'
and the dust made me sneeze.

Miz Lilly opened a creaky trunk and pulled out a pair
of shoes and a dress that musta b'longed to her daughter.
She handed them to me. I had never had no real shoes or
a pretty dress. Just the plain white pull-overs Aunt Tee
stitched up for me.

"Your mama made this dress for my Clarissa when she
was a girl. Now you can have it." I quick put the shoes on.
They were a little big, but much softer than William's big
shoes. My toes had plenty of room and the sides weren't
rough and hard. I put the dress on. It felt like it had been
mine all along, because Mama had made it. I buried my
face in it and tried to smell Mama, but it just made me
sneeze more. Miz Lilly was almost a person, but I had to
keep my wits about me. She wasn't nice just to be nice.
She was up to something.

When I showed Aunt Tee and Spicy what Miz Lilly
had give me, they looked at me with wondering faces. "I
didn't tell her nothing. Honest!" They b'lieved me, but
warned me to be careful-like.

Saturday, November 12, 1859

This study season would have been over for me, because its been too cold to fan. If it hadn't been for those

hot water treatments Mr. Harms is giving William, my learning would have ended like before. But Mr. Harms got me helping during study time. Still not a word from Mr. Harms. He sees me every day, but he walks right by me. I might as well be a shadow person. Wonder will the treatments really do William any good?

Sunday, November 13, 1859

I just hurried back to Aunt Tee's cabin to write what I just seen.

I was going back to the kitchen from the Quarters a while ago, when I seen Mr. Harms going into the woods. I followed him all the way down to the river, being quiet as I could. He put his hands to his mouth and made the sound of a bird. In a few minutes, I heard the same sound. Then out of the river mist stepped a ghostly-looking man. As the moon slipped from behind a cloud, I got a good look. He was the one-eyed man in the picture — the abolitionist — no ghost at all, but in the flesh.

My heart was beating in my chest so hard, I was sure they could hear it. I wanted to run out and tell the one-eyed man that he was my hero — like the long-ago Herquelez that Mr. Harms had read about. I wanted to tell the one-eyed man that I was an abolitionist too, and that I wanted to get rid of slavery just like him. But I decided just to watch and listen.

I know now that Mr. Harms is in with the abolitionists for sure. That means that not all abolitionists are from the Philadelphia, the New York, or the Boston. They come from everywhere — even from the south — even from Virginia. If Mr. Harms was an abolitionist, then what was he doing here at Belmont? Might it have something to do with slaves running away on that railroad that's underground?

Monday, November 14, 1859

Hince came to Aunt Tee's cabin after the dinner meal, none the worse for the beating he took. Licks heal fast on the outside, but they're a whole lot harder to heal inside.

We could hear Rufus singing down in the Quarters, *"Coming for to carry me home."*

Sunday, November 20, 1859

Today we had meeting in the Quarters same as always. I wore my new dress — Mama's dress. Everybody say how nice I looked. I tried real hard not to be puffed up, but when Missy came, I just had to strut a little. "Pride go 'fore a fall," Rufus whispered in my ear. Then he winked.

Hince came to meeting and sat 'side of Spicy. Wherever Spicy is these days, Hince aine far behind.

Rufus preached about Elijah who was taken to heaven in a fiery chariot. Home means freedom when we sing. So

Rufus's story is telling us, we're going to go to freedom one day, soon. I thought about Mr. Harms and the one-eyed man, and the Underground Railroad. Was somebody getting ready to run?

We closed singing —

Swing low, sweet chariot.
Coming for to carry me home.
Swing low, sweet chariot.
Coming for to carry me home.
I looked over Jordan and what did I see.
Coming for to carry me home.
A band of angels coming after me.
Coming for to carry me home.
Swing low, sweet chariot.
Coming for to carry me home.
Swing low, sweet chariot.
Coming for to carry me home.

Later

Wook came to Aunt Tee's cabin late this evening to talk to us. Times had changed. We hardly knew what to say to each other any more. Wook did a good part of the talking — remembering mostly. She teased me about the time we were playing hiding, and I hide in some poison ivy. That made us all laugh. Then Wook said she had to go. "Good-bye," she say, hugging Aunt Tee and Spicy. When she hugged me, she whispered softly. "Pray for me."

I haven't said anything to anybody. But Wook is getting ready to run — and the one-eyed man and Mr. Harms are probably helping her. Don't know how I know it, but I do. I do.

Monday, November 21, 1859

Things have been in an uproar all morning. Mas' Henley cain't be reasoned with. I was right! Rufus, Aggie, Wook, and the baby ran away last night. They just up and flew away.

Mas' Henley made a promise. "I'll free anybody who brings me information about Rufus and who helped him. Think of it, your freedom. I swear it!"

This aine about no handkerchief. Mas' Henley is promising freedom. If I told him everything I know about Mr. Harms and the one-eyed man, I could be free. Free. The idea is tempting. My God! I cain't believe I just had that thought. How could I even think of doing such a thing? I couldn't tell on Mr. Harms. I know there are people here at Belmont who would turn in their dear mamas for a piece of meat, let 'lone freedom. Lord, put that ugly idea out of my mind forever and ever. Amen.

Tuesday, November 22, 1859

Mas' Henley and a group of men went out looking for Rufus and his family. Rufus was the only person who has ever dared to run away from Belmont and we wanted him to make it, even though we couldn't say it — not even to each other. There was lots of singing about heaven — but we all know heaven is freedom.

Our hopes were crushed like fall leaves 'neath our feet when Mas' Henley got back this evening. Mas' Henley called all of us to him. He threw bloody pants and a shirt on the ground before us. "They're dead." He spat out the words like bad fruit. "All 'em. We had to shoot Rufus. The others drowned in the river, when the boat they was in turned over. Current took them under."

Rufus? Aggie? Wook? Baby Noah — all dead! What happened to the railroad that takes slaves to freedom? Didn't the one-eyed man help Rufus and his family?

From this day forward Mas' Henley say we aine 'llowing no more Sunday meetings, and we cain't speak of Rufus or any members of his family. Mas' might be able to tell us what we can do with our bodies, but he cain't tell me what to feel, what to think. I will remember Rufus and his family as long as I live — and he cain't stop me!

Later that same night

Even though Mas' Henley has forbidden us to gather, we mourned the loss of our friends in our own way. We raised our voices in song from our cabins in the Quarters, from the orchards and kitchen, wherever we were. We didn't need to be together to share our grief. We sang our hurt. We clapped our sorrow. We never spoke their names, but we all knew we were mourning our own, Rufus and Aggie, Wook, and little Noah. They were free at last . . .

I got a robe, you got a robe,
All of God's chullun got a robe.
When I get to hea'vn, gon' to put on my robe
And shout all over God's hea'vn.
Hea'vn. Hea'vn. Everybody's talkin' 'bout hea'vn
Aine goin' there.
Hea'vn. I'm going to shout all over God's hea'vn.

Wednesday, November 23, 1859

We woke this morning and the world looked like it's done been covered in a thin white veil. The first hard frost. Slaughtering time.

113

Saturday, November 26, 1859

The men slaughtered hogs for days. The smell of fresh animal blood turns my stomeck, so I stayed clear of the slaughtering yard and stayed close to the kitchen where pots and pans clanked and banged. The noise helped drown out the sound of dying.

As I write, the smokehouse is filled to overflowing with hams and sausage, bacon and ribs — all slow-curing in smoke from smouldering wood chips.

Later

Aunt Tee say just when you think you know the devil, he changes his face. Now I know what she means. I've always thought Mas' Henley was the worse man in the world. But then come Briley Waith. Rufus was always in charge of slaughtering, but Mas' Henley hired Briley Waith to take charge this year. He's common as dirt, tall and lean with sun-red skin. Keeps a tangle of white hair hid under a beat-up hat. The cat-o'-nine that hangs to Mr. Waith's side tells me he's a man who keeps it close, because he plans to use it.

Watching Waith makes me feel sick in my heart. There is something 'bout him that frightens me way down deep inside. We made soap today under his watchful eyes. He sees everything. To me he's a dangerment — like a snake, sly.

Sunday, November 27, 1859

Thank goodness for good days — they take the sting out of the bad ones. Aunt Tee sent me down to the stables to get Hince. When we walked into the cabin it was filled with the smell of cinnamon and apples. For days, I've been slipping sugar, butter, flour, lard — careful not to get caught. Today I got the cinnamon stick — enough to make a small apple pie.

It's first frost — Hince's birthtime. "Just for you," I say, giving him a shiny black button I had found and polished. He promised to keep it always and I knew he would.

"I don't have nothing to give," say Spicy. She stood toe to toe, eye to eye with him. Then she gave him a kiss, right on the mouth. "I'm glad you was born."

He let out a whoop that could be heard clear down to the river. We all had to laugh.

At times like these we missed Uncle Heb. But while Spicy and I worked on the quilt, we told stories about him, and about Rufus and Aggie, and Wook. That made us more thankful that we were together. Apple pie has never tasted so good.

Monday, November 28, 1859

Just as we feared, Mas' Henley liked Waith enough to keep him on. Pulled several men 'way from the tobacco drying sheds and put them on the job of building Mr. Waith's overseer's cabin. Mas' Henley chose a spot that gave him clear view of the whole plantation. He can see the Quarters out his back door, and the back of the Big House from his front door. From the left side window Waith can see the kitchen and the fields behind, and from his right side window Waith can see the orchards and woods. Clear to me, Mas' Henley has brought Waith here to be his eyes.

Tuesday, November 29, 1859

Miz Lilly sent for me today. She was lying in bed — say she had a fever.

"So you like your shoes?" she say, groaning softly. I offered to get her some water. She called to me to stand closer. Then she grabbed my hand.

"You like nice things, don't you?" I say yes, then she come back with, "You can have lots of things, but you've got to tell me what I want." She asked me question after question about Mr. Harms — so many my head went to swimming. But I was real careful not to let on to nothing. Wonder what's got her sniffing around Mr. Harms like a ol' hound dog. Missy must have brought her a bone. Now

116

she wants me to bring her another one. I say, "If I hear or see something, Miz Lilly, I'll come to you right now." All the time I'm thinking, "I'd never tell you a thing — 'specially not on a abolitionist."

Wednesday, November 30, 1859

All this time has passed and Mr. Harms still aine talked to me. But things have changed so much, I need to tell him Miz Lilly is trying to find something on him. But it's like I aine even in the room. During lesson time, I rub William's legs after they been soaked in hot, hot water. I'm still listening and learning all I can, but I wish Mr. Harms would talk to me.

Thursday, December 1, 1859

While serving the noon meal, I heard Miz Lilly tell Mas' Henley that she had written to a friend of hers in Washington. The friend had wrote back saying, "Mr. Harms's father and mother are well-bred southerners, but his uncles Josiah and Joshua Harms are hell-bent abolitionists." She sucked in as though she had spoken a word purely evil. "Who is this Mr. Harms?" she say.

This I know, Mas' and Miz Henley fights on just about everything in the world, 'cept'n slavery. On that notion they are together. They plenty mad about losing Rufus and his family. Mas' Henley say he would speak to Mr. Harms 'bout his family.

I know Mr. Harms said he would speak to me, but that was weeks ago. He never has. I got to warn him, so I'm just gon' have to speak to him first.

Friday, December 2, 1859

I took a big, big chance today. I waited outside William's room before class. When Mr. Harms came down the hall, I whispered. "Be careful. They know 'bout your uncles being abolitionists. They think you might be one, too." Mr. Harms never said a word to me — never even looked my way. I wonder did he hear me?

Later

Mr. Harms heard me all right. After supper, he told Mas' Henley about his uncles being abolitionists. It was smart for him to bring it up, before he got asked about it. I was serving them coffee in the large parlor when I heard Mr. Harms say he was sick 'shamed of his relations and wanted to forget they was ever kin. That seemed to set well with Mas' Henley. I found every reason to stay in that parlor listening. I poked up the fire as Mas' Henley was saying, "I'm trusting you to be an honorable man while you're an employee in my home." Coming from

Mas' Henley it sounded like a warning. I never took my eyes off Miz Lilly. She didn't say much. But the compression on her face told the whole story. She didn't trust Mr. Harms not a stitch. He's got an enemy in Miz Lilly — and I think he knows it.

Saturday, December 3, 1859

They finished Mr. Waith's house today. Hince say he's so glad Waith is not staying in the stables with him any more, because he snored so bad.

Waith's got a two room log cabin — one room and a sleeping loft — complete with a front and back door, and four windows. Nothing special, but the way he's carrying on, you'd think it was a Big House. Miz Lilly helped furnish his place with leftovers from the attic. Mas' Henley gave him the key to the storehouse and made him welcome.

Aunt Tee say Waith is po' white trash that aine never had it so good. That means he's gon' want to make sure he pleases Mas' and Miz Henley, to keep what he's got. I plan to stay clear of the man — he scares me.

Before going to bed, I looked out the window and saw smoke coming from Waith's chimney. The overseer has settled in for a long winter's stay at Belmont. A cold chill went up my back.

Sunday, December 4, 1859

The wind woke me up, whistling through the cracks in the cabin wall. Sounds like whisperings from the strange dream I was having. Trying, now, to write it down while I remember it. Even so it is hard to put the pieces together. I am running, running fast, but I don't know where I'm going. I see Hince being taken away in chains — Aunt Tee is begging Mr. Harms to help him, but he won't talk to her. He won't talk to me. I see a sign that says the Philadelphia, and another that says the New York, and another that says the Boston. People with no faces are holding up signs that say "We are abolitionists." I'm running to them, but I never get closer.

Sitting here in the cold darkness, I've made up my mind that I'm going to speak to Mr. Harms. I've just got to figure out how and where I can do it.

Monday, December 5, 1859

Mr. Harms and I see each other during lessons every day, but we never have time alone.

I have to say this for William, he's trying really, really hard with his lessons. No whining when I rub his legs either. I know the water is hot, and the exercises are hard for him, but he never fails to try. And today for all of his hard work, William wiggled his big toe. It was a small thing, but it made me feel big inside — good — like I'd had a part in making it happen by rubbing his legs and feet every day. It was like doctoring. I know how Aunt Tee and Spicy must feel when they help bring a new life into the world.

Tuesday, December 6, 1859

Samella, a barn cat, had a litter of three kittens under the kitchen porch. Two died. I captured the last one, a jet black one, and took it to William. I'd never heard William say thank you for anything in his life, but he thanked me for the kitten. He named it Shadow.

Later

"That was a kind thing you did for William," said Mr. Harms. He was standing in the doorway to the study. "Keep dusting."

At last, we were having that talk. My head was spinning with thoughts. What to ask? What to say? "I've been waiting and waiting for this time."

Our talk went like this:

"I had to make sure you could be trusted — and that you could trust me."

"Are you a abolitionist?" I wanted to know that in the worst way.

He smiled, but his eyes were serious. "Yes, I am. Who else knows about me?"

"Aunt Tee, Spicy, and me. But Miz Lilly's looking at you real careful-like."

"Thanks for the warning. She could be a problem."

"Are you and the one-eyed man the Underground Railroad?"

"No. Not by ourselves," he whispered. "We are conductors." He told me it was neither underground nor a railroad. It's a group of people who work together to help slaves get to freedom.

"You can read and write. I figured you learned by listening during lessons. Remarkable."

"I done learned a lot from you." Then I say, "You a southerner. Why you want to end slavery?"

He wasn't able to answer, because somebody was coming. I had more questions to ask. Later. Now it's time to take Miz Lilly her warm milk before bedtime. I got to be sure that I don't give away nothing in my face.

Wednesday, December 7, 1859

Today, Dr. Lamb came to see William — said he was improving. That still gave Mr. Harms and me a moment to talk. He told me Belmont was the first station on the Underground Railroad in this area. It was a low point in the river, where it narrows and the current is less swift. Runaways meet their first conductor here in the Belmont woods and are taken to the next point.

Why couldn't poor Rufus and his family make it?

Thursday, December 8, 1859

The days are short and cold. The fields have been laid by. Tobacco is yellowing over slow coals. Waith's put everybody to work fixing up the place for Christmas — the Big Times. Another holiday. Endless chores.

Eva Mae is making fruit cakes today. I chopped nuts and berries 'til my fingers have got no feeling. Missy got on one of Clarissa's old dresses — Miz Lilly probably promised her a hat, too, if she tells on me. Missy and me hardly talk any more except when we serving the food. She hangs under Miz Lilly like Shadow does William.

Friday, December 9, 1859

We spent the day in the barn, restuffing Miz Lilly's mattress with fresh down we've been saving all year.

Hince has been coming to Aunt Tee's cabin every night to sit with Spicy, so I can't write until he leaves.

Since our talk in the study, Mr. Harms has been slipping me things to read. I hide them under my dress until I get here. I read the papers to Aunt Tee and Spicy. A lot of it we don't understand, but a lot of my questions have answers now.

Abolitionists live everywhere, just like I thought. But, what makes me happyest is that some abolitionists are women and some are even people who done been slaves, just like me. Mr. Harms say that a used-to-be-slave named Frederick Douglass teached himself to read and write just like me. Now he's a abolitionist and writes his own newspaper up in the New York called *The North Star*. I want to read that paper some day. Maybe I will. I know I will.

Saturday, December 10, 1859

Aunt Tee sent Spicy and me to pick the last of the beets from the house garden. They're tender and sweet after the frost hits the ground. On the way back from the garden Waith jumped out and grabbed Spicy's arm. "You're right pretty for a black gal," he say, spitting tobacco juice.

He hissed at me to git, but I wouldn't go — not without Spicy. I held on to her hand. He snapped his whip in my direction. "Git like I tol' you, or I'll give you a whupping gal!"

"Mr. Harms wouldn't like you bothering Spicy. He done picked her for hisself." I surprised myself at how fast I could speak a lie. It was a good lie, because it was helping Spicy. She was frozen in fear, because she knew Waith didn't have nothing good in mind. Waith b'lieved me. He let Spicy go, and we ran as fast as we could to Aunt Tee.

I'll tell Mr. Harms what I said, and maybe he can protect Spicy until . . . until what? Dare I write it? Until we run away!

Sunday, December 11, 1859

I miss the good Sundays we had when Rufus was here. But Mr. Harms gave Spicy's Bible back. He had been keeping it in his room where it would be safe. The one he showed Miz Lilly was one of his. Spicy was thankful to get it back — it being her mama's and all. Now I read to Spicy and Aunt Tee when we get a chance.

Later

There was a big celebration at Belmont tonight. Had to work in the kitchen. Mr. Cleophus Tucker and the other men Mas' Henley supported won. The house looked beautiful, everything shining and sparkling. We'd worked hard enough to make it look that way. The guests went on and on about how they hate abolitionists and northern meddlers. Made me smile inside, seeing Mr. Harms right in the middle of them — and they don't even know he was a fox in the henhouse.

Mas' Edmund Ruffin was part of the group tonight. He was the one who talked the longest and the loudest about the rights of slaveholders. He was always talking 'bout his freedom. "We are a free nation. We fought England for our freedom. We will fight again for our freedom if we must!"

Mas'ers talk a powerful lot when it comes to their freedom. But when it comes to freeing the slaves — they gets struck deaf and dumb.

Monday, December 12, 1859

It's night. It was cold all morning, warmed up by late afternoon, and now it is cold again — a winter cold. Long hard day over. Miz Lilly fussed around in the kitchen most of the morning — setting up for the big Christmas dinner. She ended up slapping Eva Mae twice 'fore it was over.

Later, Miz Lilly gave every one in the Quarters a measure of cloth to make something for the coming Big Times. I gave my piece to Aunt Tee, because I got Mama's dress to wear. Aunt Tee is stitching up something real special while Spicy and me work on our quilt. We almost got it finished.

The cabin floor is cold, so we keep our feet wrapped in rags. We sit by the fire, so our fronts are warm, but our backs are cold. There are so many cracks in the walls, the wind whistles. And it's also getting harder and harder for Aunt Tee to piece a meal together, even though I'm slipping as much as I can out of the kitchen. Winter hard times is upon us. What keeps us going is waiting on the Big Times — our Week of Sundays. Uncle Heb always used to say, if we can last through February we can March on through.

Tuesday, December 13, 1859

Riders woke us at daybreak. Dogs barking. Torches glowing in the darkness. Aunt Tee, Spicy, and I went to the door to see who it was. Late-night riders always mean one thing — trouble.

The lead rider, Wilson, spoke first. He was quick to the point. "Two of my nigras have run away — a buck named Raf and a mulatto gal named Cora Belle. We beat it out of the gal's mama that the two was helped by a white man, what's missing an eye. If we catch him, he's gon' lose more'n a eye." The men reined their horses. "We aim to hang him."

"The dogs traced them here to your orchards. We'd like to go in, with your permission," said Higgins.

Mas' Henley raised a fist. "You have my permission. And if you'll let me dress, I'll go with you."

"Me, too," said Mr. Waith, bursting out of his cabin. "Chasing and catching runaways is what I been doing for the last three years."

I knew he was something like that — a low-lifed slave-chaser.

Wednesday, December 14, 1859

Mas' Henley come back from the hunt, telling us how they found the runaways. "We hung 'em," he hissed angrily. "My offer still stands," he said. "Freedom to the one who gives me any information about this one-eyed white man. Think about it — freedom." So they hadn't caught the one-eyed man.

I just scratched F-R-E-E-D-O-M in the ashes. I still don't get no picture. Freedom is a hard word to understand.

Thursday, December 15, 1859

Waith been pushing everybody to get Belmont cleaned up for the Big Times. After what happened with the runaways we been moving real slow-like — got no joy in our souls.

Women from the Quarters been up in the kitchen to help Eva Mae with the early cooking and cleaning. I helped put the big rug out of the large parlor and beat all the dust out of it. I got to coughing and couldn't stop. Aunt Tee made me some syrup out of honey and herbs and I finally stopped.

Later

When I went to the stables to take Hince a plate of food, Mr. Harms pulled me aside. I almost screamed, thinking it was that nasty Waith.

"Got news," he say. "Those runaways aren't dead.

They just tell you runaways are dead, so you'll be afraid to run."

"Does that mean Rufus and Aggie?" I was so hoping. But Mr. Harms say, no they didn't make it. Rufus wasn't willing to trust the Underground Railroad plan. "He never quite b'lieved that a southern man could be as against slavery as I am. But there are plenty of us." Rufus had tried to make it on his own.

"Some runaways make it alone," Mr. Harms s'plained. "They need help most times. Lots of help. I tried to help Rufus — talked to him several times when I heard he was planning a run. Rufus never really trusted me."

What happened to Rufus and his family should never happen to another family. One of them might have made it if they could swim. Mas' Henley won't let us learn how to swim, because he knows, if we stay stupid he can keep us. Come spring, I'm learning how to swim — just in case I ever need to know how.

I forgot to tell Mr. Harms about the lie I told Waith to save Spicy. I've got to remember.

Friday, December 16, 1859

Rained all day — a slow cold rain. Miserable. I sat with William in his room for a while. We played with Shadow. I pumped his legs, up and down, up and down, keeping them moving. Sadly, the hot water treatments aine helped more than to get a few toes a-going. The rest of him is still the same — nothing near walking. He's in mighty good spirits though — giggling all the time. Maybe it's the Big Times that's making him so happy. Dr. Lamb visited yesterday. Stayed for dinner. Company — even company as nice as Dr. Lamb, always means more work for us in the kitchen.

Saturday, December 17, 1859

Mr. Harms still treats me like I'm not there when others be around us.

He left me a copy of *The Liberator*, put out by a abolitionist named William Lloyd Garrison from the Boston. I read the pages to Aunt Tee and Spicy. They listened to every word — stories about black abolitionists.

I read about a woman named Sojourner Truth, who speaks out against slavery everywhere she goes. Even when the mas'ers say they gon' stone her to death, she keeps a-talking. Aine scared of nothing, because she's telling the truth. "Slavery must be destroyed — root and branch!"

I am so glad to know about Miz Sojourner. I mean to be like her one day. Maybe even meet her when I get to freedom. Maybe we could be abolitionists together. Demagine that. But will I be brave like the shepherd boy,

David? If I was with Miz Sojourner, she'd help me be strong — and we can end slavery, too.

Sunday, December 18, 1859

Waith works the people in the Quarters like dogs, won't let up on them a minute — push, work, driving night and day — painting, chopping winter wood, feeding the livestock, on and on. He's constantly yelling and screaming, and lashing that whip. I'd like to wrap it around his neck and give it a good yank! The more he yells the more Mas' Henley and the Missus feel they're getting their money's worth.

Monday, December 19, 1859

It snowed today, not enough to cover the ground. William sat by the window and longed to play once more in the snow.

"You're different, Clotee," William say matter-of-fact-like. Lord, now William is noticing me. Who next?

I made on like I didn't know what he was talking about. He say, "You don't sound like the other slaves. You say talk*ing*, instead of talk*in'*. You say, *I am* instead of *I is*. You say, *they were* instead of *they was* — and things like that. You talk almost as good as a white person. Why is that?"

I shrugged my shoulders and got out of there as quick as I could. Missy was always teasing me about talking

131

proper. Miz Lilly had spoke about it, too, and now William. Was my learning to be my undoing? I must be particular to write but not talk too proper. I could get myself into trouble.

Tuesday, December 20, 1859

Five days to the Big Times.

Two men by the name of Campbelle came to Belmont today. They stayed for supper. The older Campbelle is gray-haired with a matching mustache, stocky, but well-dressed. The son is taller, thinner. The Campbelles are horsemen from Tennessee, same as Mas' Henley.

While serving biscuits and coffee, I turned to listening. I'm piecing it all together so I can write it down.

"We've been watching you for some time," said Silas Campbelle, the older man. "We like the way your boy rides."

"I got the best jockey in Virginia right here at Belmont," Mas' Henley bragged.

"He'd be great if he had a fair mount," said Amos Campbelle, the son. "We've got the right horse. We need your jockey."

"What's your offer?"

"We'd like to buy Hince."

My heart sank! I almost dropped the plate of dessert tea cakes, but I caught them before they all slide off the

132

tray and on the floor. The men were too fixed on what they were saying to pay attention to me.

"No deal," Mas' Henley answered. "But, I'll make this bet. My jockey against your horse. I lose, you take Hince. I win, I take your horse."

"Set the date?"

"New Year's Day."

Later

Hince was shocked when I told him what I'd overheard.

"So Mas' Henley done bet on me 'gainst the Campbelles' horse?" He shrugged and went back to rubbing Can. Is that all Mas' Henley thought of Hince — to bet him against a horse?

"S'pose you lose?" I asked.

Hince talked brave. "I won't lose. Big Can is a good horse, nobody really knows how good. Mas' Henley musta planned this all along. That's why he been having me hold back a little, winning without ever letting Can stretch out. That's gon' be our edge on the Campbelles."

Once he put voice to those words Hince didn't seem worried. All I pray for is for him to be right. So does Aunt Tee and most especially Spicy. Hince can't lose.

133

Thursday, December 22, 1859

We all gathered on the porch to see the Christmas tree lights. The tree didn't look as pretty to me as it used to. Maybe Waith being here has spoiled the Big Times for us all.

As hard as everybody done worked to get the place ready for the holidays, Briley Waith went to Mas' Henley and tried to get our off-days cut short. I heard him say with all the runaways happening, he thinks we should be kept bent over working so we can't take time to study up on freedom.

Thank goodness, Mas' Henley had sense enough to realize that he'd have a r'bellion on his hands if he didn't give us the days off between Christmas and New Year's.

"Tell you what, though," he told Waith. "I won't give out any travel passes this year. That ought to cut back on any runaway attempts. Thank you for thinking ahead, Waith. You're a good man."

I just wrote M-E-A-N in the ashes. Mean. The picture of Waith is clear in my head. This is going to be a sad, sad Christmas for folks who were hoping for passes to visit their loved ones on nearby plantations.

Saturday, December 24, 1859 — Christmas Eve

Been so busy, I aine had a chance to write in a few days. Everything is ready for the Big Times — in the Big

134

House and down here in the Quarters. Even the weather is on our side. If it stays warm like it is today, we'll get to eat our dinner outside.

Everybody is home for the holidays. Mr. Harms stayed here, rather than go to his home. Clarissa and her husband are here from Richmond. The tree is up, the stockings are hung, and we've got the cream ready for Mas' Henley's famous eggnog.

The Missus led the family in singing carols. As soon as I could slip away, I joined Aunt Tee and Spicy in the stables. That's where the folks from the Quarters were having their Christmas Eve dance. All under the watchful eyes of Waith, the overseer.

Aunt Tee served him a glass of danderlion wine. Waith drank it and ate a big plate of pickled pig feet, a roasted sweet potato and ashcake. Aunt Tee winked at Spicy and me, because she had put a potion in his drink.

'Fore long, we looked for Waith. He was curled up like a fat snake, sound asleep. Slept through the whole party. He never guessed what had made him so sleepy. Thank goodness for Aunt Tee's potions — and the Afric woman that gave her the recipe.

Sunday, December 25, 1859 — Christmas Day

It is Christmas — all day. "Christmas gif'," we all shouted outside Mas' Henley's window first thing this morning. After the families from the Quarters came to the Big House to greet the family and get their gifts, they hurried back to the Quarters to begin their Week of Sundays. Us who work in the kitchen had to work all day — fetching and toting, wiping and cleaning.

Missy saw another side of Miz Lilly today. Missy was moving slow-like and whining about having to work on Christmas. All at once Miz Lilly popped Missy right upside the head. It hurt Missy's heart that I saw her get slapped.

I had Aunt Tee and Spicy bent over laughing, when I told her how Missy looked — eyes all bucked, mouth poked out — what a sight. She had it coming after what she did to Hince.

Later

Everybody in the Big House is happy because William stood up on his own today. I felt good seeing him standing up all by hisself, too. So that's why he's been all happy. He knew about this. Mr. Harms got lots of praise. Even Miz Lilly had to 'fess that Mr. Harms had helped her son stand. He'll be taking a few steps any day now.

I feel happy for William. I'd helped William come this far, too. I'd rubbed his legs and toes and sat with him when he was lonely. Nobody knew what I'd done — but I knew and that made me feel well within myself.

136

Monday, December 26, 1859

Today begins the first day of the Big Times. No work for the field hands. For us in the kitchen double work — more toting, fetching. Yesterday after we had served the big meal for the Henleys and cleaned up, we went down to the barn where there was a gathering going on.

Aunt Tee had made a cake from stuff I'd been sneaking out of the kitchen for weeks. All the elder folk stood to one side as judges. Somebody started patting the juba, clapping the tune. Then came the couples, strutting the cakewalk. Hince and Spicy come out first — high-stepping and kicking their heels. They were wearing matching shirts that Aunt Tee had made from the cloth Miz Lilly handed out. Everybody had to say they were a fine-looking couple. But they could also dance.

I had on my dress that Mama had made and the ribbon that Hince had brought me. Missy had on one of Clarissa's dresses, too. But mine was better — because Mama had made mine.

Aunt Tee 'llowed that I could dance the cakewalk this year with a boy other than Hince. Me and Buddy Barnes, Miz Clarissa's carriage driver, stepped together. He swung me up and swung me down — from side to side and up the middle.

"You look mighty nice, Clotee," Buddy Barnes said. My face turned hot and my head topped light — as light as my feet felt dancing with Buddy Barnes. As long as I live I will never, ever forget dancing with Buddy Barnes — even though Spicy and Hince were the cakewalk winners. They each took a slice of the cake for themselves, then they let everybody else have a bite.

Of course Missy was a sore loser — but she only makes herself look bad — keep pushing, pushing. Everybody knows how Spicy and Hince feel about each other. Missy should just give up.

Friday, December 30, 1859

The Week of Sundays has gone so fast. Like most holidays it's been filled with work — up the stairs, down the stairs. Bring me this, Clotee. Take that there, Clotee. Clotee. Clotee. I wish I could change my name. It is always late when we finish. Eva Mae was so tired this evening, she just fell fast asleep up in the attic. I eased out of the kitchen without waking her.

Saturday, December 31, 1859 — New Year's Eve

In the Big House all the talk is about the race tomorrow. The Campbelles are here with their horse and rider. Their horse looks like a real champion — named Betty's Son. The rider is the size of a boy, but he has a lot of years in his face. I heard one of the Campbelles call him Josh.

138

Later

The Campbelles brought along three of their slaves who stayed in the stables with Hince. They also made good dance partners for us. Missy took one look at the young man named Booker and claimed him for the rest of the evening. Aunt Tee called her a shameless hussy. I danced with the one named Obie. He was fun and had a happy laugh, but he wasn't near as good a dancer as Buddy Barnes. The one named Shad seemed shy — didn't dance, didn't talk. He left before the party ended.

After one of the dances the straw in the barn started me to sneeze. It always makes me sneeze and cough. Aunt Tee took me outside to get some fresh air — and sent me to the cabin to get some cough syrup. When I passed the stables, I saw Shad standing at Big Can's stall.

Sunday, January 1, 1860 — New Year's Day

My God. Hince lost the race!

As best I can tell, this is what happened.

This morning it was bright and sunny, but cold — not a cloud in the sky. The course was from Belmont's front steps down to the road and back, past the Big House, down to the river and back again — about a half mile.

Carriages full of people began gathering on the grounds

all morning. Hundreds were here by mid-morning. A few minutes before noon, Hince walked Can up from the stables. I could tell something was wrong with the horse. Can looked spooked, jumpy, hard to handle. I caught a look of worry in Hince's face. That spooked me.

At exactly noon, the gun fired and Can reared up, losing time that he was never able to catch up. The other horse won! We all were too shocked to believe what our eyes had seen. Hince wasn't supposed to lose.

Right away, Hince commenced to hollering that Can had been drugged. He was right. And I knew who had done it. Shad! "I seen him at Big Can's stall last night." I went running to Mas' Henley, all the time pointing a finger at Shad. He glared at me. "Please save Hince," I begged. "Shad did something to Can, I know he did. I seen him, honest!"

"I seen him, too," said Aunt Tee. "Left the dance early last night." Shad didn't say anything. The Campbelles stayed calm.

Everybody started talking to one another, whispering about what had happened during the race. The Campbelles called for several men — all good horsemen to check out Big Can. Rouse Mosby and Len Beans checked out Can. They said there were no signs of the horse being drugged. "Were they blind?" Can wasn't acting hisself. Anybody could see that — who wanted to see it.

140

The next few seconds were like hours. The Campbelles claimed that the race was fair and they had won the bet. The crowd agreed and sent up a cheer.

"You've cheated me, Amos Campbelle — you have, but I can't prove it," Mas' Henley said real angry-like. Then he ordered them off his property.

The Campbelles tipped their hats and said they had other business in the area before going home. Say they'll be coming in several weeks to pick up Hince.

"Please do something, Miz Lilly," I begged her. "I saw Shad in the barn doing something to Can. He did. Please help Hince. Please don't let them take him away. Please."

Miz Lilly snatched me by the arm and pushed me toward the house. "Hush all that crying, before I give you something to cry for. You'll say anything to save Hince." Through my tears I could see her mean eyes, and I knew she wasn't about to help Hince. She was happy to be rid of him. It's hard trying not to hate Miz Lilly — but I do hate the cruelness that lives inside her.

Later

Hince been like a wild man — walking, walking, never stopping. Say he aine going with the Campbelles. Spicy been crying all day, limp with crying. "I hope Hince don't try nothing foolish like running away," say Aunt Tee. I hope not either. I got to do something, but what? What good is know-how if you can't use it when you need it. I got reading and writing, but it can't help Hince. I feel like my head is in the big mouth of the lion, but I've got to be like Daniel. Be not afraid.

Thursday, January 5, 1860

It finally happened! Mr. Harms done been found out. Hince tattled. How did he know?

Later

We're all here at Aunt Tee's cabin. I'm trying to write down all that's been going on, so we'll never disremember.

Spicy told Hince about me, Mr. Harms, the one-eyed man, the abolitionists — everything. She asked me to forgive her. "I trusted Hince. I didn't know he was gon' tell on po' Mr. Harms."

I wouldn't a-counted Hince 'mongst the tattlers either. It breaks my heart that he has.

Would he tell on me if he got scared enough?

Still later

Hince came to Aunt Tee's cabin after the last meal, when he knew all of us would be here. "I aine going to the Deep South with the Campbelles. Why should I care about a white man? It's his life or mine." Them words didn't sound like Hince. He must be plenty scared. I would be — having to go to the Deep South.

Aunt Tee never stopped stirring the pot. She spoke. "Going to freedom this way would be a bitter road. Mr. Harms may be white but he come here to help the likes of us. Wrong for one of us to be the cause of his undoing."

"What am I s'posed to do?"

"You've got to make this thing right, somehow." Then with pleading in her voice, Aunt Tee went on saying, "Oh, son, if you gets to freedom, don't let it be on a river of innocent blood — or you'll sour yo' heart and soul."

Hince dropped his head. "I aine going to the Deep South and that's all there is to it. I'm purely sorry 'bout Mr. Harms, but it's him or me, and right now, I got to look out after me." He looked at Spicy. She didn't say nothing.

I stood with Aunt Tee. "Mr. Harms could have turned me in to win favor with Miz Lilly and Mas' Henley. He never did. I owe him something. I'm gon' try to help."

Now that I've studied on it a spell, I can't shake a stick at Hince without it pointing back at me. I told on Shad when I thought it would save Hince. And I didn't care. Now Hince done used what he knew to bargain with Mas' Henley for his freedom. He aine about to go to the Deep South. I understand wanting to be free, but telling on Mr. Harms aine the way to do it — it just aine right.

Right now I feel like we're the Israelites standing at the Red Sea. Pharaoh's army is coming in chariots. Our

143

backs are to the water. Mr. Harms is tied up in the study waiting for the sheriff to come. What we need is for God to push back the waters so we can cross over on dry land. We need a plan.

Friday, January 6, 1860

We've got a plan that might save Mr. Harms. It may or may not work, but we've got to try to save him. We can't just let him die. God, please help us like you did the three boys in the fiery furnace.

Saturday, January 7, 1860

I'm still shaking from the cold and fear. It snowed all night, so the sheriff didn't get here until this afternoon. This is what happened.

The sheriff and Waith came to the Big House. Spicy and me slipped in the side door and hid in the pantry where we could see and hear everything that was going on in the large parlor of the Big House. If Mr. Harms was afraid, he didn't show it. He looked as strange and out of order as he did the first day I laid eyes on him — not at all like the picture of a brave and daring abolitionist.

Just like we'd planned it back at the cabin — Hince said that he had seen Mr. Harms talking to the one-eyed man down by the river. "The same one-eyed man who's been helping slaves get away." Hince did a fine job.

Mr. Harms said none of it was true. "I don't know a one-eyed man." That was good. We 'spected he'd say that.

Then it was time for Spicy to come in. She was so nervous, I had to push her two times. But she burst into the room, screaming, "Oh, please, Mas' Henley, don't hurt Mr. Harms. He aine done nothing wrong. Hince be just lying 'cause he's jealous — jealous of me . . . and Mr. Harms. Tell 'em, Hince. Tell 'em." Spicy was even better than when we practiced it in the cabin. I prayed Mr. Harms would catch on to what we were doing. I had never gotten around to telling him what I'd told Waith about him and Spicy.

"No, I'm the one telling the truth," Hince say, right on time.

The room fell quiet. Mas' Henley's mouth fell open. You could have pushed Miz Lilly over with a broom straw.

"Here at Belmont? I'm so ashamed," she say, heaving a big sigh. Mr. Harms stood still and quiet.

The sheriff shifted around from foot to foot. "We got two nigras with two different stories. How do we get at the truth. Have you and this gal been together?"

Mr. Harms wouldn't answer. Waith leaned over to Mas' Henley. "Well, I heard that Harms had picked that one out for hisself." This part was going just as we had hoped. What happened next took me by surprise.

"Spicy is telling the truth," William shouted from the

145

doorway. "I've seen her go into Mr. Harms's room many times. I also heard Spicy and Hince having a fight in the stables. Maybe Hince is jealous and isn't telling the truth."

That was all we needed — two white men's word — no matter if one was a boy. The sheriff untied Mr. Harms, saying he would not take Mr. Harms — not enough evidence.

Now it was my time to heave a sigh. We'd done it! We'd saved Mr. Harms. I felt just like we'd killed Goliath.

Later

When the sheriff was gone, Mas' Henley slapped Spicy so hard she fell and slid across the room, bumping her head 'gainst the wall. I think Spicy is the bravest person in the whole wide world for doing what she did. She's braver than Sojourner Truth and all the abolitionists rolled together. Spicy knew she was probably going to get punished in a bad way, but she was willing to go under the lash to save Mr. Harms's life. I saw Hince close his eyes and clench his fists. He was at that jumping over spot. I was praying that he wouldn't jump over.

See, I remember when Mr. Barclay's Kip crossed over. He went wild on his mas'er, took the whip away and beat his own mas'er with it. They hung Kip, but he died smiling. Sometimes, I guess people get tired of being hit on, beat on, mistreated. I reckon people get tired of seeing they loved ones smacked in the face — half fed — worked near 'bout to death. I saw Hince come mighty close to that jumping over spot, when Mas' Henley hit Spicy that hard. But he held hisself, because the plan was working.

Mr. Harms didn't make a move. He hardly looked like he was breathing. I don't think I was breathing, either.

"What kind of southern-born man are you?" Mas' Henley asked, spitting out the angry words. "You come in my house and use one of my girls, and then turn around and rob me of my property? Steal my property away on some blasted Underground Railroad?"

"I am a tutor, sir —"

"No. No," Mas' say, cutting in. "I believe Hince told me the truth."

That's what I was waiting to hear. Now I could breathe.

"You know how I know? Hince doesn't want to leave Belmont — his only home. You abolitionists don't understand and you never will. Our slaves love us. They run away when you people come down here exciting them about freedom — freedom to do what? They are like children — unable to do for themselves."

Hince and Mr. Harms wisely said nothing. They let Mas' Henley rattle on, fooling himself into b'lieving we slaves was happy to be slaves.

Then Miz Lilly stood up. "You helped my son. That's

147

why I stopped my husband from killing you. So, the best thing for you to do, sir, is get off Belmont and before I reconsider." Then Miz Lilly swished away.

So far our plan had worked — all of it.

Late Saturday night

William and I were the only ones standing on the porch — cold, but huddled together, watching Mr. Harms load his buggy. All three of us knew that William had lied to save Mr. Harms. He had not seen Spicy, because she had never been to Mr. Harms's room. He had not seen Hince and Spicy fussing because they had never had a fuss. William knows that I know he lied — but we will never speak of it, I'm sure.

It's natural-like for William to be sad. Mr. Harms was above all else a very good teacher. Waith stood by a pile of books in the drive. He pointed the shotgun at Mr. Harms's head while the teacher climbed into the buggy. "Please, may I have my books. Why burn them?"

Upon a signal from Mas' Henley, Waith lit a match and the tutor's books went up in flames. At the same time, Waith slapped the horse, and the buggy lurched forward, down the drive. It was a strange sight, not unlike the first day I'd seen Mr. Harms, coming up the drive of Belmont. I was sorry to see him go, but happy he was alive to go.

148

Sunday, January 8, 1860

Aunt Tee made me tell her what happened at least ten times. Each time when we get to the part about Spicy being hit, she says, "Bless you, chile." Spicy's eye's swollen, but Aunt Tee is taking care of her.

"How do you get brave?" I asked Spicy.

"I hope I was as brave as you are smart. It was your idea. All I did was do what you told me to do — even though I was scared to death the whole time."

Later

Missy can't stop talking about what a bad girl Spicy is. "Hince won't want a girl like that." If Missy only knew.

Monday, January 9, 1860

There is no cold like January cold. It goes through to the bone. No fire is hot enough to warm the January chills. That's what the field hands spend their time doing in January — looking for something to eat and a warm place to eat it. Most of the little children in the Quarters don't have shoes or warm clothes. Mothers come to Aunt Tee's cabin to get salves and root potions. I been working hard in the kitchen and the Big House, slipping out food a-plenty.

149

Tuesday, January 10, 1860

Miz Lilly called me to her room today. Jumped right on me — talking about why I didn't tell her about Spicy and Mr. Harms.

"I didn't know."

She took my shoulders in each hand. Then she sighed. "Clotee, you could be my pet, my favorite, if you let me. You're so bright and pretty just like your mama. Did you know, we were best friends? — always laughing and laughing, like silly girls do. Then we got all grown-up. . . . She made the most lovely gowns for me and my sisters."

"Then you let her go." God, help me to keep my mouth.

Miz Lilly eyed me hard. "Go on now, get out of here," she said. "You're useless."

Wednesday, January 11, 1860

True to his word, Mas' Henley freed Hince today. I sneaked paper out of the study while dusting a while back. So, I've made a copy of the way a free paper is made up, and I got a copy of Mas' Henley's sign'ture. Hince can't leave though, because Mas' Henley say the papers have to be took to the courthouse.

Sunday

Now that Mr. Harms is gone and we don't have no more study time, I don't know what the date is. But today is Sunday.

Missy done made sure everybody in the Quarters thinks Spicy is a bad girl. Hince staying his distance for a spell. As long as Hince and Spicy know the truth, that's all that matters.

Aunt Tee's pot is mighty low. Not enough to make a meal for us, never mind anybody else. Still she tries. Sharing what we got. "This plantation makes us all kin," she say. "Not by blood, but by suffering."

January cold

My fingers are cold. My feet are cold. My nose is cold. I cough all the time. My head hurts. This is the coldest winter of my life. I stay by the fire, but I'm never warm.

In the room over the kitchen it was always warm and comfortable. I sleep in a fit and wake up tired. I will speak to Miz Lilly about getting some of the old blankets in the upstairs room of the Big House.

Everybody gathered around Aunt Tee tonight. They seem to find hope in her spirit to keep going. Somebody sang —

Rabbits in the briar patch,
Squirrel in the tree,
Wish I could go hunting
But I ain't free.
Rooster's in the henhouse
Hen's in the patch,
Love to go shooting
But I ain't free.

"We going to eat tomorrow," say Aunt Tee. "Don't you worry."

Next day

Most times Miz Lilly is cold and mean. Today, she found a little kind piece hidden away in a pocket of her heart. I told her how bad it was in the Quarters. "It has been a bad winter." She let us take quilts and shirts and shoes down to the Quarters. Boxes of stuff. It was like the Big Times all over again.

While Miz Lilly was busy helping me in the attic, Aunt Tee slipped and rung the necks of two hens and had them in the pot with dumplings before anybody could say "how-do you do." Aunt Tee was good on her word. We ate good tonight.

Day or so later

My head hurts. My arms and legs hurt. Even my teeth hurt. I can't write any more.

Early February

I don't know what day of the week it is. They tell me I've been sick with a awful fever. Aunt Tee and Spicy used teas and salves — but it was Mama's love that pulled me through.

Whilst I was in a fever, dreaming, Mama come to me all soft and gentle. "Get well, daughter. Live and grow strong." Then she told me something that's really got me studying on the meaning. She say something Rufus used to always say, "To the one God gives much, much is asked in return." Then I saw Rufus standing with Mama. He say, "You have been given much, Clotee. You can read and write, when others can't. Now, you must put your learning to good use. Use your learning."

Use it to do what?

Week later

I'm feeling better every day. Still wobbley. I'm back working in the kitchen and Big House.

After the dishes were done from the midday meal, I

walked to the woods. It's not nearly as cold as it has been. Most of the snow is melted. I passed the cemetery and spent a minute with Uncle Heb, and I remembered Rufus and Aggie, Wook, and Baby Noah who never got a chance to live. Then I moved down toward the river.

I wrote F-R-E-E-D-O-M in the mud. It still has no picture. Maybe my dream meant that I should run to freedom up in the Philadelphia, the New York, or the Boston, and then use my reading and writing to help the abolitionists. Is that what I should do, Mama? How would I run away?

Monday

I know it's Monday because Miz Lilly come to the kitchen to pass out the flour, sugar, and meal. She gave Missy a pretty scarf to wear on her head. Then she swished past me with her head in the air. Suddenly I got an understanding. Miz Lilly is like a spoiled, silly girl — playing silly games with people's lives. She's like a little girl in a big woman's body. Pitiful.

Tuesday

It's a winter thaw. Day was almost warm. But Aunt Tee say it's a fooler. I wandered down to the spot where I had seen Mr. Harms talking to the one-eyed man. No reason. Just did.

154

I heard the crackle of leaves underfoot. I stopped, stood dead still, listening, waiting — for what I didn't know.

"Clotee. Over here. It's me, Mr. Harms."

I was sure glad to see Mr. Harms and I told him so. He wondered why I had come to that place just then. "I don't know, sir. I just came." I'll always b'lieve Mama guided me there. "I thought you would be in the Boston by now," I said.

"No," he said, laughing. "But this is my last run. My partner and I are too well-known in the Tidewater. I'll move on after we take the next group out."

"Who will be the conductor here at Belmont?" I asked him.

"We won't have a conductor here. That's too bad. Belmont is an important link in the railroad."

The abolitionists will find someone, won't they?

I pulled myself tall. "Sir, I want to go with you to freedom. I'll work hard and help the abolitionists in any way I can. Please say I can come."

"Clotee, you don't have to beg. Of course you can come. Be here on the next dark of the moon. Bring fresh water but travel light — bring only what you need. It is a dangerous journey, Clotee. But you are no stranger to danger. You are a remarkable girl, and we abolitionists will be proud to have you in our ranks."

Mr. Harms hugged me. "Take care, little Clotee. Thank Spicy for what she did. I have a feeling you were

155

in on it, too." I nodded. "Tell Hince I hold no hard feelings. In his shoes I might have done the same thing." Then, "If possible, find some way to say thank you to William."

Wednesday

I've told Aunt Tee and Spicy about seeing Mr. Harms and how he was planning another runaway on the next dark of the moon. But as hard as I try, I can't get Aunt Tee to go with me. Spicy wants to go, though, because Hince is going to be leaving soon as his papers clear.

"I'm too old, chile," say Aunt Tee. "Besides, I can't leave Uncle Heb. I lived with him. I'll be buried 'side of him, too. But you go on, honey. Go to that freedom here on earth."

Going without Aunt Tee? That would be like losing Mama again.

Next day

The Campbelles came to Belmont on their way back to the Deep South. "We've come for our property," said Silas Campbelle.

"He's a free man," said Mas' Henley.

I must have polished all the brass off the mas'er's doorknob trying to hear what was being said.

"You had no right to sell what didn't belong to you."

"Take me to court," said Mas' Henley.

156

"We'll do just that." said the Campbelles and they stormed out of the house.

Now what do we do?

Monday again

Since Mr. Harms got run away, Miz Lilly been trying to teach William so he can get into Overton School. Unteach is better to say. William won't have none of it. He gets about nicely with two canes. Pretty soon, he'll be walking without them.

When William saw me watching from the hallway, he waved. Later, I stopped by his room. He was playing with Shadow.

"If Mr. Harms had had time, he would have said thank you," I said.

"I'm sure he would have," said William.

I think the message got through.

Week later

I write this with a heavy heart. The judge ruled that Hince was not free because he didn't b'long to Mas' Henley when he freed him. "The free papers he wrote aine worth a lame horse."

The Campbelles are coming to get Hince Monday-week on their way back south. I've cried dry. Aunt Tee and Spicy have, too. We got to stop crying and start thinking.

Monday (I hope)

Just when you get to thinking that times can't get no worse, something else happens. The weather's like that, too — fooled us into believing spring was almost here, but it snowed again today, all day.

While I was dusting Mas' Henley's study, I come across a paper that say he was selling Spicy to a man named Mobile, Alabama. They are coming for her on Tuesday-week.

Spicy and Hince say they won't be separated — rather be dead first. Talk like that makes a cold chill go up my back.

"What we gon' do?" Spicy asked me, right pitiful-like. "You the one had the idea that saved Mr. Harms. Can't you think of a way to help me and Hince?"

There are abolitionists and conductors on the underground railroad who want to help us — but we aine got time to wait on them. This time, we got to do it ourselves. We got to make an 'scape plan.

Saturday

I was reading Spicy's Bible when I turned to a page where somebody had written, "My baby girl was born on February 28, 1844."

I showed it to Spicy. "Mama must'a wrote that in the

Bible," she say, touching the words with her fingers. "She could read and write like you, Clotee."

"Like you, too, Spicy. You done learned how to write your name and lots of words. With a little more practicing you'll be writing real good."

"My mama wanted to name me Rose," Spicy said.

I wrote in Spicy's Bible, *Spicy's real name is Rose.*

"Do you believe that everything in the Bible is true?" I asked. She nodded. "I wrote your real name in your Bible. The name your mama wanted you to be called. ROSE. From now on you are Rose."

Shortly after midnight Sunday morning

There is a terrible thunderstorm raging outside. We had to call off the run. But we have to go no later than tomorrow.

Monday

I put my plan to work at first light. We dressed Spicy as a boy slave. I gave her a bundle. "It's our quilt," I told her. "You should keep it." She didn't have time to fuss with me about it.

Hince looks so much like a white man, we dressed him in one of Mas' Henley old suits I sneaked out of the attic. "I aine never had on a suit of clothes before," he said. We tucked Spicy's Bible under his arm. "You look like a for-

159

real preaching man," said Aunt Tee, hugging them both and giving them a biscuit and water for a day.

Time to go. "You know what to do, now?"

Just as we planned, we slipped down to the barn, Hince mounted Big Can. Being very careful not to make a sound, I eased them through the woods, past the cemetery, toward the river. I had already done my hugging and farewelling, so I just watched them ride downstream along the bank until they was out of sight.

I slipped back on the other side of the orchards, into the cabin where Aunt Tee and I sat holding each other until dawn. By then I had stopped trembling.

Tuesday

Hince and Spicy wasn't missed until the Campbelles come for Hince on Monday. Mas' Henley crashed into Aunt Tee's cabin, wanting us to tell him where Hince and Spicy had gone.

Aunt Tee stayed calm. "We don't know a thing 'bout that. We all went to sleep together and when we woke up same as you, they was gone."

"I don't believe a word, you're saying. I don't trust any of you," he shouted and carried on.

The Campbelles didn't seem too upset. "We'll take Canterbury's Watch, then." But when they went to get the horse it, too, was gone. Then the Campbelles say that

160

Mas' Henley was trying to cheat them. They say they was gon' take him to court.

Mas' Henley went to talking fast. "I'll pay you for your losses," he said, adding, "and for whatever inconven — (whatever that big word was) I may have caused you."

"Cash," said Silas Campbelle. "No marker."

Long 'bout that time, the slavers come for Spicy. "The boy and gal have run away," Mas' Henley told them. He had to pay the slavers back their money for Spicy.

I was beside myself with joy — joy in the morning. Serves him good. William and Miz Lilly came out on the porch. People from the Quarters were also gathering to see what was going on. Miz Lilly swooned, but nobody bothered to catch her when she fainted.

Mas' Henley and Waith set out to find Spicy and Hince but they are long gone. I was as happy as Daniel and David all in one.

Next day

I studied the sun today. It's different. I feel that winter is almost over. We will have more cold days, but the bitter times are over. We've made it through — in more ways than one.

Next day

Mas' Henley come back after a search saying he had

found and killed both Spicy and Hince. He showed no proof. Besides, where was Big Can? If he'd really caught them, he'd have brought back the horse, for sure. I don't believe him. I won't believe him. Spicy and Hince made it. If they hadn't, I'd feel it.

Day later

The Dark of the Moon is coming. It will be time for me to make my run to freedom. I should be happy. I'm an abolitionist and I want to end slavery. I can't do that being a slave on a plantation. Can I?

Later

Mr. Harms says there's no conductor on the Underground Railroad here at Belmont. If this station closes, what will happen to the runaways coming through here? Some might get caught. Some might get drowned like Rufus, Aggie, Wook, and Baby Noah. But if they had somebody here to help them — to show them the way . . .

Later

This station can't close.

Dark of the moon

A moonless night is scary, 'specially in the woods when it's cloudy.

I sang the Underground Railroad song — the one Mr. Harms said to signal him with.

Deep river, Lord. I want to cross over . . .

Mr. Harms met me as planned, rising up out of the darkness like a ghost. I felt better when I saw the runaways huddled together, fearing what was behind, fearing what was in front of them.

"Spicy and Hince aine going," I say, telling him how I'd helped them to get away.

"I've heard 'bout their getaway." Mr. Harms already knew about it?

"Have you heard if they safe?" My heart was pounding from wondering and worrying. I rather know a bad thing than to not know it.

"Our conductors tell me Spicy and Hince are in northern waters on their way to Canada. Where'd you come up with such a good idea?" he asked, smiling.

It seemed easy enough to me. Hince passed as a white man, traveling with his slave. When they got to Richmond, Hince sold Canterbury's Watch — to a kind man who will give Can a good home. I had made out the papers to show the horse had been sold to Hince Henley, a cousin of Mas' Henley's. I'd copied his signature, too.

163

Hince used the money to buy tickets on the first steamship heading north, just like I told him.

"Some of our people who were on the boat said Hince had won a large amount of money gambling with a group of wealthy young men who found him quite charming." I can just see him now, teasing, smiling. They never suspected he was a runaway slave.

"Now it's time to get you out of here, Clotee," said Mr. Harms.

"Have you found a person to be the conductor here at Belmont?"

"No we haven't."

"I'm not going with you, now. I want to stay here and be a conductor on the Underground Railroad at this station."

Next night

I didn't sleep last night and when I did it was fitful. Had I done the right thing? I kept seeing Mama's face. She was smiling and that made me feel better.

Mr. Harms made me promise to meet him at the river again tonight. I did.

"It is too dangerous for you to be a conductor," said Mr. Harms. "You're just a child."

"I'm young, sir, all due respect, but I'm not a child," I told him. "I'm an abolitionist. And I'm needed. Anyway, it was my idea that saved you from the sheriff. It was my plan that got Spicy and Hince away. I can do it."

"Oh, I have no doubt that you're up to the job," said Mr. Harms. "You are a remarkable young lady, and I'm proud of you. But don't you want to be free?"

I had talked this over with myself long and hard, so I knew what I felt. "Yes sir, I want to be free. But most of all I want slavery to end for everybody. I read in one of your papers that it's not right for anybody to be slaves. So, that's why I want to stay — to make an end to slavery."

Mr. Harms looked surprised and pleased. "You have a better understanding of freedom than most people do," said Mr. Harms. It was my time to look surprised. "Freedom is about making choices and learning from them," he said. "You've made the choice to stay here. The conductor's job is yours as long as you want it. But remember," he added, "the first sign of trouble you must get out of here. Promise?" I promised.

Into March

We are turning the ground for the new crop — backbreaking work. I'm not as afraid as I once was. I don't let my fear stop me from my work. I've started teaching a few trusted slaves to write. It's scary, because I know if they are ever really put to a hard test, they will probably turn me in. But I can't worry about that now. If I don't teach them, who will?

Miz Lilly has put me in the fields. I'm happy here, because I'm making more and more choices. I see why Spicy wanted to be out here, away from Miz Lilly and Mas' Henley who are mean as ever. So is Waith.

Since Spicy and Hince ran away, Waith's been very hard on us. We try not to give him reasons to beat us, but he still finds them. When it's time for me to teach school or when it's time for a runaway, we know how to handle Waith. See, he took a liking to Aunt Tee's root tea, so we just put a little sleeping herb in Waith's tea. He never knows the difference.

Sunday

Without us even noticing it, spring has pushed up everywhere. Easter came and went. We will celebrate Aunt Tee's birthday.

The orchards bloomed weeks ago. No late frost got them, so we'll have a good crop of apples this year. Uncle Heb's garden is in bloom. Mas' Henley finally realized how much work it takes to keep Belmont grounds looking beautiful.

April 1860

I haven't written in a long time . . . one month, maybe. Since I'm not in the Big House, it's hard for me to get paper to add to my diary. But I can scratch in the dirt, and I do. Practicing and teaching others.

William is going off to school in Missouri. and Miz Lilly is trying to die, because it aine Overton. I got a feeling that boy was really 'fected by Mr. Harms, more than anybody will ever know — other than me. Who knows, William might end up being an abolitionist. Now wouldn't that take the cake?

Mas' Henley finally got tired of eating Eva Mae's bad cooking. He sent her back to the fields, then brought in a new cook from New Orleans. Uses lots of peppers. Nobody will ever be as good as Aunt Tee at cooking fried chicken and whipped potatoes. And he knows it.

Miz Lilly has made Missy her pet. Missy don't speak and never comes to the Quarters not even to see her mama. Missy wears all kinds of pretty dresses but she can't be too happy — not living under Miz Lilly day after day.

Aunt Tee is busy all the time — picking wild greens, making potions, birthing babies — and helping me make plans for runaways. A group will be passing through Belmont in a few days.

Full moon, April, 1860

Aunt Tee sang the signal —

> *Swing low, sweet chariot,*
> *Coming for to carry me home . . .*

A group of three runaways found their way to the Belmont station tonight. One of them was a girl about ten. She was so scared. I pressed Little Bit in her hand. "She will keep you company," I said. The girl managed a weak smile. I had their passes written. Aunt Tee had their food and water ready.

Soon, a man dressed in black rowed up to the bank, making not a splash with his oars. "Come quickly." He was my partner, but we'd never talked or seen each other. Safer that way. He sounded like a foreigner. "See you next time," he said. I never saw his face. Quickly and quietly the runaways got in the boat and rowed away. I don't think I took a breath until they were out of sight.

Sitting here next to Aunt Tee in the cabin I feel good about staying for now. One day I'll see the Philadelphia, the New York, and the Boston. Maybe I'll make my own run for freedom next year — or maybe the next. Until then I have plenty of work to do.

Next day

I have just enough paper and berry ink to write one more time.

The morning bell will ring soon and I'll have to go to the fields. There's time to write a few words. I have decided to begin with F-R-E-E-D-O-M. Freedom. I let the memory pictures take shape in my mind. Mr. Harms is

168

safe and able to go on with his work. Hince and Spicy are free and together. I remembered the little girl I'd helped the night before and I smiled. My doll Little Bit would be free before me. Freedom. I remembered what Mr. Harms had said about choices. I looked at the letters more closely. For the first time freedom showed me a clear picture.

A picture of me.

Epilogue

During the summer of 1939, when Clotee Henley was ninety-two years old, she was interviewed by Lucille Avery, a student at Fisk University, which is in Nashville, Tennessee. Miss Avery, along with many other writers, had been hired by the government to visit aging slaves and record their stories. Clotee's story first appeared in the *Virginia Chronicle*, summer 1940.

Miss Avery visited Clotee at her home in Hampton, Virginia. And for over two months, Clotee shared her diaries, photos, and papers. From Miss Avery's research, we know that Clotee served as a conductor on the Underground Railroad, helping over one hundred and fifty slaves get to freedom, and as a spy for the Union Army from 1862–1865. She was awarded a commendation by General Ulysses S. Grant for her valor.

During the war however, life at Belmont changed forever. Briley Waith was at Fort Sumter with Edmund Ruffin, Sr., who fired the first shot. Mas' Henley lost an arm at the battle of Fredericksburg, and Miz Lilly went mad when Yankees camped on Belmont grounds and turned the Big House into a Union hospital. Aunt Tee used all her knowledge of roots and herbs to save the lives of soldiers, even when army doctors snickered and called it voodoo. They stopped laughing when she saved more lives than they did. Sadly, Aunt Tee died of cholera on Christmas Day 1864, months before the war ended. She was buried beside Uncle Heb in the plantation cemetery. When Missy's mama died, she ran off and later married a Buffalo Soldier out West.

After the war, Mr. Harms arranged for Clotee to travel up North, where she received a hero's welcome. After several business failures, Mr. Harms moved to Scotland where he dropped out of sight. Although Clotee never met Sojourner Truth, she did meet Frederick Douglass, with whom she corresponded until his death in 1895.

In 1875, Clotee returned to Virginia, where she attended Virginia Colored Women's Institute, then dedicated her life to the education of former slaves, women's suffrage, equal rights, and justice for all people regardless of race, creed, or nationality.

Inside her diaries, Miss Avery found two other interesting items that help conclude Clotee's story. One was a photo and packet of letters from Dr. William Monroe Henley, who had become a professor of philosophy at Oberlin College in Ohio. He had been disinherited by his father for taking a stand against prejudice. "Through education Mr. Harms did more to destroy slavery than all the laws on the books could legislate," he wrote to Clotee in 1891.

There was another photo of a handsome elderly couple, surrounded by a large family. On the back was written:

> *To our beloved sister-friend, Clotee*
> *from Hince and Rose Henley and family*
> *50th Wedding Anniversary*
> *Louisville, Kentucky, 1910.*

Spicy is holding a Bible in her hand, and Hince has a quilt folded over one knee. There is an old article from a Kentucky newspaper attached to the photo, praising Hince for being one of the finest horse trainers in the racing business.

Clotee never married or had children of her own, but when she died on May 6, 1941, hundreds of her former students attended the funeral. As a teacher she had challenged them. As an activist, she had inspired them. As a friend, she had encouraged them. Clotee Henley's legacy lives on in the epitaph engraved on her gravestone:

FREEDOM IS MORE THAN A WORD

Life in America
in 1859

Historical Note

The first Africans were brought to the Virginia colony as indentured servants in 1619. Slavery was a well-established institution in the United States by the 1850s. But the resistance against it was equally old and persistent.

Virginia legislators, who were often wealthy planters, took the lead in passing laws that safeguarded their rights as slaveholders, discouraged runaways, and protected themselves against insurrections. These laws were known as "Slave Codes" or "Black Codes." As a matter of record Virginia and other Southern states had hundreds of Slave Codes on their books. For example one stated that ". . . the status of the mother determined whether the child was born free or slave." Others forbade interracial marriages and outlawed the education of slaves. Blacks could not hold public meetings, or testify against a white man in court. Any slave suspected of running away was dealt with severely.

Resistance against slavery took many forms, beginning first with the captives themselves. They used work slow downs, arson, murder, suicide, and armed rebellion to gain their freedom. When they could run, most did. In fact, the runaway problem was always a pressing one for most slaveholders. As early as 1642, Virginia introduced a fugitive slave order that penalized all those who helped runaway slaves.

Even the United States Constitution contained a fugitive slave clause. Most slaves who managed to reach a free state could live as a free person. But with the passage of the revised Fugitive Slave Law of 1850, the government allowed slaveholders to go into free states and recapture their "property."

In 1854, Anthony Burns, a fugitive slave, was arrested and jailed in Boston, Massachusetts, but Bostonians attacked the federal courthouse and attempted to rescue him. Burns was returned to his master, but he was later freed. Burns' case, and others like his, brought the issue of slavery to the forefront.

As early as 1688, a group of Pennsylvania Quakers signed the "Germantown Mennonite Resolution Against Slavery." It was the first written document that protested slavery in the North American colonies and marked the beginning of a formalized abolitionist movement. Since that time, blacks and whites, men and women, Southerners and Northerners organized with the purpose of abolishing slavery. One of the largest and most effective of these organizations was the American Anti-Slavery Society, founded in Philadelphia in 1833. New York, Philadelphia, and Boston were the centers of the movement, but anti-slavery groups flourished all over the country.

William Lloyd Garrison and Frederick Douglass spoke out strongly against slavery. Women such as Harriet Beecher Stowe and Sojourner Truth also made an impact through their lectures and writing. Truth had been enslaved in New York, one of the last Northern states to abolish slavery. Stowe's book *Uncle Tom's Cabin* sold out its first printing in less than a week because people were fascinated by her depiction of slave life. Southerners tried to argue that the book was fiction, but people read it as fact.

To help runaways make the long and dangerous trip to freedom, often to Canada, abolitionists formed a network of people who served as "conductors" on an "underground railroad." It was not underground and it wasn't a railroad, but a route by which slaves were taken to freedom. Good and decent people — farmers, teachers, housewives, laborers, college presidents, and even children — risked heavy fines and imprisonment to take part in this dangerous venture. Some conductors were caught and served time in prison but nothing could stop people from running away from tyranny or assisting those who would try.

One of the best-known conductors on the Underground Railroad was Harriet Tubman, a fugitive slave. Although there was a price on her head, she continued to serve as a conductor, leading hundreds of runaways to freedom in Canada.

Slaveholders had their sights on the fertile lands out

West. They wanted to expand slavery west of the Mississippi River. Abolitionists were determined to stop them. Dred Scott, a Missouri slave, sued his master for freedom because he had been taken to live for a while in free territory. The United States Supreme Court ruled in 1857 that a slave could not sue for his freedom because he was "property." The court added that "no black man had rights that a white man [had] to respect." The decision was a bitter defeat for anti-slavery forces, because it disenfranchised all blacks — whether free or slave. Now, neither could vote, hold public office, patent an invention, serve on a jury, or testify against a white person in any court of law. African Americans were not considered citizens.

While most abolitionists chose to end slavery through peaceful means, some were beginning to think that slavery could not end without an armed struggle. Henry Highland Garnet was an outspoken black leader who called for violent resistance to slavery long before anyone else agreed with him. Another man who believed that freedom would have to be won by the sword was John Brown.

In October 1859, John Brown, along with five blacks and thirteen whites, led a raid on the federal armory at Harpers Ferry in Virginia (now located in West Virginia). Brown planned to organize a slave army made up of fugitives who would fight for their own freedom. Their suc-

178

cess would inspire others to take up arms. Colonel Robert E. Lee led the federal counterattack. Most of Brown's men were killed in the fight. One man escaped. John Brown and several others were captured and hanged. Before he died, Brown warned the South to end slavery or risk God's wrath.

To anti-slavery sympathizers Brown had become a hero, a martyr. Songs were written about him and schoolchildren honored him. In the South, Brown was dismissed as a madman, symbolic of all abolitionists.

The South was confident in 1859 that their way of life would go on indefinitely. But change was inevitable. The Republicans were a new political party, organized in 1854. In less than five years they had won numerous seats in Congress. Abraham Lincoln from Illinois was nominated to run for the presidency on the Republican ticket. He stood a fair chance of winning the 1860 election. His position seemed moderate, nothing radical. He supported Congressional prohibition of slavery in Western territories and the gradual abolition of slavery in the United States. Some abolitionist groups felt Lincoln's position was not strong enough. Some leaders, especially in Virginia, realized that slavery could not last much longer and the gradual approach seemed plausible. Sadly, these people were in the minority. South Carolina declared that if Lincoln won the election, the state would secede from the Union.

Meanwhile political posturing had done very little to ease the lives of the 4,000,000 slaves who lived on the plantations throughout the South. Most of them lived in miserable conditions, yet they never lost hope. It is reflected in the songs they sang:

Swing low, sweet chariot,
Comin' for to carry me home.
A band of angels comin' after me.
Comin' for to carry me home.

The words were coded. "Home" was freedom. The "sweet chariot" was a wagon or some vehicle that they hoped would take them to freedom. The "band of angels" were the abolitionists. Slaves sang songs for many reasons. Often, their singing was misunderstood as a display of happiness and contentment.

The conditions under which a slave lived depended largely upon the personality of his master. Planters were the masters of their estates who conducted their affairs autonomously. Their wives, children, and slaves were under their authority and could be treated any way the planters chose within the limits of the law (and the laws were always in the slaveholders' favor).

The mistress of the plantation was generally younger than her husband, sometimes by as much as twenty years. Girls married at fourteen and were expected to have children as soon as possible. But the rearing of the children

180

was usually left to slave women who nursed and cared for them through infancy.

The master's children grew up on the plantation and sometimes played with slave children because there were no other children around. Sometimes slave children were half brothers and sisters, sharing the same father. Loneliness caused some mistresses to select a slave woman to be her confidante and companion. The relationship was rarely allowed to develop into real friendship. Each situation was as unique as the people who were involved.

In 1859 most slaveholders owned no more than twenty-five to thirty field hands and four to five household servants who took care of the family's personal needs. Field slaves' lives were filled with endless misery and suffering. Death was welcomed. They worked from sunup until sundown, driven by fear and brutality. Their diets were poor, and so was their health care. People aged early and died too young. Children died needless deaths and the elderly were turned out to fend for themselves when they were no longer useful. The huts the slaves lived in were small, crowded, and filthy, and up to as many as ten people would sleep in one 20' × 20' cabin.

Those servants who worked in the "Big House" had a few advantages, but there were even more disadvantages. As grand as the old mansions were, they didn't have any of the modern conveniences we take for granted today. Work in the Big House never ceased. Servants were expected to do all the washing, ironing, cooking, serving of food, cleaning, caring for children, and even fanning. House slaves were on call twenty-four hours a day.

Even though every effort was made to keep slaves ignorant, many of them learned to read and write, using any opportunity available to them. Then they, in turn, taught others. Secret teachers — who were sometimes disguised abolitionists, free blacks, or fellow slaves — formed "pit schools." They dug a hole large enough for two to four people. They pulled a lid made of brush over the top. Down in the pit they practiced their lessons with less chance of being caught.

Being discovered was an ever-present danger. Literate slaves were usually sold to the Deep South where escape was nearly impossible. Gabriel Prosser and Nat Turner were literate men who had led rebellions in Richmond, and Southampton, Virginia. Slaveowners knew they were outnumbered on some rural plantations, so masters stayed on the lookout for budding insurrections. They used bribery, threats, and fear to coerce slaves into betraying anyone who might appear suspicious. It was not uncommon for the informer to end up being sold himself.

Frederick Douglass, publisher of *The North Star,* wrote in his autobiography that "No man who can read will stay a slave very long."

Sojourner Truth, who had been a slave in New York,

182

said, "Slavery must be destroyed. God will not stand with wrong, never mind how right you think you be."

And Harriet Tubman said, "I mean to live free or die."

Emboldened by the spirit of these and other freedom fighters, the stage was set for slaves who dared to defy their masters.

People didn't know in 1859 that the nation was on the threshold of a terrible war that would kill thousands. But the unfolding political drama would climax when Edmund Ruffin, Sr., a Virginian, fired the first shot at Fort Sumter, South Carolina, a few months after Abraham Lincoln was elected President of the United States. The war ended five years later in 1865. The cost had been high on both sides. The lives of the 4,000,000 slaves living in the United States and the 250,000 fugitive slaves that had escaped to Canada would be changed forever.

They were free at last.

The cabins in the slave quarters could be as small as 12' × 12' or 12' × 16'. They were made of wood with dirt floors and windows without panes. They had to accommodate about ten to twelve people.

Work in the fields was grueling. And slaves rarely had enough to eat to sustain them through the long, exhausting days.

Five generations of slaves on a Carolina plantation.

Slave mothers and children were often separated by plantation owners who held little regard for their family relationships, as this illustration depicts.

Slaves had to carry special passes, such as this one written by Jefferson Davis, if they went anywhere beyond the boundaries of their plantation. Without a pass, they were assumed to be attempting escape and would be severely beaten.

RAFFLE

Mr. Joseph Jennings respectfully informs his friends and the public that, at the request of many acquaintances, he has been induced to purchase from Mr. Osborne, of Missouri, the celebrated

DARK BAY HORSE, "STAR,"

Aged five years, square trotter and warranted sound; with a new light Trotting Buggy and Harness; also, the dark, stout

MULATTO GIRL, "SARAH,"

Aged about twenty years, general house servant, valued at *nine hundred dollars*, and guaranteed, and

Will be Raffled for

At 4 o'clock P. M., February first, at the selection hotel of the subscribers. The above is as represented, and those persons who may wish to engage in the usual practice of raffling, will, I assure them, be perfectly satisfied with their destiny in this affair.

The whole is valued at its just worth, fifteen hundred dollars; fifteen hundred

CHANCES AT ONE DOLLAR EACH.

The Raffle will be conducted by gentlemen selected by the interested subscribers present. Five nights will be allowed to complete the Raffle. BOTH OF THE ABOVE DESCRIBED CAN BE SEEN AT MY STORE, No. 78 Common St., second door from Camp, at from 9 o'clock A. M. to 2 P. M.

Highest throw to take the first choice; the lowest throw the remaining prize, and the fortunate winners will pay twenty dollars each for the refreshments furnished on the occasion.

N. B. No chances recognized unless paid for previous to the commencement.

JOSEPH JENNINGS.

Slave trading, like animal trading, was considered a business. This broadside announces a raffle with two prizes: a horse and a slave.

$200 Reward.

RANAWAY from the subscriber, on the night of Thursday, the 30th of Sepember.

FIVE NEGRO SLAVES,

To-wit: one Negro man, his wife, and three children.

The man is a black negro, full height, very erect, his face a little thin. He is about forty years of age, and calls himself *Washington Reed*, and is known by the name of Washington. He is probably well dressed, possibly takes with him an ivory headed cane, and is of good address. Several of his teeth are gone.

Mary, his wife, is about thirty years of age, a bright mulatto woman, and quite stout and strong.

The oldest of the children is a boy, of the name of FIELDING, twelve years of age, a dark mulatto, with heavy eyelids. He probably wore a new cloth cap.

MATILDA, the second child, is a girl, six years of age, rather a dark mulatto, but a bright and smart looking child.

MALCOLM, the youngest, is a boy, four years old, a lighter mulatto than the last, and about equally as bright. He probably also wore a cloth cap. If examined, he will be found to have a swelling at the navel.

Washington and Mary have lived at or near St. Louis, with the subscriber, for about 15 years.

It is supposed that they are making their way to Chicago, and that a white man accompanies them, that they will travel chiefly at night, and most probably in a covered wagon.

A reward of $150 will be paid for their apprehension, so that I can get them, if taken within one hundred miles of St. Louis, and $200 if taken beyond that, and secured so that I can get them, and other reasonable additional charges, if delivered to the subscriber, or to THOMAS ALLEN, Esq., at St. Louis, Mo. The above negroes, for the last few years, have been in possession of Thomas Allen, Esq., of St. Louis.

WM. RUSSELL.

Posters announcing a reward for the capture and return of runaway slaves were very common.

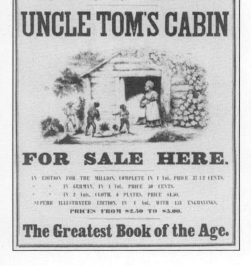

Harriet Beecher Stowe wrote Uncle Tom's Cabin *in 1852 to expose slavery as "a system so . . . cruel and unjust." By 1856, over two million copies had been sold, second only to the Bible in sales. When President Lincoln met Harriet Beecher Stowe, he said, "So you're the little lady who started this big war."*

Charles T. Webber's famous 19th-century painting, The Underground Railroad, *which depicts refugee slaves arriving at Levi Coffin's Indiana farm, an important station on the railroad.*

A pass for the Underground Railroad. It reads: "My Dear Mrs. Post: Please shelter this Sister from the house of bondage till five o'clock — this afternoon — She will then be sent on to the land of freedom. Yours truly, Fred K." Fred K. was Frederick Douglass, the famous escaped slave. He became a well-known lecturer and founded the abolitionist newspaper, The North Star.

Harriet Tubman was the most famous conductor on the Underground Railroad. A runaway slave from Maryland, she made about twenty trips from the North into the South and rescued more than three hundred slaves.

A freed slave, Sojourner Truth was one of the most famous abolitionists and activists for the rights of blacks and women. Although she was illiterate, Truth could quote the Bible word for word and was a powerful and affecting preacher.

Words and music to "Go Down, Moses." While slaveowners believed religion had a placating effect on slaves, the Bible and its stories were a great source of strength and inspiration to seek freedom. In this traditional negro spiritual, the slaves identified with the Jews of Egypt who were also held in bondage by the cruel Pharaoh. Harriet Tubman was said to be the Moses of the slaves' song, helping runaway slaves escape from "Egypt's land."

SWEET POTATO PIE

Two big sweet potatoes grown in the garden patch out back.
2 cups of sugar (trade with the Big House cook).
          If not available use 1 cup of molasses or honey.
1/4 pound of butter–scrape from the insides of the butter churn.
2 tsp. vanilla
1 tsp. of cinnamon
1/2 tsp. nutmeg
If you can't get spices then use a tablespoon of rum.
1/2 cup of milk, if somebody you know gets to milk the cow.
4 eggs. Send the children to gather eggs in the hay.

Peel cooked sweet potatoes and mash them together with butter, sugar, and spices. Beat eggs and milk together in a separate bowl, then slowly add mixture to the potatoes. Beat mixture briskly until it is creamy and smooth.

Pour potatoes into a pie crust shell. Cook until firm. If you can stick a knife in the middle of the pie and none of the mixture sticks, it is ready. Serve after it has cooled.

This recipe is based on information from slave narratives and plantation diaries.

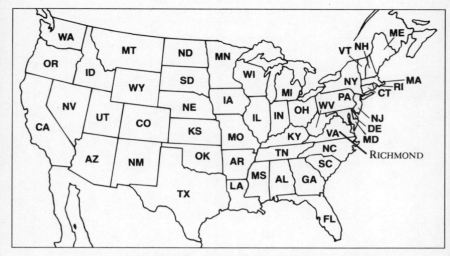

Modern map of the continental United States, showing the approximate location of Belmont Plantation, near Richmond, Virginia.

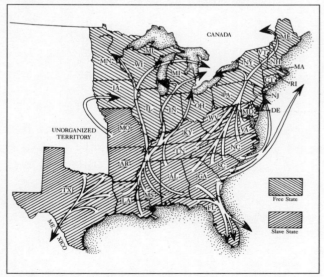

This map shows escape routes on the Underground Railroad, as well as which were slave states and which were free states in 1859.

About the Author

Award-winning author Patricia C. McKissack says, "I was inspired to write *A Picture of Freedom* by the story I grew up hearing about my great-great-great-grandmother, Lizzie Passmore, who had been a slave in Barbour County, Alabama. Although it was against the law, she had someow learned to read and write. After the Civil War ended, she started teaching children in her home near Clayton, Alabama. Unfortunately that is all I know about this remarkable woman, but it gave me the foundation upon which I built Clotee's story."

Although this is McKissack's first full-length work of fiction, she has written over sixty books for children, including *Flossie and the Fox, Mirandy and Brother Wind*, a Caldecott Honor Book, and *The Dark-Thirty: Southern Tales of the Supernatural*, a Newbery Honor Book. She has co-authored with her husband, Fredrick, numerous nonfiction books, which include the Coretta Scott King Award winners, *Sojourner Truth: Ain't I a Woman?* and *Christmas in the Big House, Christmas in the Quarters*. She also co-authored with her son, Fredrick, Jr., *Black Dia-*

mond: The Story of the Negro Baseball Leagues, which was a Coretta Scott King Honor Book.

While researching *Christmas in the Big House,* the McKissacks visited six plantations in the Tidewater area of Virginia. "It was natural for me to set the Clotee story there because it was so fresh in my mind and we had tons of material that found a place in this book."

McKissack says her teaching experiences helped her understand how Clotee might have learned to read and write. "Finding Clotee's voice was the most difficult problem I had to overcome. Once I heard, in my head, how she would say things, then the story was easy to tell. She told it to me."

McKissack lives with her husband in Chesterfield, Missouri, a suburb of St. Louis. When they aren't traveling for research, they travel for fun.

*Honoring Lizzie Passmore
my great-great-great grandmother
who dared to learn and teach*

Acknowledgments

Grateful acknowledgment is made for permission to reprint the following:

Cover portrait: A detail from *The Cotton Pickers* by Winslow Homer. United States, 1836–1918. Oil on canvas. Acquisition made possible through Museum Trustees: Robert O. Anderson; R. Stanton Avery; B. Gerald Cantor; Edward W. Carter; Justin Dart; Charles E. Ducommun; Mrs. Daniel Frost; Julian Ganz, Jr.; Dr. Armand Hammer; Harry Lenart; Dr. Franklin D. Murphy; Mrs. Joan Palevsky; Richard E. Sherwood; Maynard J. Toll; and Hal B. Wallis. Los Angeles County Museum, Los Angeles, California.

Cover background: A detail from *The Underground Railroad* by Charles T. Webber, Cincinnati Art Museum, Subscription Fund Purchase, Cincinnati, Ohio.

Page 185 (top): Slave cabin, The Library of Congress.

Page 185 (bottom): Cotton pickers, ibid.

Page 186: Slave family, Schomburg Center for Research in Black Culture, The New York Public Library, New York, New York.

Page 187 (top): Slave mother separated from her child, Culver Pictures, New York, New York.

Page 187 (bottom): Visitation pass, The Museum of the Confederacy, Richmond, Virginia.

Page 188: Raffle broadside, The New-York Historical Society, New York, New York.

Page 189 (top): Reward poster, The Library of Congress.

Page 189 (bottom): *Uncle Tom's Cabin* poster, The New-York Historical Society, New York, New York.

Page 190 (top): *The Underground Railroad* by Charles T. Webber, Cincinnati Art Museum, Cincinnati, Ohio.

Page 190 (bottom): Pass for the Underground Railroad, Department of Rare Books and Special Collections, University of Rochester Library, Rochester, New York.

Page 191: Harriet Tubman, The Library of Congress.

Page 192: Sojourner Truth, The Library of Congress.

Page 193: Words and music to "Go Down, Moses," from *Songs of the Civil War*, Dover Publications, Inc., New York, New York.

Page 194: Recipe, courtesy of the author, based on information from slave narratives and plantation diaries.

Page 195: Maps by Heather Saunders.

Other books in the *Dear America* series

A Journey to the New World
The Diary of Remember Patience Whipple
by Kathryn Lasky

The Winter of Red Snow
The Revolutionary War Diary of Abigail Jane Stewart
by Kristiana Gregory

When Will This Cruel War Be Over?
The Civil War Diary of Emma Simpson
by Barry Denenberg

Across the Wide and Lonesome Prairie
The Oregon Trail Diary of Hattie Campbell
by Kristiana Gregory

While the events described and some of the characters in this book may be based on actual historical events and real people, Clotee is a fictional character, created by the author, and her diary and its epilogue are works of fiction.

Copyright © 1997 by Patricia C. McKissack.

—ɱ—

All rights reserved. Published by Scholastic Inc.
557 Broadway, New York, New York 10012.
DEAR AMERICA®, SCHOLASTIC, and associated logos
are trademarks and/or registered trademarks of Scholastic Inc.

No part of this publication may be reproduced, or stored in a retrieval
system, or transmitted in any form or by any means,
electronic, mechanical, photocopying, recording, or otherwise,
without written permission of the publisher.
For information regarding permissions, write to Scholastic Inc., Attention:
Permissions Department, 557 Broadway, New York, NY 10012.

Library of Congress Cataloging-in-Publication Data available.

ISBN 0-590-25988-1;
ISBN 0-439-44559-0 (pbk.)

10 9 8 7 6 5 4 3 2   02 03 04 05 06

Printed in the U.S.A. 23
First paperback printing, October 2002

—ɱ—

A Light in the Storm

The Civil War Diary of Amelia Martin

by Karen Hesse

Scholastic Inc. New York

Fenwick Island, Delaware
1860

Gains for All Our Losses
by R. H. Stoddard

There are gains for all our losses —
    There are balms for all our pains;
But when youth, the dream, departs,
It takes something from our hearts,
    And never comes again.

We are stronger, and are better,
    Under manhood's sterner reign;
Still we feel that something sweet
Followed youth with flying feet,
    And will never come again.

Something beautiful is vanished,
    And we sigh for it in vain;
We behold it everywhere —
On the earth and in the air —
    But it never comes again.

Monday, December 24, 1860
Stormy. Wind N.E. Light.

I rowed across the Ditch this morning. Wish there were some other way to reach the mainland. Wind bit at my knuckles and stung my nose. Pulled hard at the oars to keep warm, landing Bayville beach in record time.

Bayville looked festive in its wreaths and ribbons and windows gold with candle glow.

Visited with Uncle Edward briefly. He has shaved off his beard! He looked so new with his whiskers gone, his chin so pale and tender. Beardless, he resembles Father less, but still enough. Even now, a stranger would know the two fair-haired men as brothers.

Uncle Edward slipped a package to me from under the counter. "Merry Christmas, Wickie," he said. "Open this tonight."

I hugged and thanked him, then handed over my present to him. He weighed it in his good hand, guessing.

It is *On the Origin of Species* by a man named Charles

Darwin. Mr. Warner recommended Darwin's book for Uncle Edward particularly.

At the confectionery, I purchased sweets for Father. Bought handkerchiefs for Keeper Dunne, and for William. Bought gloves for Grandmother.

But Mother's gift is best of all. I picked it up after finishing Grandmother's chores. Dear diary, let me tell you. Mother loathes the sea. Even though our rooms and the Lighthouse set back a good distance from shore, still we hear the waves breaking, the bell-buoy boat clanging. Mother longs to move back to the mainland, to Grandmother's cottage, away from Fenwick Island and the Light.

I expected Reenie O'Connell to do a good job. Day after day, she would arrive at the schoolhouse, her hands smudged with charcoal. But this afternoon, when I saw the finished drawing Reenie had made for Mother, it exceeded even my hopes. A charcoal window, captured in just a few strokes and smudges, the heavy hinged door, all in shadow, opening onto Commerce Street. "You have got the cottage just right," I told Reenie.

I paid her and brought the sketch to the Worthington house to show William, and to deliver his Christmas gift. All the Worthingtons approved of Reenie's sketch. Even Daniel.

William walked me back to the skiff. "Can you come skating with me and Daniel this week?"

I asked if the ice was thick enough for skating.

William grinned. "Not yet."

William! He is forever taking risks. That is how we became such good friends. Because of his risk taking.

It's almost nine now. Near the end of my watch. Father insists I take first watch. I don't mind. Sometimes the colors of the sunset paint the sky beyond the balcony of the Light. Then all the sea is awash with orange and dappled rose.

Only three hours more until midnight, until Christmas.

Father should be out to relieve me soon. The lamps are all burning well. The wind remains low. An occasional fit of rain slicks the glass surrounding the Light, but it is not a freezing rain and not too worrisome.

All the Christmas gifts are ready and waiting for tomorrow.

You, my diary, were in the package from Uncle Edward. Written upon the brown paper parcel, in Uncle Edward's peculiar script, was this note. *Open while you are on watch tonight, Wickie. You need a friend on the island. This might do.*

On the first page Uncle Edward has copied out a poem. It is a sad poem about gains and losses, about fleeting dreams, and the end of youth. I wonder why he chose to begin my

7

diary with such a poem, but Uncle Edward is wise. Someday I will understand. My uncle knows me well. I do need a friend on Fenwick Island. You, dear diary, should do perfectly.

Tuesday, December 25, 1860
Stormy. Wind S.E. Moderate.

Christmas morning passed pleasantly. While Father, Keeper Dunne, and I cleaned the glass in the lantern room, Mother baked and made a good meal for us. Her happy presence in the kitchen cheered me mightily.

We gathered for Christmas dinner in the early afternoon, downstairs, in Keeper Dunne's quarters. Everything is dark there. Heavy draperies hang across his windows. Not even the light of the sea gets through. And Keeper Dunne looks just like his surroundings. Dark eyes droop at the same angle as his mustaches. But our Christmas was so pleasant, even Keeper Dunne smiled during our party.

Mother was at her best today. Sometimes she is waspish with Father. She can't seem to forgive him for landing us on this island off the coast of Delaware where the work never ends and the wind never ceases, where the sand is forever scratching at our skin and grinding between our teeth. Where nothing she plants survives the restless Atlantic and the ever-hungry water rats.

Keeper Dunne ignores the trouble between my parents. I try to do the same. I dream that things will be good again between them, the way they were before we came to live here, when Father commanded his own ship and came home to us at the cottage in Bayville, after months at sea. Mother and Father never fought then.

After our meal of pork, corn cakes, and beans, at last we opened Christmas gifts. Father gave me ribbons, one a dark, dark brown to match my hair, one the gray-green of the sea when it runs wild with spume. He also carved a model of our Lighthouse, hollowed out, so I might place a candle within its walls. I told him I loved his gifts and threw my arms around him.

Mother says that at fifteen I am too old to be so affectionate. When I am at school, assisting Mr. Warner, I try to behave as Mother says. But even then it is hard not to hug a child who has just read his own name for the first time.

Father has a way of smiling with his eyes when he is happy, and today his eyes were as gay as ever I can remember. "I'm pleased you like your gifts, Wickie," he said.

Though my Christian name is Amelia, Father has called

me Wickie for more than a year now, since he became Assistant Lightkeeper and we moved here to Fenwick Island. Wickie is a name of affection bestowed upon lightkeepers — I suppose because we are always tending the wicks. Mother hates to have me called so. She fears it will bind me to a lightkeeper's life. But I am already bound . . . in my heart and my soul, I am bound!

Mother handed me a small bundle. "Merry Christmas, Amelia," she said.

I opened her package to find two new aprons. What a sacrifice such a gift was for her. To sew when her hands and fingers often ache these days.

"Thank you, Mother," I said, coming over and kissing her dark hair. She blinked up at me, tears pooling in her eyes. "It is a wonderful gift," I told her. And I meant it.

Then I gave Mother Reenie's drawing of the cottage.

I could tell right away how very much she liked it. She sat in silence for several moments. Then, "Oh, Amelia, how lovely, how very, very lovely," and she would not let the little charcoal drawing out of her sight the rest of the afternoon. Father offered to fashion a frame for her and Mother thanked him, and there was a flicker of warmth between them in that moment that was for me the greatest gift of the entire day. If only the day could have ended then.

10

But we tarried by Keeper Dunne's fire. Father and I sang "Jingle Bells" and "Listen to the Mockingbird" and Mother and Keeper Dunne joined in. But then Father sang "The Old Gray Mare," the song used for Abraham Lincoln's campaign, though Father sang the original words, not the words about Lincoln coming out of the wilderness. And then he sang "Darling Nelly Gray," a song Mother abhors because of its abolitionist sentiment. Shortly after, Mother retired upstairs to our quarters, carrying Reenie's drawing. The spots on her cheeks told everything. She was angry at Father again, for bringing up the troubles so much on our minds these days.

Like Mother, I once believed unquestioningly in the institution of slavery. Then, a little over a year ago, a storm shipwrecked a family of fugitive slaves here on the island. That is when I first truly noticed the difference between my parents. Father wished to help the fugitives along to Philadelphia, to freedom. Mother insisted we turn them over to the authorities immediately, so they might be returned to their owner. You see, dear diary, Delaware is a border state. There are those here who oppose slavery, but there are also many who uphold it.

I remember rescuing the five limp, salt-streaked bodies clinging to their battered raft. A male, a female, and three bedraggled children. I had always thought Mother was right, that slaves were simpleminded. But these slaves, there was something in their eyes, in their way with one another, that made me question how simpleminded, in fact, they were. Still Mother insisted that getting them back home was the greatest kindness we could do them. Father disagreed. While they argued, our neighbor, Oda Lee Monkton, turned the fugitives over to the slave catchers and collected the reward.

Such a memory to recall on Christmas Day!

I left our rooms well before dark with a saucer of tasty bits for Napoleon. This past summer, Mother lost her entire garden to rats. I rowed to Bayville that very day and found Napoleon. He was a half-grown barn cat, then.

He is full grown now and worth his weight in gold. Our rat problem is greatly reduced. And he is my dearest companion on the island. Father and Keeper Dunne, too, find he makes for good company in the long, quiet hours on watch.

Napoleon ate the drippings and shreds of Christmas dinner eagerly, then scrubbed the saucer and himself, purring all the while. I stayed to play with him as long as I dared before running up the spiral stair to assist Father and Keeper Dunne in our nightly kindling of Fenwick Light.

Thursday, December 27, 1860
Fair. Wind S.W. High.
Inspection at 2:30 P.M. Condition very good.

No time to write yesterday. Today the Inspector from the Lighthouse Board came. He made no complaint against our work. He declared the Lighthouse trim and tidy, though he recommended a fresh coat of paint come spring. The salt, sand, and wind have been unusually hard on the buildings.

He was so pleased with our care of the station, remarking on the condition of the brass, on the polish of the glass. With his compliments coming so freely, he took us all by surprise at the very end of his inspection when he spoke unkindly of me.

He said Father and Keeper Dunne should alter their watches to eliminate the need for mine. He said I should not be standing watch over the Light. "She is little more than a child. And a female, at that. How can she make decisions in time of emergency?"

My temper sparked. How dare he question my ability? It is Father's opinion that in this year alone at least three men would have drowned but for my actions. I wear a scar across my cheek from rescuing William Worthington the September before last, when I was fourteen. Yet it would do me no good to show my anger to Inspector Howle.

13

Father defended me. He told Inspector Howle of my position as Assistant Teacher at the Bayville School. "She has been teaching two years," Father said. "If her work here at the Light does not demonstrate her reliability to you, contact Mr. Warner. Let him speak for her."

The Inspector looked into my face. I wished I could make the freckles across my nose disappear. Wished I could slim the lines of my cheeks, round as a baby's bottom.

Inspector Howle said if I was in service as an assistant teacher, then I must have enough to keep me occupied without the additional work of a Light station. How could I possibly get enough sleep standing five-hour watches?

"My work at school ends at one in the afternoon," I told him. "I am always back here in time to take first watch. I begin at four, finish at nine. I get by well."

The Inspector stared at Father disapprovingly. "You have raised your daughter to contradict a representative of the United States Lighthouse Board?"

Father put his hands on his hips and looked the Inspector directly in the eye. "I've raised my daughter to be honest, Inspector Howle. A quality the Board values highly, if I am not mistaken."

I do not overlook a single task, from the filling of the oil wells to the polishing of the doorknobs. Not a speck of dust do

14

I leave. There isn't a single situation for which the Lightkeeping manual does not give step-by-step instructions, and since we came here nearly one and a half years ago, I have read from that manual as often as the tide has turned. If I drop oil on a lens, I clean it with spirits of wine. I know precisely how to trim a wick and adjust a flame. Precisely.

I don't ask for pay for my work. Nor even acknowledgment. I simply ask to be allowed to attend the Light. It is enough for me to know that by my actions, men are guided safely to port. I am good at my Lighthouse duties. I should continue.

When he left, Inspector Howle did not cite us for one single thing. Nor, in the end, did he instruct Keeper Dunne to relieve me of my watches.

So I am allowed to continue, unofficially, as assistant to the Assistant and Head Lightkeepers.

Inspector Howle shall see. In time I shall show the entire United States Lighthouse Board. I can keep the Light as well as anyone. And someday, I shall be given a Light of my own.

Friday, December 28, 1860
Clear. Wind N.W. High.

Cold has set in early. The millpond in Bayville is frozen over and William has started skating upon it, though I have yet to find time to join him.

A skin of ice borders the edges of Fenwick Ditch, making my daily trips to and from the mainland more difficult.

If the Ditch freezes fully over this winter, I shall walk across the water from island to mainland and back again. Mother would shackle me if she caught me. But wouldn't it be fine to do such a thing!

Crossed the Ditch this afternoon to pick up supplies in Bayville and see to Grandmother.

On my way to her cottage, I passed some men who were drinking in the street. One chased after me. I ran from him, my skirts hiked up. He didn't stand a chance of catching me. Even in my skirts and cloak I run faster than most boys. I thought first of running to Uncle Edward, but made Grandmother's in less time.

Didn't dare tell Grandmother what had happened. The man who had chased me came puffing past her window several minutes later, shouting drunkenly. He seemed already to have forgotten me. I asked if Grandmother knew the cause of the man's midday revelries.

Grandmother said three Negroes were hanged earlier today in the jail yard. At one o'clock. Just an hour before I passed.

After I did the washing up and the ironing, brought in wood and cleaned out the ashes, Grandmother asked me to sit and visit awhile. She asked after Mother. I told her about the inspection and how Mother and I received excellent scores on our housekeeping, and Father and Keeper Dunne and I on the accuracy of our logs.

Grandmother wanted to know if Father was treating Mother well.

I struggled to keep from losing my temper.

Grandmother said, "The captain of a vessel shall be not governed by his mate. But a married landsman shall." She said Father was not captain of his vessel anymore and he should remember that.

Grandmother is angry because Mother is too busy to come ashore often. But she is also still furious with Father. Five years ago, Father was stripped of command of his ship.

He knowingly broke the law by transporting north the leader of a slave rebellion. When the rebel slave was discovered on Father's ship, Father lost everything.

17

I was so young when it happened, only ten. But I remember feeling shame. I managed at last to put it out of mind. That's where it stayed until last year when we plucked the family of fugitive slaves from the sea and the whole question rose up again.

After washing up from tea, banking Grandmother's fire, and preparing a light meal for her dinner, I ran all the way to Uncle Edward's store. Uncle listened to my talk about the executed Negroes.

"That's the way it is here in Sussex County, Wickie."

Now, on watch, I remember again the fugitive slaves we rescued. Remember the expression on the children's faces as the slave catchers took them away.

Were they hanged, too?

Monday, December 31, 1860
Stormy. Wind S.W. Moderate.

Hard weather the last few days. No time to write. Today Napoleon followed me along the high tide line as I collected driftwood. Mother and Father argued again.

Napoleon keeps very close at my heels lately. He was waiting for me, outside the Lighthouse, when I came for my watch. Brought him up the stairs and dried his wet fur in my apron before Father and Keeper Dunne arrived to help me kindle the Light. This dark and stormy evening, I feel so deeply alone. Napoleon is even more a comfort in his own way than you, my diary, particularly as I read over the poem Uncle Edward placed in the beginning, particularly in view of the news he gave me today.

Uncle Edward heard that South Carolina voted to leave the Union! A state can't just stop being part of our country anytime it pleases!

Napoleon keeps nosing under my hand as I write, making me smudge my letters. He is purring and needling my lap with his claws. Outside the storm blows, whistling around the Lighthouse. The tower sways, buffeted by high winds. But Napoleon, at least, is happy for the moment.

I wish I could be happy. I wish Uncle Edward was wrong about South Carolina. But Uncle Edward is seldom wrong about anything.

Thursday, January 3, 1861
Rain and Fog. Wind S.W. Fresh.

Won't make excuses. Some days I simply cannot write. Enough said.

19

This morning, Father and I left the station at 9 A.M., heading for Frankford on our big expedition to buy monthly supplies of flour, sugar, coffee, and the like.

In Frankford, the talk was everywhere about South Carolina. It alarmed me to hear the pleasure taken by so many at the idea of secession. Our country's history has been my fascination since I was small. I know at what sacrifice our nation was born. To consider undoing the country over the issue of slavery and where it shall be permitted is unthinkable.

Saw Mr. Warner in Frankford. At least he spoke of something other than secession. He spoke of the new school term beginning next week. "I've heard from several parents that their children miss you," Mr. Warner said. "And I miss you too, Miss Martin. Did your uncle like his book?"

I told him how much Uncle Edward was enjoying Darwin. Mr. Warner said he had a book for me to read. *Fifteen Decisive Battles of the World* by Edward Shepherd Creasy. I shall have it when school resumes.

I am eager to return to my post as Assistant Teacher at the Bayville School. I miss the children very much.

Father and I returned across the Ditch just in time for my watch. Keeper Dunne had already begun preparations to kindle the Light. Because we returned from Frankford so late, I missed dinner. Father brought a basket from Mother out to me. I listened, with pleasure, to his steady steps climbing the spiral stair.

Now, with Father back at the house, sleeping, I eat my cold pork and biscuits, alone, gazing out to sea. As the light sweeps across the dark, I strain my eyes, watching. I have just you, my diary, for company tonight. And I'm afraid I have made a grease stain on you.

Monday, January 7, 1861
Clear. Wind S.E. Moderate.

Helped Mother with breakfast chores, then joined Father and Keeper Dunne in the Light. Cleaned soot from the lantern, trimmed wicks, and polished brasswork before heading across the Ditch for school.

The current swept me down channel, but finally I made my way across.

Reenie O'Connell and my young Osbourne scholars joined me on the path. Bayville School is not much to look at. A low, unpainted building furnished with double seats, a single blackboard, a woodstove, and Mr. Warner's desk. The boys tend the woodstove, each bringing a stick with them in the morning. Even little Jacky Osbourne carries a chunk of firewood for the stove.

I wish I could speak with someone at school about all the matters troubling me. William is no longer a student. Both he *and* Daniel work now. But even if William came to school, lately, as I question slavery more and more, William gets thorny with me and I with him.

I wish I could speak with Reenie, but I can't. Reenie's father sides with the secessionists. Her family has no love for Abraham Lincoln.

Today I began my third year as pupil teacher, assisting Mr. Warner. Mr. Warner says I should continue my studies at the University next year. He says I would make a very good teacher.

I haven't mentioned Mr. Warner's idea to Father or Mother. I'd very much like the opportunity to learn more about history and teaching, but I have no wish to leave Fenwick Island.

After school, I took care of Grandmother's chores. She has begun making a list for me each day and the lists get longer and longer with every visit. It's confounding. She generally can't abide having me in the same room. I'm a big and muscled girl, not at all the dainty lady she'd wished for in a granddaughter.

I finally broke free of Grandmother and visited Uncle Edward but I had only a few minutes before heading back to

22

the Light. We discussed Mr. Darwin's book and I showed Uncle the *Fifteen Decisive Battles* from Mr. Warner.

I felt I must talk with Uncle Edward and give voice to the trouble in my heart.

Uncle called for Daisy to look after things and took me aside. Last year, Daisy was Reenie O'Connell's house slave. Uncle Edward bought her from the O'Connells, then freed her. Daisy stayed on to work for Uncle Edward. She could go as a free woman wherever she pleased, but she pleased to stay at Uncle Edward's store, sleeping downstairs in a room she fixed herself.

Uncle Edward frowned under his smart mustaches. "What is it, Wickie?"

"South Carolina leaving the Union," I told him. "I'm frightened."

Uncle Edward's eyes showed understanding.

"I'm a little frightened, too, Amelia."

He stretched his good hand over the top of mine. His withered hand hung at his side.

I stopped at the church for one moment before rowing home. The ropes of evergreens from Christmas still hang along the galleries. Knelt and prayed, for the preservation of our country and for the preservation of my parents' marriage.

And now I stand watch. I've been tracking the lights from

23

a small ship heading south. Have made note of its progress in the log.

I wonder if there are any corn cakes left from dinner. I am hungry.

Thursday, January 10, 1861
Clear. Wind N.W. Moderate.

Oh, my diary, Uncle Edward gave me the most horrible news today. Three drowning deaths. Children venturing on ice not thick enough to support their weight. The first two deaths were my scholars, Winfield Pearce, six years old, and John Moore, eight. The boys died last night, together. I knew of *their* deaths already, before Uncle Edward told me. Children at school could speak of nothing else. The boys fell through the ice at Churchman's Pond. I am bereft to lose those little boys.

Yet, the third death Uncle Edward revealed to me tore truly through my heart. William Worthington, my William, drowned in Sharp's Millpond last night.

I couldn't believe it when he first told me. Surely if such a thing had happened I would have known.

"William was skating at the head of the pond," Uncle Edward said. "He ventured too far out, where the ice was still

24

thin. He broke through and drowned before Daniel could reach him. I'm sorry, Amelia. I know you were friends."

Friends! Oh, much more than friends.

I sat with Uncle Edward. I could only think of the way William unwrapped his bread from its cloth before he ate, and the smell of the woods the day we went out gathering chestnuts, and how William's eyes widened when I told him about storms at the Lighthouse. How we argued about stupid things. How alive he was. Oh, how will it be without William?

Uncle put his arm around my shoulder.

"I should go see Mrs. Worthington, and Daniel, and the little girls." But I couldn't make myself move.

William had asked me to come skating with him. If I had been there he would still be alive. I would have kept him from the thin ice, I would have kept him from falling through. But even as I thought it, I knew it wasn't true. William was stubborn. He went where he pleased. I couldn't have stopped him any more than Daniel could have.

Uncle Edward said, "Wickie, we should take a holiday. Just the two of us. Professor Armes is speaking in Smyrna this weekend." I tried paying attention but I could only think of William.

I told Uncle Edward no. I could not leave my school

25

chores, I could not leave my Light chores. I could not walk away from William Worthington.

I rowed back to the island. Napoleon greeted me as I pulled the skiff to the boathouse. I walked along the strand, holding Napoleon against me.

Oda Lee Monkton appeared suddenly on the beach, her arms crossed at her chest, her short hair sun-streaked and wind-tossed. I was close enough to see the puffiness under her eyes, her face with its four deep lines, two connecting her nose to her mouth, two connecting her mouth to her chin. She was close enough to see my tear-streaked face.

Napoleon, startled by Oda Lee's sudden appearance, paddled free of my arms and ran through the dune grass.

I ran, too.

Back to the house. I found Mother upstairs, sewing in the front room, a blanket over her lap, her long hair spilling across her shoulders. Father sat carving in his corner.

"What is it, Amelia?" Mother asked the moment she saw me. "What's wrong?"

I was too upset to talk.

"Come with me," she said.

I followed her to her bedroom. She lightly touched my face. It was enough to open the door on my sorrow.

26

When I returned to the front room, Father was preparing to take my watch. "I can manage," I told him. We headed down together.

Light spilled pink across our faces, the pink of sunset. Wrapping my cloak around my shoulders, I raised my hood for the short walk to the Light. Father and I climbed the Lighthouse steps together, joining Keeper Dunne in the lantern room, where we lit the wicks. Keeper Dunne pulled the chain until it hung at its longest, down through the center of the stairs, then started the clockwork. The heavy Light began to turn, floating on its greased base.

As if this were any night, the Light began its nightly circle of darkness and flash.

Keeper Dunne returned to the house. Father and I descended one flight below, to the watchroom. We stepped onto the balcony, the wind snapping at our cloaks. In the twilight, we watched a ship steam past several miles out. No doubt the captain took comfort in the flash of our Light.

Father nodded to the distant ship. "Safe passage," he whispered.

I thought of William. Safe passage, I prayed.

Friday, January 11, 1861
Rain. Wind N.E. Light.

Buried William Worthington.

Thursday, January 17, 1861
Cloudy. Wind N.W. Moderate.

Visited Uncle Edward after school. There was an earthquake in South Carolina! The quake sent people running into the streets. They thought their houses were falling down.

Uncle Edward said their houses *were* falling down, from a different kind of earthquake altogether. "For pity's sake, the very house of America is falling down because of their actions."

Mr. O'Connell was in Uncle Edward's store testing the weight of hoes, close enough to hear Uncle Edward's words. Mr. O'Connell still treats Daisy like a slave. She works in back when Reenie's father comes in. After hearing us speak out against South Carolina, Mr. O'Connell pitched the hoe he'd been favoring back against the wall. He left without buying a thing.

This afternoon, the wind pulled at my cloak as I made the quick passage from our quarters to the Lighthouse. I left for the Light early, to keep from hearing my parents argue. I can no longer stop them, no matter how I try.

Keeper Dunne was first to join me in the lantern room. He has been looking gray lately, gray smudges under his eyes, gray smudges under his cheekbones. I fear he is ill.

Father joined us moments later.

"Shall Father and I take your watch tonight?" I asked.

Keeper Dunne shook his head no. "Just need some rest, I think."

Father guided him toward the head of the stairs, offering again to stand double watch as Keeper Dunne prepared to descend.

"No thank you, John," Keeper Dunne said. "I'll leave you two to kindle the Light, though. Just see I'm awake before you go to bed, Amelia." And he climbed slowly down the stairs, his steps ringing like a dull bell.

As we lit the wicks, I spoke almost in a whisper. "Father, it feels as if the world is coming to pieces."

Father harrumphed.

I looked down on our house through the lantern glass. Mother used to stand and watch us kindle the lights as night fell. Tonight there was no sign of Mother.

Saturday, January 19, 1861
Clear. Wind N.W. Moderate.

Mother nearly burned the house down last evening, though she doesn't know it. Father was in the lantern room; he'd come early to relieve me. When I returned to the house, I smelled smoke. Mother had washed my extra stockings for me and hung them by the fire before retiring for the evening. By the time I reached them, my stockings were ablaze. Throwing water on the fire, I put it out quickly. Except for ruined stockings, a scorched fire-board, and a lightly toasted arm, all is well. Another five minutes and we might have lost everything.

Today Mother said she kept smelling smoke. To settle her mind, Keeper Dunne promised he would write the Lighthouse Board and request a visit from the chimney sweep as soon as could be arranged.

Mother insisted we not wait. That we must clean the chimney ourselves.

Father surprised me by agreeing to Mother's demand. He must still care for her. Why else would he spare her feelings by hiding the truth . . . that she, not the chimney, had caused the house to smell of smoke.

Tomorrow, though it is the Sabbath, we shall tie several stones onto ropes, climb to the roof, and let the ropes down

30

the chimney, raising and lowering the stones until the worst of the black crisps of soot are scraped off the chimney's inside walls. We shall have twice the mess to clean when we finish, but Mother should be satisfied.

I wish I could help her somehow. Her moods rise and fall with the pain in her joints, with the battles with Father. Most of the time she simply seems sad. As if she finds no beauty, no joy in this life. How can she live in such a place and not see its beauty?

I love Mother. I want her to feel gay again. To laugh. To be content. But she seems determined to be unhappy with Father and with our position at the Light. I should not say this, and I could not say this to anyone but you, my diary, not even to Uncle Edward, but there are days when I am angry at Mother. Because she is so blind to Father's goodness, because she hates the Light and the sea.

Sometimes, what I write here is all that keeps me calm. Putting the tumble of anger and fear down on paper gives me power over it. Then I don't feel so helpless.

I record the wind, the weather, the ship sightings in the Keeper's log, but here, in my own diary, I write all the rest.

Sunday, January 20, 1861
Clear. Wind N.E. to S.E. Light.

Keeper Dunne led us in prayer this morning. We have reached the lowest point of cold so far this winter, the thermometer standing at 4 degrees.

We cleaned the chimney this afternoon.

No more time to write. The oil congeals and will not pour. I must warm it before I can refill the wells that feed the Light.

Monday, January 21, 1861
Cloudy. Wind S.E. Light.

The sudden rising of the temperature brought relief, even to Mother, who spent the day doing wash.

The only relief it has not brought is to Mr. O'Connell's bad humor. Reenie's father has forbidden her from talking with me. This latest outburst, I fear, comes from his presence in Uncle Edward's store the other day when we were discussing South Carolina. At first Mr. O'Connell threatened to withdraw Reenie from school. But she spent the weekend calming him. She promised she would not listen to any talk of Abolition, from anyone. And in particular she would have no conversations with me. She explained

32

everything to me this morning, quickly, without looking at me once, before she slipped to the back of the procession of Osbournes.

As soon as I returned home from Bayville this afternoon, I worked beside Mother. She had such energy. Her humor was so good. Her knuckles were hardly swollen.

I dare to hope she is recovering and all will be well from now on.

Thursday, January 24, 1861
Clear. Wind S.E. Moderate.

Father and I made the mistake of discussing politics within Mother's earshot.

She colored and grew angry. "I will not listen to this talk," she snapped. Without looking back at us, she retreated to her room.

I heard her weeping. Father heard her, too.

A little later, when she grew quiet, I went in to her. She was sitting at her dressing table, gazing at the charcoal drawing of the cottage, which Father has not yet framed for her. I promised I'd row her to the mainland to visit Grandmother this weekend.

"Thank you, Amelia," she said.

I am heavyhearted. How could Father and I have made such a mistake, when Mother was doing so well?

Tuesday, January 29, 1861
Cloudy and Snow. Wind S.W. Moderate.

A covering of snow has transformed Bayville into a soft, white plain, but here, on the island, the wind blows the snow away before it has a chance to settle. Just now, for the second time on my watch, I have had to inch up the ladder onto the narrow balcony that runs around the outside rim of the Light. The wind blew strong enough to rattle the ladder so that it shifted in the buffeting gusts, even with my weight upon it. Clinging with one hand to the slick balcony rail, I scraped ice and snow from the glass, keeping my eyes averted so as not to be blinded by the flash. Below and beyond, the sea thunders, the wind howls, and the snow has scoured my cheeks and hands with its stinging pins. Clearing ice off the outside of the lantern glass is dangerous; it is the chore that most frightens me. I would rather take on a rescue on the stormy sea than face the ice-slick ladder and the beastly wind.

I hope the glass does not ice up again tonight.

Thursday, January 31, 1861
P. Cloudy. Wind N.W. Light.
Received a delivery of whale oil.

Uncle Edward and I sat quietly in the afternoon and gazed out at the patches of snow remaining from the storm two days ago. I stopped at the Worthingtons' before coming to Uncle's. Mrs. Worthington seems to find me too much a reminder of William. I fear my visit made her grief more difficult to bear. Daniel avoids me entirely. Only the little girls seemed pleased when I came. Perhaps I should not visit soon again.

Uncle told me that the states of South Carolina and Mississippi have ordered all their residents to pay a $12 property tax on the head of each and every slave. The rebels figure that's the best way to raise money to run their new country.

A $12 tax on every slave!

I don't dare tell Father what else Uncle Edward told me. Uncle and I actually laughed over it, but I'm not certain Father would find it funny. It seems the Delaware senate, in an effort to settle down our hotly divided state, has proposed intermarriage between Southerners and Northerners to hold the Union together. That is what my mother and father have, a marriage between South and North; she from Sussex, the southernmost county in Delaware, and Father from up north in New Castle.

They might as well be from Charleston and Boston, as different as they stand on the issues of slavery and secession. All I can think is the Government had better have another plan in mind, because I do not think this intermarriage idea is going to work.

The paper Uncle Edward read from says now Georgia has seceded from the United States. Dear Lord, if you add Georgia to South Carolina, Mississippi, Florida, and Alabama, we have five states now that have left the Union!

Thursday, February 7, 1861
Cloudy. Wind N.W. Moderate.

A flock of birds hit the glass last night. It must be over four months since the last time. They are blinded by our Light and crash into the lantern room. I hate cleaning up their bodies afterward; all frozen stiff, their necks broken. The dead birds were everywhere this morning, strewn over the ground, piled on the Lighthouse balconies. I discovered a crack in the lantern room glass on the seaward side before I left for school. Reading through the log tonight, I see that Keeper Dunne has made a report. Someone from the Lighthouse Board will come to inspect the damage soon. I hope it won't be Inspector Howle.

We must get the station sparkling before the Inspector comes. Mother did the scrubbing today while I was at school. She could barely get down on her knees, barely hold the brush when I bid her good-bye this morning. But she worked all day anyway, in spite of the pain in her hands and her knees.

Tonight, though, after my watch, I must retrace Mother's footsteps and clean all the places she missed because, for the first time, she did not scrub well enough to pass inspection.

Friday, February 8, 1861
Cloudy and Rain. Wind S.E. Light.

Temperature in the fifties.

Saturday, February 9, 1861
Stormy. Wind N.W. Light.

Temperature within one degree of zero this morning.

Monday, February 11, 1861
Clear. Wind W.N.W. Light.

Temperature up around sixty.

Thursday, February 14, 1861
Cloudy and Fog. Wind N.E. Moderate.

Chill again. This restless weather is much like Mother's moods, high and low, and never a clue as to what each day might bring.

After morning chores I rowed across the Ditch and walked to school with the Osbourne children at my heels. Reenie, good to her word, maintained a safe distance behind.

I miss William Worthington. I see Daniel in passing. He is two years older than I. Daniel has taken his brother's death hard. Perhaps if we spoke together of William, it would bring comfort to us both.

I did the marketing for Grandmother, filling her cupboards. Grandmother sat in her hearth chair, a blanket up around her neck. She crossed her arms under the blanket and cursed Mr. Lincoln. The bones of her elbows poked inside the blanket like a pair of fishhooks.

The name of our President-Elect enters most conversations these days. Down here in Sussex County, the comments are mostly unkind.

In the paper, Lincoln's route to Washington was mapped out for all to see. "He won't be traveling any straight lines,"

Grandmother said. "Probably run the Government just as crooked."

I banked her fire, wished her good day, and stepped into the fog.

No time for Uncle Edward. Rowing home across the Ditch, I tensed against the tide. The current in the channel was stronger than usual. The current inside me, too.

The paper says that down south, in Montgomery, Alabama, the Confederates have elected Jefferson Davis as President of their "country." They declare a new President and Mr. Lincoln isn't even to Washington yet.

Friday, February 15, 1861
Cloudy. Wind N.E. Fresh.
Inspection. The cracked glass must be replaced.

The air has turned as mild as mid-April. Got my young scholars to point out the spring birds: the robin, the black-bird — children and birds, all chattered away as merrily as if they believed spring really had come. I am delighted with the sight of a single robin. Grandmother said she saw one under her fence and heard it chirping through the closed window. There are no robins at the Lighthouse yet.

I promised to row Mother across next Sunday so she might attend services with Grandmother and see Grandmother's robin with her own eyes.

Wednesday, February 20, 1861
Fair to Rain. Wind E. to N.E. Fresh.

Opened the windows, even in the Lighthouse, before leaving for Bayville this morning, hoping the warm breeze would freshen the stale winter air in our rooms.

But the sun disappeared midmorning. As I rowed back home across the Ditch, the station took on an eerie light. Rain began, with the wind driving the downpour like an attack of spears.

I ran to the house, up to Mother's room to help her with the windows, and found her facing out to sea. She was wet with rain and salt spray, her hair and her gown blowing wildly about her frame. Paper, hair combs, and silks tumbled about the room.

"Mother, what is it?" I asked.

"Amelia," she cried. "I will go mad with the din of that bell. Stop it, please! Stop it." Mother cried for the pain in her head.

I fashioned cloths in a muff to protect her ears.

Closing her windows, I remained long enough to see Mother wrap herself in a dry gown. Reenie O'Connell's drawing of Grandmother's cottage was under Mother's dressing table, water-spotted and curled with the damp.

Made haste down to the cellar to lift the boulders onto the lid of the cistern. It is my duty to keep the sea out of our supply of fresh water.

Closing windows along the way, I rushed round and round, up the Lighthouse stairs. Though it was still early, the sky had darkened to where the Light needed kindling.

Father, Keeper Dunne, and I pulled away the protective curtains, trimmed the wicks in the fourteen lamps, filled the wells, and lit the Light.

We had not finished when the storm hit full force.

As I squinted into the gloom, a gull blew past, beating its wings, struggling to stay aloft. The bell-buoy boat clanged at its mooring just offshore. Poor Mother.

But thank goodness for the din. I pray sailors will hear the clanging above the scream of the storm, for I don't know how far the Light can reach through this weather.

Can't sit still. The storm has caused a restlessness in my mood. Even in this diary I write in fits and starts, checking the Light, trying to peer through the storm to the sea, watchful for ships, watchful for danger.

Quickly I must put you away, my diary. There is the sound of footsteps on the stair. I hope it is Father coming to stand watch with me.

I have been listening, waiting, for half an hour. No one has come. I keep waiting for someone to appear. But no one comes.

My hair stands up on my spine. Perhaps a ship has gone down and the ghost of a sailor has come to haunt me because the Light did not show brightly enough, the bell did not clang loudly enough, to save him.

Thursday, February 21, 1861
P. Cloudy. Wind N.W. High.

I looked around the island this morning for something, anything, that might explain the footsteps I heard last night in the Lighthouse, but I saw nothing out of the ordinary. I am grateful the footsteps have not come again tonight.

Mother's head was still pounding this morning. I consulted with Father and Keeper Dunne. It was decided I should leave early and stop at Dr. McCabe's before going on to school.

Told Dr. McCabe about Mother. Told him about her swollen joints and her head.

He asked if there wasn't a certain time of day harder on Mother than others.

Morning, I told him. The worst is always morning.

While Dr. McCabe made a powder for Mother, he asked my age.

"Sixteen in May, sir."

We talked about the Lighthouse chores, about school, and such.

"And you look after your grandmother, too, don't you?"

Dr. McCabe suggested we give Mother a vacation from the Light and let her remain awhile on the mainland. He thought perhaps she might stay briefly at the hospital in Frankford.

"Is she so sick?" I asked.

Dr. McCabe said he'd like to examine her first but he thought Mother's joint problems might benefit from additional medical attention.

Finished *Fifteen Decisive Battles* and returned it to Mr. Warner. He pulled *A Chronological History of the United States* from his desk and handed it to me.

I was no good in classes today, worrying about Mother.

Mr. Warner noticed I was not myself. "Where is that fine, sharp mind today, Miss Martin?" he asked, tapping his own head. He asked if I wished to leave early, and I did.

Uncle Edward told me not to fret over Mother.

I noticed a lack of customers in Uncle's store.

He explained that some of his neighbors had stopped coming to make purchases there. He has the national flag flying and Daisy, after all.

When I asked how many customers he'd lost, Uncle Edward said, "Most."

"Funny, isn't it. I have no business, while up in Connecticut, Colonel Colt's pistol factory is running day and night."

I lifted a jar, dusted it, dusted the shelf beneath it, then put the jar back down. I needn't have bothered. Daisy keeps the shop spotless.

Now I am in the third hour of my watch. Mother was grateful for the powder from Dr. McCabe, and when I left her to come on watch, she was resting comfortably. Father and Keeper Dunne made repairs on the bell-buoy boat, which suffered a leak during Wednesday's storm. Everyone agrees they must get the bell back in commission as quickly as possible. Everyone but Mother, that is. Mother would just as soon the boat broke its mooring and sailed away, or sank to the bottom of the sea. Mother says the bell ship is like a tethered whale with a gong in its gullet.

But to me the bell is a good and comforting sound.

Tonight I can hear music. It is eerie and beautiful. I have heard it before. It comes to me on the wind. I don't know if it is really music or just a trick played by the sea. If it is a trick, it is a very good trick, indeed.

Wednesday, February 27, 1861
Clear. Wind W. Fresh.

What a beautiful day. The mild weather calls forth the caroling of birds. In Bayville, the blooming faces and bright eyes of my young scholars swell my heart with joy.

It is hard to be without hope when the weather is so kind. Even the sea seems at peace.

Thursday, February 28, 1861
P. Cloudy. Wind N.W. Fresh.

Mr. Lincoln has arrived at last in Washington. He took the final leg of his trip secretly, by carriage, because of threats on his life.

In one week, he inherits the trouble of this great, unhappy country. In one week, the responsibility will be his — whether we come together again as a Union, or fall entirely to pieces. And here we sit, in Delaware, on the border between North and South, half the state holding slaves, half the state opposed to the practice. I do not envy our President-Elect. It is hard enough to hold a family together. Poor Mr. Lincoln. It is in his hands to hold a whole country together or watch it fall apart. My hands are calloused and strong from rowing and working the ropes, from lifting and carrying barrels of oil and scrubbing stone floors and spiral stairs, but I do not know if they are strong enough to hold Mother and Father together.

Mr. Lincoln's hands . . . they must be a thousand times stronger than mine. Please God, give Mr. Lincoln strong hands.

Monday, March 4, 1861
Fair. Wind N. Fresh.

The weather is rare indeed for the season and would have done credit to May or June; in fact, yesterday and today the thermometer rose to 80 degrees — 4 degrees above the average summer heat. The consequence is the blooming out of crocus and other early spring flowers, and a general bursting of the

46

buds and spreading of leaf everywhere, even here on Fenwick Island.

Mother hummed today as she washed.

Thursday, March 7, 1861
Cloudy. Wind N.E. Fresh.

Now we can say *President* Lincoln, for his presidency is official as of Monday last. I wish him good luck.

Our new President says the Union is not broken. He says this issue is a matter of law, and he shall see to it that the law is faithfully followed.

Mother despises President Lincoln. Father and I sat with her this afternoon as she prepared dinner. I read her articles from the paper that promise our President will not interfere with the practice of slaveholding in the Southern states, nor obstruct the return of fugitive slaves. But she would not listen.

"He will have the whole country overrun with colored," she said. "You just wait. How can anyone trust a man so ugly?"

Father turned red. "Damn you, woman. You judge everything by appearance!"

My cheeks burned.

Father's fury mounted. "If the Negro seems stupid it is because he has not been given the opportunity to learn. The fact that so many Negroes can read and write and handle themselves in this world is a testament to how great they might be."

"Do not speak this rubbish to me," Mother screamed.

I stood between them. Helpless.

Friday, March 8, 1861
Fair. Wind S.E. Fresh.

Before I left Bayville this afternoon, Uncle Edward offered to treat me to ice cream from the confectionery. I caught sight of William Worthington's mother as we crossed the street. I ran to inquire after her health, and to see the little girls, and have news of Daniel. Mrs. Worthington took me in her arms and held me. Her hand stroked my hair. "How I have missed you, Amelia," she whispered in my ear.

Oh, Mrs. Worthington, I have missed you, too.

Thursday, March 14, 1861
Cloudy and Rain. Wind N.E. Fresh.

Father and I took Beans and the wagon across the Ditch while the weather was still balmy. We rode to Frankford for supplies.

In Frankford we heard politics discussed everywhere.

Perhaps this sounds strange, dear diary, but I am growing used to it all. At the Lighthouse, we go on, performing chore after chore. We trim and light the wicks, opening each mantle, adjusting the height of each flame, swinging the doors shut, and fastening the catches. We wind the clockwork of the lantern carriage. We watch through the night, ensuring that the beacon stays lit. And at dawn we extinguish the Light. This is the only way I know to go on.

Perhaps it is because of the constancy of the Light that my heart can grow used to the uncertainty of everything else.

Tuesday, March 19, 1861
Cloudy and Rain. Wind S.E. Moderate.

Caught a shad.

Caught sight of Oda Lee Monkton, too, while fishing out in the skiff.

Oda Lee's husband deserted her years ago. He went to sea and never returned. Since then she has kept to herself, living on what she can scavenge. She would prefer for us to fail in our duty of keeping the good Light; she lives at cross-purposes, waiting only for ships to founder on the sandbars and shoals.

Oda Lee lives off wrecks. She has become a pirate. And she keeps company with slave catchers.

Keeper Dunne calls Oda Lee "the mooncusser." When the moon shines, a ship is far less likely to run aground. So people who make their livelihood from scavenging wrecks curse the moonlit nights.

Mother forbids me to have anything to do with Oda Lee, and on this matter I have no difficulty complying.

Thursday, March 21, 1861
Clear. Wind N.W. Fresh.

Last night the millponds froze over to the thickness of an inch — the thermometer being at 11 degrees this morning. I fear the peaches on the mainland are destroyed.

Tonight I am so tired. Must force my eyes to stay open, force myself to remain alert. If I let the Light go out, even for a moment. . . . Reenie O'Connell said once she would never want such responsibility. She said it was hard enough to look after a family, how much more difficult to look after the sea and those who sail upon it. But it doesn't seem difficult to me. Except when I am so tired.

Sunday, March 31, 1861
Clear. Wind S.W. Fresh.

Keeper Dunne led us in morning prayer.

Dr. McCabe came out later and stayed for the noon meal, complimenting me on my pie. He is a talkative man in this place where we say so little. We all listened to his stories. Even Mother. Especially Mother.

He told of two patients lying ill in one room. One had brain fever, the other an aggravated case of mumps. They were so ill, Dr. McCabe said, that watches were needed at night, and he thought it doubtful either would recover.

Mother dabbed at her mouth with a napkin, listening. I had not seen her so attentive in months. She was absorbed in Dr. McCabe and his stories, forgetting her own discomfort.

Dr. McCabe told us he engaged a gentleman to watch these two patients through the night. The gentleman was to report any change in condition and wake the nurse periodically to administer medication. But the gentleman and the nurse both fell asleep. The man with the mumps lay staring at the clock and saw it was time to give the fever patient his medication. Unable to speak, or move any portion of his body except his arms, the mumps patient seized a pillow, and threw it as best he could, striking the watchman in the face.

Thus suddenly awakened, the watchman fell to the floor, startling both the nurse and the fever patient awake with the sound of his fall. Dr. McCabe grinned and, to my delight, Mother laughed aloud.

Dr. McCabe said the gentleman's fall to the floor struck the sick men as so ludicrous, they laughed heartily at it for some fifteen or twenty minutes. When Dr. McCabe came to see them in the morning, he found both of his patients improved . . . he said he'd never known so sudden a turn for the better. And now they are both well.

Mother joined us as we walked Dr. McCabe back to his skiff. She spoke to him in a way I had not heard her speak in some time. She spoke to Dr. McCabe as she would to a friend. Suddenly I was struck by how lonely Mother must be here.

Though Father was some distance away, inspecting the doctor's skiff for seaworthiness and preparing it for the short return back across the Ditch, I was close enough to hear Mother's words.

She asked Dr. McCabe to excuse the condition of the house. She told him she had not been well.

Dr. McCabe said he found nothing wanting but asked Mother to speak at greater length of her illness.

Mother said, "I detest the sea. It smashes and stinks and tears everything apart. It beats down my gardens and has left

52

my health in ruins. My head aches, my joints ache, and every morning I wake swollen. My hands are useless."

To hear Mother speak this way pierced my heart.

Mother said Father should have taken a stag station, a station where the men live without their women, without their families. She said Father should never have brought us here. She told Dr. McCabe she was surely dying of damp and loneliness.

My heart reached out to Mother, but if Father had applied to a stag station as she said, I would never have seen him.

Oh, my diary, can't Mother see how much I need Father? Father understands the bigger world. He has brought the dawning of that understanding to me. There is a knowledge that reaches beyond the little cottage on Commerce Street, beyond Fenwick, even. Father's knowledge is more like the histories I read. To know the world only as Mother and Grandmother know it . . . perhaps that would be simpler. But my heart is filled with so many questions. And I am not certain I can find the answers in Mother and Grandmother's world.

Thursday, April 4, 1861
Rain. Wind E. Fresh.
Received and installed new glass to replace the cracked piece.

Fine fishing weather. Brought in a good catch of shad. The run of fish is so plentiful, there is enough for us to eat and shad left over to sell. Assistant lightkeepers do not command much of a salary. It is good to help out.

Thursday, April 11, 1861
Clear. Wind N.E. to E. Moderate.

There is much activity on the water to record.

Uncle Edward says a large number of troops — 3,000 men — have gathered in New York. Steamers and men-of-war stand in readiness.

The papers report that at Fort Sumter, in South Carolina, the supplies of the U.S. Government troops stationed there have been exhausted, and receiving fresh provisions will be a great risk. The Southern Confederacy might attack the Federal troops at any moment or at the very least force our Government to abandon the fort!

When I sleep, when I wake, when I watch over the Light, when I wind the clockwork or haul the barrels of oil, when I sit in the skiff, fishing, when I look across the great sea, when I watch over the children in the classroom, I feel in my heart a collision is about to take place somewhere.

I am beginning to think President Lincoln can't force the Southern states back into the Union any more than I can force Mother to be happy at the Light station.

That Jefferson Davis, so-called President of the Southern states — I like him less the more I hear of him. He knows President Lincoln can't abandon our men at Fort Sumter. President Lincoln won't leave our men there to die. It is a simple act of humanity. We have to bring supplies through to Fort Sumter.

Uncle Edward says telegraphic communication with the South has been cut off below Petersburgh, Virginia.

We may already be at war and not yet know. At war! With ourselves!

Saturday, April 13, 1861
Clear. Wind E.S.E. Moderate.

Keeper Dunne arranged to have the Light tower and the oil house whitewashed.

The painters arrived from the mainland early this morning. They rigged a barrel and tackle and swung out from the top of the tower to work. I did not believe when I saw who was part of the crew. Daniel Worthington. He nodded to me from the barrel.

When I finished my chores in the Light, I climbed down the spiral stairs to the observation deck. Daniel called to me and asked if I could bring him some water at lunch break. I was busy with housework through the morning, but I did not forget Daniel's request.

I brought him a big slice of pie in addition to the water he had asked for.

We sat on the beach with our backs to the dunes, and the Light, and my house.

"I still miss William," I said.

Daniel stared out to sea. "He never listened to anyone."

"He listened to me."

Daniel laughed. "And then he went and did exactly as he pleased."

I laughed, too. I knew he was right.

We talked about William and Mrs. Worthington and Daniel's little sisters. Daniel kept his eyes on the sea as he spoke. I noticed how long and thick his lashes are.

"I'm going to war as soon as President Lincoln calls," he said.

I told him perhaps there would not be a war.

Daniel turned his face from the sea a moment to look at me. His eyes were laughing. "Really, Amelia."

I could feel myself blush.

"Your mother might wish you to stay, you know," I said. "Your sisters need you."

"I can't stay," Daniel said.

His lips are full like William's were and his nose, like William's, straight and fine. And he has those pretty eyes, prettier than William's, I think. Big and gray with those long, thick lashes.

Daniel said he would work through the noon hour on Monday, and eat with me when I returned from school, if I liked.

I am eager for Monday.

Monday, April 15, 1861
Rain. Wind N.W. High.

The tide is the highest measured in nearly ten years.

Oda Lee has been out scavenging night and day. The sea leaves her gifts. Her cloak whips around her legs. She moves slowly, bending into the wind. Sometimes the sheer power of the wind lifts her off her feet, and she is a goodly weighted woman. She flaps like a crow from one piece of flotsam to the next.

The weather today was no good for painting Lighthouse towers. But Daniel came anyway. Just to see me. Because he'd promised. We ate our meal on the beach in our rain cloaks, watching Oda Lee.

Thursday, April 18, 1861
Clear. Wind N. to E. Fresh.

The weather for the past few days has been rainy, making painting impossible. With all his free time, Daniel rowed out every morning while I was doing my Lighthouse chores. Tuesday morning he said it was good to get out of a house filled with women, and his eyes laughed as he said so. It gave me an oddly pleasant feeling, knowing he sought refuge from the mainland in my company.

Yesterday morning, as Daniel rowed me across the Ditch from Fenwick to Bayville, we talked about slavery. "This fight over owning slaves has been too long in coming," he said. "Slavery is wrong, it always has been wrong, always will be wrong, no matter what color a person's skin." Daniel likes talking history as much as Uncle Edward, as much as I.

And I am always eager to hear what he thinks. I told him about the *History of the United States* I am reading and he listened with great interest and asked questions I had not thought of.

Monday, Tuesday, and yesterday, after school, we went together to visit Uncle Edward and Daisy. Daniel treats Daisy as if she never was a slave. I so enjoyed myself, I delayed returning home each day until the last moment, but Daniel had promised I would get back to Fenwick in plenty of time for the Light.

I would not mind if the weather kept the painting crew home all spring. It has made for very fine conditions for me to get to know Daniel better.

Today, though, it was lovely and clear, and Daniel worked while I rowed myself to and from Bayville.

Friday, April 19, 1861
Cloudy and Rain. Wind S.W. Fresh.

The War is begun!

Uncle Edward said Fort Sumter was attacked by General Beauregard of the Southern Confederacy on Friday last and though the Federal troops resisted, Major Anderson, the commander at the fort, had no choice but to surrender. Fort

Sumter has fallen to the secessionist rebels and the Stars and Stripes have been replaced by the "Stars and Bars" of the Southern Confederacy.

When I heard the news I felt a roaring inside my ears, a roar of outrage. That our country should come to this moment.

Sunday, April 21, 1861
Cloudy and Rain. Wind N.W. to N. High.

Keeper Dunne led us in prayer.

Uncle Edward said President Lincoln made a proclamation calling for 75,000 militia. He urges those in defiance of the law, all Secessionists, to return to their homes, and retire from this disagreement peaceably, and within twenty days.

President Davis says he is ready for President Lincoln's 75,000 Northerners.

Where is Delaware to stand? Kentucky refuses to send troops to fight for the Union. Yet in Rhode Island, the very Governor has offered his own services to President Lincoln. Men from all across the North prepare to put away their daily lives and march to war to uphold our Union.

Daniel is among them. But he is not without concerns. He worries about the welfare of his mother and sisters, as well he might. "Who will support them when I am away? Who will see to their needs?"

I did not know how to answer. But I could see the matter was of great concern to him, though it was not so great as to keep him from joining the Federal army.

Uncle Edward cannot go, because of his bad hand. But what of Father? Will Father join?

Monday, April 22, 1861
Cloudy to Rain. Wind N.E. High.

The schooner *W.B. Potter* foundered on the shoals north of Fenwick Station. Father and I brought all hands ashore safely and they stayed at the Fenwick quarters overnight.

The schooner went aground on Keeper Dunne's shift. He rang the alarm and woke Father and Father woke me and Mother. Father and I pulled on our storm clothes and fought the waves to push our boat off the island. We struggled to reach the distressed vessel. There were six aboard. All were glad to be rescued, but for the owner. The owner did not wish to leave his ship. What a foolish man. As if any possession could be more important than life itself. He screamed at Father, demanding a guard for the foundering ship. Father could hardly hear his words as the wind screamed in our ears, and the hungry waves swelled around us. The owner's mates, yelling into the storm, made the schooner's owner see the folly of his request. The schooner was already breaking up, being lifted and torn to shreds on the shoals. We were in danger of suffering the same fate, the storm was so wild, the waves and wind so high.

We got the crew and passengers safely back to Fenwick, though we had as difficult a time landing as we had pushing off. It took several attempts to bring the boat safely to shore.

Keeper Dunne remained at his watch at the Light, and Father and I led the men up the beach to the house and gave them blankets.

To my surprise and great relief I discovered that Mother, in our absence, had prepared food and warm drinks. My own body was so tired and so cold from the relief effort, I don't know how I could have done by myself all Mother did for us.

I can't remember when I've seen her so active, nor so beautiful. Do we need a wreck to make Mother happy?

Saturday, April 27, 1861
Clear. Wind S. Moderate.

I persuaded Mother and Father to attend Van Amburgh's Menagerie and Fair with me today. We stopped to inquire if

62

Grandmother might like to come with us. She declined. We next asked Uncle Edward, but he could not get away. He said we might see Daisy there, though. He had given her the day off.

The day was mild. By two o'clock, it seemed as if thousands were assembled on the grounds, all shades, colors, complexions, degrees, and kinds. I did not see Daisy, nor did I see Daniel, but there were so many people in attendance, they might have been there and I could easily have missed them.

I attended an exhibit in the Agricultural Booth. The exhibit featured the latest in farming equipment, tools that will replace the old reliable implements farmers have used for centuries. As I left, searching for Mother and Father, I wondered if in the future, lighthouses and their keepers would be replaced, too, just like farm tools. It does not seem possible. But I couldn't help fretting that someday there will be no Light, and no need for a keeper to tend it. That, and not seeing Daniel, turned my mood toward a dark and irritable humor.

Not only that, but if I had hoped to bring Mother and Father closer by this diversion, I was gravely mistaken. They quarreled all day — about the crowds, and what to eat, and where to go, and how long to stay there. And all their bickering, I realized, was not about the fair at all, but about something else, something unsaid. I did not see any point in remaining, but Father stubbornly insisted we stay.

When we finally returned home this afternoon, Mother's eyes were red and her hands swollen.

Before my watch, I walked carefully through the grasses where the plovers nest. I sat on the beach, thinking, as the long Atlantic rollers came in.

A little ways down the shore, Oda Lee stood in men's light trousers, her hands on her hips, talking to herself.

Tuesday, April 30, 1861
Fair. Wind S. Moderate.

Much depends upon Maryland. She grows more and more agitated, fearing a battle will soon be fought on her soil. Some of our neighbors, like Daniel, are joining the Union army, but many are not. At least our fellow Delawareans resist enlistment in the Confederate army. But if words were weapons, the North would surely suffer defeat in Sussex County.

The reports I hear in town are that the Confederate armies are in Virginia, preparing to make an attack upon Washington, our very capital.

In the newspaper, it states that Southern children of ten and twelve years of age have joined the regiments! Southern women, who never before turned their hand to anything because they had slaves to do their chores, now work day and night in the preparation of their men's equipage.

I work day and night, too. Not in preparation for battle. Just to keep the Light.

Wednesday, May 1, 1861
Fair. Wind S.W. Moderate.

The month of flowers, instead of bursting in all gay and sunlit, came in cold and blustery, more like February than May. The wind whipped up sand into a pelting storm. I checked the cover on the cistern to make certain sand would not foul our drinking water. The day was so disagreeable we were forced to light fires and wear hip boots, oil pants, overalls, layers of shirts, heavy sweaters, and overcloaks.

Uncle Edward said that in northern Delaware it was recommended that citizens raise money for the families of those who volunteer to defend the Government. "How else shall their families survive?" he said. "Men can't rise up and leave their homes without some support to make up for their absence." Daniel was greatly cheered by this proposal.

I am not surprised the idea originated in the north of the state. I wonder how our neighbors down here will take to it.

Mrs. Worthington is dependent on Daniel. He works not only as a painter. He will take any odd job to bring in money for his mother. I think about Father. What will we do if Father enlists? Will the Lighthouse Board pay me Father's salary? I doubt it. Mother and I would be destitute. And so would Grandmother, for Father supports her as well.

Uncle Edward said that Virginia has chosen to secede after all. The men of western Virginia are so unhappy with the situation, they have proposed separating their part of the state from the east so they might remain faithful to the Union.

So much anger, so much resentment. If only the two sides would sit down and discuss this sensibly. But how?

Mother cannot be sensible, nor can Grandmother. And Father, he is like a man deprived of his reason when the topic of slavery comes up. "There should be no slavery," he yells at Mother. "Not in the existing states, not in the territories."

Grandmother and I do not discuss politics. When I visited her today, she could speak of nothing but the mad dog that appeared in the street on Monday. A crowd of men went after the mongrel, but it managed to bite several dogs before it was killed. Unfortunately, those bitten also had to be destroyed. I think the mad dog is like South Carolina. It is biting its neighbors and forcing them into the position where they, too, must lose their lives.

Reenie O'Connell no longer comes to school. I wonder if she will continue to study on her own. And to draw. Her picture of the cottage is rain-damaged, but it is not ruined. I made a frame for Mother myself. The frame is not perfect. It irritates Father to look at it. Mother has it hanging in the front room.

Thursday, May 2, 1861
P. Cloudy. Wind N.W. Fresh.

Finished *A Chronological History of the United States.* Uncle Edward let me take his Darwin home with me.

The weather continues exceedingly cold for the season. Snow and hail and heavy frosts.

Governor Burton has proclaimed to the people of Delaware that the 780 men requested by the Secretary of War shall be assembled, though he does not command these men to obey President Lincoln. Rather, he suggests the men voluntarily offer their services in defense of the capital and the Constitution.

A request for arms has been sent to Europe. It seems we have more soldiers than weapons. Daniel said that will not stop him. He will take his father's musket down from the wall where it has hung all these years. Daniel will use his father's musket until the Government can issue him a weapon from its armory.

Daniel was one of the first to sign up. I am proud he is willing to fight for the Union. But I am so very frightened for his safety. I rely greatly upon his friendship and counsel. I shall miss him too dearly if he should truly leave.

I untied the bow from my hair and gave him the ribbon to carry with him, the green one Father gave me for Christmas, the one the color of the restless sea. Daniel laced the ribbon through his buttonhole and tied it in a knot. "I will keep it always, Amelia," he said.

I lowered my head. I did not wish him to see the pleasure on my face.

Friday, May 3, 1861
Clear. Wind N.W. High.

Today is my sixteenth birthday.

Mother's joints were so swollen, she could not get out of bed. I tended her, the house chores, and the Lighthouse chores. I rowed alone to school. . . . Daniel did not come out to meet me. I taught school, looked in on Grandmother and Uncle Edward. Picked up the mail. Then rowed myself back home. It was a day like every other day. Like every other day.

68

Uncle Edward was busy with inventory. He and Daisy worked together, counting the hoes and the shovels, the boots and the hats. They were discussing the War. What else? It is all anyone speaks of these days.

Daisy told me the slaves of Maryland are fleeing by whole families and in great numbers into Pennsylvania. Uncle Edward thinks this is just the beginning. He says not less than 500 slaves have escaped the South in the past few days.

Tonight, the thought of that tide of Negroes haunts me.

As I was writing this, standing watch at the Light, I heard a step on the stair below and I remembered when I heard steps but no one came. My whole body listened. I feared a ghost might appear at any moment. Whose ghost? Who is haunting me? And then I recognized the sound of the footstep.

It was Daniel. He came with a gift, a shell, delicate, polished, with a ribbon strung through it. He tied it around my neck. He wished me a happy birthday and left.

It happened so quickly, I'm still not certain I didn't imagine the whole thing. But here is the shell and the velvet ribbon.

Monday, May 6, 1861
Clear. Wind S.E. Moderate.

Both frost and ice this morning.

Wednesday, May 8, 1861
Rain to Fair. Wind N.E. Fresh.

A violent rain fell, quite deluging the lowlands, impeding the work of the farmers and bringing the sea to our doorstep.

Thursday, May 9, 1861
P. Cloudy. Wind N.W. to S.E. Moderate.

Volunteers are being interviewed in the state of Delaware.
    When I asked Daniel what the interview was like, he said,
    They ask:
    Are you a married man?
    Daniel's answer was no.
    Have you anybody that cares anything about you?
    No.
    Oh, Daniel.
    Do you believe in God?
    No.

70

Daniel?

Do you believe in the Devil?

No.

Daniel!

Are you afraid to die?

No.

Have you ever been in the penitentiary?

No.

Have you ever stuck a knife in a man?

No.

Will you swear to bring home a lock of Jeff Davis's hair?

Yes.

You will do.

I asked Daniel is that truly the way the interview went? He smiled. I am not entirely certain but I believe he was teasing me.

Uncle Edward is going away for a week. He is traveling north, to Wilmington, to attend an abolitionist rally.

Before he left, he gave me the most wonderful new book, a belated birthday gift. It is a geography and atlas, published by Messrs. J. B. Lippincott & Co. Full-page maps of countries, states, and cities, maps of rain and winds and races of men . . . altogether the most satisfying book I have ever seen. Have set aside the Darwin for the moment. Before my watch I took the atlas out on the beach and, bundled up against the uncommon chill, sat reading as I faced out to sea.

The atlas does not fit inside my cloak as nicely as you, my diary. It is far too big. I cannot carry it up with me on watch. Anyway, I might become too engrossed and forget my duties.

North Carolina, Tennessee, and Arkansas have turned toward the Confederacy.

Maryland, it is settled, will stay with the Union. I am so relieved. If Maryland fell, Delaware could not have remained steady. We are just a stone's throw from the Maryland border. If Delaware fell, we would have lost the Lighthouse. It would have gone to the Confederates. And where would that have left us?

As far as I can figure, this War is not so much about the destruction of slavery as it is about the preservation of the Union. Yet if slavery should vanish from this country as a result of the Union's victory, I will not grieve.

I have spent my entire life in Bayville with Mother and Grandmother. I was wrong in my beliefs about slavery. Mother still is wrong, and Grandmother. But even if I did not think slavery wrong, it is pure selfishness to tear asunder what our forefathers struggled so hard to establish. Pure selfishness!

Monday, May 13, 1861
Cloudy. Wind N. Moderate.

It is rumored in town that women and their children are fleeing their Southern homes to avoid the danger of slave insurrections. The planters are loathe to leave their land unprotected from rebellious slaves. They refuse to let any of their white hands enlist in the Confederate army. They are arming them and keeping them as private guards, instead. The news is also that the Cotton States, particularly Mississippi and part of Louisiana, are running short of necessaries. Cornmeal, in small quantities, is the only food to be had.

I miss Uncle Edward. I should like to talk this over with him. I am eager for his return from Wilmington. Perhaps they are discussing the difficulties of the South at the abolitionist rally even now.

We should not be jubilant over the suffering of our Southern neighbors. It is a cruel thing to go hungry, no matter what your political beliefs. What does the stomach know of politics? It knows only that it is empty.

Tuesday, May 14, 1861
Clear. Wind N.E. Fresh.

In the paper appeared this Counsel to our Volunteers.

1. Remember that in a campaign more men die from sickness than by the bullet.

2. Line your blanket with one thickness of brown drilling. This adds but four ounces in weight and doubles the warmth.

3. Buy a small India rubber blanket (only 50 cents) to lay on the ground or to throw over your shoulders when on guard during a rainstorm. Most of the troops are provided with these. Straw to lie upon is not always to be had.

4. The best military hat in use is the light-colored soft felt, the crown being sufficiently high to allow space for air over the brain. You can fasten it up as a Continental in fair weather, or turn it down when it is wet or very sunny.

5. Let your beard grow, so as to protect the throat and lungs.

6. Keep your entire person clean; this prevents fevers and bowel complaints in warm climates. Wash your body each day if possible. Avoid strong coffee and oily meat.

7. A sudden check of perspiration by chilly or night air often causes fever and death — When thus exposed do not forget your blanket.

I presented a copy of these instructions to Daniel, at his house, along with a pair of socks I've been knitting in the evenings, a blanket lined with drilling, and a small India rubber blanket I purchased with money I have made selling the fish I catch.

Daniel examined my package, bowed, and thanked me like a proper soldier.

Mrs. Worthington was not so formal. She hugged me and thanked me many times over.

I felt confused by Daniel's polite distance, but then he ran after me as I headed to the skiff. He caught me, swung me around, and taking my shoulders in his two large hands, gave me a kiss right on my forehead. Then, without a word, he ran back home.

Even now, as I stand watch, my cheeks flush with pleasure.

Thursday, May 16, 1861
P. Cloudy. Wind S.W. Moderate.

Pulled up five blue crabs from one pot and three from another this afternoon. Mother, though she is out of bed, is still painfully swollen and not able to get her fingers to work. After I steamed the crabs, I picked the meat. Mother smiled to see all the crabmeat. Her smiles come so infrequently, I felt as if a ray of sunlight had fallen across me.

Uncle Edward was delighted with the crabs I brought him. The rest sold marvelously well in town.

It is good to have Uncle Edward back from Wilmington and his abolitionist rally.

He said most of Delaware hates the Abolitionists.

I am disappointed to my very soul.

Uncle Edward said one side recognizes the rights of all men. The other side is based upon the domination of one race over another.

When put that way, how can so many stand against abolition? Yet a year ago, I stood against abolition.

I hardly see Daniel at all now. He does not come out to the island in the mornings. He is caught up in preparations for war.

Monday, May 20, 1861
Clear. Wind N. to E. Moderate.

Mother spends hours with the papers I bring her from Uncle Edward. She sits in silence, her hands so cramped she can barely turn the pages. Her chores are neglected. I would like to

76

sit with the paper as she does. I would like to rest for an hour after school. Instead I run from one chore to the next. The only time I have to myself is on watch. And even this time isn't truly my own, for I must be always vigilant.

I don't know what is wrong with me. I feel angry much of the time. Peace is too often a stranger, except when I am here in the Light, or rowing across the Ditch, or with the children at school. But even the schoolchildren are stirred up by the War. Mr. Warner is enlisting in a few days, when school ends. He says he will be back in time for the commencement of fall classes. But what if the War doesn't end this summer? What if the War ends and Mr. Warner doesn't return?

My mind goes like this, in circles, angry at the North because they stubbornly corner the South, angry at the South because they pigheadedly challenge the North. Angry at my father because he has given up everything for his lofty principles. Angry at my mother because she cannot love him in spite of those principles.

This afternoon I lashed out at Mother when she ordered me to wash her underthings. And then I looked at her face, saw the pain in her eyes. And I knew suddenly what it cost her to ask me to do such a chore for her. Then I grew angry at myself.

Grandmother isn't well, either. I gave her rum to ease her aches. Rum is what she prefers. I did her heavy and light cleaning and asked Dr. McCabe to look in on her.

Seeing my stormy mood this afternoon, Uncle Edward searched for the words to cheer me. He told me not to brood about the War.

But how can I not brood?

Daniel came to see me last night to say good-bye. This time, when I heard the footstep on the stair, I knew it would be Daniel's face coming through the watch room door. And then he was there, his eyes shining, his fine frame proud and straight. He held me only a moment. "Good-bye, Amelia," he whispered in my ear. "Wait for me."

Then he was gone.

Thursday, May 23, 1861
Fair. Wind E. Moderate.

The fishing is the best I can remember. Rowed my catch to shore this morning and sold it in Bayville. Uncle Edward got first choice. Brought the rest to sell at the hotel. The additional money eases Mother's fretting. Mother always loved to look fashionable. She has not picked out new cloth for over six months, except perhaps for the aprons she made me at

Christmas. She is unable to sew now anyway because of the swelling in her fingers.

School ends tomorrow. Mr. Warner urged me to keep up with my reading and made a gift to me of several history books from his own collection. I shall miss Mr. Warner. I hope he fares well.

Uncle Edward said that oat and wheat crops have recovered exceedingly well from the unseasonable cold earlier this month. The yield promises to be heavy. Perhaps this will help keep the Union army fed.

The Delaware Regiment is assembling. Daniel is on the march.

Thursday, May 30, 1861
Clear. Wind S.E. Moderate.

Daniel's regiment is encamped one mile from Wilmington. I hope he is getting enough to eat. I hope his feet don't hurt. I hope that he is able to stay dry and sleep well.

The Stars and Stripes fly over Uncle Edward's store, though I see the flag nowhere else in town except at the post office and at school.

Traded my fish today for strawberries, which are large and ripe and sweeter than wild honey. Wish I could share them with Daniel. Instead I brought them back home and made shortcake for Father and Keeper Dunne.

Mother has lost interest in sweets. She has lost interest in most everything.

I fear this will not be a fast war. The Government is looking for more men. Men to fight for three years rather than three months. Father mumbles to himself. I overheard him this morning as he rubbed lamp rouge into the reflectors. Will he try enlisting?

If Father enlists in the Union army, that will push Mother away from him forever.

Thursday, June 6, 1861
Cloudy. Wind N.E. Fresh.

Uncle Edward has had word from his friend Warren Harris, who shipped out last August for Buenos Ayres on *The Pride of the Ocean*. Mr. Harris's ship had been at sea since before Mr. Lincoln's election and the unhappy events that have followed. Her crew had no knowledge that we had become, in their absence, a country at war with itself.

Warren Harris wrote Uncle Edward that when *The Pride of the Ocean* pulled into Apalachicola, in Florida, she was boarded by privateers under letters of marque issued by

Jefferson Davis. The captain and crew, including Mr. Harris, were taken prisoner and kept for over a week in a room without furniture or bedding, and fed only rice and water. With the help of the National Government, the captain and crew were at last able to regain their ship, but the privateers had stripped it of everything movable, including all clothing and food, except for a supply of rice for the trip back home to Boston. Those privateers are as thorough as Oda Lee. Uncle Edward said Mr. Harris's captain was lucky to get away with his ship. I think Uncle Edward is right.

As I write this on my watch, I look out toward the sea. Day and night, there are increased sightings of ships moving from North to South. Our log is filled with sightings and we must be ever watchful for signs of trouble. To see so much movement on the water excites me, but it also fills me with fear. Those ships are carrying boys as beloved to someone as Daniel is to me.

I purchased a copy of *The Soldier's Companion* in Bayville today for 25 cents and sent it to Daniel so he might know I am thinking of him.

Sunday, June 9, 1861
Rain. Wind S. Fresh.

Keeper Dunne led us in prayer.

Caught a feast of crabs. It felt good, out on the water, the rain falling softly.

Now I stand watch.

This war between neighbors means nothing to the sea. It is a very good lesson.

Thursday, June 13, 1861
Cloudy and Fog. Wind S.W. Light.

The shoals are shrouded in fog and we have kept the Light burning all day.

So far, no wrecks. Oda Lee sits like a cormorant out on the rocks, waiting for trouble. I cannot see her now. But I believe she is there still.

Mrs. Worthington had word from Daniel yesterday. His company left its encampment last Sunday, along with the other five companies in the Delaware Regiment.

Daniel will go to Maryland now. Three months is not so long.

I visit Mrs. Worthington every day. Today I helped her

pack a box of letter paper, envelopes, stamps, soap, and towels for Daniel. Being with his family, in his rooms, brings Daniel into my heart so that I can imagine him right beside me; I can almost smell him sometimes. Perhaps I miss him a little more when I am there. But I am still happy to be there, to be useful in Daniel's home.

Uncle Edward had news of a battle near Norfolk, Virginia. Two Federal regiments fired upon each other by mistake, killing two boys. Then the Federal troops united, only to be attacked by a rebel battery. Is it possible that thirty to forty Federal boys lost their lives, and nearly one hundred more were wounded?

The Government says the troops in the field, the three-month volunteers, shall be paid for their duty. This will ease Daniel's mind, and Mrs. Worthington's. Now, in addition to the pay for duty, the Government offers a $100 bounty if the three-monthers will enlist for three years before they are mustered out of service. Daniel's mother could live well on $100. But I wish Daniel would not sign on for so long. What if the War actually lasts three years?

When I stopped for the mail, there was a letter for me, from Daniel! I made myself wait until I could be alone here, in the Light, to read it.

Daniel's letter is most polite. But in one paragraph I see a flash of the Daniel I have come to know so well. This paragraph I shall copy out.

> *The health of the camp is good. The men are merry and happy as men can be. We have just enough work to make us relish sport. Target-firing, fishing, bathing, quoits, newspapers, &c fill up the time between drills and guard duty. At night all the noises of the barnyard can be heard from the quarters of Company D. Such crowing, Amelia, and cackling, and grunting, and bellowing were never surpassed by any living animals. The Kent boys are gaining a reputation of being great cooks. We have our batch of hot bread daily. It is not as good as your pie, nor my mother's duck, but it is mighty good anyway.*

Thursday, June 20, 1861
P. Cloudy. Wind S.W. Moderate.

Mother is not interested in the garden this year. Where last year she supervised me in the planting and weeding, this year I alone tend the roses, the turnips, the tomatoes and cucumbers.

I do not mind the extra work, particularly now that school

is out. It does not take much to tend this sandy garden. I am able to keep it weeded and watered. I love working in the garden. It holds me out of doors for hours with the wind and the smell of the sea and the sound of the breakers singing in my ears.

Why can it not be the same for Mother? Why can't the sea bring her the peace it brings me?

Friday, June 21, 1861
Clear. Wind S.W. Light.

Dr. McCabe's brother came into Uncle Edward's store while I was there today. He has known almost a week now about his son, who was killed in Maryland while on guard at the railroad bridge over the Big Elk. Dr. McCabe's nephew was killed by an oncoming train. His body will be returning to Delaware any day now. The McCabe family had hoped he would be home soon. But not like this.

Saturday, June 22, 1861
Rain and Fog. Wind S.E. Light.

We are having a fine fall of rain. The heavy clouds and sheeting downpour kept Father, Keeper Dunne, and me busy all day and now into the night on fog shift at the Light. The log is filled with entries recording wind, conditions, behavior of the lamps, &c. The bell-buoy boat, repaired and freshly painted, clangs out its warning. Mother has kept to her bed with the curtains drawn and the windows shut.

Tuesday, June 25, 1861
Rain and Fog. Wind S.E. Light.

I cannot explain how I knew a ship had gone aground on the sandbar last night during my watch. I could not see it. And yet I felt it like a scraping inside me.

I'd been watching the lights of passing ships the best I could, but the fog made tracking nearly impossible. The crew of the yacht did not hear the bell-buoy boat ringing its warning.

I hesitated to wake Father and Keeper Dunne. I had no proof that anything was amiss. Just a "feeling." I hesitated, also, to bother Mother unnecessarily.

Standing out on the balcony, the rain slashing against my face, I thrust my head toward the sea and listened. It was then I heard the shouts of men and a faint sound, a ghostly sound, like a woman crying from the depths of the sea.

86

This time I did not hesitate. I rang the alarm bell and within minutes Father and Keeper Dunne joined me.

When their hearts and their breathing stilled enough, they heard, too, the cry of terror from a woman, the calls for help from deep-voiced men.

Keeper Dunne and Father rowed out toward the sound. Fortunately the waves were not high and they did not have to fight anything more than the fog and the rain. But I could hear the cries of panic increase as the pleasure yacht slowly gave way and slipped under the water.

Father and Keeper Dunne brought back the four crew members and all five of the passengers, including the woman I had heard. She wept softly as Father helped her up the beach to the house. I could see the lamp burning upstairs in the kitchen window. Mother could be counted on even in her sad condition. She cared for our unexpected guests through the night until this noon, when they were all questioned by the insurance company and returned to the mainland.

Last night, after all the members of the sailing party, their crew, Father, and Keeper Dunne had disappeared inside the house, a deadly quiet settled back over the Light. The sea hardly moved. Nothing moved.

Until I saw the lantern. Oda Lee, floating through the fog, seeing if there was anything left to scavenge.

Thursday, June 27, 1861
P. Cloudy. Wind S.E. Moderate.

Uncle Edward said today that several of the area farmers are arranging to take a day off for observation of the Fourth. This is not an easy time for them to be away from their fields. Both the hay and wheat are heavy and ready for the scythe. Yet for these men it is important to show their loyalty. I am so glad to know of them.

Daisy has gone off to Pennsylvania for a week and Uncle Edward asked if Father and Mother and I might like to come across the Ditch this evening and share a meal with him. I rowed back excitedly and asked, but Keeper Dunne had other plans and could not let both of us go. I suggested that Mother and I could go without Father. Perhaps we could bring Grandmother to Uncle Edward's with us. Mother hesitated. I could see how much she longed to get off the island and see Grandmother. But she had kept to her bed most of the day because of the swelling in her joints. In the end she did not think she could bear the motion of the boat across the Ditch.

The only thing that keeps my spirits buoyed is this letter I received from Daniel.

Here I am in Maryland, a high private in the U.S. army, a place a few weeks ago I had no expectation of seeing. I had hoped to make it at least to Washington but rumor has it the Government isn't sure it can trust those of us from Delaware.

We are getting along very well on the feed we get. Hard crackers and salt pork are not the most palatable viands, but I remember, Amelia, how you told me of the sufferings of our Revolutionary sires, and I am careful not to complain. You and your great mind full of history, you take all the fun out of being miserable.

Our victuals are not set before us by servants, or by a sister or mother, I assure you. We wash our own dishes, and, for that matter, sometimes our own clothes. Ah well, I am happy, for I am here for my country's sake.

Our Sundays are not spent here as at home. That day is like all others to us. Plenty of drill and very little church.

The floors on which we lie are made of peculiarly hard wood — not a soft plank to be found. All the better, it will accustom me to hardships. But what a fall it is from a comfortable bedstead and mattress. Never mind. If I had to fall in this life, at least I did not fall from the barrel at the top of your Lighthouse.

The sights of Maryland are not so different from our own state, though there are places from history that might interest you. As for me, I wish I could be back in Bayville for a few hours. Here we are surrounded by men, no ladies' society whatsoever. It is hard to imagine I ever looked for an excuse to leave my sisters and mother in that gracious house of women. I am afraid, with respect to my present companions, I will become a regular bear and lose all my refinement — that is, if I ever had any.

I cannot help but smile, even as I copy this. Bless Daniel. To make me smile at such a time.

Thursday, July 4, 1861
Clear. Wind S.W. Fresh.

Last night, I kept an even more careful watch than usual as all through the night the crack of pistols and guns could be heard across the Ditch, announcing the arrival of our country's Independence Day. It was all in good fun, but my ear listened to every noise, lest it warn of danger and duty. The firing of guns may mask another sound that would tell of disaster on the shoals. Fortunately no such disaster occurred through the night. At sunrise the church bells rang.

Father and I cleaned and polished the big panels of bull's-eyes and prisms in the lantern room as quickly as possible so we could get a start on the day.

I asked Mother last evening if she would accompany us to the Fourth of July program in Lewes and she agreed. But when she woke this morning, she found it a particularly bad day. She urged us to go on without her. Keeper Dunne agreed to look in on her from time to time.

Mother's hand trembled when I came to say good-bye, but she said I must not be concerned. I must have a lovely day.

Uncle Edward had posted a notice that his shop would be closed. Daisy has not yet returned from Pennsylvania.

We arrived by wagon in Lewes just before ten, in time to watch the long procession of clergymen, orators, choirs, committees, cadets, citizens on foot, citizens on horseback, citizens in carriages, and a company of guards. Two large American flags draped the archway under which the orators spoke. Evergreens and flowers festooned the whole platform. The Reverend prayed for our country, for a happy issue out of its present difficulties, for a pardon of our individual and national sins, and a blessing upon the troops defending our liberties. The Declaration of Independence was read and more speakers addressed the crowd.

Late afternoon, Father and I left Uncle Edward off in Bayville, returning to the island in time to light the lantern. I regretted we could not stay in Lewes for the fireworks, but as I walked out on the narrow gallery, I saw the displays of brilliant lights at sea and on land.

Sunday, July 7, 1861
Fair. Wind S.E. Moderate.

President Lincoln is calling for 400,000 more men.

Tuesday, July 9, 1861
P. Cloudy. Wind S.E. Light.

General Scott says, "Make haste slowly."
    It is advice that works equally well at a lighthouse.

Thursday, July 11, 1861
Clear to Rain. Wind S.E. to N.W. Moderate.

Grandmother wanted to gossip when I came to do her chores. She said that Ann Blackiston has left her husband, and he has posted notices everywhere that he will not be responsible for any charges she contracts. I beat the rugs ruthlessly from the porch and weeded Grandmother's flower beds in the rain. But I could not escape the fact that wives leave husbands, husbands leave wives. If a country can break its bonds, why not two people?

But Mother and Father must reconcile. When a storm comes, everyone is needed to run the Lighthouse station. Father, Mother, and I work together alongside Keeper Dunne, each with our own tasks, to meet the storm head on, and to survive it. And might not another country act like a storm? What if England, or France, or Spain decides we are weak now? It would be easy for them to come blustering in and conquer us.

I feel as if I am the Light in my family. I must keep my hope burning, so that Father and Mother, even in the darkness that seems to engulf them, might find their way back.

Monday, July 15, 1861
Clear. Wind S.E. Fresh.

A comet appeared recently in remarkable brilliancy, although now it is fading. It is called Thatcher's comet, after the man who discovered it last April. But everyone calls it the "war comet." Every night, after my watch, I go out and sit on the beach and send up my troubles to it.

The weather has been very warm for several days, the mercury rising to the suffering altitude of 96 degrees in the shade. As hot as it is, the chill never leaves the room where Mother and Father are present.

Thursday, July 18, 1861
Clear. Wind N. Fresh.

I thought it would be Father leaving, to fight for the Union, but it is Lightkeeper Dunne who has left us. He said nothing to us of his intentions until this very day. He simply waited for the arrival of the new Keeper and departed. I never did grow fond of Keeper Dunne, though he was a good enough Lightkeeper. Still I don't know anything about the new Keeper. Father and I will be busy until Keeper Hale is accustomed to this station. I am most relieved that Father is staying, at least for the moment.

Mother hoped that Father would be promoted from Assistant Lightkeeper to Head Keeper, but the Lighthouse Board will never consider such action because of the mark on Father's record.

I am not certain how I shall stand with Keeper Hale. He has a handful of rosy children, and he and his wife are as big and boisterous as whales. They treat me as a child. Keeper Hale laughs when I tell him I am an equal in the keeping of the Light. I cannot suffer the thought of losing my place here. I shall never relax around him. Fortunately his children are not old enough to help with the Lighthouse duties, and they will keep his wife so busy she will be no help, either. Soon enough, Keeper Hale will see the value of my extra hands, my extra ears, my extra eyes.

Oda Lee cut through the piney woods in front of me while I was gathering kindling for the house.

She stopped and stared at me. She had never held still so close to me before. I didn't know what to do. Finally, to break the silence, I told her Keeper Dunne had left.

Oda Lee was quiet awhile. "I know," she said. "They all go in the end."

95

Sunday, July 21, 1861
Clear. Wind S.E. Light

A flock of black skimmers rested out on the shoals, making a great noise this morning as Keeper Hale led the lot of us in prayer.

I played with Keeper Hale's children this afternoon. I was not certain we should be so noisy on the Sabbath. But Keeper Hale did not discourage us. There are five little Hales, three girls, two boys, none older than eight. The oldest girls, Sarah and Alice, have a gift for fancy. They make up games all day to keep the three smallest ones, Mary, James, and William, entertained. They cheer me. They are so full of laughter and life. Even their rooms, so dark when Keeper Dunne occupied them, are dappled now with sea light. Mrs. Hale asked if there were not any berries on this whole island, and Keeper Hale came along as we went on a hunt for them.

Keeper Hale acted like a great bear as we marched through the woods, and the children ran screaming back to me every time he growled. They peeked around my legs, drawing my skirts about them. We ate plenty of berries during our outing. But we brought back enough to satisfy Mrs. Hale's recipe for berry pie.

Monday, July 22, 1861
Clear. Wind N. Moderate.

Keeper Hale, Father, and I talked as we polished the lenses and the reflectors this morning. With each passing day Keeper Hale permits me to do more of my normal Lighthouse chores.

There is an ease between Father and Keeper Hale. I believe they are friends already in a way Father and Keeper Dunne never were. I have never known Father to have a friend other than Uncle Edward. It is good for him to have someone here to speak with.

As we worked, Keeper Hale told us of his sister who lives in South Carolina. She grew up in the North and has no fondness for slavery. Nor does her husband. They have servants, but they are paid, much as Uncle Edward pays Daisy.

Father said, "Imagine living in South Carolina and supporting the Union, Wickie. If the rebels despise the Union at a distance, how much more they must despise their Union neighbors."

He asked if Keeper Hale's sister and her family were safe in South Carolina.

Keeper Hale opened his huge arms and said jovially that she could come here and stay with him if she wanted. I do not know where he would put one more person. His rooms are filled to the edges with children and books and the most fascinating possessions.

Later, when Father and I were alone working in the garden, we came close to each other as we moved down the rows, plucking out weeds. "It must be like that for Mother," I said. "The way it is for Keeper Hale's sister. Surrounded by people who feel different from you."

"It is hardly the same, Wickie," Father said. But he would say no more.

Tonight, as I stand watch, I have so much to think about.

Keeper Hale's sister has made a life for herself in South Carolina. She loves her home there as I love mine here. We have been at Fenwick Light from the start. We were here when Keeper Dunne touched the lucerne to the very first wick for the very first time. I remember the tiny flames growing behind their prisms. I remember those flames within their glass lenses. . . . Those lenses reminded me of flower petals when I first saw them. I remember the lantern room becoming a cage of light.

We have kept the Light burning here ever since, so that no more lives would be lost in the dangerous waters off our stretch of the Delaware shore.

Mother says that Father has no understanding of his

98

responsibilities. When she speaks to him at all, it is to remind him of his past mistakes. To accuse him of present mistakes. She says if Father understood his responsibilities, he would never have stranded us on Fenwick Island.

I wonder about Mother's words, about Father's choices. Does responsibility to family weigh more than responsibility to something greater?

I have never seen Father do anything but honor his responsibilities at the Light. He would sooner die than let Fenwick Light become a Dark House, an extinguished lighthouse. A Dark House is deadly. The Lightkeeper must carry the consequences of that darkness for a lifetime.

But what of our own lives? Are we a Dark House, Mother, Father, and I? After watching Keeper Hale and his family, what else can I think? And if our life is a Dark House, whose responsibility is it? And what are the consequences? And how long must those consequences be carried?

Saturday, July 27, 1861
Clear. Wind N.W. Fresh.
Inspection at 10 A.M. Condition very good.

From Manassas Junction, Virginia, along Bull Run, there is word of a slaughter of Union soldiers. The Union troops were vastly outnumbered and exhausted. They panicked and rushed into retreat. The losses are frightful. Wagons are arriving in Alexandria and Washington, carrying dead and wounded.

I pray Daniel was nowhere near the action.

Thursday, August 1, 1861
Clear. Wind S.E. Light.

Keeper Hale has decided that on Sunday we shall raise a pole here at Fenwick Island from which to fly a large national flag. All citizens from on and off the island who are loyal to the Union are invited to attend the flag raising. Keeper Hale thundered up our stairs this morning to ask Mother to help Mrs. Hale provide refreshments. Generously, he gave her an allowance with which to do so. I do not know where he found the money to undertake such an affair.

After he bounded down the stairs again, Mother muttered, "I'll not labor with that abolitionist wife of his. Nor will I lift a finger to help the man who has taken your father's position."

Mother is weary beyond her limit, and present circumstances have not improved her temper. Keeper Hale's children are noisy, night and day. To me it is a joyful sound, but the precious little sleep Mother once got is lost to her with all the commotion of those busy children.

Keeper Hale does not know how to deal with Mother. He believes everyone enjoys the same good health and robust constitution he and his family enjoy.

I told Mother I would take the money and go to Bayville and get supplies for her. "I'll work with the Keeper's wife."

Mother shook her head. She would not part with Keeper Hale's money.

"Mother, you can't just take it."

"Why not? We have so little. Your father should be Head Keeper."

I do not have enough money to buy supplies for Keeper Hale's refreshments myself. The money I earn selling fish disappears as soon as I purchase more medicine for Mother from Dr. McCabe.

But Keeper Hale is expecting refreshments contributed by our family.

Rather than fighting with Mother, I decided I'd better catch some fish to sell, in the hopes of earning what Mother would not part with. I picked my way over the ribbons of rotting seaweed, dragging the skiff down to the water's edge. The gulls wheeled overhead.

Oda Lee appeared from nowhere just as I prepared to push off.

"Fine day," she said.

I jumped. Then tried to hide the fact that she had startled me. I brushed wisps of hair back from my face, speechless.

Oda Lee asked me if I had a crab in my knickers.

I laughed.

Then I told Oda Lee about the new Keeper and his party on Sunday.

Oda Lee asked if the new Keepers were Abolitionists.

I nodded.

She wanted to know how Mother felt about her new neighbors.

I looked down and said I didn't know.

This time it was Oda Lee's turn to laugh.

I always thought Oda Lee so peculiar. But today, she understood not only what I said to her, but what I did not say, as well.

Sunday, August 4, 1861
Cloudy. Wind S.E. Light.

Keeper Hale led us in prayer at dawn. Services with Keeper Hale are unlike any services I have ever attended in all my life.

Keeper Hale's words are full of glory and goodness and bounty and life. Not a dark or somber word escapes his mouth.

Saw Oda Lee out on the beach early this morning. While she scavenged, Father, Keeper Hale, and I carried oil up from the oil house and filled the reservoirs. We cleaned and brightened every pane of glass and every reflector, polished every piece to brilliancy, the brasswork, too. Then I drew the curtains and washed down the rooms. When I looked again, Oda Lee was simply sitting on the beach, her arms resting on her knees, staring out to sea. Napoleon sat beside her.

When I came out of the Lighthouse, Oda Lee motioned to me.

I looked back at the house to see if Mother might be watching, then came across the dunes, my hands stained and smelling of lamp rouge.

Oda Lee never looked at me once, the entire time I approached her. Instead she kept her eyes on the sea. I kept turning back toward the second-story window of our house. The window where Mother stands.

While I turned to look back the last time, Oda Lee slipped away. For a moment, I thought of the time in the Lighthouse when I was on watch and I heard a footstep on the stair, but then no one came to me in the watch room.

I walked through the dune grass to where Oda Lee had

been sitting and nearly tripped over a basket set right in the path. The basket was filled with supplies. I had managed to purchase a few things. But in the basket was all I needed to help with Keeper Hale's party. The basket came from Oda Lee. Who else?

But why did she leave it for me? I am much unnerved by her.

For a moment I hesitated, uncertain about whether I should take the basket or not. These supplies were from Oda Lee's scavenging expeditions.

But then Mrs. Hale called to me.

And without a second thought, I lifted the basket and ran all the way back to her.

Mrs. Hale and I set straight to work with the baking. The party was set for four in the afternoon.

We had help from the children, who were sticky up to their elbows and streaked with flour across their cheeks and foreheads. Even Keeper Hale was put to work after he and Father had set the pole.

At four, with everyone cleaned back up, we waited, looking across the Ditch. Uncle Edward came with Daisy, though he was reluctant to leave the store unattended. Still, he said it was important for both of them to come. While we waited for the others, Uncle Edward told us that someone sent a parcel to the

104

editor of *The Smyrna Times*. It looked as if they were returning a copy of the paper from several days past, but when the
bundle was unwrapped, a yard of brown domestic cloth with
blood and scabs fell out. Smallpox! Someone had attempted to
infect the editor and his staff at *The Smyrna Times* with smallpox. They are a pro-Union paper. Fortunately no harm was
done.

No one else ever came to Keeper Hale's party.

Keeper Hale never lost his good spirits. Nor did Mrs. Hale.
We made a picnic out of it and had a wonderful time.

Mother stayed in her room.

Oda Lee came out and stood a good distance down the
beach. When we raised the national flag, she turned her back
on us and walked away.

Thursday, August 8, 1861
Clear. Wind S.E. Light.

I saw what Keeper Hale wrote about me to the Lighthouse
Board. He says I am a sturdy girl, frugal in all things, even language. He states that I carry equally one-third of the Keeper's
responsibilities, and my logs and attendance to duties are beyond reproach. He recommends not only that I be retained in
the service of the Fenwick Light, but that I be compensated

for my work. I was not certain I would like Keeper Hale or his noisy family when they first arrived. I was not certain he would permit me to remain at my Lighthouse duties. I judged him wrongly.

Grandmother has come out to the station to help with Mother as Mother's health has taken a turn for the worse. Grandmother complains about the children downstairs at every opportunity. Yet I am so fond of them.

The change the Hales have brought to this island is wonderful. Downstairs, in Keeper Hale's quarters, there is always a river of voices. There are thumps and bangs and shouts and laughter. It is a sweet sound. But Grandmother criticizes with every breath. I feel as if our rooms are suddenly too small.

I wake to the sound of the Hale children singing and chattering. Those happy sounds fill me with a contentment I have never known before. Today Sarah and Alice raced up the Lighthouse stairs as I was polishing the brass. They would not leave me alone until I promised to come swimming with them. Yesterday, I took little Mary out in the skiff and taught her to fish. The children are forever drawing me into their games. James and William spend hours and hours building forts in the sand, only to bash them down in a matter of seconds, gleefully, with their plump little feet. Mary and James take particular pleasure in chasing Napoleon around the

106

house, across the dunes, along the beach, and I chase after them . . . to make certain no harm comes to either child or cat. Napoleon could escape from them in a moment if he was truly annoyed, but he likes their attention as much as I.

Father has given his cot to Grandmother and is sleeping here at the Light. That gives us more time together, though now I must steal time to write in you, my diary. In silence, this afternoon, Father and I watched the gulls and herons. From high above we studied the movements of the sandpipers and the sanderlings, the knots and the yellowlegs, the curlews and the oystercatchers. I tried to talk with Father about Mother. But Father stopped me. He said there are certain things that should not be discussed between father and child. I will try to respect and obey Father. But it is hard to live with so many questions.

The news is full of skirmishes in Missouri and Kansas, and in Maryland. The Delaware regiment is not involved. People in Bayville continue to speak of the devastation done to the Union troops at Bull Run last month. I am grateful for every day Daniel is not in battle.

Grandmother brought peaches with her when she came. I baked three peach pies. Mother's favorite is peach pie. But I could not get her to take even the smallest taste. Happily, Grandmother succeeded where I failed.

Keeper Hale and his family were delighted with the extra pie I made for them.

I do not know what Oda Lee thought of hers. I left it on the path in the basket placed precisely where I had found it filled with supplies a week ago.

Sunday, August 11, 1861
P. Cloudy. Wind E. Moderate.

Keeper Hale led us in prayers of celebration this morning.

This afternoon, Uncle Edward explained the Confiscation Bill to me, the one just passed in Congress. If property is discovered, especially property devoted to the uses of the Rebellion, that property may be confiscated and sold. When the property involved is a slave, the United States Government will not take the role of slave trader. The slave shall be set free.

I wish no one would come to the island for a while, and that I did not have to leave it. I wish that Father and the Hales and I could just keep the Light and not see anyone, not talk to anyone until this lunacy is over, until the country is the country again, and there is peace. I wish we could go back . . . back to before South Carolina seceded, back to before Mother and Father began their fights. But how far back would we have to go?

108

Beginning tomorrow, school resumes. How odd it will seem without Mr. Warner. The new head teacher is from Maryland. I do not know how we shall manage together.

Five companies of the Delaware Regiment returned to Wilmington Saturday, their three months having expired. The report is that they are in good health. They have been engaged in watching bridges in Maryland and have not seen even a skirmish. They will be paid off in a day or two, then mustered out of service.

Daniel has signed on with the Second Delaware Regiment for three years, but I believe he must be mustered out of the three-month regiment first. Mrs. Worthington had a letter from him on Friday. We don't know where he is now. I brought Mrs. Worthington some shad yesterday and visited with her a spell. Daniel's little sisters like to climb into my lap. They want stories about the barefooted Hale children. They want stories about Daniel. They miss their big brother. I miss their big brother, too.

I try to be civil with Grandmother. She has softened a little. Watching Mother in such pain has softened us all. Grandmother pats Mother down with a cool dampened cloth in the dark bedroom. Outside the curtains is the brilliant light of the sea, but in Mother's room it is as still and dark as a grave.

Rain has fallen every day since Grandmother arrived. Today

the decision was made to take Mother back to town with Grandmother. It is a decision we all knew would come, though Father put it off as long as possible, I think, for my sake.

Mother and Grandmother shall leave as soon as the weather clears. In the meantime, I have kept the fire stoked for Mother though it is August.

Abraham Lincoln has asked us to set aside the last Thursday in September as a day of prayer and fasting for all the people of the nation. It will be difficult to perform our duties and keep to the President's proclamation, but we shall try.

Thursday, August 15, 1861
Fair. Wind S.W. Fresh.

Mother left with Grandmother this afternoon. Father and I took them across the Ditch. I looked over my shoulder at the familiar lines of the Lighthouse, the white conical tower topped with its black balcony. Mother looked back at it, too.

Father lifted and carried Mother easily to Commerce Street. We settled her comfortably in Grandmother's bed.

After taking care of her at the Lighthouse through all these months of bad spells, I did not know how I could leave her today.

"Should I stay here with Mother?" I asked Father as we stood in Grandmother's front room.

Father shrugged.

If I stayed, it would be just like before, when Father was gone at sea, and the three of us lived in the cottage together. I looked at Grandmother, more active than she has been in a long time. She has revived with Mother's needing her. I realized it would be better for her to nurse Mother without me.

I chose to come back to the Light.

How odd it feels here on Fenwick without Mother.

Thursday, August 22, 1861
Clear. Wind N.E. Fresh.

Daniel is back! I am so filled with joy. He will be here for three weeks. Three weeks! I forced myself to do justice to my chores before Father and Keeper Hale told me I had done enough.

I rowed quickly to the mainland and stopped in at Grandmother's, but Mother was sleeping. Then I raced to the Worthingtons' in the moments I had before school. Daniel and I were awkward at first with each other.

But then we went out in the skiff after school, fishing. I dropped my line and sat quietly, waiting for Daniel to speak.

Knowing if I could be still long enough he would eventually talk.

And he did start talking. He said it is so different here in Delaware. The way people talk about the War, the way they talk against President Lincoln. "The War is easier to understand when you discuss it with like-minded people."

I asked him to explain it to me.

He told me the things I already knew. That the slave states wanted to expand slavery into the new territories, that their pride forced them to turn their backs on the Union when they could not have their way.

"Nothing can be accomplished by secession," Daniel said. "The South has nothing to gain. This could have been worked out without leaving the Union. If they felt their rights were being invaded, the Constitution was there to aid them."

I sat in the skiff, my line in the Ditch, the marsh and reed birds singing. And Daniel. It is a moment I shall always remember.

Daniel thought he might switch regiments. He said some of the officers are good men, but not all. "It helps to know the man who's leading you. I've been lucky so far. There was a colonel I knew who didn't care a fig about his men."

Daniel gazed across the water. He sighed deeply, more deeply than the first time we really talked after his brother,

112

William, died. "Our Government didn't plan this War as well as it might have." Daniel tilted his head, listening to the call of a reed bird. I could have watched him like that forever.

He said the rebel army is growing daily. But the three-monthers from the Federal army are being sent home. The capital is not adequately protected. Everywhere, there are too few Federal troops. They must bring the three-monthers back into position immediately. And the press must cease printing where the troops are, where they are heading, how many. "No wonder the rebels are taking the advantage."

We sat in the boat a long time, quiet. "When do you think it will end, Daniel?"

"Prepare for a long war, Amelia. Bull Run was lost because everyone up North thought the War would be short. We thought that victory would be easy. We were wrong. We need a vast army, we need ample supplies. That's the only way to win. The battle at Bull Run extended over seven miles. Seven miles of soldiers! Seven miles of death."

We brought the fish we caught back to Daniel's house. I shared an early meal with his family before heading home for my watch. When I shut my eyes, even now, I can see Daniel in the boat with the reed birds behind him.

Sunday, August 25, 1861
Clear. Wind S.E. Fresh.

Keeper Hale led us in a celebratory service before chores.

Daniel rowed over early to help with the brass. He gets on well with Keeper Hale. I almost felt left out. But then Daniel had to rush back to attend regular church with his mother and sisters. I am glad for Keeper Hale in a hundred different ways, not least of which is the way he keeps the Sabbath.

Father brought Mother back to the station today for a visit. I was overjoyed to see her here, in her own home. We spent the day together. She looks better. I have watched her steady progress each day during my visits to Grandmother's cottage.

How much better she is than when Father carried her out of here ten days ago.

She did not enjoy her time back on the island, though. Keeper Hale's children buzzed curiously around her and Mother swatted them away like they were bothersome insects.

Father came upon us while I was brushing Mother's hair in her old bedroom. She had made a new dress for me and I was wearing it. Father stood in the doorway a moment, watching us. His expression clearly showed what pleasure he took in seeing the two of us together like that. Then Mother caught sight of Father standing there and told him to leave at once. A

114

wounded look crossed Father's face for only a moment. Then he straightened, bowed, and was gone.

I took Mother back myself to Grandmother's cottage and returned to Fenwick before sunset. I tried talking with Father about Mother when I returned. Father turned away.

Thursday, August 29, 1861
Fair. Wind S. Fresh.

School this morning. After checking on Mother this afternoon, I met Daniel and we hurried off to Uncle Edward. Uncle Edward visited with us for nearly an hour. He has a great deal of time on his hands these days. He says it would be so even if he was surrounded by Unionists. It seems the only businesses doing well in Delaware are those supplying the army — makers of shoes and coats and weapons.

He told us of a new business recently sprung up in the South — slave stealing. Uncle Edward says hundreds of men are descending on the eastern section of Virginia. There are plenty of slaves running loose there, slaves who have been deserted by their masters. These men take the abandoned slaves and convey them down to South Carolina, Georgia, and Alabama, where they are condemned to slavery forever.

I was hardly able to take in that news when he told us that

115

Jeff Davis has issued a proclamation ordering all Union sympathizers to depart within forty days. He means to seize their property, to fill his treasury.

What will happen to Keeper Hale's sister and her family?

I tried to ask Father about this earlier tonight. He is still sleeping below, rather than in the house. In spite of his nearness, there is a great distance between us. It grows greater by the day. I asked him to come and sit with me awhile on my watch. He came but he hardly listened, not when I spoke of Union sympathizers in the South, not when I spoke of Daniel. When I was little, and he was a stranger, someone I saw only briefly with months of absence between, he used to pull my braid in teasing when I was hesitant to speak to him. He would look straight into my eyes. "Go on, Amelia," he would say. As if everything on my mind was important to him.

There is no "Go on, Amelia," now. Only distance.

Thursday, September 5, 1861
P. Cloudy to Rain. Wind S.W. Moderate.

I am an official Assistant Lightkeeper with a salary, small but steady! I picked up the letter today at the post office. When I showed the letter to Father and Keeper Hale, they held a little

116

ceremony for me. Then Father placed the letter in a box containing his most important papers.

I am considering giving up my duties at Bayville School in order to take on more here at the Light. It is hard for me to imagine not being in the classroom with my little scholars, but everything has changed since Mr. Warner's departure. Perhaps I could help teach the Hale children here on the island, instead.

I stopped in on Mother and Grandmother this afternoon and the Worthingtons, too, to show Daniel the letter from the Lighthouse Board, but signs of a storm made me head back to the Light early, without a visit to Uncle Edward.

Daniel has one week more. The time passes too quickly.

Daniel walked me back to the skiff in the rain this afternoon. He had heard from someone in his regiment that the English were seeking, among their possessions, a place where cotton might be grown. Once they have a source of cotton other than our Southern states, the English will not need to wait for our blockade on the Southern cotton export to lift.

But what happens to the Negro who knows no other work than picking in the cotton fields if the cotton supply is no longer needed? Look what has come of the rebel's temper.

In less than a month, all the people of Tennessee who adhere to the General Government shall lose their property.

117

Those same Union sympathizers, if they choose to remain in the state of Tennessee, shall find themselves jailed.

Father, Keeper Hale, and I cleaned and inspected all the gutters and joints in anticipation of a strong blow. The cistern in the cellar is low. A good rainfall will do wonders for our supply of fresh water.

The storm is gaining strength, lashing around me now, as I stand watch. The wind is gusting, buffeting the tower. Spears of lightning are cast quickly toward the lantern room, then are swallowed by the bright flashing beacon of light. Thunder rolls in, regular as the wild waves, one crack rumbling into the next. The sky is fitful, with long legs of lightning kicking out every few seconds. The bell clangs for all it is worth. I cannot hear the bell in a storm without thinking of Mother.

Thursday, September 12, 1861
Fair. Wind N.W. Fresh.

Father left before dawn this morning, while Keeper Hale was on last watch. Father did not speak with me about the purpose for his leaving. He has not talked much with me since Mother came to visit last month. I have been thinking a lot about that visit. Mother was cruel to Father, crueler, in fact, than she was to the Hale children.

It troubles my spirit, these changes. The longer Mother is away from the Light, the happier and stronger she appears. But Father is not at peace. Even with Keeper Hale and his family around, Father rarely takes pleasure in the simple joys.

Daniel rowed out to tell me he has been given one more week before he has to leave. I am so grateful.

Monday, September 16, 1861
P. Cloudy. Wind N.W. to N.E. Fresh.

Daniel and I pulled in a good number of crabs this morning before crossing the Ditch. The crabs fetched a fine price in town. I offered to give Daniel half but he refused. I gave the money to Grandmother, instead, to help pay Mother's expenses.

This afternoon Keeper Hale handed me a copy of Harriet Beecher Stowe's book *Uncle Tom's Cabin*. He said I may keep it.

Thursday, September 19, 1861
Clear. Wind N.E. Fresh.

Father left the station early again. He gives no explanation. I wish he would have waited and crossed with me on my way to school. Perhaps in the skiff he would have talked. Daniel always talks in the skiff.

Saturday, September 21, 1861
Fair. Wind S.E. Moderate.

Uncle Edward says the crop this year was abundant after all, in spite of the late spring. So there will be enough for soldier and civilian to eat. France and England, suffering from rains and ruined crops, and Ireland, with its blight on the potatoes, are eager to purchase the sum of our surplus agriculture. Their purchases will place needed money in President Lincoln's coffers.

Grandmother and Mother, with all that is going on around them, talked today only about the impertinence of shop girls. Mother's color rose with anger as she described the Negro girl behind the counter at the millinery shop. Mother was angry because the girl's dress was of a nicer cloth than she can afford.

A certain quality in Mother has been awakened by Grandmother. I am not certain I admire that quality, though I am grateful for what Grandmother has done.

Daniel's regiment left today for Maryland. He did not come to see me this morning. There was no time.

I stand this watch, knowing Daniel is gone. That I might never see him again. That is a hard and constant ache.

But I stand my watch.

Sunday, September 22, 1861
Cloudy. Wind N.W. Moderate.

Keeper Hale led us in prayer, a more sober and plaintive service than he has held for us before. Two hundred thousand men, women, and children in the single state of Tennessee have received notice to leave the state of their birth because of their Union sympathies. Those who own stores have been assaulted as they resist the theft of their goods by the rebel pirates. I fear for Uncle Edward in a town where he is surrounded by secessionist sympathizers, at a time when emotions are running so wild.

Daniel has been gone only a day and already I miss him sorely. Who may I confide my troubles to now? Not to Uncle Edward. He has troubles enough of his own. Not to Father. He is silent as the floor of the sea. Not to Keeper or Mrs. Hale. I do not wish them to think me unstable and therefore ill suited for my job. That leaves only you, my diary. And Napoleon.

121

Earlier today, I gathered the five little Hale children around me and read to them from the Bible. They were good and quiet for at least three minutes. And then they were off chasing Napoleon, who is allowed to come in the house these days. Now that Mother is not here.

Thursday, September 26, 1861
Fair. Wind S.W. Moderate.

The glass was broken in Uncle Edward's shop last night. And a fire set. I had a feeling something like this would happen.

When I saw what was done to my uncle's shop, I feared for his life. I raced through the open door.

There was Uncle Edward, perched behind his counter. The lingering smell of smoke stung my eyes. "We're fine, Wickie," he said. "Don't worry. Daisy and I extinguished the fire before it did any real damage."

Uncle Edward sat straight, his eyes glittering. Daisy had a bandaged hand.

"They won't drive me out," Uncle Edward said.

I thought about the people in Tennessee. They were being driven out.

Our Governor refused to proclaim today as a day of fasting and prayer for deliverance from our troubles, as President

Lincoln wished. The Mayor of Wilmington stepped forth and issued the proclamation instead.

The damage done to Uncle Edward's store was meant to send a clear message about how the people of Bayville feel about President Lincoln and his proclamation.

Now I am on watch. I try not to notice the burn of hunger in my stomach as the hours of my fast go beyond fourteen

I dozed off!

The alarm bell woke me, letting me know that the clockwork had run down. Immediately I attended to my duties. My heart pounding, I checked everything, everything from the Light to the oil reserves, from the inky night sea to the bell-buoy boat.

All is well. Nothing amiss. I am lucky. I am so lucky that nothing went wrong in the moments I slept. That the Light stayed lit, that no ship went aground.

If anything had gone wrong, it would have been my fault. Lost property, lost life, it would have been my fault.

Thursday, October 10, 1861
P. Cloudy. Wind N.E. Light.

I came softly upon Mother standing in Grandmother's garden this afternoon. I studied her before she was aware of my approach. She is so beautiful. Seeing her standing there, wrapped in her cloak, a bush of flaming red leaves behind her, it was easy to imagine how Father first fell in love with her. He used to tell me the story whenever I asked, about meeting Mother in Grandmother's garden, and knowing the moment he saw her that she would be his wife. . . .

The weather, up until yesterday, has been hot to the point of oppression, even with the ocean winds to cool us. The lantern room has been insufferable. But today it is cold, almost to freezing. And Daniel sleeps outside.

Thursday, October 17, 1861
P. Cloudy. Wind S.E. Moderate.

Uncle Edward has let me work in his store in exchange for a flannel undershirt for Daniel. It is easier to find an extra hour or two for Uncle Edward now that Mother is with Grandmother. Together the two are able to handle the sewing, the ironing and baking, all the light chores I had been doing for Grandmother myself. They only need me now for heavy chores, lifting and carrying.

I have tried to send a package or letter to Daniel every week. He writes back nearly as often.

I think of Daniel among the long lines of fires flickering and glowing in the night — all the tired soldiers, eating their suppers, settling into sleep while only the sentinels keep watch.

I am one of the sentinels.

Thursday, October 24, 1861
Clear. Wind N.W. Fresh.

Father woke me at dawn, at the conclusion of his watch. As I climbed the spiral stairs to the Light to begin morning chores, Father took the scow across the Ditch.

Please, I thought then, please, I have thought all day, do not let Father enlist in the army. Please do not let that be what he is doing when he leaves like this.

Perhaps I have lost Mother to her politics and her pain. Perhaps I have lost Daniel to his politics and the War. Must I lose Father, too?

There are things a father and daughter cannot discuss. But there are things a father and daughter must discuss. Tomorrow I will ask Father where he was today.

Friday, October 25, 1861
Clear. Wind N.E. Moderate.
Inspection at 4:45 P.M. Condition very good.

When I asked Father about his trip to the mainland, he grew angry. "Why can't you be a proper girl, Amelia? Why must you always question me?"

He might have tossed me over the balcony and dashed me to pieces on the ground below. But Keeper Hale came upon us and I pushed the hurt down deep where no one could find it. And that is where I shall keep it, as God is my witness.

Keeper Hale, Father, and I were briefed on precautionary measures during inspection today. We were told we must be vigilant throughout our watches for ships flying foreign flags.

There is a smell to the air on the mainland. Long ago I gathered chestnuts with William when the air smelled just this way. William will not gather chestnuts again. I would have liked to gather chestnuts with Daniel. Perhaps Daniel would have found my hurt and soothed it for me. But Daniel is not here. So I gather chestnuts alone. I once might have asked Reenie O'Connell to come with me, but Reenie will not speak to me now, because of her father. Is Reenie the proper kind of girl Father wishes me to be?

Thursday, October 31, 1861
Cloudy. Wind S.E. Moderate.

The frosty mornings of the past week have hastened my trips across the Ditch. I always row faster when I am cold.

I brought pumpkins back from Bayville as Mrs. Hale requested. Because the pumpkin crop is large this year, I was able to buy quite a few at a very good price. The skiff was so heavy with the enormous orange globes, it is a wonder I did not sink.

As I played with the Hale children, Mrs. Hale mixed a teacup of grated pumpkin, a pint of good milk, an egg, a little salt, two large spoons of sugar, some cinnamon, and some nutmeg. She lined a tin with pastry, filled the shell, and set the pie in the oven to bake. I asked if she would mind if I took some pumpkin to bake a pie or two of my own.

Mother loves pumpkin pie, almost as much as she loves peach. Father loves pumpkin pie, too. I am so angry at the two of them, tonight, after my watch, I shall bake two pumpkin pies and I shall eat them both myself.

Friday, November 1, 1861
Clear. Wind W. Fresh.

When I returned from Bayville today, Napoleon met me on the beach. He rubbed against my legs and mewed. Each time I started for the house, Napoleon ran toward the woods, then turned and ran back to me again.

I worried that perhaps one of the Hale children had gone to play in the woods and met with some mischief. But all five children were accounted for.

I threw myself at my house chores, for the dark comes quickly now and my shift at the Light comes early. When I headed to the Light at dusk, there was Napoleon, waiting for me, mewing, catching at my skirts and playing his game of running to the woods and back.

I had not time to go after him before my watch, but I promised myself I would follow him if he still waited when my watch ended.

Keeper Hale relieved me at nine and I had almost reached the house when Napoleon shot out of the darkness and yowled at me. Lifting the lantern, I followed him into the woods.

We had gone quite a way when I heard cursing, cursing such that I have heard only once before, and that from a sailor during a rescue. How he apologized for his language later when he found I was a girl.

I held my lantern aloft and continued toward the sound. To my astonishment I found Oda Lee Monkton leaning against a small tree. I knelt beside her and saw her face was bruised.

"What has happened?"

She stared at me, her face a mix of anger and pain.

"The girl looked white to me. Talked like she had money. I thought there might be some come my way if I helped her. Dang slave catchers caught me. The leg's hurt."

I did not understand anything but the last.

I fashioned a crutch for her from a green branch and with the crutch on one side and me on the other, we slowly made our way out of the woods to Oda Lee's.

I had never been inside Oda Lee's house. She was not happy to have me there now. Supplies were stacked everywhere. There was no place to walk, no place to sit, no place to lie down.

Oda Lee steered herself toward a pile of boxes.

The room was bitter cold.

I started a fire for her.

"I will row across and bring Dr. McCabe."

129

"Don't you dare."

She cursed at me and told me to get out. I stopped at the door, looked back at her. She was licking her hand and rubbing it over and over across a bruise on her cheek.

She screamed at me to leave.

Keeper Hale was still on second watch. I woke Father and told him about Oda Lee. I handed him the lantern and one of the pumpkin pies. He thanked me, sent me to bed, then left.

Oh, my diary, I don't know what to make of anything anymore.

Saturday, November 2, 1861
Fair. Wind N.W. High.

Father said Oda Lee helped an escaped slave last night and was beaten by the slave catchers as a reward.

I do not know what possessed Oda Lee Monkton to help a fugitive slave. But then I do not know what possessed her to help me last summer with the supplies for Keeper Hale's party, either.

Monday, November 4, 1861
Cloudy. Wind S.E. Fresh.

Father arrived at Grandmother's today while I was there. He stood in front of Mother and handed her a sheaf of papers. Mother took the papers, read down the first page, then shut herself in her room.

When after awhile Mother did not reappear, Father turned and left and I followed him. In silence I shadowed him across the Ditch, he in the rowboat, while I took the skiff. Once we had landed, I caught up with him and asked about the papers he had handed Mother.

Father kept his head down as he dragged his boat up out of the Ditch. He would not look me in the eye.

Oh, my diary, I think not knowing will drive me out of my mind.

Tuesday, November 5, 1861
Stormy. Wind S.E. High.

One of the highest tides I have seen in all my life. The marsh embankments have overflowed and fences have washed away. A number of houses along the Ditch are flooded by the invading tide. At least Mother and Grandmother are far enough inland that they are in no danger.

Father has checked on Oda Lee twice. She, too, is safe for the moment. He still says nothing about the papers, and I dare not row the Ditch today to see Mother and ask her myself.

Keeper Hale and his family have moved in upstairs with us until the storm and high tides run their course. We have given them Mother's room. Our quarters have never been so full of life. The children's sticky fingers and noisy activities are everywhere.

The sea has managed to get into the cistern. It was unavoidable, and now our water is salty. But the Lighthouse has weathered the storm so far, and though we lost our fence, the house remains undamaged and the Light continues to burn.

Here on the island, when a storm hits, nothing protects us from the mighty Atlantic. We have no barrier to buffer us the way we protect the mainland. We have only one another.

We must stand and take whatever the sea throws our way. And we do.

Mother could not.

But we do.

Thursday, November 7, 1861
Fair. Wind W. Moderate.

Mother was sleeping when I came. Grandmother said I was not to disturb her with any of my nosy questions.

Nosy questions!

I carried water and firewood in, but I did not do one lick of housework. Not one lick!

Thirty victims of the battle at Ball's Bluff were found Monday in the Potomac River near the Chain Bridge. They were much mutilated. No sooner did we have news that Daniel was at that very battle, fighting with the 71st Pennsylvania, but we had word he was one of the survivors. Daniel was not the only one to survive the fight. It seems the boys who were good swimmers managed to escape. I taught William to swim two years ago, after he nearly drowned. William must have taught Daniel. It makes me wonder why things happen as they do. I am filled with gratitude. I am filled with awe.

The beautiful Indian summer has come, with its soft and melancholy days. After the brush with winterlike weather, which set everyone to making provision for the coming frost and snow, the mild temperatures and balmy breezes have returned. This afternoon, the sunset blazed with a thousand hues.

133

Thursday, November 14, 1861
Cloudy. Wind S.E. Moderate.

A steamer wrecked on the shoals today. She was badly stove, with four feet of water in her hold. The Hale children wasted no time when I returned from school in describing to me in great detail how the steamer hit square and broke in two. Father and Keeper Hale took all aboard into the house and, because it was still early, delivered them across the Ditch, where they made their report. The insurance company will continue its interrogations here tomorrow.

The steamer struck in full daylight. Father and Keeper Hale saw her coming, saw there was nothing they could do to stop her. All that was left for them was to be ready for her. She was loaded with provisions. The cargo was strewn all along the shore. Oda Lee, still limping, has been busy all day. My guess is, she is still at it. She will be provisioned for a year on what she can take until an inspector arrives. I wonder where in those rooms she will stuff it all?

The army is now requesting woolen mittens, an article almost as useful to the soldiers as stockings. The mittens should be fashioned with a forefinger, otherwise they would be very unhandy in actual service.

I have found that cast-off woolen clothing, usually cut into carpet rags, is an excellent material for making mittens. I have been cutting mittens out from discarded cloth in every free moment I have had, and stitching them up in no time. I have finished three pair already. It is only want of material that keeps me from making more.

About 5,000 blankets for the army have been contributed by the people of the North. I have sent my own blanket along.

I sleep just as well in my cloak.

Thursday, November 21, 1861
P. Cloudy. Wind N.W. Fresh.

Daniel has written and asked for a likeness of me.

There are few more homely on the face of the earth. My ears are too big, my chin too small, and my cheeks always raw with the weather. I have never been one to dwell on appearance, a trait that has driven Mother and Grandmother to distraction. I do not intend to start dwelling on appearance now.

Daniel is a better friend than I imagined, to request a likeness of a face uncomely as mine. He says if he could look on my face each day it would bring him comfort. If having such a likeness brings him comfort, then I suppose I had better go to Frankford and have one made. But I would think such a thing would give him a start when he looked upon it. It certainly would me.

Thursday, November 28, 1861
Stormy. Wind S. High.

We had a fall of snow.

It gets dark so early now that we must kindle the Light in the afternoon and keep it burning well into the next morning.

Uncle Edward and I finally had a chance to talk yesterday. I have not had much time to spend with him. We caught up on events close to home. I asked after Daisy. She was away again, for a week. I asked if business had improved any. It had not. I did not mention the papers Father gave to Mother. It seemed disloyal to speak of them somehow. What do I know to speak of, anyway? Nothing! And besides, it was clear Uncle Edward wanted to talk about war. He said the rebel capital has been removed to Nashville, Tennessee.

Then he got onto the subject of slaves and cotton. He said the value of a field slave has always been measured by the price of cotton. When the price of cotton goes up, so does the price of a good field hand. When the price of cotton goes down, a field hand can be bought for a pittance.

136

With the blockade there is no way to ship out cotton, and no need for the slaves to grow more.

"Wickie, it is becoming a burden to be a slave owner. If we only persevere in our purpose for a year or two, no Southern man will be found rich enough nor foolish enough to wage war over the keeping of slaves."

I hope Daisy comes back soon. Uncle Edward seemed sore lonely yesterday with her gone.

Because of the weather, I was not able to cross the Ditch to see Mother on this day of Thanksgiving. After some consideration, I pulled on my storm clothes and ran to Oda Lee's shack and invited her to share the meal with us, but she chased me away.

I left a pumpkin pie on her step.

Keeper Hale led our prayer of thanks in the lantern room this afternoon. He said that all at sea on this day had taken their day mark from us, from the white column rising to the black tower topped by the lightning rod. He said all at sea this night would take their mark from our bright and steady flash.

We gathered at dusk for the lighting of the lamp.

Sarah and Alice entertained us in the tower, reciting a poem called "The Knitting of the Socks." I shall not forget the way Alice looked to Sarah with each line and the brightness of their eyes as they stood at the center of our attention. In that moment I understood the bond between loved ones. Why can it not be that way for my family?

I am standing my accustomed watch, first watch over the Light. Napoleon is here with me. Earlier, I fed him scraps from dinner and he licked the tips of my fingers.

I stroke his soft head and gaze out to sea, missing Daniel, missing Uncle Edward, missing Mother, missing the feeling of family after being with the boisterous Hales.

Wednesday, December 4, 1861
Stormy. Wind N.W. High.

December has come in raw and cold; the clouds are dark and threaten snow. Ice grips everything; the sides and decks of passing ships shine with an icy crust. The clapper on the bell has frozen again, and soon Father or Keeper Hale will go out to loosen it.

The conditions tonight are some of the worst. The windows of the Lighthouse rattle incessantly. They are encrusted with ice. I have come down again from scraping the glass surrounding the lantern room.

Just as I finished scraping this last time, I foolishly forgot to shield my eyes from the flash. In that moment of carelessness I was blinded. Suddenly I could see nothing as the wind tore at me. It howled and grasped at my cloak and my hood. I clung with desperate hands to the side of the Light. Such a wind, it fought to throw me from the balcony. I could not see at all. Blindly I crawled to the opening in the floor of the lantern balcony, groping for the top rung of the ladder. With the greatest care I struggled to make my way down to the safety of the watch room. As I descended, using only my numbed hands and feet to feel my way, the wind in all its fury plucked at me.

My legs and arms, my hands and feet, my face and ears are bitten through by ice and cold. But I am safe inside the watch room now and my sight has returned.

I must be more careful next time. The Light is not without pain. Life is not without pain. This I have learned.

As I sit here, my hands cramp with the cold and I struggle to hold my pen. I look at these hands, so miserable, so raw. I am humbled by the knowledge of the pain Mother must live with every day.

Friday, December 6, 1861
Clear. Wind S.W. Fresh.

Uncle Edward and I talked about the ending of slavery and the freeing of the Negro people. I have made it a practice never to speak politics at school. Everyone from the littlest Osbourne to the new teacher would turn from me. They all sympathize with the Southern states. I have yet to resign my position, but I grow increasingly unhappy at the school with each passing day.

This afternoon, Uncle Edward asked, how is slavery to be extinguished? By act of Congress? By edict of President Lincoln? How do you make a country stop such a habit, forsake such an institution? How do you legislate a people to give up not only its slaves, but the very concept of slavery?

Uncle Edward makes me think. While I am up here in the Light each night, I ponder his words of the day.

What he said today made me think of Father, when he was a captain. He could not discard all thought of winds and currents and intervening rocks and shoals, and simply steer by the North Star. Such a voyage could end in no other way but disaster. Nor can the Government simply declare an end to slavery and expect the country to sail safely through the shoals and rocks and currents along the way.

Nothing is simple, nothing is simply done.

Uncle Edward said, the real battleground of this rebellion is in *our* states, the border slave states. It is upon us that the burden of this War has fallen the heaviest. It is here that

140

families are divided, that households are broken, that hearth-stones are wet with blood and tears.

Father has become a ghost. He lives in the Lighthouse. He comes to our quarters only to eat or wash or change his stockings. I think he cannot stand the sound of the Hales any more than Mother could stand them, though I think their reasons are quite different. But in the end they are the same. Mother could not tolerate their joy, nor can Father. For one the sound is too much an imposition, for the other the sound is a reminder there is not imposition enough.

"I don't want Father to go to war," I told Uncle Edward today. Suddenly the words spilled out of me. I simply could not hold them inside anymore. And if I could not discuss the turmoil in my heart with Father, I had to discuss it with Uncle Edward. "Father has given Mother some kind of papers. I do not know what they mean. Either Father is going to war, or he is going to leave Mother and me. I do not want Father to leave. Not for war. Not for anything."

Uncle Edward held me close.

"Am I wrong to tell you this?"

Uncle Edward looked carefully down at me. His eyes were bright.

"No, Amelia," he said. "It's about time you did."

141

Thursday, December 12, 1861
P. Cloudy. Wind S.W. Moderate.

I weep at times here, when I am alone at the Light. I weep at times when I fall into bed at the end of a watch.

Tonight, an hour into my shift, while I was tracking a lumber ship, I heard footsteps on the spiral stair. I remembered when I heard footsteps and no one came. I thought it was a ghost then. Now I think it was Oda Lee.

I remembered when I heard footsteps on my birthday and it was Daniel.

I looked to the door, wondering who might be coming. It was a ghost this time. A ghost of a different sort. Father. Father surprised me, entering the lantern room.

I wiped at my cheeks but he could tell I had been crying. I busied myself checking the oil reserves.

Father put his hands on my shoulders and turned me to face him. We did not talk for a long time. So long that I am afraid the Lighthouse Board would have found me negligent had they been watching. And yet at the moment I did not think of the Lighthouse Board. I thought only of the weight in my heart.

As we stood there, so many thoughts went round in my head, like leaves in the wind. I could not catch hold of any of

142

them and yet I knew them all. I knew them a hundred times too well.

Father led me down the ladder to the floor below. He guided me to the window and stood by my side, his arm around my shoulder. We looked out into the dark and blowing sea. In the flash, I saw a tall swell forming into a wave. Though darkness followed, I knew the story of that wave, how it would swell and curl and rush over the sand and through the grasses. Father and I both knew what that wave would do, even in the dark when we could not see it.

When the flash came again, the water was rushing back, back to the sea.

"I wish we could go back," I whispered.

Father nodded. He said he had been fighting against the tide. He was tired of fighting.

My hand tightened on the frigid sill. How cold it must be for Father to sleep here. How could he stand it?

Father said, "I spoke with Edward today. He said I have been selfish. He is right. I am sorry, Wickie. The papers. You should know. The papers I gave your mother. They are divorce papers."

I did not dare look at Father's face. Instead I studied his coat.

Father said he would take care of Mother as long as she lived.

143

"What will become of me?" I asked him.

Father asked what I wanted.

"I want to stay here, at the Light, always."

Father nodded, not to say I shall have what I want, simply to say he had heard me.

Thursday, December 19, 1861
Clear. Wind N. Fresh.

A letter from Daniel.

> *1st December 1861*
> *Near the Potomac*
>
> *Dear Amelia,*
> *With guard duty, picket duty, and a severe illness, your correspondent has been prevented from writing you for some time. If you will excuse the procrastination, he will endeavor to be more faithful in future.*
> *We have now every assurance of staying here all winter, and the prospect is anything but flattering. 'Tis bleak here — the wind howls dreadfully, and the white, heavy frosts of early morn warn us that winter is coming.*

We have picket duty in abundance, but we all rather like it. There is only one thing that mars our pleasure in service, and that is the cowardice of the rebels. If a few would only sneak up to us and get shot once in a while, it would ease the monotony that otherwise clings around us. Still we cannot blame them for their love of life, can we?

I will not deceive you. There is a great deal of sickness prevailing now in the regiment. The Doctor has had his hands full.

We have devotional singing and praying in one or more of the tents every night, and, as "Voice after voice catches up the strain," the effect is truly inspiring.

Your little packages are received with every demonstration of delight, and I take this opportunity of returning to you a soldier's thanks. I carry your likeness with me everywhere and often look to it for advice as I might look to you if you were near.

After next payday, which will be on the first of January, a furlough of ten days' duration will be given out, and one or two from each respective company given leave to travel home. Hope it shall be me.

Yours truly,

Daniel

Wednesday, December 25, 1861
Fair. Wind N.E. Light.

Christmas. It was an unusually quiet day. I went early to the mainland. Mother seemed strangely animated. But now it is late. Mother and Grandmother are alone by their hearth, Father and I alone, but for the boisterousness of Keeper Hale's brood. How grateful I am for their brightness. This morning Keeper Hale's youngsters found their stockings filled with goodies from Old Kriss — sugarplums, nuts, candies. I cannot imagine how Keeper Hale manages with so many mouths to feed, but he is not supporting his wife and her mother at a separate address, and Mrs. Hale, big-hearted as the sky, is most clever. She used tin patterns and baked fancy cakes for her family as well as for Father and me, and even one for Mother and Grandmother. At the noon meal together we untied the bag of chestnuts and ate the goose that we had kept and fed on corn.

Daniel is spending Christmas miles from home. Last Christmas I barely gave him a thought. This year is different. I look at the carving Father made for me last year, the carving of the Lighthouse. That little carving has brought me hours of comfort in this trying year. That and you, my diary. One of the aprons Mother sewed for me last Christmas I wore this

Christmas to bake cookies for the Hale children. Wearing the apron makes me feel that Mother is close by. And the drawing Reenie sketched hangs over my bed. Mother does not need it now. Not the way I need it, to hold her near.

I wonder what Christmas is like in the camps. Are the tents decorated with evergreens and colored lanterns? Do the ones receiving packages share with the others? Is there enough to go around?

Daniel, wherever you are, however you are, I wish you a merry Christmas.

Saturday, December 28, 1861
Clear. Wind N.W. High.

We are having a good deal of trouble with frozen feet in this terrible weather. Father bathes my feet in kerosene and rubs them every four hours, day and night. He does not let me do the same for him. He says his feet do not bother him.

Father feels guilty that I should have frosted feet. If I did not live in this buffeted Lighthouse station, if I did not work like a man beside Father and Keeper Hale, if I lived in the manner of a protected young lady, as Mother would have it, I would not have to concern myself with frozen feet.

But I have chosen this life. Frosted feet and all.

147

We are fighting a war of our own here. To keep the Light, in all weather, under every adversity. The other night when I struggled to keep the glass free of ice and Father struggled to restore the voice of the buoy bell, then we were soldiers in battle against the elements. Certain battles must be fought. I will fight to keep the Light. I will fight to keep Mother, too, in whatever way I can have her. I have lost something immeasurable in Mother's departure. But I have gained something immeasurable, too.

I read that some bachelors go to war because they like the fighting, some married men because they like the peace. I am not certain where Father falls within those lines of reason, but somehow, he has managed to find a peace of his own.

And I, though I have paid a price as dear as a lightkeeper's lifetime of wages, I, too, have found a certain peace.

I reread Uncle Edward's poem at the beginning of this diary and I understand.

Epilogue

Oda Lee Monkton continued looting ships until she died of cholera in 1866.

Keeper Robert Hale remained as Head Lightkeeper at the Fenwick Island Light until 1871, when he moved his entire family, except daughter Alice, to Alaska to accept a Government position.

After furthering his education, Edward Martin, Amelia's uncle, left Bayville in 1872 to teach at the newly founded University of Oregon in Eugene. Upon his death, in 1887, Edward Martin left all of his worldly possessions to his common-law wife, Daisy.

Mildred Martin, Amelia's mother, died in 1862, after suffering a seizure. Dr. McCabe ruled the cause of death as asphyxiation.

John Martin, Amelia's father, resigned as Assistant Keeper in 1863 after suffering a stroke. Alice Hale, Keeper Hale's second daughter, remained at Fenwick Island, looking after John Martin, from 1869, until his death in 1878. Alice Hale married Creighton Sydney of Ocean City, Maryland, in 1871, and she and Mr. Sidney brought great joy to John Martin's last years, surrounding him with their seven lively children.

Daniel Worthington survived the War and returned to Bayville and to Fenwick Island to marry Amelia in 1863. However, Daniel did not remain at the Light for long. Though they were never divorced, Amelia and Daniel lived only briefly together as husband and wife. Daniel went west, working as a supervisor on the Transcontinental Railroad. On the night of his death in December 1913, Daniel Worthington asked that a candle be lit in an old wooden carving of a lighthouse. The wooden carving was sent back to Amelia Martin along with a chest containing Daniel Worthington's personal effects and a rather large sum of money. The remainder of his estate was distributed between his two sisters.

Amelia Martin took over from her father as Assistant Lightkeeper at Fenwick Light in 1863, at the age of eighteen. She was appointed Head Keeper of the Ragged Island Light, a stag station off the Maine coast, in 1869, saving twenty-two lives over the course of her career as Head Keeper and receiving various commendations and awards, including the Medal of Honor. She retired from the Lighthouse Service in 1920. At the age of seventy-seven, Amelia began a new career, bringing books by boat to island residents up and down the Maine coast. Amelia Martin died in her sleep in 1940 at the age of ninety-five.

*Life in America
in 1861*

Historical Note

The tiny state of Delaware occupied an unusual position during the Civil War: It was officially a slave state, yet its citizens chose not to join the Confederacy. Instead, Delaware remained in the Union and fought with the North. Small as it was, the state lay on the border between North and South, between freedom and slavery, and those who lived there found room for disagreement and division among themselves.

The causes of the Civil War date to the founding of the United States, when Northern and Southern delegates to the Constitutional Convention disagreed over slavery. The framers of the Constitution compromised by writing about slavery without ever using the words *slavery* or *slaves* in their famous document. As a result, the first seventy years of the new nation were marked by continual tensions and negotiations between North and South, most notably on the question of whether or not slavery should be permitted in new territories and in new states admitted to the Union. As the North moved toward industrialization and wage labor, and the South developed as an agricultural society supported by staple crops and enslaved labor, the clashes between these vastly different economic systems grew more intense.

When Abraham Lincoln won the presidential election of 1860, Northerners were ecstatic, for they felt certain that Lincoln would prevent the Southern states from gaining more power in Congress. The white South, however, reacted to Lincoln's election with alarm because Lincoln believed that slavery should not spread beyond its present borders. Three months after the election, the seven states of the lower South voted to secede from the Union — to leave the United States. These states (South Carolina, Mississippi, Florida, Alabama, Georgia, Louisiana, and Texas) formed the Confederate States of America and elected Jefferson Davis as their own president. The Constitution of the Confederacy was similar to the Constitution of the United States, but with two significant differences: states' rights were strengthened, and the institution of slavery was recognized and protected.

At his inauguration in March 1861, Lincoln assured the white South that he would not attempt to end slavery in states where it was already legal. Although Lincoln personally judged slavery to be morally wrong, he did not believe it was his duty as president to impose those views on others. Lincoln did make clear, however, that the federal government would enforce the existing laws of the United States, which meant that the South did not have the constitutional right to secede, and the formation of the Confederacy was considered an act of treason. At the same time, because Lincoln's first resolve was to preserve the Union, he would not go so far as to declare war. In his inaugural address, he announced to white Southerners, "In *your* hands, my dissatisfied fellow countrymen, and not in *mine,* is the momentous issue of civil war. . . . You can have no conflict, without being yourselves the aggressors."

Fort Sumter, in the harbor of Charleston, South Carolina, belonged to the federal government. Lincoln had refused to surrender the fort to the Confederacy, for to do so would have condoned secession. But by early April, the United States soldiers stationed there were running out of supplies. Sumter would either have to be resupplied or evacuated. Lincoln made a careful plan, announcing that he would resupply Sumter with food only; there would be no resupplying of weapons, and the provisions would be carried on unarmed ships. These actions were intended to demonstrate that Lincoln refused to play the aggressor in a civil war that would tear the nation apart.

But the Confederacy interpreted Lincoln's plan as a declaration of war. On April 12, 1861, at 4:30 in the morning, the Confederates fired on Union ships that had arrived at Sumter. After thirty-three hours of bombardment, the federal government surrendered the fort, and the next day, President

Lincoln called up 75,000 soldiers from state militias to serve in the Union army for three months. Lincoln, and almost everyone else, felt sure that this would be a short military conflict.

In the spring of 1861, Virginia, Arkansas, North Carolina, and Tennessee seceded from the Union to join the Confederacy. White Southerners who owned the greatest numbers of slaves were the loudest supporters of secession and war. However, in the upper South, portions of the white population sympathized with the Union, notably in areas where the poor soil did not support the staple crops of a slave economy. Most white Southern Unionists lived in Delaware, Maryland, Missouri, and Kentucky. These were the "border states": slave states that bordered on free states and remained with the Union during the Civil War. The white populations of the border states were divided by the war.

Although Delaware permitted slavery, its economy shared more with the North than the South. Delaware farmers had always shipped their crops to northern markets on the Delaware River, and in the 1850s, the railroad solidified ties to Philadelphia and New York, while mills and factories were built in the Wilmington area. Wilmington had also served as an important stop on the "Underground Railroad," a network of black and white activists that provided food, shelter, and safety to fugitive slaves fleeing north to freedom.

156

By 1860, the vast majority of African Americans in Delaware were free, and a thousand black Delawareans joined the Union army. Delaware whites fought on the Union side ten to one. Still, many in the southern part of the state sympathized with the Confederacy. Tensions could run high within communities, and in each of the border states families found themselves on opposite sides of the war.

African Americans, in both the North and South, supported the Civil War as a means to create a nation without slavery. People who wished to abolish slavery called themselves "Abolitionists," and in the North, a minority of whites agreed that slavery was morally wrong and should not be tolerated anywhere in the United States. While Abolitionists were extremely critical of President Lincoln because they felt he wasn't doing enough to end slavery, the majority of Northerners supported Lincoln wholeheartedly. Most white Northerners backed a war to preserve the nation and were initially satisfied to restore the Union to a country half slave and half free. But that, too, would change as the war raged on.

The first major battle of the Civil War took place in Virginia in 1861. At the time it was fought, the First Battle of Bull Run was the largest battle ever in American history. The Confederate victory at Bull Run confirmed the confidence and righteousness of the white South. To the North, the defeat brought shock and fear. Finally realizing it would not be a short war after all, President Lincoln soon asked men to enlist in the Union army for terms of three years.

After Bull Run, the North worried that Confederates would invade Maryland, and Union soldiers stood guard on the north bank of the Potomac River. In October 1861, the Battle of Ball's Bluff, fought on the southern bank of the Potomac, ended in a dramatic Confederate victory. Although the year came to a close with considerable uncertainty in the North, 1862 would bring a number of important Union victories, most notably the Battle of Shiloh, the bloodiest battle in the entire western hemisphere at the time it was fought.

On both sides of the war, men who had enthusiastically signed up to fight — and had envisioned themselves returning home as war heroes — now experienced horrors on the battlefield such as they had never imagined. Those who survived witnessed death and destruction of tremendous magnitude and at close range, and many wrote home to tell their families what they had seen. Those on the home front suffered hardships as well, ranging from the daily miseries of food shortages to the overwhelming grief of losing loved ones.

As the second year of the war opened, it had become abundantly clear that neither side was going to surrender except in the face of total military defeat. Union soldiers now fought to

158

destroy all enemy resources — and slavery was just such a resource. The goal of destroying the Confederacy therefore came to include the destruction of slavery. The Emancipation Proclamation, which Lincoln issued in 1863, forever changed the purpose of the war: All Northerners were now undeniably fighting to end slavery, and the official aims of the war now matched Lincoln's personal beliefs. The Proclamation also confirmed just how much the institution of slavery had already been weakened by the war. From the start, enslaved men, women, and children had seized the opportunity of wartime chaos to escape from their masters and run behind Union army lines. For slaves and their sympathizers, the Civil War had always been a war for freedom. Now that was official, too.

In 1861, very few Americans could have predicted that the Civil War would last four years and that 620,000 lives would be lost. In the course of those four years, North and South traded victories and defeats, but following General William Tecumseh Sherman's marches in 1864 and 1865, the Confederacy collapsed and surrendered in April 1865. The nation was united once again, but the bitterness of civil war would last for generations to come. In the United States, the institution of racial slavery had ended forever, but racial equality would prove to be a long way off, both in the North and in the South.

For years, mariners complained about the treacherous waters off the coast of Delaware known as the Fenwick Island shoal. Situated six miles east of Fenwick Island, this dangerous sandbar caused many shipwrecks. In 1855, the newly established United States Lighthouse Board investigated complaints and deemed this area in need of a lighthouse to guide vessels safely to shore. Today, the lighthouse's appearance remains very similar to when it was first built.

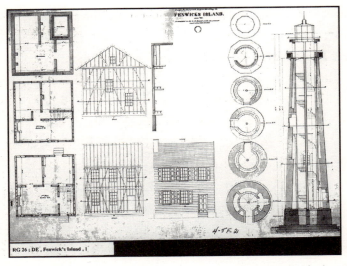

A blueprint of the Fenwick Island lighthouse details its unique construction: Two brick towers, instead of one, comprise the structure. The outer tower is conical, slanting inward as it ascends, and the inner tower is cylindrical. The interior and exterior tower walls measure seven inches thick and twenty-seven inches thick, respectively, making the lighthouse a secure fortress against even violent seas and storms.

The Fenwick Island lighthouse was first illuminated on August 1, 1859. The tower rises eighty-seven feet above ground, and its light is visible fifteen miles out to sea. Keepers and their families lived in the two-story house (right) located on the ocean side. The house's most unique feature is its cisterns, located in the basement. These concrete tanks are made to hold rainwater, collected through gutters, providing occupants with fresh, clean water for drinking and bathing.

The interior of this lighthouse emphasizes the proximity of the keeper's family quarters to the ocean. Girls' daily responsibilities in a lighthouse dwelling required the same chores—sweeping, scrubbing, and laundry—as did homes on the mainland. Whether working or relaxing, girls tied their hair back with ribbons and wore long skirts, usually sewn from fabric purchased at general stores.

1911 MONTH	DAY.	RECORD OF IMPORTANT EVENTS AT THE STATION, BAD WEATHER, ETC.			
January	1	Cloudy & Rain	Wind	S. E.	Fresh
"	2	Cloudy & Rain	Wind	S.	Fresh
"	3	Rain & Fog.	Wind	S. W.	Fresh
"	4	Clear	Wind	N. W.	Fresh
"	5	Clear	Wind	S. W.	Mod.
"	6	Clear	Wind	S.	mod.
"	7	Clear	Wind	S. E.	mod
"	8	Fair	Wind	S. E.	Fresh
"	9	Clear	Wind	N. W.	Gale
"	10	Clear	Wind	N. W.	mod
"	11	Fair	Wind	S. W.	mod
"	12	Cloudy	Wind	W.	mod.
"	13	Foggy	Wind	N. W.	Light
"	14	Cloudy & Fog.	Wind	W.	Light
"	15	Cloudy & Rain	Wind	S. E.	mod.
"	16	Clear	Wind	N. W.	High
"	17	Cloudy	Wind	N. W.	mod.
"	18	Cloudy & Snow	Wind	N. E.	Fresh
"	19	Clear	Wind	N. W.	mod.
"	20	Clear	Wind	N. E to S. E	Light
"	21	Cloudy	Wind	S.	Light
"	22	Rain	Wind	N.	Fresh
"	23	Clear	Wind	N. W.	Light
"	24	Clear	Wind	S. E.	mod
"	25	Clear	Wind	S. W.	Light
"	26	Cloudy & Rain	Wind	S. W.	Light
"	27	P. Cloudy	Wind	S. W.	Light
"	28	Clear	Wind	W. N. W.	Gale
"	29	Cloudy & Rain	Wind	S. W.	mod
"	30	Clear	Wind	W. N. W.	High

As shown in this 1911 log from Fenwick Island, keepers and their assistants continued to keep daily records of the weather the same way they did when the procedure began in the late 1850s.

In 1861, public schooling for children took place in small, one-room schoolhouses heated by wood-burning stoves. Teachers instructed all students in the same room, but provided varied lessons for different ages and abilities. Assistant teachers, usually former pupils, sometimes taught alongside them.

During the mid-1800s, ice skating was a favorite pastime among young girls and boys in cold northern climates. Skating took place on naturally frozen outdoor ponds, which put skaters at risk of falling through broken ice.

Abraham Lincoln was elected President of the United States in 1860. At the time there were well over three million slaves in the South. White Southerners did not want a President who opposed slavery, because their whole way of life—economic and social—depended on it. As a result, southern states seceded from the Union and formed their own government, known as the Confederate States of America.

In desperate attempts to evade their captors and escape to the free states, slaves used the Underground Railroad—a network of secret routes north. On January 1, 1863, President Lincoln's Emancipation Proclamation outlawed slavery and declared all slaves free. In actuality, however, this decree liberated few people because it did not apply to border states siding with the Union or to southern states already existing as part of the Confederacy.

Union boys' reasons for enlisting in the Army ranged from seeking change and adventure in their mundane lives, to preserving the Union, to abolishing slavery in the South. The minimum age requirement for boys was eighteen, but soldiers in the North and South were often as young as twelve. A typical Union soldier's uniform consisted of a navy four-button sack coat and navy wool pants.

A FAMILY QUARREL.

This 1861 cartoon expresses the conflicting political sentiments of families living in the border states. Dissension over the abolition of slavery was so widespread that even members of the same family fought about it.

The Smyrna Times.

ROBT. D. HOFFECKER, EDITOR.

SMYRNA, DEL.

THURSDAY APRIL 18, 1861.

THE "TIMES" is published Every Thursday, by Robt. D. Hoffecker, Editor and Proprietor, at Smyrna, Del.

SUBSCRIPTION.—One year, $1.50 in advance, or $2.00 if not paid till end of the year. No paper discontinued until all arrears are paid—only at the option of the Publisher.

ADVERTISING—For every square of 12 lines, or less, first insertion, 50 cts.; each subsequent insertion 25 cts.— Liberal arrangements made with yearly and half yearly advertisers.

Civil War--The Feeling Here.

The curtain has fallen upon the first act of the great tragedy of the age. Fort Sumter has fallen before the fury and prowess of a rebellion, and the "Stars and Stripes" of the great American Republic give place to the "Stars and Bars" of the Southern Confederacy. Civil War, that most horrible of all Wars, is now fully inaugurated. When it will end, God only knows. We have now the sad spectacle of a divided Country, broken confidence, prostration of business, and, instead of the busy hum of trade, we are greeted on every side with the tocsin of war and the resounding of the cry To Arms! To Arms!! The news of the bombardment of Sumter, though expected, was nevertheless received with a shock.— All hoped that something might yet be done to avert the desperate impending strife, but, as it had to come, the feeling seems to have been, let it come—anything but this dread suspense. We do not think the fall of Sumter produced any more, if as much, depression here as the passage of the ordinance of secession. Our peculiar situation in regard to locality has tended to counteract any decided feeling either way; but the last act of the drama commenced in November last has had the tendency to draw tighter and tighter the line of demarcation here as elsewhere, and the people are fast dividing for one side or the other. While there

The Smyrna Times, *a Delaware newspaper, announces the start of the Civil War following the Confederacy's attack on Fort Sumter, South Carolina—a United States military stronghold—on April 12, 1861.*

PUMPKIN PIE FILLING

Pare pumpkin, take out the seeds, and slowly boil until soft. Strain or rub it through a sieve or colander. Mix this with good milk till it is thick as batter; sweeten it with sugar to taste. Allow three eggs per quart of milk used. Beat the eggs well, add them to the pumpkin, and season with ginger and other spices to taste. Roll the paste rather thicker than for fruit pies, as there is only one crust. If the pie is large and deep it will require to bake an hour in a brisk oven.

Adapted from a mid-nineteenth century cookbook, this recipe details an old-fashioned method for making pumpkin pie. The crust, also homemade, would have been made separately.

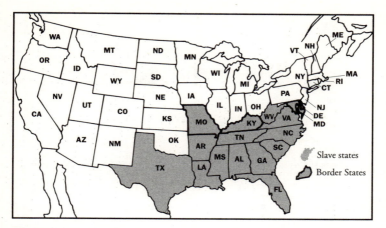

This modern map of the United States shows the slave states at the time of the Civil War.

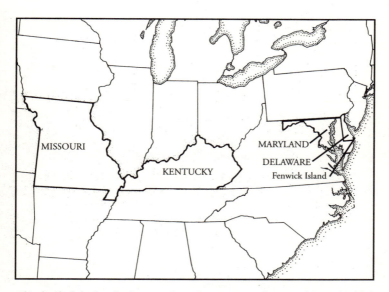

This detail of the four border states shows the approximate location of Fenwick Island, Delaware.

About the Author

KAREN HESSE says about writing this book, "While researching in the 1911 *New York Times,* I came across a series of articles written about Ida Lewis. Ida Lewis kept the Lime Rock Light burning off the coast of Newport, Rhode Island, during and after the Civil War, taking over her father's duties when he became too ill to serve. Ida Lewis never hesitated to go to sea in a storm, placing her own life in peril numerous times to rescue those who would otherwise have perished. She saved twenty-two people in her career as Lightkeeper. Yet she hated the attention her heroism brought. Ida Lewis saw herself as a Lightkeeper doing her job, nothing more, nothing less. Her story inspired me. To think of a female given such responsibility at that point in history! And the image of a light burning in the darkness of a Delaware night was so fitting when I looked at the darkness spreading over this country as the Civil War unfolded. Amelia Martin was created in Ida Lewis's image, and in the image of the other female Lightkeepers who sacrificed and struggled to keep their Lights burning through some of this country's darkest hours."

Karen Hesse is one of the most distinguished children's book authors in America today. Her acclaimed novels include *Out of the Dust,* winner of the 1998 Newbery Medal, the Scott O'Dell Award, and many other awards and honors; *The Music of Dolphins,* an ALA Best Book for Young Adults; and, most recently, *Just Juice.* She lives with her family in southern Vermont.

Acknowledgments

This book could not have been written without the assistance of Gladys Kennery, Wayne Wheeler of the U.S. Lighthouse Society, Paul Pepper, Tracy Mack, Jean Feiwel, Bernice Millman, Zoe Moffitt, Martha Hodes, Liza Ketchum, Bob and Tink MacLean, Eileen Christelow, Kate, Rachel, and Randy Hesse, Ken Black, Florence Thomson, Dr. John Straus, The State of Delaware Public Archives, The Library of Congress, Tim Harrison, Lorinda White, and Richard Shuldiner of the Brooks Memorial Library.

Grateful acknowledgment is made for permission to reprint the following:

Cover portrait: *The Umbrella* by Maria Konstantinova Bashkirtseva (1860–84). Oil on canvas, 1883. Collection of State Russian Museum, St. Petersburg, Russia. The Bridgeman Art Library International Ltd., New York, New York.

Cover background: *Desert Rock Lighthouse* by Thomas Doughty, 1847. Oil on canvas, 27 x 41 in. Gift of Mrs. Jennie E. Mead, 1939. Inv. #39.146 Collection of the Newark Museum, Newark, New Jersey. Art Resource, New York, New York.

Page 160 (top): Fenwick Island lighthouse, National Archives (RG Z6-LG-20-11)

(bottom): Fenwick Island lighthouse, blueprints, National Archives

Page 161 (top): Fenwick Island lighthouse and keeper's house, Delaware Public Archives, Hall of Records, Dover, Delaware

(bottom): Interior of lighthouse, Culver Pictures, New York, New York

Page 162: Weather journal of Fenwick Island lighthouse, National Archives

Page 163 (top): Schoolroom, Culver Pictures, New York, New York

(bottom): Ice skating, Brown Brothers, Sterling, Pennsylvania

Page 164 (top): Abraham Lincoln, Culver Pictures, New York, New York

(bottom): Slaves, Library of Congress

Page 165 (top): Union soldier, Library of Congress (LC B818410697)

(bottom): Civil War cartoon, New York Public Library Photograph Collection, New York, New York

Page 166 (top): *The Smyrna Times,* Delaware Public Archives

(bottom): Recipe for pumpkin pie filling, adapted from *Early American Cookery: "The Good Housekeeper"* by Sarah Josepha Hale, Dover Publications, Inc., New York, New York

Page 167: Maps by Heather Saunders

Other books in the Dear America series

A Journey to the New World
The Diary of Remember Patience Whipple
by Kathryn Lasky

The Winter of Red Snow
The Revolutionary War Diary of Abigail Jane Stewart
by Kristiana Gregory

When Will This Cruel War Be Over?
The Civil War Diary of Emma Simpson
by Barry Denenberg

A Picture of Freedom
The Diary of Clotee, a Slave Girl
by Patricia C. McKissack

Across the Wide and Lonesome Prairie
The Oregon Trail Diary of Hattie Campbell
by Kristiana Gregory

So Far from Home
The Diary of Mary Driscoll, an Irish Mill Girl
by Barry Denenberg

I Thought My Soul Would Rise and Fly
The Diary of Patsy, a Freed Girl
by Joyce Hansen

West to a Land of Plenty
The Diary of Teresa Angelino Viscardi
by Jim Murphy

Dreams in the Golden Country
The Diary of Zipporah Feldman, a Jewish Immigrant Girl
by Kathryn Lasky

A Line in the Sand
The Alamo Diary of Lucinda Lawrence
by Sherry Garland

Standing in the Light
The Captive Diary of Catharine Carey Logan
by Mary Pope Osborne

Voyage on the Great Titanic
The Diary of Margaret Ann Brady
by Ellen Emerson White

My Heart Is on the Ground
The Diary of Nannie Little Rose, a Sioux Girl
by Ann Rinaldi

The Great Railroad Race
The Diary of Libby West
by Kristiana Gregory

The Girl Who Chased Away Sorrow
The Diary of Sarah Nita, a Navajo Girl
by Ann Turner

This book is dedicated to all Lightkeepers — past, present, and future — who kindle their lamps of hope against the darkness.

While the events described and some of the characters in this book may be based on actual historical events and real people, Amelia Martin is a fictional character, created by the author, and her diary and its epilogue are works of fiction.

Copyright © 1999 by Karen Hesse.

All rights reserved. Published by Scholastic Inc.
557 Broadway, New York, New York 10012.
DEAR AMERICA®, SCHOLASTIC, and associated logos
are trademarks and/or registered trademarks of Scholastic Inc.

No part of this publication may be reproduced, or stored in a retrieval system, or transmitted in any form or by any means, electronic, mechanical, photocopying, recording, or otherwise, without written permission of the publisher.
For information regarding permissions, write to Scholastic Inc., Attention: Permissions Department, 557 Broadway, New York, NY 10012.

Library of Congress Cataloging-in-Publication Data available.

ISBN 0-590-56733-0;
ISBN 0-439-44557-4 (pbk.)

10 9 8 7 6 5 4 3 2 1   02 03 04 05 06

The display type was set in Garamond Semibold Italic.
The text type was set in Garamond.
Photo research by Zoe Moffitt and Pamela Heller
Book design by Elizabeth B. Parisi

Printed in the U.S.A. 23
First paperback printing, October 2002